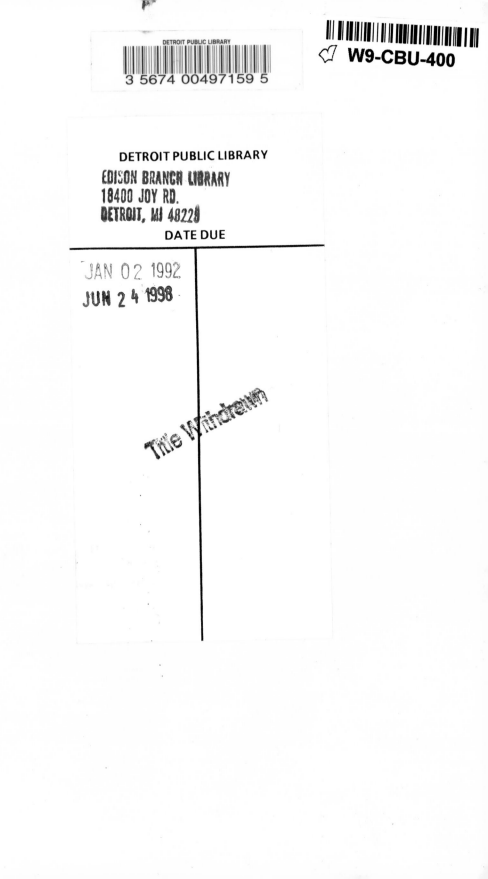

PEGASUS
IN FLIGHT
...

THE DRAGONRIDERS OF PERN®

The author respectfully suggests that books in the Pern series be read in the order in which they were published. Which is:

Dragonflight	*Dragonsong*
Dragonquest	*Dragonsinger*
The White Dragon	*Dragondrums*

Moreta: Dragonlady of Pern
Nerilka's Story

Dragonsdawn

The Renegades of Pern

THE ATLAS OF PERN *by Karen Wynn Fonstadt* and* THE DRAGONLOVER'S GUIDE TO PERN *by Jody-Lynn Nye with Anne McCaffrey* both provide additional interesting information as companion texts to the main novels.*

*Available from Ballantine Books

OTHER TITLES BY ANNE MCCAFFREY
Published by Ballantine Books:

Decision at Doona
Dinosaur Planet
Dinosaur Planet Survivors
Get Off the Unicorn
The Lady
Restoree
The Ship Who Sang
To Ride Pegasus

THE CRYSTAL SINGER BOOKS
Crystal Singer
Killashandra

Edited by Anne McCaffrey:
Alchemy and Academe

PEGASUS
IN
FLIGHT

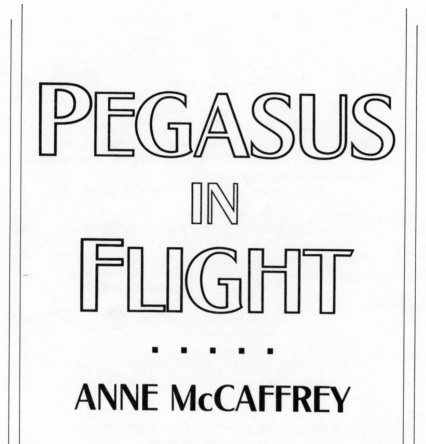

ANNE McCAFFREY

A DEL REY BOOK

BALLANTINE BOOKS ■ NEW YORK

A Del Rey Book
Published by Ballantine Books

Copyright © 1990 by Anne McCaffrey

All rights reserved under International and Pan-American Copyright
Conventions. Published in the United States by Ballantine Books, a division
of Random House, Inc., New York, and simultaneously in Canada by
Random House of Canada Limited, Toronto.

THE DRAGONRIDERS OF PERN
is a trademark of Anne McCaffrey. Reg. U.S. Pat. & Tm. Off.

Library of Congress Cataloging-in-Publication Data
McCaffrey, Anne.
Pegasus in flight / Anne McCaffrey.—1st ed.
p.   cm.
"A Del Rey book."
ISBN 0-345-36896-7
I. Title.
PS3563.A255P44   1990
813'.54—dc20   90-92901
CIP

Manufactured in the United States of America
Designed by Ann Gold

First Edition: December 1990
10 9 8 7 6 5 4 3 2 1

OCT '91

This Book is respectfully
and gratefully dedicated to
Diana Tyler
and
Diane Pearson

PEGASUS
IN FLIGHT

. . .

P R O L O G U E

During the late twentieth century's exploration of space, a major breakthrough occurred in the validation and recording of extrasensory perceptions, the so-called paranormal, psionic abilities long held to be spurious. An alternate application of the Goosegg, an extremely sensitive encephalograph developed to scan brain patterns of the astronauts who suffered from sporadic "bright spots," temporarily diagnosed as cerebral or retinal malfunction, was inadvertently discovered when the device was used to monitor a head injury in an intensive-care unit of Jerhattan. The patient, Henry Darrow, was a self-styled clairvoyant with an astonishing percentage of accurate "guesses." In his case, as the device monitored his brain patterns, it also registered the discharge of unusual electrical energy as he experienced a clairvoyant episode. For the first time there was scientific proof of extrasensory perception.

Henry Darrow recovered from his concussion to found the first Center for Parapsychics in Jerhattan and to formulate the ethical and moral premises that would grant those with valid, and demonstrable, psionic talents certain privileges and responsibilities in a society basically skeptical, hostile, or overtly paranoid about such abilities.

Extrasensory perception—or Talent, as it came to be called—came in varying strengths and forms. Simple, short-range telepathy was fairly common, once inhibitions were discarded. But there were also one-way telepaths, people who could send their thoughts but not receive those of others, and people who could receive thoughts but not send. Others were empaths, able to adjust immediately to the moods of those

3

around them, sometimes quite unconsciously. Telempaths could sense and react to extreme or more distant emotions; some of these were able to redirect emotion, by broadcasting other emotions or by neutralizing the negative—such Talents proved to be invaluable in crowd control, for they could keep a throng from turning into a senseless mob. But the most valuable of the telepaths were those who could both receive and broadcast thought, speaking to other minds anywhere in the world.

Telekinetics—Talents who could move physical objects by sheer mental power—were also invaluable, their abilities ranging from lifting heavy machinery to manipulating on micro levels.

Clairvoyants or precogs could see future events, either close at hand, or at some remove from their present. Very often their visions allowed the future to be altered and disasters to be averted. Some clairvoyants had special affinities: some sensed events revolving around fire, water, or wind; others were more apt to perceive children, or violence, or criminal intentions.

Finders also had affinities—some could locate people or animals, while others were able to sense inanimate objects—and their abilities could vary greatly in range.

Talent came in many forms and guises, and not all of the viable types had, as yet, been recognized. The various centers, worldwide, constantly searched for the less dramatic gifts because the need had now far outstripped the supply. For those potential few, the training was arduous, and the rewards did not always compensate for the unswerving dedication required by their taxing positions.

And yet to be found Talented became the aspiration of many, and the triumph of few.

*They have been at a great feast of languages,
and stolen the scraps.*
                              —William Shakespeare.

CHAPTER 1

Tirla took a quick look from the alley into the Main Concourse of Residential Linear G, then pulled back instantly, flattening her thin twelve-year-old body against the plas-slab wall. Public Health officials were swarming all over, rounding up the early-morning crowd of able-bodied workers who had been scanning the employment board for a day's work, the mothers with their handicapped kids making their way to the Rehab centers, and the legal children on their way to the Linear's physical-training facility.

Cautiously she took another look, to see what the PHOs were setting up on their tables: vials and the big compressed-air bottles that operated the hyposprays. She withdrew, having seen enough to recognize another wholesale vaccination effort. Strange, she hadn't heard of any new 'mune plagues. To give them their due, PHO was swifter than rumor to avert disaster.

Rapidly Tirla ran through her head her current list of those mothers of illegal children whom she should inform: first, because they would pay her for warning them to hide the kids; second, because those who could afford to would pay her for stealing whatever vaccine was being administered. She counted on her fingers: Elpidia, certainly; the old bouzma, Pilau; Bilala, and Zaveta, Ari-san, and Cyoto—and she had better ask Mama Bobchik if there were newborns, for they would need the Five-shotter. She would want one for herself, as well, and could possibly finagle a box, depending on how the current stuff was packaged. It all depended. Mirda Khan, yes—she had best tell that old wagon right after she warned Mama.

She would have to change into clean clothing issue—she

5

had washed, but this week's issue was five days old and looked eight. Public Health were quick to notice details like that. Mama Bobchik was always good for fresh wear, especially if Tirla went to her first with her news. This could be a very good day, Tirla thought with a rise of spirits as she slipped back down the alley for the center-shaft emergency stairs on her way down to Mama Bobchik's pad.

Most of Tirla's twelve years had been spent in scrounging a totally unofficial living in the multi-ethnic thirty-storied community of the Linears. She could not afford to miss a single trick, like today's unexpected Public Health roundup, to escape the stringent controls, clever obstacles, and little traps ingeniously set up by the Jerhattan Complex Administration Council and the Law Enforcement and Order Organization to identify and control each member of the restless population.

Officially there had never been a record of Tirla's birth. She was, however, the fifth child born to Dikka—only the first, Tirla's brother, Kail, was legal. The government tied a woman off when she gave birth to a second child. Consequently Firza, Lenny, Ahmed, and Tirla had all been born in Dikka's single-parent squat with the aid of Mama Bobchik, who had had an illegal child every year until her womb had dried up. Kail had been official until Dikka had sold him at ten. Firza had had the use of Kail's wrist ID for two years until she was profitably disposed of. In the next year, Dikka, Lenny, and Ahmed died of one of the immune plagues that sporadically flared up to decimate the Linears. In the haste and confusion of body disposal, Dikka's death had not been officially noted. So Tirla had been left with two ID bracelets—a fine legacy. Self-sufficient and resourceful, she had managed to retain the squat, drawing two subsistence rations, until Dikka's ID was canceled after her failure to appear for a routine medical examination.

Wise in the ways of her society, Tirla had not been caught short by the lockout. She knew Tenancy Articles, Paragraphs, and Subsections by heart, so figuring out the cancellation date had been no problem. Two days prior to the eviction, she moved her few possessions—hotter unit, the best of the sleep sacks, the 'corder, and the pretties Dikka's men had given her from time to time—into new quarters five levels below the Main Concourse, in the maintenance segment of Linear G, right beside the charged security grille that protected the engineering section from unauthorized entry. Only a slight and agile person like Tirla could reach the eyrie, where massive ducts formed a broad platform before bending up the inner wall. She patched her hotter and 'corder wires into the overhead cables, certain that her small use of electricity was unlikely to be discovered, and settled in. She did miss the all-night informational programs on the squat's tri-d. The big public tri-ds on the Concourse stopped 'casting at the midnight curfew. Tirla, with her clever, shrewd, and organized mind, was thirsty for knowledge. She even used Kail's ID to log into school. One of Dikka's men had said that one had to know the rules before one could break them. Tirla had never forgotten.

For another two years, Kail's bracelet supplied his small sister with daily subsistence, weekly clothing issue, and other amenities until "Kail" failed to appear at Evaluation Center within three weeks of his sixteenth birthday. The cancellation caused Tirla no problem, for by then she was well-established, almost indispensable to most of the Residential clients and gang bosses in the neighborhood industrial complexes. Her ability to translate any of the nearly ninety dialects and languages used in the subsistence-level Residential Linears saved clients hours at official transspeech centers, or worse, misunderstanding. She knew when to be ingratiating or stand firm. She knew what courtesies were due whom and never failed in performing them. Everyone who knew her knew very well that she was illegal. Because she was so useful to the residents of Linear G, as she would be today with her warning about the Public Healthers, and because officially she did not exist anyway, there was no profit—yet—in reporting her illicit existence.

The various errands she did—and she was scrupulously silent about them—often brought in "floating" credit chips. Floaters were legal tender—*Pay to Bearer*, untraceable chips that changed hands frequently. Jerhattan Treasury and all the merchant and banking houses wisely ignored the circulation of minor amounts of floaters, just as they ignored the petty small traders as long as they made no trouble and their merchandise was harmless. Tirla, and others like her, relied on floaters to support their illegal existences in the Linears.

Linear G thrust thirty massive levels above the squat, featureless F and H commercial blocks where residents of Linears E, G, and I worked. Once, on a Free Day, while Tirla still had her brother's ID, she had gone with Mama Bobchik to the Great Palisades Promenade, where thousands upon thousands of people had swarmed to enjoy a brilliant spring day, to overlook the exclusive hives, platforms, and great cone complexes of Manhattan Island, and to ooh and aah at the monorail cars, large and small, that zipped along the tracks which garlanded the buildings like colored tinsel strands. That was the first time Tirla had seen ships floating on water or the great pleasure skycars. There had even been a special issue of holiday food, yards above the standard fare, at dispensing banks. Buril, Mama's son, had a tripper key that he used on the dispers, so they had managed to stuff themselves before the mechanism's malfunction alarm was triggered. It had been a super day for Tirla. She had never dreamed that the world was that big.

That was the same day that Buril explained to her all about the space platform that was being built, which needed so many workers. When it was completed, he said, all the people living on Manhattan who had enough credit and were the "right kind" would be able to go off into space and find other worlds to live on. Then all those beautiful buildings would be empty and there would be enough space for everyone crammed into Linear squats to live in proper big apartments with a bedroom for each family member and no more Public Health or LEO men and women tying men and women off, shaming a virile man.

This morning, as Tirla scratched on Mama Bobchik's door to tell her of the PH presence in the Linear, she heard the old woman gasping and groaning as she struggled off the bedshelf.

"Kto stuchitsya? Perestan'te udaryat'sya. Okh, kak bolit golova!"

Tirla grinned. So Mama had a big head this morning, caused by the vodka she had made from the potatoes Tirla had nicked for her. In that state, she would be easy to wheedle out of a credit.

"It's Tirla, and the Public Health are already on the Concourse."

"Boje moi! Eto tak? Have I not enough pain in my life?" But the door was pushed open wide enough for Tirla to slip inside. "What have you said? The Public Health again? So soon? Why?"

"Another vaccination by the looks of it. They're grabbing everyone, able-bodies, students, handies and their mothers."

"Ah, we must hurry. Elpidia, Zaveta . . ." Mama Bobchik began reciting the names of her usual maternity patients.

Tirla tugged her arm.

"Nu, what do you want from me?"

"I cannot help unless I have clean issue," Tirla said, managing to look piteous and sound efficient at the same time.

Buril had fixed the clothing-issue slot in his mother's squat so that it could be coaxed to extrude more than it ought. His taking ways had been very useful until Yassim—Tirla made the warding sign at just the thought of *that* man—had paid Mama a huge sum for him. Buril's unusual talent for "fixing" official equipment made him quite valuable—he had not gone the usual route of Yassim's purchases, and Mama had been paid enough floaters to keep her comfortable in her old age.

Mama Bobchik blinked her reddened and bleary eyes and

looked at the tiny girl. *"Da,* that is so!" She patted Tirla's head before she went to the clothing slot and did something that her heavy frame obscured from the girl's sight. When she turned back, she had a packet in her hand.

"I washed this morning," Tirla said, immediately unfastening and stepping out of the old suit. She had to roll up the sleeves and legs of the fresh issue, but when she had neatly folded each roll over wrist and ankle and pressed the edges to seal them, sleeve and leg bloused out nicely to give her apparel more style. She retied the pretty braided rope belt that she had inherited from her mother and tucked the excess material neatly back. "Now, I'll tell Mirda Khan, do this level, and then up and down. That'll be all I think I have time for. What'll I do for an ID? They'll grab me if my wrist's bare."

What Tirla wanted most in her life was a genuine, valid ID bracelet that would allow her a squat right, the use of a tri-d, three meals a day, and a fresh weekly issue of clothing. An ID that was all her own and had never been anyone else's! One that would allow her into the school programs that so few of the kids she knew seemed to care about at all.

Now she cocked her head at Mama Bobchik, knowing perfectly well that an ID was essential when the PHOs were swarming the Linear. Mama Bobchik pretended to consider, giving Tirla just a few moments of anxiety.

"Eto tak! For PHOs, we use one." With a flounce of her skirts, for Mama would not wear the single-piece coverall without proper skirts to conceal her limbs, she turned her back on Tirla again. No matter how hard Tirla listened, she could not tell where Mama secreted those precious counterfeit IDs that Buril had also contrived. They were good for one day's use only—one day, because while the band would be accepted by a portable reader such as the PHO would have to record vaccinations, it would show up as a fraud later, when the day's entries were checked.

Mama Bobchik turned around, dangling the precious ID band. "You split the take for the warning with me. As usual."

Tirla nodded solemn agreement to the terms, her eyes watching the swing of the band.

"And if you can steal enough vaccine, I will give you thirty percent of that take," Mama added.

Tirla gave an incredulous snort. "Sixty. I could get caught stealing."

"Forty, then. No one has caught you yet. After all, I gave you the ID at no cost to you and have the expense of the spray gun."

"Forty-five!"

The two hagglers eyed each other, and then Mama's broad face beamed down at Tirla's unyielding expression. She spit in her palm and engulfed Tirla's delicate hand in her own to seal the arrangement.

"You are a clever one. You must hurry now."

The girl was already slipping through the half-opened door and down the hall to spread the warning.

D espite her speed, Tirla barely finished her route before the PH officers began to penetrate the levels, checking the IDs of each squat's occupants and herding them out and down to line up for their hypospray. She soon learned that the health threat was not a 'mune plague but a virulent intestinal disease that had started in Linear B with devastating results. All Linears were being vaccinated in an attempt to stem the spread of the ailment. The PH public-address system droned on constantly giving a short explanation in all the languages registered in Linear G; Tirla did some rapid translations of her own when requested by nervous mothers.

"It's only another food contamination," she assured the

skeptical. "They've isolated the source, who have been heavily fined and lost their license."

"Huh!" Mirda Khan said, her dark eyes glistening with skepticism. "That will be gone as long as it takes to send in enough credit to reissue it. How long will the protection last us?"

"Oh, this one'll do us for a year!"

"A year? They are improving."

Trudging forward step by step in the long line, Tirla and Mama Bobchik finally reached the PH, dropped their wrists across the reader, and received their shots. Immediately Mama pretended to become faint and staggered against the table. While the PH woman was coping with that, Tirla swept an entire tray of the vaccine ampoules into the shopping sack Mirda Khan had ready as she, too, came to Mama's assistance.

"*Okh, kak bolit golova!*" Mama said in an appropriately wispy tone, the back of her fat hand against her head. The pain in her voice was not entirely faked, considering the hangover headache.

"What's she saying?" the PH officer asked, hovering between concern and annoyance.

"Her head hurts," Tirla replied.

"Not from this injection," was the callous response of the PHer. "Now move along!"

Solicitously Mirda Khan and Tirla propped up Mama Bobchik as she made her way slowly toward the nearest side aisle. Once safely out of sight, Mama immediately reached for Mirda's sack and peered inside it.

"One whole tray? Miraculous, Tirla, truly miraculous. There are more than enough. Run ahead and tell them to come in small groups. The PHOs have already checked our three levels. It will be safe."

In the course of her errands, Tirla tried her ID bracelet on as many public dispensers as she passed, no matter what commodity emerged from the slot. She tucked each purloined item

1 2

into the extra material at the back of her coverall, or into a sleeve or a trouser leg. It became harder to move quickly, but she managed. By evening, she had enough small floaters and illegally acquired items to keep her well fed and content for the next month. If she stretched a bit, it might even be six weeks before she need bother about working again.

CHAPTER 2

"There was no aura of menace or threat," Rhyssa Owen told Sascha Roznine as he stood glaring down at her. To reduce his threatening glower to a more productive, thoughtful mood, she touched his arm, reinforcing her statement with a mental *See? Curiosity. An impingement, not a threat.*

Sascha subsided, but he continued to glare at the graph recording of Rhyssa's early-morning sleep pattern, where the wide black mark of the spoke showed that she had been roused from an REM dream sequence to full alertness by a mental intruder.

As the director of the Center for Parapsychic Talents on the North American East Coast, Rhyssa Owen lived on what had been the Henner estate, a reserve of trees, lawn, and mature gardens above the Hudson River on the Palisades. This archaic remainder of the twentieth-century residential suburbs interrupted the flow of Linear structures that housed the millions who lived and worked in the massive Jerhattan complex. Rhyssa's quarters were undistinguished from any of the other three-story apartment blocks set among the gardens and trees. As with all dwellings for the Talented, these were secured and shielded from unannounced entry. In fact, even those who tenanted the Linear constructions running on the long sides of the Center's extensive grounds did not know of its existence, so artful were its screens. No one should have been able to intrude on Rhyssa, much less in her sleep.

"Awkward, rousing you so thoroughly. You need all the rest you can get." Sascha projected a vision of himself and Rhyssa curled together in her bed, the double-thick duvet tucked around their spooned bodies.

Yes, yes, Rhyssa replied. She responded with a vision of a firm foot pushing the Sascha body out of the bed. *But even if you had been there physically, you couldn't've helped, Sascha-bear. It was all in my mind, in my dreams. And that's your duvet, not mine. I never use plaids.*

Rhyssa smiled up at him, fluttering her eyelashes to mock his projection. He raised his brows in resignation. They both enjoyed this game. They had been playing it for years.

Picky, picky. Don't avoid the issue, Sascha said. "Who, I'd like to know, could knock in on your mind? And why?"

"Indeed!" Rhyssa crossed her arms and stared off into a view of the lowering clouds and dismal rain that obscured a usually breathtaking view of Jerhattan. *That's what perplexes me.*

Don't range, Streaky. Sending your mind out searching for him takes too much out of you. You're going to need all your energy to deal with the Zealots. He projected the vision of three persons with limbs so entangled they resembled an Oriental fetish, each caricatured face wearing an expression of mixed intransigence and skepticism.

Oh, don't! She laughed as her return image untangled arms and legs and set each person upright, a whiskbroom smoothing tunic and trousers while emblems of rank were straightened. *I can't remember that when I have to deal soberly with their urgent requests for Talents I don't have. They're laughable enough as it is.*

"Good. That's all they deserve. Shall I have Sirikit check back and see when this phenomenon first registered?" *Sheer impudence!* Sascha snorted his annoyance.

"That's an idea." Rhyssa smiled ruefully as she pulled

clothes from drawer and closet. She continued to talk as she dressed in the bathroom. "I only thought of checking my graph this morning. I really do need my sleep."

"Probably some emergent Talent who doesn't understand protocol. I do wish they didn't always feel required to over-react to their newfound mind-powers."

"Damned strong one!" Maliciously, Rhyssa projected an image of a very young Madlyn Luvaro, mouth wide open, and the circle of people cringing away from the waves of sound emanating from her.

Sascha grimaced. Madlyn Luvaro had a mental shout that could penetrate to the space station and any of its peripheral dockyards. It had been Sascha's task, as he was nominally in charge of Training and Development, to teach her how to fo-cus and moderate her mental voice. Madlyn adored him pas-sionately and was embarrassingly possessive of him, an adulation he was finding increasingly difficult to discount—it was the reason that he assiduously cultivated the notion that he and Rhyssa were on the brink of a total partnership. Kindly, Rhyssa did not disclaim the rumor.

"I'll have Sirikit run a check on possible emergents," he told her, then sent the request to Sirikit in the Control Room, also asking her to check Rhyssa's encephalograph charts for the previous months.

Emerging washed and dressed, Rhyssa beckoned Sascha to follow her through to her office, which adjoined her living suite. She yawned as she sat down at her desk, kinetically pulling some pencil files into her reach, fanning them out, and turning each until the index-code side was visible. She selected the one she wanted and neatly piled the others in front of her, code side outward, as her first selection inserted itself in the reply slot. Simultaneously the reader net came off its hook and settled lightly on her head. With one finger, she poked the left contact pad against her temple in a final adjustment.

"We won't find him there," she said, and was as startled as Sascha was that she used a gender. "Well, I know a trifle more than I thought I did from that fleeting nudge."

"A secret lover?"

"Could be," Rhyssa murmured, projecting an image of a sly grin and a come-hither expression directed at an amorphous shadow. Although her tone was light, Sascha perceived that her surprise at making any kind of an identification went deep.

"I'll follow through," Sascha said, and left her office. As he took the antigrav shaft down from her tower to the vast basement complex where most of the Center's training and research was conducted, he carried with him a vivid mental picture of Rhyssa Owen at her desk, the reader net covering her black hair, a spiderwebbing across the wide silver lock that she had had since her early teens. That streak grew broader every year, and by her late thirties her hair would be all Celtic silver.

Rhyssa would always have a young face, Sascha thought, as both her father and her illustrious grandfather, Daffyd op Owen, had had: young, vibrant, with dark blue eyes that sparkled and gleamed with intelligence, humor, and unassailable energy. Rhyssa was nearly as tall as the males in her family and a shade too thin; she clothed her long bones in elegant, if often bizarre styles: generally long flowing garments that set her off in a society which had stripped apparel to the minimum.

She was not pretty—her features, though small, were too uneven and mismatched, her right eye socket canted above the cheekbone, giving her a gamine expression that no one who knew her would misjudge. Her nose had a slight bump, making her profile look haughty, and her mouth was too generous above a strong jawline. Still, one forgot such details within moments of meeting her. She had inherited the full measure of charismatic personality, as well as the strong psionic talents, of

her parents—and of the grandfather who had battled to secure
the position of Talents in the present socioeconomic-political
atmosphere.

Sascha Roznine, himself a third-generation Talent and
younger than Rhyssa by three months, preferred his current
role as chief trainer and recruiter in the Center. Not for him
the petty power ploys that Rhyssa coped with admirably, for
he had struggled all his life to manage a quixotic temper. The
nerve-racking sessions with Jerhattan's managers and all the
picayune details she had to deal with would have set him
raging in five minutes. Sascha, on the other hand, had immense patience with emergent Talents, coaxing, cosseting,
and curbing, gently allaying their doubts and building their
confidence. When Rhyssa had once pointed out that, in their
own way, emergent Talents were as obnoxious as managers,
Sascha had replied that at least Talents learned from their
mistakes.

There were so many strengths and varieties of Talent. Of
the precogs, there were those who could foresee events, generally those which would have a major effect on a large number
of other people; those whose prescience was limited to people
they knew or were assigned to watch; and those whose pre-
cognitions had affinities with fire, water, males or females, children—there was as wide an assortment of focus points as there
were strengths of perception.

Telepathy was the most common Talent, though some people could only receive thought, and others only send it. Telempaths felt emotions and responded to the pervading ones. A
trained telempath could either dampen negative auras or rein-
force positive ones, a Talent useful for altering the tension in
a crowd, preventing rampaging emotions from turning groups
of people into disorderly mobs.

Finders were those Talents who could locate things, using only a facsimile of the desired item, or, in the case of a

missing human or animal, a garment or some other personal
object.

Telekinetics could work on the largest objects, or the most
minute particles that could not be seen with the naked eye or
even a microscope, though there had only been one known
genetic manipulator, Ruth Horvath. Telekinetics were invaluable in so many walks of life that those with this Talent were
encouraged to have as many children as possible.

The rarest of the Talents were the pure and double telepaths—like Rhyssa, who could send and receive communications across the world as long as she had met the person she
wished to contact. She could penetrate any mind not shielded
by the thin metal caps the nervous wore or by the natural mental shield that some normal people were born with.

Sascha, also a strong double telepath, lacked the phenom-
enal range that Rhyssa possessed, but he never resented her for
it. Once her strength had been established by her grandfather,
Rhyssa had been committed to a Center directorship and all its
responsibilities—responsibilities that Sascha would never want
to take on. As far as he was concerned, Rhyssa was welcome
to her Talent.

He heard Madlyn Luvaro before he landed on the shaft
cushion at the basement level. She was trying to be quiet, but
she was as successful as if she had been tap-dancing across a
sound-resonant surface.

*Until you learn to damp down your aura, it won't work,
Madlyn,* he told her. *Improper flow! Low positive energy is
what you need to be 'silent.'*

Dammit, I thought that's what I had! Her mental response
was contritely discouraged.

Sascha pushed out of the shaft and there she was, flattened
against the wall.

"I did 'hear' you coming," she said aloud.

Sasha: *Giant step forward!* Madlyn was a powerful sender,

but generally she could "hear" only those in her immediate vicinity.

He tugged a strand of her tangled mane of black hair as he passed, and she fell into step behind him, her large and expressive eyes rueful. Madlyn was a voluptuous eighteen-year-old with a sensual nature to match her appearance. She, and her Talent, had matured at fourteen, and since then Sascha had been struggling to teach her the necessary discipline that any Talent had to master, and that she would certainly require before her penetrating mental shout could be utilized.

Sirikit's already checking Rhyssa's Goosegg readings. Sascha had not tried to dampen his immediate concern. With so many telepaths aware of the alarm, keeping the investigation under wraps had been impossible.

Someone actually intruded on Rhyssa? Madlyn projected an image of herself throttling a large, amorphous intruder and squashing it into a little ball which she then flushed down the toilet.

Sascha snorted. Madlyn was quite capable of attacking anything that threatened Rhyssa. Who in the Center wasn't?

They found Sirikit already scanning Rhyssa's Goosegg encephalographs for the previous month. Several were paused at the spoking that indicated intrusive wakenings. The Goosegg, initially developed to monitor the odd light flashes experienced by astronauts, was especially sensitive in registering delta brain waves, which had been discovered to be the seat of paranormal or extrasensory perceptions. A Talent, trained to recognize his or her own slight mental alteration prior to paranormal activity, slipped on a net that could read brain activity. Many Talents, particularly the precognitives and clairvoyants, wore them night and day. They were lightweight, of a strong fine mesh matching the wearer's hair color. The net transmitted to the Center's main banks, so that Incidents of paranormal activity could be officially recorded, studied, and consulted. It was proof positive to any skeptics that the extra-sensory perceptions did occur.

"Look at Rhyssa's recordings, Sascha. There's no question that the Incidents have been increasing," Sirikit said as Sascha strode to the bank of horizontal spindles used in such comparisons. "First one three weeks ago, second four days later, then three, and this past week once a night—about four-ish."

Sasha: *Odd time for a voyeur!*

Sirikit: *With three-quarters of the population asleep in bed.*

Madlyn: *Insomniac?*

Sascha smiled, for not only was her mental tone appropriately soft but she had caught the quick exchanges.

Sasha: *An adolescent generally has to be pried from his sleep. Rhyssa thinks it's an emergent Talent.*

Madlyn: *You keep telling me that emergent Talents follow no rule.*

"Any statistics on insomniacs?" Sirikit asked.

"I'll program it," Madlyn said, flipping her hair back as she seated herself at a monitor, keying in directories that could access any computer bank in the world under the special concessions granted the Centers. She was cleared for normal use, although passwords were needed for any sensitive files. Madlyn might have been blatant in her sexuality, but her mind, open to inspection at all times, was as transparently guileless as a child's. "Well, this won't be productive. Anyone can have insomniac phases. Anxiety is the biggest cause. There are some people, the elderly in particular, who can get along on only four hours of sleep a night!" Her mental picture was of a horrified grimace superimposed on a tossing body in a rumpled bed. "I'm wrecked without eight hours!"

Sirikit leaned back from the spools, which had all paused to display the telltale spoke of intrusion.

Sirikit: *Three-thirty to four, predawn, too early for most shift workers, even air and road haulers.*

Sascha bent over her shoulder, studying the reels as if he could glower the riddle into the open.

Sascha: *Rig her net.*

Madlyn gasped and stared at him. Sirikit blinked, sighed, and then, rising from her stool, went to the main board to enable the necessary program.

"Some early-morning joy seeker *has* to be overflying the Center. Set an alarm through her net, and we can catch the bugger in the act." Sascha's voice was vindictive.

Madlyn shot him a worried glance. She could feel the wave of high negative energy he exuded.

CHAPTER 3

archenka, Duoml, and His Highness Manager Prince Phanibal Shimaz arrived promptly for their meeting with Parapsychic Center Director Rhyssa Owen at the Jerhattan City Manager's Tower, a massive structure in the center of Central Park, the last vestige of nineteenth- and twentieth-century Manhattan. The tower, rising above the tallest of the mercantile buildings, was crowned by ziggurats of communication dishes, giving it an appearance from any distance of a grotesque bunch of stiff daisies rammed into an immense glass brick. Skycars of varying sizes at the landing level stuck out like a fringe of angular, multicolored leaves.

Space Station Construction Manager Ludmilla Barchenka entered first, her odd bouncing gait indicating that she was wearing her antigrav boots. Her infrequent visits back to surface gravity were difficult for her—but they tended to be worse for those she confronted. The woman's appearance did nothing to mitigate her abrasive personality: she was stocky, big-boned though not fleshy, with a flat, broad face and unexceptional features. Pale blue eyes and short-cropped hair only added to the image of a tough persona—cold, inflexible tenacity. To top that off, Ludmilla invariably wore a thin metal skullcap, a shielding device that was almost an insult to Rhyssa in her capacity as director of the Eastern Center. Rhyssa was not sure if Barchenka used the shield merely out of concern for security or because she was pathologically wary of the Talents whose services she desperately needed even as she deplored their abilities. Sascha was convinced that Barchenka had some sort of

Talent, even if it could not be scanned, and that she refused to acknowledge the possibility.

Despite her total lack of social graces, the Exalted Engineer's dedication could not be faulted. Padrugoi Station was due to be completed, and on budget, at the end of the current year.

With interstellar voyages now possible and habitable planets located in two near systems, the pressure to implement the colonization program was incredible. But first the Padrugoi Station, the essential springboard to the stars, had to be completed. The project had worldwide priority and the enthusiastic support of every political and economic faction on Earth.

Considering that the first laboratory station had gone over budget by trillions and had been five years late in completion, Barchenka's achievements so far were considerable. But Rhyssa knew the truth: that the Exalted Engineer was beginning to fall behind schedule despite all her efforts. It was rumored that the woman slept no more than four hours a night and daily accomplished a prodigious amount of work—but that she expected the same dedication from everyone on the project. Unfortunately she did not have the charisma or leadership ability to generate either loyalty to herself or to the project. Initially many Talents had volunteered to assist, but one after another they declined to renew their contracts. The many enticements to return with their unique capabilities to work on Padrugoi Station had met with failure.

Personnel Manager Per Duoml, coming in behind Ludmilla, moved with the heaviness of someone accustomed to lighter gravity, but he managed without the antigrav assists. A Finn, as capable and dedicated as Barchenka, he was slightly easier to deal with. And though he, too, tended to wear a metal shield, the Talents had liked working with Duoml: he was fair, competent, and had succeeded in persuading a few Talents to return for special, short-term assignments. But still most had declined to extend their employment, and they could not be conscripted. And though Rhyssa had dutifully asked the directors of every Center in the world, she had no takers to offer Duoml.

Program Manager Prince Phanibal Shimaz pounced in behind Per Duoml, and his presence was neither essential nor welcome to Rhyssa. Peculiarly arrogant and impervious to her continued, and lately overt, distaste for his company, he used any excuse available to press his suit on her. Rhyssa often wondered why he had bothered to develop an impenetrable mind shield when his face revealed all that most men would have had the courtesy to hide. The prince was a computer genius— some said he had thought in binary codes in his creche and teethed on chips—and when he was barely out of his teens, he had mastered the use of the Josephson junctions in what he termed an "idiot proof" application to regulate with complete safety the vast flow of skycars and drones in and out of major Linear depots and over densely populated areas. He was currently applying his efforts to create a similar basic and safe flow of spatial traffic.

Rhyssa composed her face and her mind, smiling with a warmth she did not feel as the three settled themselves.

"I do *not*," Ludmilla began with no preamble, her deep voice guttural with only a slight trace of her native language, "have the required personnel." Her pale eyes accused Rhyssa.

"As I have told you repeatedly, Manager, I cannot and will not order the Talented into space."

Ludmilla brought her fist down with a wince that revealed that, in her frustration, she had forgotten the gravitational differences. She brought the bruised hand up in a gesture that in the space station would have been flamboyant but was less graceful on Earth.

"You *must* insist—"

"I can insist, but they can resist," Rhyssa replied equably.

"How can I maintain schedules without the personnel to perform the necessary tasks? Day by day we fall minutes behind: minutes which your diffident workers could make up in seconds. I will not fall behind the schedule. We will make our completion deadline. We must have the suitable personnel. You told me that you have them, and I have here the proof." Triumphantly Ludmilla extracted a pencil disk from her tunic and brandished it at Rhyssa.

"In that reply I said that I would certainly approach all Centers with your specific requirements. I most certainly did not promise to fill the vacancies."

Barchenka narrowed her pale eyes into a basilisk stare. "You recruit constantly. It is public knowledge that you find new Talents—"

"It does not follow," Rhyssa inserted smoothly, "that those we recruit are the kinetics that you specifically request. Certainly I could not ask untrained Talents to go into the hazards of space."

"Why not?" Ludmilla dismissed that consideration with a broad wave of her hand, inserting the pencil file back into its pocket at the end of the gesture. "We will train them on the job—to be useful, to be careful, to be specialists. They will love space. They will make many credits and be wealthy."

"The Talented do not accumulate wealth, Manager," Per Duoml stated in his flat, nearly toneless voice, his patient eyes never moving from Rhyssa's face.

"Nonsense! Everyone acquires wealth." Ludmilla had more than the usual contempt for altruists. "In the beginning we had many Talents working for us."

"We wished to assist the world project," Rhyssa said. "But you would not accept their stipulations when their contracts came up for renewal."

"Stupid clauses, untenable for us. Shifts of no more than six hours when we work twenty-four on the platform. Special shielding for noise. There is *no* noise in space." Her scornful gaze rested hotly on Rhyssa.

"No noise which is audible to you, Madame Engineer, but which is extremely unpleasant to sensitives."

"Bah! Sensitive!" Once again Barchenka summarily dismissed that consideration. "Spoiled, pampered, catered to."

"No, Madame Barchenka, not pampered or spoiled, but yes, catered to," Rhyssa flashed back. "The Talented are skilled personnel and require some minor considerations to enable them to perform at their best in the hostile environment of space."

Barchenka plowed on as if she had not heard. "It is incredible that such a minority can exert so much influence on the economic life of our world. In the airport, in the spaceport, in industry where, while I order matériel, I see the very Talents I must have to complete the most important project of the world, a project which has universal approval, which means mankind may reach beyond the limits of this solar system and explore the very stars themselves. Yet you and the other Center managers do not permit me to hire the specialists I need."

"It is not the permission of the Center directors that is required, but the consent of the employed," Rhyssa reminded the engineer. "Center directors negotiate the individual contracts with the necessary safeguards."

"I can buy the contracts." Barchenka's challenge was also a threat.

"Such contracts cannot be sold, Engineer Barchenka, and if you would accept the necessary safeguards, you might be more successful in attracting Talent!" Rhyssa replied sternly, beginning to lose patience with the woman's dogmatic pursuit. She could ignore Per Duoml's mournful expression and even keep her gaze averted from Prince Phanibal's hot eyes, slightly wet lips, and nostrils that flared slightly from his rapid breathing; but all three glaring at her were an unnerving combination. She kept a smile on her lips, deliberately increasing the flow of her limbic system.

"You can insist," Ludmilla repeated. "It is in all your contracts that 'it can be voided at the discretion of the Center in emergencies.' "

Rhyssa suppressed a rush of anger that Barchenka had been given access to a Parapsychic Contract and had to remind herself that such contracts were public knowledge. "My fellow directors do not consider that you have a true emergency, Engineer Barchenka."

For the first time Barchenka flared angrily. "I say this is an emergency! I say I must have a larger work force to complete this world priority project."

"You have unlimited access to the conscriptable pool of workers."

"Bah! They are useless—sterile, uneducated, untrainable grunts! I cannot build a space platform only with grunts. I will have the kinetics I need. I promise that, Director!" With that she wheeled and, in a dangerous imbalance, made a lurching exit, Prince Phanibal following her.

Per Duoml took one step forward, bowing slightly at the waist. "Even half a dozen kinetics would improve the situation tremendously."

"As I have explained repeatedly, Per Duoml, insure the Talents shielded quarters and a six-hour maximum shift and they will be amenable. Surely if there's credit enough in your budget to support the number of trips back to Earth that have been made for the purpose of recruiting Talents, the funds can be found to supply their basic needs on Padrugoi!"

"Engineer Barchenka must adhere to the budget. No alterations can be made to existing staff accommodations."

"Then Engineer Barchenka is stuck with the result." Rhyssa fervently wished that Per Duoml would relax his mental shield long enough for her to place directly in his mind the information her words patently did not convey. "You require kinetics to shift objects of mass proportions in the assembly of Padrugoi. You also need kinetics who can assemble chips of the most complex delicacy in the total vacuum of space. The kinetic energy required by both tasks is the same and exhausting. They need quiet to restore their strength—they are sensitive to the metallic vibrations of Padrugoi itself, the inhumanly close quartering, the lack of privacy, and the appallingly bad rations which are insufficient to replenish their bodies and minds."

Per Duoml nodded impassively and then shrugged, unwilling to comment before he, too, turned to leave.

His departure left Rhyssa with an uneasy sense of foreboding. She directed a query to Sirikit on duty in the Control Room of the Center. *Any precogs in just now?*

Sirikit: *None. You're expecting one?*"

Rhyssa projected an image of Ludmilla Barchenka's grim visage: *Possibly!*

CHAPTER 4

The boy blinked three times, and the channel on the ceiling screen changed again. He sighed. Yet another oldie he had already seen often enough to have memorized the good parts. He blinked the switch signal again, and realized that he had been through enough of the channels to be sure that there was nothing on to catch his attention—not even an educational program unfamiliar to him. The first few weeks he had been in the ward it had been lots of fun, watching the tri-ds all through the long nights. Kept his mind off—things—after his headaches had eased. Sometimes he almost missed those headaches, because at least then he had been feeling something in his body.

He sighed. He could do that, too, he reminded himself, thinking positively as Sue, the therapist, said he must. He didn't understand a lot of what she told him, like imagining himself walking and running, thinking hard of how he used to do it—before he had run alongside the ruins and that brick wall had collapsed on him.

Why? The agonizing question made him gasp. He had thought he had stopped thinking about that. Asking "why" was definitely negative and always depressed him terribly. Why had that wall come down just as he, Peter Reidinger, had been running past it? Had he kicked a stone that had been enough to trigger the collapse? Had one of the boys chasing him lobbed a stone at the wall? Why, since it had been standing for fifty or a hundred years all by itself, why had it picked that moment to come down? Three seconds later, he would have been safe—safe from both the wall and the boys chasing *him. Why had he turned into the forbidden area, anyhow? He'd had a choice at the end of the alley: over the wall, only it seemed very high to him and he had nothing to give him a leg up; to the right, only that took him back into the Alley Cats' territory and possible ambush; or to the left, weaving his way through the ruins, making it more difficult for them to know which way he would go. Why?*

Negative! Negative! Peter screwed up all his face muscles and then made them relax, group by group. Then he smiled, slowly and consciously spreading his lips and bringing the corners of his mouth up, stretching them until his cheeks lifted, his chin dropped, and his lips parted over his teeth; willing the nerve impulses in his face to change the limbic system. As Sue had taught him, he pulled his most happy moment out of his mind: his eleventh birthday, when his father had come home on leave from the space station in time for the party.

Planting that memory firmly in front of "why," Peter rehearsed the details of that happy experience until he could relive the entire scene from the moment the door chime had announced that his father had made it home until Dad had tucked him into his bunk. He had gotten so he could even feel the touch of his father's hand on his forehead.

Good thing Dad had touched him there—one of the only places he still had feeling. Peter sighed again and refelt the touch. Then he closed his eyes and "heard" his father leave the room, "heard" the muffled sounds of his parents talking and laughing. He expelled another deep sigh.

He was lucky. He could breathe on his own now. Sue had been so proud of him when that autonomic reflex had returned. He filled his lungs, knowing that his chest was rising, his diaphragm tightening. He could feel the air in his windpipe. He held his breath until spots came in front of his eyes; then he expelled it.

Immediately he heard the steps of the duty nurse. Miz Allen did not like to be disturbed, especially when he knew that they

31

had a critical case on Pie 12. He counted ten steps and then she was peering down at him, making eye contact. She then peered at the wall panel that displayed the readings from his monitors.

"Why was there a respiratory fluctuation, Peter?"

"Aw, I was just doing my breathing exercises."

"You were not." Miz Allen glared at him a moment, and then her long thin face relaxed. She laid a light hand on his forehead and then drew one finger down his cheek to press it against his lips. "You were fooling. Don't fool with your breathing, Peter. Your brain needs oxygen. And it needs sleep, too. It's quarter of four. You should sleep. You know how to achieve relaxation, Peter. Do your progressives, there's a good boy."

They both heard the sudden whimpering of the burn girl on the other side of the circular ward.

Miz Allen, reproving smile and all, disappeared, and Peter counted her steps, twenty-one, to get to the critical case. Then he counted to thirty, and the whimpering ceased. He knew burns hurt. He wished he felt something, *even burns!*

He immediately put his mind to the few progressives available to him: the relaxation of every muscle in his face, head, and neck. He could not move his head, but he had sensation in his neck. He reached total slack and thought carefully of his place, feeling the spring of grass under his feet, hearing the shimmer of leaves as a wind soughed through them, smelling the fragrances of the garden, gazing up at the sky above, the sun warm on his back. He began to float again. He had the sensation of drifting up, out of the supine body resting on its cushion of air, amazed and annoyed at the various tubings and wires shunted into him that he never felt.

The garden of his dreams was miles away from Jerhattan. It had been part of the vacation farm to which his parents had taken him when he was eight. For someone raised in Linear Jerhattan, surrounded constantly by the noise and smell of

people and maintenance machineries, he had been totally en-
tranced by the farm. Peter knew that there were small green
belts throughout the Jerhattan complex; he had even been to
several, trying to relive that vacation, but none had evoked
the same response in him, being too small and cramped to
close out the eternal noise of the city.

He had found a place, though, where he could float when
he got to the proper state of relaxation. It had grass and trees,
barely visible in the eerie predawn light. And he was strangely
attracted by other inexplicable strands, comforting wisps of
thought, enticing him to linger. One in particular intrigued
him, and he hovered as close to it as he could, tantalized by
a sense of tranquil familiarity.

All of a sudden he was nearly blinded by powerful lights
that flooded the scene. He felt a moment of terror. He could
not suppress his scream, steadying only when he heard Miz
Allen's steps. He did not open his eyes until he felt her hand
on his forehead and knew *he was safe back in Bed 7 of Pie*
Ward 12.

"What's the matter, Peter?" Miz Allen always knew if a
patient was shamming and she did not tolerate false alarms.
Her eyes flicked to the wall panel. "Bad dream?"

"Yes, bad dream." Despite himself, his voice quavered,
and her expression softened.

"Yes, your endorphin level shot up. I think you'll have to
have some sleep."

Peter nodded, relieved at her decision. "I've got VMR to-
morrow . . ." He began, but then darkness overwhelmed him.

You scared him off! Rhyssa accused Ragnar, fuming that
someone had triggered her net to alert the Center's security forces if her pattern spiked during the night. The field lights
had blazed up. Moments later she had heard the thrumble of

the skycars, shooting off in all directions. *Sascha!* she roared.
He was the only one empowered to set surveillance on her!

Sascha: *We'll catch the bugger!*

Not that way! Rhyssa forced controls on herself to disperse
the white-hot fury. Sascha had exceeded his authority—even
the boundaries of friendship.

Sascha: *I have not!*

She inhaled deeply, aware that she was still trembling with
anger. She expelled the breath right down to her toes, continuing to press downward until her belly muscles were taut. *There
was* NO *threat!*

There was *intrusion!* His mental pattern broke briefly as he
responded to some exterior stimulus. *That's bloody strange,*
he said a moment later. *There* was *no intrusion. Not a physical
one. Not a blip on any screen that can't be accounted for. And
nothing—read that—nothing in our airspace.*

An emergent! Rhyssa colored the thought with satisfaction.
That is, if you haven't scared him out of his Talent! She sent
an image of herself turning back onto her stomach, hauling the
duvet in its pastel print tightly around herself, and dragging a
matching pillow firmly over her head—which was what she
did.

A n emergent from where?" was the question that circulated
the Control Room.

"Who's awake at four o'clock in the morning?"
Sascha asked.

"I can do a probability curve," Madlyn suggested, "elimi-
nating all the obvious shift workers."

"Why eliminate them?" Budworth asked.

"If they're working, they're not doing o.o.b.," she replied.

"And who says this is an out-of-body job?" Sascha asked,
turning on Madlyn with surprise.

"What else could it be?"

Sascha grinned. "You may very well be right, Madlyn, and it's so obvious I wonder none of us thought of it before. Okay, who would go o.o.b.?" It was a leading question to which he already had an answer.

"Someone who doesn't like the bod they're stuck with," she replied.

"But o.o.b.'ing *is* Talent," Budworth said, "and all of 'em are registered, so they have better things to do than o.o.b."

"*If* they're registered," Sascha pointed out.

"I see, so we run a check on new ones."

"That's right. With the hospitals."

Madlyn groaned. "D'you know how many hospitals there are in Jerhattan?"

"Not intimately," Sascha said with a grin, and pointed an index finger at her. "Think of it as a survey question in your training. Ask for paralytic cases, teen, preteen, insomniacs . . ."

"Why blame the teens?" Madlyn asked, bridling.

"They won't have been scanned for Talent yet. Okay," Sascha added graciously, "try anyone faced with a sudden lack of mobility. I'll add the prison systems, too." He grinned at Madlyn's groan. "One of the most famous was a guy escaping a sadistic jailor."

Madlyn's eyes widened. "Can the Center get prisoners released?"

Budworth chortled. "Don't you remember your Center history? This place was started by rejects from prisons and mental institutions—" He shot a sly look at Sascha. "—and all kinds of otherwise asocial and/or eccentric personalities."

"If my brother were here . . ." Sascha waggled an admonitory finger at Budworth.

"Huh!" Budworth snorted. "I'm not afraid of your brother even if he is the high-and-mighty Law Enforcement and Order commissioner."

"I would be," Sascha replied. "Which reminds me, I'm late for that appointment. Get the program started on checking hospitals and prisons. And buddy boy, you can do the mental institutions. I appreciate the reminder.''

"Ha!'' Madlyn said to Budworth as Sascha left the Control Room.

H ow can there be that many illegal children in the Residentials?'' Jerhattan City Manager Teresa Aiello demanded of Medical Chief Harv Dunster. "Your people are supposed to tie off after a second pregnancy.''

Harv's angular face was grim. "Only if we get to deliver 'em. You know that some ethnic groups still refuse to practice contraception. Until we have the right to use infertility drugs in subsistence-level food, there'll be unreported births—and continued traffic in preadolescents for sexual perversions, or cheap labor in illegal factories. And the ones with the right blood factors and healthy organs will still be stashed away by the very rich for transplants as needed.'' He gestured at the fax sheets on Teresa Aiello's desk.

"And ruthless people will still dispose of the used ones,'' added Boris Roznine, commissioner of Law Enforcement and Order. "Even illegal kids have rights.'' He glanced obliquely at the faxes scattered on the worktop.

Teresa inadvertently glanced down. She was a tough-minded woman, but she had a ten-year-old daughter, and the fax of the bloated bodies discovered as flotsam off the North Shore of Long Island spared no one's sensibilities. She averted her eyes. The coroner reported that the oldest had been twelve, the youngest five.

Boris Roznine had contacted her the moment the appalling discovery had been made. The temper of Jerhattan was always uncertain when faced with such news, and Teresa had called an emergency meeting of her commissioners to prepare for a possible eruption if the news was leaked to the media. Boris's twin brother, Sascha, was due to arrive with the Parapsychic

Center's suggestions. To insure the tight security around the tragedy, the four were meeting in the shielded privacy of the city manager's tower office.

"Ah," Boris interrupted what Teresa had been about to say, his right hand lightly touching his temple in indication that he was receiving a telepathic message. "Positive ID of one, the Waddell girl who was kidnapped six weeks ago . . ."

Teresa winced and let out a groan. The Waddells were acquaintances of hers, high-tech executives; the child, bright and extremely pretty, had been a school friend of her daughter. Teresa had put a top priority on the abduction, and had officially requested that Rhyssa Owen assign her best finder to the case.

"Two others are listed as runaways, reported missing two months ago. Of the others . . ." Roznine shrugged, glancing at the medical officer. "The best the lab can do is genotypes, and it's all-sorts."

Every citizen of the United World was permitted—provided they did not carry the proscribed genetic recessives—to produce a replacement. One parent, one child. Two parents, two children. ZPG was stringently enforced until the pressure of Earth's population could be released on the new habitable worlds, identified but not yet attainable. The Propagation Laws were easier to enforce in rural communities than in the huge residential warrens of cities like Jerhattan, with its population of over thirty million.

Teresa turned to the LEO commissioner. "You haven't stopped the spot checks, have you, Boris?"

"Hell, no, but we're still not locating the early pregnancies no matter how we try. If I had the personnel to mount simultaneous level searches, we'd catch more." Boris brought his clasped hands together as if closing a net. He gave a ghost of a grin. "We did pretty well at the Residentials, six weeks after the last big power outage, but that was a once-off." Then he spread his hands wide, matching Dunster's resignation. "You know our situation. We manage to keep a lid on most of the trouble—if we're all sitting down as hard as we can. It isn't as if we need more bodies.''

"The ones that ignore the legal control," Harv said dejectedly, "are exactly the ones educational and hygiene programs don't reach—in any language.''

Teresa grimaced. "So there's no indication where the rest of those poor kids were snatched?''

Roznine shook his head. "Could have come from any subsistence level.''

"In the last gruesome chucking, three months back or so, only four were recognizable ethnic types," Harv Dunster said grimly. "Near Easterners—Lebanese and Arabic. Two were Tay-Sachs, ten were dark-skinned, and one was an HIV carrier—which may well be why they were all . . . disposed of.'' The medic sighed heavily. "I suspect Lab may also find anti-body positives among this latest—''

"Spare me, Harv," Teresa said firmly, and called up the main Jerhattan map on her screen. "We've just had a go-round of the Residentials with Public Health. We haven't got the funds available for another. Exactly where were the bodies found, Boris?'' Her fingers hovered over the terminal as she waited for an answer.

"Washed up out by Glen Cove, not far from some of the more exclusive residential hives bordering the Sound.''

"Great!" Teresa's frustration came out as sarcasm. "No Incident logged?'' she asked Boris, though that would have been included in the initial report.

"The storm, yes. The flotsam, no.''

"Shouldn't your brother be here by now?" Teresa frowned, glancing at the clock ticking off the seconds in the corner of the main screen. "We need all the help we can get on this.''

The focus of Boris Roznine's blue eyes locked briefly as he linked minds with his younger brother. "Traffic snarl's breaking up. But he says"—his voice suddenly deepened as the Talent peculiar to the twin brothers allowed one to speak through the other—"Look, I want to save time—yours and mine. These murders go deeper than the loss of thirty juveniles. Forget the HIV factor—it's irrelevant here. They were disposed of because we'd got too close to them, but not close enough, soon enough. Teresa, Carmen's been on search-and-find duty ever since you handed us the Waddell kidnap file. She got a whiff or two of terror, but never enough light to pinpoint. Except that she got a hint of water." Boris's wide mouth quirked briefly, reflecting his brother's chagrin. "Most of those children had to be illegals. We all know that that group of pederasts is active—and supplied—despite international efforts to eradicate that sort of traffic. We know that kids are bought as cheap labor and shipped who knows where. And that some are also secreted as possible transplant donors.

"We haven't been idle," Sascha's voice continued. "This could, in fact, be the break we've been waiting for. We got too close. It'd be nice to know—" and at that word the door to Teresa Aiello's office swung open and Sascha Roznine strode in, smiling at everyone. As he gave his brother's shoulder a grateful squeeze, he continued, "where exactly we got so close. We're working on it, and with your assistance, Harv and Teresa, I think we have a line to throw out to those sharks." His smile took in each of his listeners, but he cocked his head at his brother and winked.

Slowly a smile began to lighten Boris's face as he read the detailed thoughts in Sascha's mind. "Tag kids with strands through the school system? That might just work! We might even catch the bastard child-stealers this time." Boris leaned forward across the table. "You are all familiar with the restraint filaments that were recently developed? Sometimes those we tangle with the strands escape before they can be secured. A second application has been made with a slightly altered formula, and now the altered strand can be traced for up to six months. There're certain anomalies to be resolved, but it's worth the effort to tag every child in the vulnerable group."

"You mean, this side of the river?" Teresa waved at the panorama visible from her tower office, the uptown cluster of beehive, cone, and single-tower Residential buildings clearly visible on this bright morning. "But statistically, it's the illegals in the Linear Residentials who are more at risk."

"If we could catch Linear kids to strand 'em," Boris said, raising his hands palms-up in resignation, "we'd be way ahead. Meanwhile we'll strand as many kids as we can on both sides of the river and hope."

"Hope?" Sascha asked softly.

*R**hyssa!* She recognized the mental touch of John Greene, the Talented bodyguard of Secretary of Space Vernon Altenbach.

We got problems? she asked.

Girl, you really deserve all the headaches of administration if you can guess that much from just hearing me speak your name.

No precog needed, JG, because you never bother me unless there's political pussyfooting. What is it this time?

A bill to draft the Talented into whatever position the government needs them!

Not again? Rhyssa's response was half-amused, half-irritated.

Concerted attempts had been made in the past by government agencies to circumscribe the freedom of choice originally granted to the Talented. That was prior to the point at which the government began to appreciate the applications of Talent—after the days when Daffyd op Owen, her illustrious grandfather, abetted by Senator Joel Andres, had fought to gain legal immunity for Talents exercising their abilities.

Immunity had been particularly vital for precogs because, when they warned of disasters which were, by those warnings, averted, they had been subjected to expensive and time-consuming lawsuits. There had been attempts since then, from the ridiculous to the deadly serious, to regulate or restrict, all manner of Talents to military, civil service, or mercantile uses.

But the Talented had always managed, quite legally and with no untoward exercise of their particular abilities, to circumvent such attempts. Many Talents had willingly sacrificed personal freedoms to serve in the public sectors, some on a lifelong basis, to preserve the right for their peers to choose. Rhyssa's parents had done that, to give her the opportunity to achieve the position she now held.

Again, and this isn't funny, Rhyssa, Johnny Greene went on, *space is in a bind. The platform has to be finished on schedule before the sheer weight of numbers on Earth becomes more unmanageable than it already is.*

So Ludmilla's been lobbying?

She's got some hefty help, and Vernon's got tremendous pressure on him. I'm the loudest of the Washington/Luxembourg voices, so I'm making the contact with you for the rest of the minders. We've been excluded from far more sessions than we ought to be—sessions that have been attended by some of the most antagonistic Right Mutes that have ever been lined up against Talents. And when you think that I helped him develop his shields against unauthorized peeking, I could spit! The nerve of him closing me out!

One of the more sensitive professions open to empathic Talents was that of "minding" vulnerable top-ranking officials. Terrorism was still a fact of political life, and although the problem of the displaced and the minorities had been somewhat eased by the mass resettlements and the institution of the Linear developments near every major urban area, and the incidence of assassinations had been drastically reduced, empaths were still employed to "mind" those officials who might be targets for the fanatics who still occasionally emerged.

Rhyssa could hear the hurt in Johnny's voice that Vernon Altenbach had been shielding his thoughts from his minder, especially since Johnny was also Vernon's best friend, as well as his brother-in-law. In his official capacity, Johnny served as under secretary in the Space Secretariat. Prior to that he had been a trained etop—earth-to-platform—pilot with twenty successful launches . . . until the twenty-first had grounded him forever. His Talent had saved his crew from death but not himself from losing both left leg and arm. Despite state-of-the-art prostheses, a new career had seemed advisable. So far Johnny had already prevented four attempts to kill or kidnap Secretary of Space Altenbach.

Johnny: *I shoulda been included in these latest talks, but I wasn't.*

Rhyssa: *Which means that Talent was being discussed. Barchenka and Duoml want more kinetics on the platform in the worst way. I'm doing my best to help . . .*

Johnny, in an uncompromising tone: *Anyone thought of telling Barchenka that she's the reason why Talents won't work up there?*

Rhyssa: *Lance Baden did. He thinks she has selective amnesia. Can't even get her replaced, not with the performance record she's got!*

Vernon's tried! She's so bloody good at what she does—it's only how she does it. I'll keep in touch, but we felt you ought to be forewarned. There was a hint of criticism in his voice.

Nothing has come up with any precog, Johnny.

I know, I know. That worries me as much. This thing could be very very big, and not even Mallie's got a whiff!

Rhyssa: *Then obviously the matter is solved before it reaches critical.* She tried to sound firmly optimistic even as a little shudder rippled down her backbone. Someone should have been sensing something! Mallie Vaden was one of the most sensitive precogs the Center had ever produced, and her lack of foresight—if Johnny's reading of the situation was correct—was surprising.

I'll be in touch, Johnny assured her. *I'll even see what the ghosts think. You know how they'd like to see our Talented noses out of joint.*

I think I'll try a frontal attack, Rhyssa said. *Might jog a few brain cells loose.*

When'll I see you then? Johnny asked, his tone brightening.

If possible, today. Run me through Vernon's schedule. When Johnny did, Rhyssa stopped him at the lunchtime engagement. *I like the food there. I'll just drop in!*

Rhyssa always experienced a mild shock when she encountered Johnny in the flesh, for the light tenor of his mental voice was at variance with his strong physical appearance. Medium tall, he kept himself physically trim, and one would never guess his serious injuries from seeing him walk or manage eating utensils. Some latent kinetic ability had proved to be an asset with his prosthetic limbs. He rose as he spotted Rhyssa approaching the table where he, Secretary of Space Vernon Altenbach, Exalted Engineer Ludmilla Barchenka, and Padrugoi Personnel Manager Per Duoml were seated. Johnny's broad smile welcomed her, and they exchanged touch and a kiss.

Would you have dared look so stunning if the amorous Phanibal had come, too? Johnny's green-flecked amber eyes twinkled with devilment.

Rhyssa: *Why doesn't that odious man go back to the Pacific island that spawned him and attend to the family's plantations?*

Johnny: *All you need is a strong handsome man who'll*

scare him off. Right now you've got this lot embarrassed by your appearance, and yet they haven't said a thing out of line, he added, all in the split seconds of the greeting.

Rhyssa gave Altenbach a genuinely glad smile, then nodded politely to the fiercely scowling Barchenka and the bland-faced Per Duoml. "Just the people I hoped to see. When I saw you were to be in Washington, Madame Barchenka, I realized that I should put in an appearance before matters get out of hand."

"Now, Rhyssa," Altenbach said, signaling a waiter to bring a chair and set up another place for his unexpected guest, "you can't disrupt the established procedure of lobbying. That's not the way to play the game."

"Nor is going behind my back," Rhyssa said, smiling to take the sting out of her criticism. She turned to Barchenka. "You have a schedule to keep. What you will not appreciate is that one cannot schedule Talent or lobby it. The kinetics you so desperately need cannot materialize to help you meet your schedule. That many kinetics don't exist. Talent is a random and highly individual trait, not an imposed one. No one can dictate to a Talent and expect the person to perform to the best of her or his ability. That dictation inhibits the Talent as surely as seasickness inhibits appetite. There is no legislation in the world that may chain the mind."

"There is legislation that will recruit those needed to do the job that the entire world has decided must be done." Barchenka's stolid words complimented her uncompromising expression. "The platform *will* be finished as scheduled. The kinetics *will* participate."

Rhyssa caught another strong emanation, this time from Per Duoml, who nodded solemnly to support Barchenka's statement.

"There are ways," Barchenka added, her cold eyes scanning Rhyssa's whole appearance from the elegantly coiffed hair and subtle makeup to the couture outfit.

"Legal?" Rhyssa asked with a slight smile.

The secretary cleared his throat and handed Rhyssa a menu. "I'm still of the opinion that this—impasse—can be negotiated to the satisfaction of all concerned."

Barchenka made a monosyllabic noise of disbelief and resumed her perusal of the menu. After only seconds, she tossed it negligently to the table. "I would prefer nutritious food to this . . ."

Johnny Greene beckoned to the maitre d', who was famous for his poise under the most trying situations that Washington could produce. "D'Amato, Manager Barchenka requires the *other* menu."

At a snap of D'Amato's fingers, an underling appeared and handed him a slim folder, which he presented to Barchenka with a flourish. She gave him, then Johnny, a sardonic look that turned to agreeable surprise as she scanned a menu composed of the foodstuffs available on the platform.

"Five, twelve, and twenty, taken with tea," she said in a voice that still vibrated with controlled anger.

Watch it, Rhyssa! Johnny cautioned. *Did you catch that flash? She's poison-sure she's got us where she wants us.*

Simultaneously three other minders, dining with their charges in the same room, sent Rhyssa similar warnings. She was particularly glad to feel the mental touch of Gordon Havers, the youngest Supreme Court justice ever appointed, whose expertise might be extremely useful.

Fine! Now discover what? Rhyssa said mentally as vocally she chose her luncheon of cold fruit, soup, and salad. *Gordie, are you available for some quick scans of obsolete statutes that could cover such a contingency?*

Been driving myself and my clerks all hours trying to find one, Rhyssa, replied Gordon Havers. *There's nothing in our constitution, but since the Russians won the contract for Padrugoi, there may be something in the Russian section that does! Their legal system is as convoluted as their grammar!*

"You can, of course, invoke some forgotten but still active statute," Rhyssa remarked all too blandly, waiting for reactions, "to conscript Talents . . ." Both Barchenka and Duoml looked startled.

Bingo! Gordie cried. *I'll concentrate on the Russian end of space law.*

"But," Rhyssa continued soothingly, "it has always proved unwise to force Talent to perform in an area that is either personally or professionally distasteful to them, and under punitive conditions."

"We have been too lenient with your temperamental tricks and traits," Barchenka said, leaning across the table in anger. "You will do this, you won't do that!" She affected a child's petulant tone. "Many concessions were made to cater to the whims and fads of your Talents, and still no significant numbers will volunteer for the most important world project of all history. Your attitude is unacceptable."

"I am protecting my colleagues, not being obstructive. I must repeat," Rhyssa continued smoothly, "it has always proved unwise to force Talent to perform duties unacceptable to them and under punitive living conditions."

"That will change! Will be changed! The platform will be finished on schedule!" Barchenka's voice had risen with each sentence until it stopped conversation throughout the opulent dining room. She pushed herself from her chair, wobbling slightly as her movements, more suited to half grav, brought her stocky body ponderously to an upright position. She kicked the chair away from her. "I do not tolerate insubordination!" And she clumped away from the table.

"I was doing my best for you," Vernon Altenbach said to Rhyssa, his face and manner resigned as he rose, his chair pulled back by a hovering waiter.

"You do not understand our position, Director Owen," Per Duoml added, but he made no move to leave the table. "We

are forced to use unpleasant alternatives to avert far more serious disasters overtaking the world!"

"I'll see if I can calm her down, make her see reason,"
Vernon said with a gesture for Johnny to remain. "D'Amato,
send my meal and hers to the private room. I'll be there."

"Do you believe, in your own heart, Per Duoml," Rhyssa
asked, leaning across the table to the man, "that we are *evad-
ing* our duty to the world?"

He shrugged, his mind, with its metal shield, as impervious,
Rhyssa thought, as his unwillingness to understand the nature
of Talent. "It is the opinion that this—reluctance—puts the
whole platform project in jeopardy."

"It is Ludmilla Barchenka who puts it in jeopardy," Rhyssa
said with more heat than she had intended. She smiled quickly,
hoping to repair the damage of her candor. Per Duoml might
not be Talented, but he was scarcely stupid.

"Ah! My esteemed colleague was correct," he said.

"I am *not* standing in her way. I am protecting my professionals even as she is protecting her project."

Well, she is why Talents won't work for her, Johnny said
in swift reassurance. *And we all know it!*

Gordie: *Yeah, but she stays! This will be an interesting
power struggle, speaking from a purely legalistic viewpoint.*

"I admire Barchenka's unquestionable abilities as a spatial
engineer. I would prefer that she return the professional compliment," Rhyssa said amiably. "This soup is excellent, Per
Duoml. Let us enjoy it."

B*ingo!* Gordie Havers told Rhyssa the next day. There was
absolutely no joy to his tone.

You mean Barchenka can conscript Talents? Rhyssa felt a
cold paralysis grip her.

You've got it! I've been over the statute—and it is *Russian,* *from the pre-*glasnost *days, and should have been repealed long ago it's so archaic. In the good old Bolshevik days, it was illegal—get that, illegal—to be unemployed. The State was the only employer—not the employer of last resort—but the only employer. Ergo, everyone worked. Consequently, the only employer in a system that makes it illegal to be unemployed can certainly do whatever is deemed necessary with its work force. Legally, it gives Barchenka the right, under Padrugoi's International Charter, to draft any technicians, professionals, or workers required by the space effort—the space effort in terms of the original law being the Russian one. But the statute is still in effect, and, by legal crook, she can apply it to Talents. We can fight it, of course!*

And? she prompted.

With a glib-tongued attorney like Lester Favelly, we might just win. But the trial would take years, and could be construed by Barchenka to prove her contention—that the Talents are obstructing the Good Work. He paused significantly. *We could just give her enough rope to hang herself?*

The Talents will be miserable, and they won't perform well. That was what rankled Rhyssa's fine sense of integrity. Talents did the best they could no matter what the circumstances. To give the slightest suggestion that they skimped was against the most stringent of tenets for the parapsychic. But, in space, worn down by punishing hours and psychic static they could not avoid, inevitably their performances would suffer.

Exactly, Gordie said. *Ask the other directors. You must appear to be accepting the inevitable.*

The sort of press this could give Talents would undo the work of the last century, Rhyssa said despairingly.

I know. Although to sweeten this very bitter pill, Rhyssa, Mallie Vaden sees nothing going wrong.

Whose side is she on? Rhyssa could not keep the bitterness out of her tone.

Ours, as you well know, was Gordon Havers's crisp reply. *Ergo, it has to work out by our compliance. But I've initiated some investigations that might just give us a lever against Barchenka. Meanwhile, consult, Rhyssa. Quick action might shift public support to us.*

CHAPTER 5

Some of the fourteen other Center directors were not best pleased to be roused by her urgent request for conference in the middle of their nighttimes, and there was some grumbling. Though all Centers were theoretically equal, no director decided issues that would affect all Talents without consulting the others first, and Rhyssa—in charge of negotiations for the Talents because Padrugoi's administrative headquarters was in Jerhattan—deemed a meeting necessary. As soon as all were attending, she explained the situation.

And from what equally critical positions does this Russian think we can draft these essential kinetics? Lance Baden, the Australian director, demanded. Rhyssa always found it odd that his mental voice was devoid of the Aussie accent. *We sent everyone we could bribe or blackmail up there. Sheer bloody-mindedness keeps some of 'em in place, but my staff's down to nubbins or feather-movers.*

I have told Ludmilla Ivanova, said Vsevolod Gebrowski of the Leningrad bureau at his most apologetic, *time and again, that there are few kinetics not already doing double, triple work in order to supply essential services in Russia. Believe me, I have tried to educate her to the practicalities . . .*

We do believe you, Geb, we do, was the mass thought that reassured him.

What's the levy, Rhyssa? Miklos Horvath, the West Coast director, asked.

She's demanding one hundred forty-four kinetics! Rhyssa said grimly, and threw up a buffer against the cries of outrage.

The number of registered Talents in every Center was open knowledge to every director, as transfers constantly shifted key Talents at need from one Center to another.

We don't happen to have a handy gross of kinetics, the Brazil director said angrily. *And I spent six months up there, in the most godforsaken barrio I've ever seen. Constant noise! Dreadful food—nutritious food could at least have a distinctive flavor. How she can expect us to function . . .*

If we use the discretionary clause, we can remove the required number from commerce and industry, Max Perigeaux of the large European bureau began in his slow, thoughtful way.

Ignoring the howls . . .

Under the circumstances, at least we're not liable to penalties . . .

That's a real comfort to those forced up to Padrugoi . . .

Well, Commerce and Industry want this station—they'll have to suck lemons along with the rest of us . . .

Max went on, his message weaving inexorably among the asides: *. . . put the trainees where at least they can be overseen, we could just about manage it. But how can we expect our people to endure the conditions up at the platform and still perform creditably? To do less than our best reduces our reputations, but how can anyone operate at his best in that milieu! And the noise!* The tall aesthetic man imaged a shudder of revulsion.

But something *must be done to give those who are conscripted some relief!*

Barchenka believes we set up the conditions of shielded quarters and short hours to be obstructive! Rhyssa said. *I was informed that there is no noise in the vacuum of space, and, because there is also no gravity, there is less physical stress and* longer *hours can be worked, not fewer.*

The woman is utterly without a shred of understanding or empathy, the director of Africa North said.

Has anyone tried *to adjust her thinking?* Hongkong Jimmy asked.

You've never met Barchenka, have you? Shields tighter'n a chastity belt! Baden said in an acid tone.

What's a chastity belt? Hongkong Jimmy flicked back in genuine innocence.

Images from nine helpful telepaths enlighted his ignorance. Rhyssa was grateful to him for easing the growing tension in the linkage with that byplay.

We are compelled to comply, are we not! Perigeaux said, at his most mournful. *And without delay, so that we can bargain on the best possible conditions for those who must sacrifice themselves. A rotation scheme, perhaps . . .*

If she's after the gross, that makes rotation impossible!

I can try to insist on some sort of short-term stretches, Rhyssa said.

Let us also issue some publicity, Miklos Horvath suggested, *about conditions up there.*

Of dubious value when she needs to recruit so many grunts. You know she has to go to the shelters for anyone below Civil Service–8.

But the public must see that Talent's objections to working in space are valid!

The most valid being Barchenka herself . . .

Can no one *lean on her?*

It's been tried . . .

Who's the best we've got?

What about her associate, Per Duoml? Any chinks in him?

It isn't that we don't want to help with the project, but she is her own worst enemy.

Did she specify kinetics only?

No one's told her that some kinetics are also telepaths!

Don't anyone mention that! Lance Baden said with unusual vehemence.

Wouldn't dream of it!

You mean, she doesn't know?

Ludmilla Ivanova knows what she wants to know, Vsevolod said wearily. *She only hears the explanations she wishes to
hear.*

In twelve minutes of rapid-fire exchanges, the Talents arrived at a grim but workable course of action. Max, Baden, and
Jimmy would do the actual selection of suitable kinetics. Some
Talents could be excused on grounds of infirmity, pregnancy,
or unsuitable skills—though two of Baden's "feather-dusters"
were well able to handle the fine tunings. Rhyssa, Miklos, and
Dolores of the Brazilian Center would attempt to achieve
shielded quarters and work shifts of six hours maximum, four
for the less experienced kinetics. Barchenka might be running
her operation twenty-four hours a day, but eight hours of tele-
kinesis were impossibly draining, even in space and in 0.5-grav
conditions.

What we must also organize, for ourselves, Kayankira of
the Delhi Center said as the main issues had been resolved, *is
an emergency system in a disaster situation.* In her mind
churned images of the previous year's catastrophic floods in
the northeastern sections of the Indian subcontinent, mitigated
only by the rapid mobilization of hundreds of kinetics when
the precog had come in.

*Kayan, you've had far more experience with that sort of
thing than anyone needs,* Baden said with unexpected humil-
ity. *Advise us and we will comply.*

*You always do! We'll have to strip all nonessential indus-
trial firms and reduce Port Authority staff to a dangerous
minimum. But we shall be very short of those we most need.*

Weather permitting! was Hongkong Jimmy's droll remark.
When are we going to find a weatherman?

If we weather this one, Miklos said, *we can all apply!*

The mindlink was dissolved, and despite the massive task

ahead, the Center directors were much heartened by the contact. When Rhyssa informed Gordie Havers of the results, he gave a loud mental cheer for solidarity.

There're going to be some mighty unhappy kinetics! she told him. *Every Center is going to be stripped, and I'm steeling myself to endure the slings and arrows of outraged businesses.*

Machinery predated kinetics, and men used their muscles before that. Let 'em go back to traditional ways. It'll make 'em appreciate us more than ever. Gordie imaged an archaic block and tackle to move matériel usually hoisted by a kinetic. *Who's handling the publicity?*

We're going to have to be careful about that—don't want Barchenka to say we're interfering with her ongoing employment drive.

The man I have in mind is not a valid Talent, but he's a brilliant publicist, Rhyssa. Let me get Dave Lehardt to wave the flag for us.

Dave Lehardt?

He put our honored president in the White House.

And he's not Talented? That's unfair! That campaign was sheer genius!

We have to allow the Mutes a few prerogatives, you know. Shall I approach him on this delicate matter?

Please do. I'll give him all the help I can.

By the by, did you realize that most of what you do is totally illegal in Scotland, which still has antiwitchcraft laws on the books?

Spare me!

I had, and look what it got us. I'd been working up to the Russkis by way of the British Isles and Scandinavia. Sorry about that! You never know where to start in nullifying age-old bigotry, do you!

When Gordie had broken their mental link, Rhyssa spoke to Sascha.

You got touched again? he demanded.

In the head, but not by my peeper. She put in his mind all that had happened in the past half hour.

He whistled in a descending scale. *We're going to get a lot of flak from Commerce and Industry!*

They can't have it both ways. They're the group that gave Barchenka such punitive fines if she doesn't deliver on time. That clause is just coming home to roost where they didn't expect it. They'll have to dust off their machinery and toughen up their muscles. We've made it far too easy for them.

What if they like the old-fashioned ways and don't want to rehire our people?

Rhyssa snorted derisively. *Just consider how much money kinetics save industry every year in equipment and maintenance costs—the arguments we used to get them to take kinetics in the first place!*

Yeah, but how do we explain it to our kinetics?

Rhyssa projected an image of her on her knees, tearing her hair out, pleading to amorphous faces, offering jewels and ingots of gold. *Enlistment has always been preferable to conscription. And then we can insist on shielding and short shifts. We can't if she implements that blue law. We're over a barrel, and every Talent will realize that!*

Vsevolod can't help us there? Sascha asked.

He was appalled, apologetic, and all, but apopleptic that one of his nationals was doing this to us.

Nothing mentioned about getting the law wiped off the books?

Gordie's working on it! Rhyssa did not bother to lighten the grimness she felt.

D ave Lehardt swung into Rhyssa's tower office at the Henner estate within an hour of the Talents' reluctant acceptance of the inevitable.

"My God, do you have wings?" Rhyssa commented as the

energetic Lehardt shook her hand. He was a full two meters tall, athletic in build, and he emanated a competence and geniality that could only come from a secure, well-adjusted personality. He was handsome enough, with mid-brown hair, blue eyes, and regular but not remarkable features, and he dressed with conservative elegance.

"Not wings! Vanes! More reliable," he said with a charming grin. He began sorting through the papers in his attaché case. "Gordie said it was urgent, and I watch the news." He stopped when he noticed her baffled expression. "What's the matter? Did I break out in spots?"

"No, but you haven't an ounce of Talent, and you ought to."

"Why?" Dave Lehardt shrugged. "I've never needed it. Astute student of human psychology and keen observer of body language."

He also had an impenetrable natural shield. With all her skill, she could not read his mind.

"Now," he said, hauling a spare chair up beside hers and spreading out hard copy of advertisements and graphics, "we get in there before Barchenka even thinks of crowing in triumph, so the public will see that Talents are graciously mobilizing all available personnel to be sure Padrugoi Platform is finished on schedule—with phrases that imply she can't make it on her own without Talented help."

"That's true enough," Rhyssa said grimly.

"Ah, but there are ways and ways of saying the same thing," Dave Lehardt said with a truly malicious smile. "I tangled briefly with the Barchenka Stonewall for another client, and believe me, I'm on your side!"

Rhyssa smiled to herself. Dave Lehardt did have something like a Talent—a self-confidence that radiated from him like an aura. She had never met someone like him before: someone whose mentality she could not delve into, however discreetly. It was a new experience, and she found herself watching his

expressive face, noting the way his hands emphasized points
and how he occasionally added a shoulder movement that reinforced what he said. He also kept glancing at her, meeting
her eyes as few non-Talents would. Clearly he was not the least
bit in awe of being in the presence of one of the top telepathic
Talents.

Oblivious to her reactions, he went on. "I've been yearning
to score on our gracious 'Milla." A flicker of some quickly suppressed emotion shot across his face, but Rhyssa could not
decipher it. "All-out Talent assistance, even at the expense of
long-established links with the public sector, at considerable
personal sacrifice—'Milla doesn't pay the going rates, since hers
is a priority contract and has worldwide backing."

"She will not believe that money is not a consideration . . ."

"Are you aware of the size of her bonus if she gets the
station fully operational on time?"

Rhyssa grinned. "One of the best-kept secrets of the Talents. We also know the percentage she has to cough up if she
doesn't."

"You are well informed!" He paused with a hopeful expression and then sighed as she merely smiled. "No, I didn't
think you'd tell me." He snagged the corner of a graphic sheet
from the pile and spread it out. "To address your two points:
six-hour shifts and shielding—very alliterative. I'm going to be
able to use that as a slogan, you know . . . Have you *demonstrated* the problem?"

"How do you mean 'demonstrated'?"

"Time and motion studies, energy expenditures—that sort
of recordable data. Remember, I've seen your kinetics in action, but I doubt that Ludmilla or even Per Duoml have taken
the trouble to watch them work. They've been too busy bitch-
ing about weightlessness and the silence of space to appreciate
the effort kinesis actually takes. I thought you might not have
thought of that gimmick. So I had a chat with a Talent I know
who was up on the platform, and he gave me some remarkable

insights into the actual shift mechanics. *If* the day's matériel was properly organized, the kinetic could put everything in place for the grunts to lock on and weld.

"Then, the noise element. Samjan ran some of the 'noises' past me—" He grimaced and crossed his eyes in sympathy. "—and I think if we did a tape simulation of what a sensitive hears in unshielded quarters and played it back . . ."

"Not to Ludmilla. She insists there is no noise in space."

"She's more of a Mute than I am."

"But I take your point. I hadn't thought of a trick like that."

"No trick, my dear, just presentation—and that's where I'm the expert." His grin was a mixture of impudence and malice.

For the first time in her Talented life, Rhyssa found herself fascinated by a Mute, and half of that fascination was due to the fact that she could not predict what he would do or say next. It was fun matching wits with him during subsequent interviews, giving the onerous task an unexpected exhilaration.

Dave Lehardt was at her side for the initial meeting with a Barchenka who oozed smug satisfaction that she made no attempt to disguise. Rhyssa was hard put to remain civil. Dave Lehardt talked so fast that the engineer had to listen attentively to catch his points. Per Duoml was, as usual, with her, but Rhyssa had been spared another confrontation with Prince Phanibal.

"All we have had is talk, empty talk," Ludmilla Barchenka said when Dave had explained the dual problems of short shifts and shielding. "Even the physically impaired are able to work proper shifts in space: no gravity, no sound!" She shot an accusatory look at Rhyssa.

"Ah, but it is not gravity which is a problem, nor the vacuum. Ludmilla Ivanova, I have arranged a demonstration . . ."

"I have no time for demonstrations," the Exalted Engineer stated dismissively. "I must return to the platform. Already there are delays which must be rectified."

"Understood, Engineer Barchenka," Dave said soothingly, with just the right amount of respect and understanding. "Perhaps Per Duoml will attend. This demonstration is likely to put the basic problems into proper perspective, and thus help us all resolve the main problems with the maximum benefit to your project."

Duoml would be much easier to deal with—his mind was not totally closed, although he was as dedicated to the project as Barchenka. If they could *prove* their points to him, they would be halfway to victory.

"I think she's disappointed she didn't have to invoke that wretched statute," Rhyssa told Sascha later.

"D'you think we gave in too easily?" he asked. "The news quotes Barchenka calling it the 'cowardly capitulation of the effete.' "

"Let her. If we can just swing Duoml to our side." Rhyssa frowned. "I don't see what else we could have done. Dave Lehardt is running public-opinion polls. One point is clear: *Everyone* wants Padrugoi to be finished, *everyone* wants someone else to work up there, and *everyone* thinks people who volunteer for anything are crazy."

The next day, Dave Lehardt and Rhyssa Owen took Personnel Manager Per Duoml to the most prestigious exercise complex in Jerhattan, a facility that occupied the first nine floors of a Residential ziggurat near Central Park. The largest gymnasium was set up with three sets of stress-monitoring paraphernalia and technicians, three pyramids of standard-size packages, a forklift, a bevy of impartial observers, and the Complex director, Menasherat ibn Malik, who had been a multiple Olympic gold medalist for four times running.

Per Duoml was suitably impressed by ibn Malik. So was Rhyssa, for the man exuded physical vitality and competence. He also had no more Talent than Dave Lehardt, who appeared well acquainted with him. Dave stood by, a slight smile on his face, while ibn Malik accepted Per Duoml's homage and conversed amiably with him.

"Now, Manager Duoml," the Complex director said, gesturing to the three men who entered from the side. Stripped down to their shorts, they were all festooned with wires, which were in turn hooked up to the machines. "Let me introduce you to Pavel Korl, bronze medalist in heavyweight boxing; Chas Huntley, a forklift operator with International Canning; and Rick Hobson, the kinetic."

Rhyssa was almost as bemused as Per Duoml as ibn Malik made the introductions. Korl and Huntley were big men, towering over Duoml and certainly making Rick Hobson, who was average in height and build, look insignificant.

"Now, if you would care to check the movables in each pile, Manager Duoml, to assure yourself that they are equal in weight . . ."

Duoml complied, and it was clear that he had to struggle to lift any of them.

"Then once our guinea pigs' wires are double-checked, we can start the test—which is rather simple. By muscle, by machine, and by mind, our subjects will transfer their piles across the floor. The energy levels required, the stress factors, and calories consumed will be displayed on the monitors. Now," ibn Malik said, moving to the big screen set in the wall for use at sporting events, "on Padrugoi, three men will be doing exactly the same in Q hangar." He spoke into his collar mike. "If you're ready up at Padrugoi?" The big screen lit up with a scene not dissimilar to the one around them, except that all the men wore space suits. "In space, our hand shifter is Jesus Manrique, the lifter is operated by Ginny Stanley, and the kinetic is Kevin Clark. Are you all ready? On your marks—" The gold medalist raised his arm. "Get set—go!" His arm came down, and the activity on the gym floor and in Q hangar commenced. "This test will last an hour," he informed Per Duoml, gesturing for the observers to take seats to one side.

After the first few minutes, Per Duoml stopped watching the burly figure of Korl manhandling the packages down the floor, or Huntley zipping back and forth on the loader. He kept his eyes either on Rick, who had seated himself at a table and, with no visible effort, kept a steady stream of packages flowing, or on the platform kinetic, who was doing his work while leaning against a stanchion. Occasionally Duoml flicked a look at the monitors chattering out their hard copy.

Both Talents worked their way through their piles in half the time it took the others. The instrumentation proved that they had expended half again as much energy and used up twice as many calories.

When the test had been completed, Dave Lehardt stripped the hard-copy sheets from all six printers. Neatly folding them, he handed the sheaf to Per Duoml, who took it without a word. The test subjects were all thanked and left the gym, Rick Hobson throwing Rhyssa an impudent wink as he walked by.

"You will, of course, wish to analyze the results of this test with your own motion experts, Manager Duoml," Dave Lehardt said, "but I'm sure you recognized the fact that weightlessness grants no bonuses to the kinetic. As to the noise factor . . ." The publicist took a compact recorder from his hip pocket and thumbed it on.

At the babel and squeaks and metallic groans, Per Duoml covered his ears in defense and stared in shock at Rhyssa.

"*That* is what a sensitive 'hears' on the station," Dave said, raising his voice and inserting his words in between the worst of the noise. It was a fair selection, representing the streams of consciousness of eighty mentalities: resentments, complaints, shouts, pains, angers, and myriad metallic noises that some of the kinetics endured. "With ten thousand people living up there already, the mental noise is never-ending. So all that garbage is a constant secondary drain on their nerves, reducing their efficiency if they have no respite from it in shielded quarters."

Having set the decibel rate herself, Rhyssa knew that covering his ears gave Duoml frail protection, but she did not reduce the volume until Dave had finished his little speech.

"I see that you hadn't realized just what we meant by

noise," she said finally. "But the cost of shielding personnel quarters for the kinetics is going to be less than the cost of matériel lost or damaged due to tired minds."

"You have made your points," Per Duoml said with a grim expression. "I shall present them to Ludmilla Barchenka."

"Present them and insure their implementation, Per Duoml, and you will have the kinetic assistance you require. Oh, and one other minor point," she added, smiling to take the sting out. "Barchenka is to relay all orders to the kinetics through the regular channels. We will have no more of her rousting Talents out of their quarters at inappropriate hours and insisting on 'extra duty' because her schedule is two minutes out of line! Have I made myself clear on that point?"

He nodded, his expression solemn.

Rhyssa hoped he could convince Barchenka.

CHAPTER 6

N o, *please!*" Peter Reidinger cried as the electrician was
about to disconnect the tri-d in the ward. His cry was
echoed by the other children.

"Look, kids, there's some kind of freaky drain on the hospital's power supply, and we've finally traced it to this ward. I
gotta fix it, or some of your support systems will go down
when they shouldn't," the electrician said with a hint of exasperation in his tone.

"No, wait, please," Peter said. "The program's all about the
space platform and the Talents."

"Huh?" The electrician took a better look at the monitor.

"It'll only be a few minutes! Just the newscast!" Peter
pleaded.

"Wal, I guess—"

"Shhhh," Peter interrupted, straining to hear the commentator. Not that he really needed the voice-over to identify the
scene as the estate of the late George Henner, one of the ear-
liest supporters of the parapsychics. As the camera panned
across the trees and lawns, the boy was startled by the place's
eerie familiarity. *This* was the place he had sought—a place of
tranquil greenery and huge old trees and vine-covered buildings. The place that had scared him away. And now he knew
why. *They* would not want to have their precinct invaded. *They*
needed their privacy to do all the wonderful things they did.
Like help to finish the last three spokes of the Padrugoi Platform so that mankind could, at last, reach for the stars.

"It's not only the Talented who are making a sacrifice,"
the commentator went on, still standing in that marvelous oa-

sis, "for Industry and Commerce have granted leave of absence
to their Talented employees to assist with this final push out
to space. Platform Manager Ludmilla Barchenka announces that
the most ambitious world project yet undertaken will be completed on schedule. And now to other news in the Jerhattan
district . . ."

"Okay, mister," Peter said, relaxing against his frame.
"That's what we wanted to see."

"You're not looking for a career in space, are you?" the
electrician asked, half-teasing. He was always a little nervous
around kids who were so badly injured.

Peter cocked his head at him. "Why not? With no gravity,
I wouldn't be stuck in this frame, and a push of my toe or my
little finger—" He waggled the two extremeties, which were,
after months of therapy, all he *could* move. "—I could float
about."

"Yeah, I guess you could. Now, nurse, can I start with this
frame?" the electrician asked, gesturing to the multiple-tasking
device that gave Peter what independence he had in his condition.

"Yes, it's time for Peter's body-brace session anyway," Sue
Romero said. "C'mon, Peter."

"Aw, do I have to? Couldn't I watch what he does?"

"No, the moment for positive thinking has come. Let me
see that limbic-system smile on your face."

Peter hated the body brace and the morning's 'torture session,' as he mentally categorized the therapy. He felt heavy in
the frame, his body more lifeless than ever. "But see, I can
move my big toe and my little finger. Please . . ."

"Hey, what the—?" the electrician exclaimed. The diagnostic reader he had just hooked up had unexpectedly registered a blip.

While Peter gamely concentrated on his body-brace drills,
the electrician checked out the bed's wiring, but except for
that one brief blip, he could find no short, no dysfunction in

any of the circuitry. By the time an exhausted Peter was back in his bed, the electrician had done a thorough test of all the specialized treatment electronics in the ward. Baffled by the continual surges on the ward's circuits, the man left a small monitor attached to the one piece of equipment that had registered an abnormality, slight though it had been, and left.

Peter knew by her face that Sue Romero was disappointed in him. He did try to make his body remember how to move. The frame sent electrical impulses into his atrophied muscles, the theory being that the little jolts would restimulate neural and muscular activity. He hated that intrusion into his body even more than he hated being paralyzed.

"Peter, if you would only stop resisting the mechanism," Sue said reproachfully. "If you would only go with it, instead of denying the help it could give you. You could, you know, even get to the platform. Your schoolwork was excellent—there'd be no problem with the educational end . . ." She trailed off, fighting her own dispiritedness. Sometimes with the very badly damaged children, she felt she was pounding at the well-known immovable object—generally, as in Peter's case, the child itself.

The boy was exhausted, eyes closed, arms and legs sprawled just as he had been rolled out of the body brace. Sue Romero could not afford to pity him—it was unprofessional and helped neither of them in his rehabilitation—but she did. As she turned away, she thought he was sleeping. She would have been amazed to learn that he was reviewing that vision of the Center, with its trees and lawns and . . . Rhyssa Owen.

That night, Rhyssa was wakeful, going over and over that telecast. She had felt good about it during filming. Dave Lehardt had done his job well. They would, of course, have to wait until opinions had been sampled, but Rhyssa felt that Barchenka was coming out a poor second at the moment, despite her apparent triumph at the cowardly capitulation of the effete Talents. Rhyssa fretted that she had somehow weakened the consolidated strength of Talents and wondered how she could rectify what was still, in the minds of most Talented, an untenable position with Barchenka getting her way.

She felt then the gossamer touch—envious, yearning, wistful, and so terribly sad that a sob clogged her throat.

Wait, little friend, she murmured in the softest of tones.

Say what? With the voice came mixed impressions of startlement, sense of apology-denial-rejection, and an astringent smell. And then the touch—timorous and reluctant—was gone.

Rhyssa tried to follow, her touch feather soft, but the retreat had been too swift, like a flicker of shadow across the moonlight outside her window. She made a quick note of the time: 3:43. Then she lay there savoring that touch, examining it, letting her perception analyze it.

Such swiftness suggested a young mind—no old thoughts or experiences to slow the instantaneity of action. A boy on a prank . . . A boy? Doing an out-of-body maneuver? A boy in a hospital—yes, a hospital would account for the astringent odor—his movement constrained so that only his mind could travel?

That fit the pieces together so perfectly that Rhyssa got out of bed and paced over to the console.

"Bud, I want a call out to all hospital Talents," she said, unable to keep the elation out of her voice.

"The peeper caught you again?"

"That's right. An adolescent boy, quite likely crippled or paralyzed. I want to see who was awake on the wards at three-forty-three this morning."

"The last thing you need tonight is some pimple-faced nerd rousing you."

"On the contrary, Bud, I think that's exactly what I did

6 6

need. A youngster able to go out of body? He's got to have fantastic potential.''

"For what?" Budworth wanted to know.

"That," Rhyssa said with a surge of hope, "is what we'll have to find out.''

As she climbed back into bed, she had a lot to think about before she could compose herself for sleep. How long had it been since a new Talent that strong had been identified? And what sort of a Talent was it? Even strong telepathy did not leave an image, however transparent. A new type of kinesis? Very few kinetics could move themselves! Inanimate objects, yes, but animate ones, no. Most out-of-body experiences were the results of traumas and useless in a commercial sense—and theorists still argued over whether the out-of-body phenomenon was a kinetic manifestation or a strong telepathic projection.

Just remember, she told herself that it was the commercial applications of Talents that provided us with legal immunities, good jobs, and special status for the past four score years . . . and let us get marvelously complacent. Maybe it wasn't really "noise" that even kinetics heard in space but some other form of interstellar communication, a multilingual garble that they were picking up. Open your mind up, gal. Look around you. Look at Dave Lehardt. He has to be Talented, even if it won't register on a Goosegg graph.

Why, Rhyssa Owen, she asked herself, does Dave Lehardt *have* to be Talented?

And that was the quandary she fussed over as she finally slipped into an uneasy sleep.

I discovered some interesting new facets of employment on the platform,'' Dave Lehardt told Rhyssa in her office two days later. "Came out in further talks with my platform contact, Samjan, and a few judicious inquiries." He gave her a humorless grin. "The casualties."

"Yes, the total is horrific." Rhyssa shuddered. "But working in space there were bound to be some."

"Some?" Dave raised his eyebrows. "Some, yes, but when I checked with Johnny Greene in Altenbach's office, we found several different sets of figures on the casualty rate."

Rhyssa straightened. When Dave had arrived unexpectedly, she had been busy reshuffling the rotas of the Center's kinetics, steeling herself to endure their understandable reproaches and arguments. Any interruption was welcome.

"Then I got JG and Samjan together, and they both did a bit of research," he went on, "and, using their security clearances, they came up with what we think are the real statistics." His expression was bleak, and there was a stillness about his body that forewarned her. "You know how the unemployed are terrified to be conscripted to Padrugoi? They may not be Talented, but they've got an instinct about baaaaad situations. They have good reason not to want to get conscripted. She loses grunts at a frightening rate, far beyond the allowable. The major reason is because Barchenka's so bloody-minded about keeping her Sacred Schedules, she won't interrupt a shift to retrieve drifters!"

To be sure she understood his meaning, Rhyssa unconsciously tried to read his mind. It was like stubbing her toe on a stair raiser, and she blinked. "Run that past me again, please, Dave," she asked, struggling with confusion at her inability to read him the way she was used to reading most of her friends.

"Surely you've seen the promotional footage," he said, "with the grunts suited up and pushing gi-normous sections of a spoke with the tips of their fingers or a spare foot?"

"Yes . . ."

"In the *real* working situation, not that mockup they did for recruitment, a worker'll push too hard, and with every action causing a reaction in space, the poor sod goes spinning off into the dark deeps.''

"Yes . . .''

"Well, Barchenka doesn't stop work to rescue them. Oh, no, anyone that stupid has to wait until the shift is over before his buddies are allowed to go after him. That is, *if* a skiff is available, and *if* the bod's been tracked.''

Appalled at the vivid scene his words evoked, Rhyssa stared at him. "Is this public knowledge?''

He gave her a cynical look. "Why do you think the grunts never take surface leave? It's not the fact that they're paid so little that they can't afford surface leave, or that there's no available space on shuttles for mere grunts, or that they're un- likely to have any family to visit on Earth. It's that they're plain not allowed back down to tell *anyone* what's happening. The grunts are also segregated so that even the observant among the more elite employees don't know exactly what's going on. It took both JG and Samjan and some long program analyses to piece fact out of the publicly available fictions.''

"But all the recruitment films show safety lines and . . .'' Part of Rhyssa crowed with delight at discovering Barchenka resorting to very questionable tactics, while another part balked at the enormity of the crime.

"That's *promo* footage, my dear director. The theory is great. In practice, Barchenka dispensed with safety lines—they kept getting tangled in equipment, slowing down her precious work schedule. So safety lines are a space myth.

"And Barchenka has such saving ways.'' Dave Lehardt perched his lean frame on the edge of her desk. "For instance, we discovered by an analysis of records that a suited grunt is given only enough air in his tanks for that shift and maybe a sniff or two left over. Oh, there's plenty of safety regs for the engineers and supervisors and skilled technicians—but not the grunts. She doesn't care what happens to them. There're plenty more where they came from.''

Rhyssa was outraged. "You just validated my instincts about that woman. Law be damned, I won't ask my kinetics to face such risks!"

Dave gave a snort. "*They're* far too valuable to be risked. There'd be too much of a stink kicked up if a drifting Talent wasn't retrieved right then. Overworked, yes. Samjan confirmed the notion that eight-hour shifts are another platform fallacy.

"On top of that conspicuous savings of consumables, I uncovered several other little anomalies: grunt suits have limited-range com units. They can't be heard shrieking for help! Might disturb their fellow workers."

Rhyssa stared at him aghast.

"There's also a high incidence of agoraphobia among the grunts and genuine space cafard. But ailing grunts are never transferred down. They just disappear! Accidental death! Never suicide! Always accidental. After all," he said, taking on a mock Russian accent, "everyone knows how dangerous it is to ignore safety warnings and procedures. And then there appears to be a neat little system which causes unexpected casualties during the routine drills they so conspicuously hold from time to time on Padrugoi." Dave paused again. "Checking through medical records, it becomes apparent that the unfortunate victims of those drill 'accidents' are always either the injured or the headcases."

"Oh, my God, Dave!" Rhyssa propelled herself from her chair to pace agitatedly up and down the tower room. "*Why* haven't any of the precogs caught this?"

"According to your brief summary on Talents' capabilities, precogs usually latch onto large numbers, Rhyssa. There are never enough—"

"Numerics is no excuse!" Rhyssa was surprised by a vehemence that answered the despair in his voice. She wondered if his mind, too, was filled with faceless forms, twisting and turning in space, drifting farther and farther from the network of lights that was the oasis of air and warmth in the blackness, and a violent shudder seized her.

A warm hand cupped her shoulder. "Easy! Talent spreads itself thin enough as it is. You're not God, or gods, to mark each sparrow's fall."

She blinked and looked up at him. Though his mind was as closed to her as ever, the sympathy and understanding in his warm blue eyes was obvious. She would not tell him that Talents generally disliked tactile contact—surprisingly enough, she had discovered that she liked him touching her.

"Armed with this information, however, you can spread Barchenka over a barrel." His voice was soft and teasing. "If you see what I mean. Or, maybe you Talents are too simon-pure to lower yourselves to outright blackmail."

"Not when the lives and safety of my Talents are at risk, I'm not," Rhyssa declared stoutly. "Not to mention those poor sods who've not even been given half a chance to survive. I'll insist on short shifts and shields, and we'll increase that ante to safety lines for everyone working on the platform and the deployment of rescue skiffs. Or do skiffs have limited power and air on them, too, so as to save costs?"

He crossed his arms on his chest, grinning at her. "Your Talents wouldn't be at risk anyway, unless I've misunderstood their capabilities. There's no way Barchenka can pull the same tricks on *them* that she does with the poor grunts. And unless your response is unique among your ilk, I can't see your folk standing by for some of her tricks, once they know what to look for. Some of the kinetics are telepaths, aren't they?"

"Quite a few." Rhyssa gave a sardonic chuckle. "A fact we haven't actually mentioned to Barchenka, whose understanding of Talent is severely limited."

Dave let out a bark of laugh. "Not the whole truth nor even half the truth, huh? Good girl, Rhyssa!" He playfully knuckled her chin. "Is distance a problem? Or the vacuum of space?"

When Rhyssa shook her head, he went on. "Well, you guys could sure be popular with the grunts because *you*"—he waggled his finger at her—"could be *their* insurance. A Talent could haul back a drifter, couldn't he? Without asking for permission during his shift, or waiting for a skiff?" He gave her a broad smile. "That'll help a lot of ways. Damned good PR, too. The best, because it proves that the Talents will help the ordinary grunt where Barchenka just simply hasn't!"

Rhyssa suddenly turned away, not wanting Dave to see her expression. *Sascha?* she called. *I've just found the perfect job for Madlyn! Tell you later!*

I can read your evil mind, Sascha said, *and she's not even on the list for the platform.*

She is, as of right now, Rhyssa replied. *How often have you said that Madlyn could be heard at the space platform? We'll just put it to the test!* She smoothed her expression and looked up at Dave Lehardt, who was eyeing her keenly.

"Who were you talking to just then? And don't hold out on me. I'm getting used to your ways, woman!" His voice rippled with an odd emotion, and the gleam in his eyes intensified.

Rhyssa's grin was half embarrassment at his scrutiny and half delight with her inspiration. "We've got a telepath with an extraordinarily loud voice. We'll send her up in an administrative capacity. Put her on a radar scope, and she'll locate and reassure any drifters for the nearest kinetic to haul back to safety."

"Lady, you don't realize what a difference that could make to morale up at the platform." Dave's grin was so infectious that Rhyssa had to grin back. "Not only is Barchenka unaware that she's her own worst enemy, but her ignorance about Talent in general will prevent her from realizing that she's just hired a battalion of undercover agents."

"*That's* the beauty part!" Rhyssa said, grinning more broadly. "Does Duoml? Or Prince Phanibal?"

Dave Lehardt considered briefly. "Prince Phanibal might, but he's not on the platform as much lately—some crisis in Malaysia that occupies a lot of his time. Besides, I read him as being just ornery enough not to tell her something as crucial at this time for the sheer pleasure of watching her squirm. Now what's this emergency clause Lance Baden wants added to the contracts?"

"In case of a major emergency, we must be able to bring Talents back down. You remember the floods last monsoon on the Indian continent and that major shake in Azerbaijan? We knew about each of them ten days before, so we were able to muster help and reduce the effect of the catastrophe. Sending her a hundred and forty-four kinetics has wiped out our disaster-squad organization. We want a twenty-four-hour clause—to bring key personnel back to Earth in time to cope here."

"Can't you teleport 'em down?"

Rhyssa laughed. "No, more's the pity. Our Talents are finite, definite, and nowhere near such a fantasy application as instantaneous transmissions. That takes more power than a human brain can generate."

"I thought the Moral Code on legitimate bio-engineering permitted—"

"Hold it right there, Dave." Rhyssa held up a warding hand. "Read the Code: congenital defects, yes—manipulations, no. And I doubt any genetic engineer would monkey with the brain yet—even a monkey's brain."

"If you can find one. Though don't you think it's likely that someone has been doing illicit experimentation, the world being what it is these days?"

"That's cynical of you, Dave."

"Sometimes saying no is registering a challenge," he replied with a shrug. "I wouldn't rule out the possibility."

"Meanwhile," Rhyssa said, bringing the discussion firmly back to relevant matters, "I'd very much like to see a full report on what JG and Samjan have been discovering about platform personnel problems."

Dave grinned, taking three diskettes from a breast pocket. "I thought you might. Gives you a stronger bargaining position for shields, short shift—"

"Safety lines and skiffs," Rhyssa finished, taking the diskettes but letting her fingers linger on his a little longer than the transactions required. "I thank you, sir." What on earth was happening to her in Dave Lehardt's presence? She felt as giddy as—as Madlyn could be in Sascha's company.

When Per Duoml, Prince Phanibal Shimaz, and two other minor officials, one of them the accommodations officer, arrived to settle the minor details, Dave Lehardt had another presentation that altered the proceedings. Rhyssa, sitting with Max Perigeaux, Gordie Havers, and Lance Baden, found the meeting eminently satisfying.

Showing the accurate fatality statistics—figures that bleached all color from the faces of Duoml and the prince—Dave Lehardt talked knowledgeably of some of the "minor" problems that the Talents would be willing to undertake, such as the retrieval of any suited workers experiencing "malfunction of suit jets," and telepathic contact "with those using short-range com units," plus monitoring systems; they would also include among the Talents two with broad diagnostic capabilities. Dave pointed out that the savings on skiff fuel and man-hours required for retrieval would more than compensate for the cost of shielding required in Talent accommodations.

Nor was there any discussion about the emergency clause. Lance Baden announced that he was to be Talent liaison with the engineering staff and that was that.

And what were they saying about cowardly capitulations? Lance commented.

Rhyssa was so weary from accumulated stresses that she experienced no elation at having forced every single concession out of the Padrugoi officials. She wanted nothing more than a quiet supper and some mental peace. Per Duoml had a natural shield, but the other project representatives at the meeting had not, and when their initial euphoria at coercing Talents onto the work force was burst by hard facts and figures and compromises, their emotional responses of anger, horror, and embarrassment had been hard to deflect.

Sascha: *I've cleared everyone out of the first floor. Relax!*

Rhyssa: *Oh, you are a pet!*

Sascha: *Lot of good it does me!* But she knew he was only teasing.

Rhyssa entered the Henner house, appreciative of the deep silence in the elegantly appointed rooms. Very little had been altered from the days of George Henner, the parapsychics' first benefactor: all had been lovingly preserved in his memory. The subterranean offices, the annexes, and her tower were modern, with state-of-the-art technology, but the main reception rooms were reminders of more leisurely times. The kitchen, where modern appointments were hidden behind old-fashioned cupboards, exuded an aura of comfort—it was spacious, with an archaic but working fireplace, a huge table, and comfortable chairs. The dining portion faced onto the gardens at the rear of the main house, bright with blooms and bushes.

Some thoughtful kinetic had activated the kettle. She made herself a cup of tea, found sandwiches in the crisper, and kicking off her shoes, curled up in one of the wing chairs.

There was something amazingly restorative about looking out onto the garden, watching the flowers move in the light breeze. She set her mind adrift, savoring the quiet, despite the deep-seated nagging presentiment.

"I'm not a precog," she told herself and sipped her tea. "What I am feeling is just reaction to the last few hectic days. A quite natural depression."

Then she felt the touch, once again colored with wistfulness and a deep sadness that pierced her to the heart, making her own malaise seem insignificant.

She dared not reach out for fear of startling the boy. Boy he was, and despairing. Had her transitory unease triggered a response from him midday? Or was it his need seeking consolation? What could so desolate a young person? One could endure detached misery—tragedy happening at a distance to people one had never met—but to *feel* the palpitating misery of another person was an intense experience.

Delicately she impinged on the boy's mind, hoping to gain some clue to his whereabouts. He was dreading something, and the yearning for trees and lawn and flowers and *someplace* that was not hospital had precipitated the nebulous contact. And her mind, less controlled than usual in its weariness, had attracted his. Dreading what? She inserted the question.

The body brace!

Rhyssa had not expected an answer. She tried to keep the lightest of contacts, though, oddly enough, he felt very close at that moment. *Isn't it meant to help?* she asked cautiously.

It doesn't. It hurts. It's artificial, it's awful. It's a cage. The bed is bad enough. I don't want to. I—don't—want—to!

A wail from the depth of a forlorn and comfortless mind reached her—then it was abruptly cut off.

W e got another one of those surges this afternoon—usually we get 'em at night," the hospital's maintenance man said as he held up the printout to the consultant engineer whom the concerned hospital administration had finally called in.

The engineer peered at the peak, a sudden sharp deviation lasting seventy-two seconds. He asked for the other anomalies and was presented with further examples. "Shouldn't be any drain on the systems at three-forty-three, three-oh-three, three-fifty-two, or three-thirteen. You've checked all the equipment?"

"I put meters on several floors. Got a blip on PedOrth Ward Twelve when I was installing it. So I took everything apart on that ward and there wasn't nothing malfunctioning. Craziest thing I've ever seen. And you know how Admin is when you got outages and anomalies with all them life-support systems hooked up. Funny though, nothing in the ICUs."

"Okay, screen me your schematics for all the equipment on PedOrth and see what's being used there." The engineer sighed heavily—he could see it was going to be one of those days.

A stir around the beds in the circular ward alerted Peter Reidinger, and he blinked away the screen that blocked his view. A very old lady stood in the doorway, Miz Allen hovering with her "you'd-better-behave" look on her face as she glanced around the ward to be sure everything was in order for the visitor.

Instantly Peter's attention was riveted on the lady. She was different. That became more apparent to him as Miz Allen began to introduce her to the kids in the ward. Cecily even smiled and answered the lady. Cecily was a spina bifida case who "ought" to have been corrected in utero but had not been. Osteomyelitis had caused her to have one leg amputated, and her recovery from that operation was very slow. She rarely opened up to other people—and particularly not to strangers—so her response to the old lady was a minor miracle. Peter was in a sweat of anticipation by the time the lady reached him.

"This is Peter Reidinger, Ms. Horvath." The way Miz Allen cocked her right eyebrow told Peter that he had better behave himself.

Ms. Horvath just smiled down at him, her eyes twinkling, and they were not at all old, or rheumy, or hard. He wondered she let herself look so old.

I promised my husband that I would grow old gracefully, she startled him by saying. *That way I wouldn't surprise people so much when I don't act my age.*

Peter goggled at her. She had not moved her lips—and yet he had heard her voice clearly in his mind.

"Peter . . ." Miz Allen prompted him.

"Pleased ta meetcha!" Peter managed to get out. Miz Allen cleared her throat warningly.

"Thank you, Mrs. Allen, I'll just chat a bit with Peter," Dorotea Horvath said, pulling a chair to Peter's bedside and dismissing Miz Allen in a manner that astounded the boy. *Miz Allen doesn't really believe in telepathy and Talents. And we just haven't had the chance to go around the pediatric wards lately. So we missed you.*

"Missed me?"

Dorotea smiled again, a smile that was magical because it seemed to envelop Peter with warmth and caring. The hard knot of self-pity and resentment that had been building up at the thought of another body-brace session dispersed.

"That is, until you started visiting Rhyssa."

"Rhyssa?"

Into his mind came a new touch. *I'm Rhyssa. I sent Dorotea to you because you run away from me. Dorotea says you can't run away from her right now, Peter Reidinger. Please come live with us where I know you long to be.*

"Now that you've had an official invitation, will you accept?" Dorotea asked, brimming over with amusement at his stunned reaction.

"But I can't. I'm crippled. I can't go anywhere . . ."

Ahahahaha! Dorotea chided him, still smiling. *A boy who can go out of body on tours of Jerhattan at three in the morning is no cripple!*

"But I can't *use* the body brace!" Peter was horrified to hear himself blubbering and to feel tears streaming down his face. He had not cried in months.

Crying's a natural release for emotional pressures, Dorotea said as she blotted his cheeks matter-of-factly. *All that manly repression has also been blocking Talent. I do believe that the brace also posed an inhibition. I think it short-circuited natural ability. We'll sort it out. Of that I'm positive.*

And suddenly Peter had no doubt at all.

"First, of course, we have to get your parents' permission." Dorotea was always practical. "Do you think they'll mind?"

"Mind?" Peter nearly shouted. He knew that the hospital fees, even with the huge compensation the city was forced to pay since he had been injured on city-owned property, had been a terrible financial drain on his parents. His mother came to see him regularly, but his father's visits grew fewer and shorter. His mother always had some plausible explanation for Dad's absence, but Peter had not been fooled.

Suddenly Dorotea's eyes widened in pleased surprise. "I don't think you'll need much training after all," she said, pointing at him.

"What?" And at that moment Peter realized that he was hovering above his bed—and that an alarm just beneath it had gone off.

*R*hyssa! Dorotea's mental shout was a very welcome diversion for Rhyssa.

The Eastern director had not been able to make that first contact for several reasons, the foremost one being the Padrugoi priority. The other reason was that Dorotea was still the most accurate Talent diviner in the entire world, with the deftest touch to allay fear and suspicion.

Rhyssa, Peter Reidinger reeks of Talent. I can't imagine why the resident didn't tumble to it a long time ago, despite the fact that Peter's been suppressing his natural feelings to be considered a brave boy. Being in a hospital situation, he'd have to blank out all peripheral static or get wound up in everyone else's pain. Though he's not your garden-variety kinetic or telepath. In fact, I've never touched anyone quite like him. One thing's sure, he no more needed a body brace than you need a videophone.

Can you expedite his release to us? Rhyssa asked.

In my best granny mode! I don't anticipate any trouble with the family—they've been struggling under the medical costs. I gather the father has trouble visiting his "crippled" son. They should regain some perspective now that Peter'll be able to pay his own way.

How medical is he?

Dorotea gave a mental snort. *With a little help from his friends, he won't be medical past the gate of the Center. Whoops! We've just been charged by an irate electrician and a stupefied consultant, and—my God!*

Dorotea broke off contact, startling Rhyssa—Dorotea usually had no trouble double-talking. Rhyssa waited for the old woman to come back and explain her abrupt disappearance. After three minutes with no further word from her, Rhyssa reluctantly resumed her immediate task.

Worried about Dorotea and the boy, it was difficult for her to keep her mind on the reassignment of kinetic Talents, but the matter had to be cleared up as soon as possible. The Eastern Center would be left with just ten to do the work of thirty, along with five trainees who could be slotted into some of the less exacting hoist work. Airshuttle clients, passengers or commercial, were just going to have to wait longer to collect their luggage; all construction firms would lose kinetics, save those on two nearly completed projects where kinesis was the only way to safely install heavy equipment on the uppermost stories.

She and Miklos Horvath, Dorotea's grandson on the West Coast, also had to arrange "fetch and carry" teams, telepaths and kinetics who could work in tandem and at long distance. But such skills were exhausting and would have to be reserved for emergencies.

Dave Lehardt had come up with yet another valid suggestion that might not improve relations with Barchenka and Duoml but would certainly make more effective use of the four-hour shift of each kinetic.

"I looked at some of the motion studies," he had told her, "and some videos of an actual working day. Samjan mentioned that he spent a good portion of every shift on Padrugoi doing nothing—waiting until matériel was organized from the storage yard or bins, or while the engineers sorted out minor discrepancies. So I got Samjan and Bela Rondomanski, who was Space Lab designer, together with Lance Baden, who's a trained engineer. Bela said a lot of the delays on Space Lab were caused by a chronic disorganization in Supply. Lance said that the problems hadn't been completely solved when he did two tours at Padrugoi, but one of Barchenka's strengths is her organizational skills. Take them one more step forward, and, in a four-hour shift, a kinetic can get everything in a spoke section lined up so that all the grunts need to do during the next twenty hours of shift time is give a tiny shove and the elements will fall into place.

"Of course, it'll mean a good deal of reorganization in the stores and matériel already up at Padrugoi, and maybe some shipment rearranging, lighting a fire under the tardy suppliers, but the time spent doing *that* will cut down on the man-hours upstairs."

"Duoml's returned to the station," Rhyssa said.

"We'll just borrow Hangar Q again for another handy little

demonstration. I'll work out the details. Hey, you're looking mighty good today. New hairstyle? Sure shows off your skunk streak.'' Her screen diffused on another of his famous confidence-inspiring grins.

Skunk streak indeed, she thought, her fingers smoothing it back. At least he had noticed. With a sigh, she went back to her analyses, until she realized that she had not heard another squeak from Dorotea.

Then, as abruptly as the contact had been broken, Dorotea returned.

Well, I said I'd come back as soon as I could. It's too soon to be sure what he does do, Rhyssa, but he apparently taps into electrical sources. He's been glitching the hospital circuits fit to drive the electrician and a high-priced consultant barmy. And it also explains why he couldn't cope with the body brace: the impulses which were fed directly into his synapses were short-circuiting inherent abilities, so the poor lad was trying to cope with an overload. Sue Romero is in bits thinking of all she's been doing to Peter, and he's in a state because he had no way of explaining why the body brace was all wrong *for him . . . and the head nurse, Miz Allen, is one of those by-the-bookers and compounded the problem. Oh, his family are delighted, especially to know that Peter will not be "handicapped"—but their heads read "crippled, useless, financial drain." It'll be standard contract until he's eighteen and fully trained. Here's one kinetic Barchenka won't get her space gloves on!*

When can you bring him home?

We're on our way! Dorotea replied triumphantly. *Get Roddy's room in my house ready.* She shot Rhyssa a mental glimpse of Space-Force posters on every wall, models of space shuttles, mass passenger hotols, stealths, space labs, and generation ships depending from the ceiling, and a bunk bed with desk space below. *Nothing could be more distant from the antiseptic environment he's been living in for months.*

The physical meeting between Rhyssa Owen and Peter Reidinger was not quite an anticlimax. Dorotea had warned her that Peter's mother and older sister were accompanying him in the heli-amb, excited but slightly apprehensive at his new circumstances.

Ilsa Reidinger was a pleasant enough woman, terribly concerned for and certainly extremely proud of her Petey. She struggled with a less than congenial job in order to help meet the medical bills. The sixteen-year-old sister, Katya, was what Dorotea called "pushy," trying to figure out how her brother's good fortune might spill over on her and disgruntled that Peter had Talent and she had none. Dorotea said that Katya resented Peter because the cost of his hospitalization had kept her from having many of the things that she, the elder child, ought to have been able to enjoy. *Perfectly understandable reaction,* Dorotea told Rhyssa as the women deftly maneuvered Peter's gurney into Dorotea's house and on through into Roddy's room.

Both telepaths could feel Peter's spirit lifting as he saw the unmedical furnishings and artifacts.

"But how'll you do all that has to be done *for* him all the time?" Ilsa Reidinger began in surprise.

"Oh, Peter'll only need a little help in the beginning, Mrs. Reidinger," Dorotea said. Her mental *Alley oop* was the signal for Rick Hobson to "lift" Peter up into the bunk bed. "Now, let's all clear out and let him settle himself in. And," Dorotea added as she shooed everyone before her, "the heli-amb is waiting to take you and your daughter home. Here's the vid number. As you saw, Peter has a set in the room. Call him any time. Unlike the hospital, here you can see what mischief he's getting into. All right?"

Dorotea's positive manner made refusal impossible, and soon the heli-amb was thunking its way up out of the Center's grounds.

Rick, hook me up a line from the 4.5-kpm generator in the

garden shed and bring it right into the room with Peter, Dorotea requested.

What is this all about? Rhyssa demanded.

I told you, Dorotea said, then added aloud since they were now alone, "he seems to tap into the electrical system and use *that* for power. Some sort of a gestalt. I want some of our engineer Talents to link with me when he's rested enough for us to do some testing. But it'll have to be you and me for a while, Rhyssa. He's had such a terrible time."

Dorotea's eyes welled with tears, and automatically Rhyssa gathered the older woman into her arms, smothering her with love, affection, and admiration.

"I'm sorry, dear," Dorotea said with a little sniff, pulling herself away. "You've had a lot to cope with now, and you don't need me turning into a watering pot, but—" She poured into Rhyssa's mind the jumble of pain/despondency/anguish/guilt, the self-accusation, and the soul-destroying terror that Peter had been enduring.

Easing Dorotea to the couch, Rhyssa sat beside her, shaken by that accounting despite years of dealing with the bizarre mental states of emergent Talents.

"I think a spot of tea would go down well right now," Dorotea said, and Rhyssa gave a weak little laugh at Dorotea's ever practical mind. *Peter? A cup of tea? Lemon, milk, sugar?*

Yes, please, was Peter's answer, surprising Rhyssa.

You see? He needed only a little help to project his thoughts instead of squashing them down. Dorotea's face wore an exaggeratedly smug smile.

They were all enjoying a cup of tea when Rick Hobson bounced in, festooned with an electrician's belt and heavy-duty cable.

"I don't know what kind of an outlet or receptacle you need, Dorotea," he said, winking at her, nodding to Rhyssa, and then waving a hand at Peter, who was watching it all from his bunk.

"Well, Peter, what do you think you need?" Dorotea asked. "He'd just been sort of hooking in to the electronic gadgets of the bed," she told Rick.

Both women caught Peter's hesitation and concern.

"Oh, well, it's as easy to sort the specifics out later," Rick said easily, catching Rhyssa's warning look. "At any rate, the generator's right outside and powered up. Any time you need it, it's there." With a cheery wave to all, he left.

"It's all a bit much, isn't it, Peter?" Rhyssa said gently.

"I don't know what I did that makes you think I'm any good at all," Peter said in a voice as pale as his complexion just then.

"Dorotea thinks you used available electrical power to assist those dawn visits you made to me," Rhyssa told him. She gave him a mischievous smile to reassure him. "I'm honored that it was my mind you linked with to bring you where you wanted to be."

"You are?" Peter turned his head away from the drinking straw in his teacup so that he could look down at Rhyssa.

"I don't get many men invading my bedroom, I assure you."

Subtly Dorotea was supporting her, increasing for Peter the sense that his intrusion had been clever and original. Both women generated subliminal thoughts to bolster his perception of himself, reversing the low self-esteem that was currently inhibiting any forward progress.

"I didn't *mean* to intrude."

"You will soon understand that among telepaths a midnight knock on the door isn't considered an intrusion."

"But all those lights . . ."

Rhyssa let her thoughts echo the annoyance she had felt at that proprietary supervision. "You didn't hear me chewing them out for scaring you off, either."

"Ooooh, Rhyssa was angry," Dorotea added.

"You were doing what many have tried and failed at miserably," Rhyssa went on.

"I was?"

"It's what we call an out-of-body experience," Rhyssa went on. "Very few people ever achieve that degree of mental control."

"They don't?" Peter was wide-eyed in awe. "But it's not hard."

Dorotea and Rhyssa exchanged amused glances.

"Nothing's hard when you know exactly how to do it, Peter," Rhyssa said, "and you've apparently mastered the art. Dorotea and I are both hoping you can teach us. I don't have much kinetic ability . . ."

Sascha: *And aren't you glad of that right now?* He sent an image of a space-suited Rhyssa whirling about Padrugoi chased by a whip-wielding Barchenka.

Rhyssa: *Don't you dare interfere, Bearman! This is tricky enough as it is without you in my mind! Oh, my God!* And suddenly Rhyssa began to fathom the potential of the boy. Give young Peter Reidinger access to sufficiently powerful electronic sources, and his kinetic Talent might boggle the mind of the most optimistic theorist. Why, his Talent was as far from spoon bending as modern precognition was from priestly auguries divined from ox intestines!

There was an instant response from Sascha, Dorotea, Sirikit, Rick, and Madlyn. *Damp it down, Rhyssa. Have a heart!*

Dorotea: *Well, you've all got the picture now, so leave us alone with the boy. We can't mess this one up.*

Rhyssa had to take a deep breath, hoping that the sudden revelation she had been unable to keep from other strong telepaths in the Center had not also been picked up by Peter Reidinger's still-emerging skill. He was certainly not reacting.

Dorotea: *I blocked him, Rhyssa. Get ahold of yourself.*

"So, Peter," Rhyssa managed to go on, "if I could get the hang of what you're doing with the generators, it could be an extremely valuable added whammy."

Dorotea: *I couldn't have put it more discreetly myself.*
Rhyssa: *Thanks.*

"I don't know what I'm doing," Peter said sadly.

"It's the sort of thing you don't *think* about doing, Peter. You just *do* it—because you want to, because you need to. And Dorotea and I will help." Rhyssa grinned at him. "Communication is where telepathy excels. The spoken word sometimes isn't as clear as it should be: words can be misused, inappropriately assigned muddy meanings. You're accustomed to a word meaning one thing; someone else will think it means something else entirely and misunderstand what you just said. Speaking mind-to-mind clears up a lot of such confusions. Or have I just confused you more?"

Peter began to smile suddenly. "Like how I couldn't explain to Miz Romero just *why* I hated the body brace."

"That's a very apt example, Peter. You just didn't have the words for the concept of that sort of interference."

"But how'll I move without a brace?"

"By the power of your mind alone, which is exactly what you did when you were going out of body. Only we'll teach you how to take your body along with you! *And* manage most of your daily care. You won't be dependent on nurses or orderlies or anyone. In one sense it was what Sue was trying to get you to do—make your mind motivate your body to remember what it once could do. Only you took it one step beyond that, and neither of you knew you had latent kinetic ability. So, of course you couldn't do what she wanted. You were a good jump ahead of her."

He was still skeptical. "I'm kinetic?"

"Do you know what the word means?"

"Sure. But I didn't think I was."

Rhyssa rose. "Well, you are. So think about it."

Dorotea retrieved his cup. "You take a rest now, dear. Then I'll show you about the house so you'll know where everything is when you want it."

CHAPTER 7

Although Sascha usually handled training, the affinity established between Peter and Rhyssa made it sensible for her to guide his initiation.

"I'll help as much as I can," Dorotea told Rhyssa, a look of resigned disappointment on her face, "but I am eighty-four, and I've slowed down a lot." Then she smiled with bright mischief. "Of course, I've always liked cooking for a male appetite. And he'll be able to do most things for himself in short order. I'm sure of it. I know a strong Talent when I bump minds with it."

So Rhyssa, Dorotea, and Sascha made a little ceremony of adding Peter Reidinger's name to the Registry of Talents at the Eastern Center. Peter was still not quite certain of his great good fortune. Rick Hobson, who was empathic as well as kinetic, monitored the kinetic aspects; Don Usenik, the Center's versatile medic, kept a close check on the boy's physical condition; and the boy resided in Dorotea's house.

"I can still handle the mothering bits," the old woman said staunchly, "especially since Rhyssa has enough to administer."

By the end of the first week, Peter was able to handle all his intimate problems, a success of immeasurable proportion for a sensitive boy. The morning he managed to take a shower all by himself was celebrated by his mentors as the achievement it was. The first time he had attempted a shower, he had nearly scalded himself and then overcontrolled and had to be rescued from icy water by Dorotea.

It also took time, and finesse, to descend from his bed without hitting the floor in a heap. Or to keep from colliding with furniture as he reeled around the house. Gradually he achieved a delicate control of the gestalt and managed to imitate walking; only the really observant would notice that his feet never quite touched the ground and that the bend of his knees only approximated a normal walk. He could not grasp things, but he arranged his hands in appropriate positions so that he appeared to be carrying objects. With such accomplishments, he was a different boy altogether, and the change astonished his mother on her next visit.

"There's never been any Talent in our family, on either side," she confided in Dorotea at one point. "I just can't imagine where he got it from."

"Necessity, Mrs. Reidinger," Dorotea said at her most grandmotherly. "The accident has forced him to transfer motor functions to another part of his brain. Even the best of us only utilize about two-fifths of our brain potential."

Ilsa Reidinger did not really understand Dorotea's explanation, but she accepted it because Dorotea spoke with such authority.

"The human body learns to compensate, Mrs. Reidinger," Dorotea went on soothingly. "All Peter needed was a chance to train in new ways. Which, I must say, he has done extraordinarily well. We're very pleased with his progress." She beamed placidly at her guest.

"Yes, but what will he *do?*" Ilsa Reidinger asked plaintively.

"Why, Peter will do very well here at the Center, helping other youngsters—and adults, too—who have to learn to compensate for drastic handicaps." Sensing the woman's reservations on that score, Dorotea added, "Oh, the work pays very well. He's on a training scholarship right now, of course, but his profession pays very well indeed. He's all set for a fine career at the Center. You're going to be very proud of him."

Dorotea chose to ignore Ilsa Reidinger's other dominant thought: that if Peter was Talented, Katya must be, too. The girl was being ever so difficult, wanting to know why Peter got all the luck and she was stuck in a boring school, doing boring studies while Peter was getting everything his way just because he had gotten lucky.

"Can he read minds?" is what Ilsa Reidinger asked out loud. The idea made her uncomfortable.

"Peter has a very limited range," Dorotea replied mendaciously, intimating regret. "He can hear very strong thoughts, but his projections are short-range. His Talent lies in kinetics. Do you understand that word?"

"Yes, it means people can push things about without having to touch them. Like the ones going up to Padrugoi Station to help get it assembled so we can colonize the stars." The glib phrasing came from Dave Lehardt's clever publicity campaign on the tri-d.

Then Ilsa asked more timorously, "Would Petey go into space?" In her very audible public mind, Ilsa decided that whatever the answer, she would not mention that to Katya.

"Quite unlikely. The platform will be finished before Peter's received all his necessary training." The very thought of Barchenka conscripting Peter Reidinger made Dorotea queasy. Ilsa Reidinger was disappointed, however, suffering from the usual maternal syndrome of wanting *her* son to be unique, which he was; famous, which the Center would not wish on him; and perhaps rich, which Peter would also be, in that, as a Talent, he could purchase through the Center anything he really desired. "He shows a truly unique Talent." Let that be a sop to her pride.

"Yes, but what exactly *does* Petey do?"

"Well, you saw him walk and serve us tea quite by himself. That is all accomplished by his kinetic Talent. So you see, he is no longer dependent on mechanical or prosthetic devices to conduct normal activities. When he's surer of his abilities, we'll add more complicated tasks."

"He'll be able to hold down a job?"

Ilsa Reidinger really had not even grasped the basics, Dorotea thought, or comprehended the obvious achievements. She had barely grasped the fact that Peter would no longer be a financial or an emotional burden to his family. She was just a nice woman who had certainly been devoted to Peter during his convalescence, but the strain had taken a toll on her, too. Dorotea ventured to wax more enthusiastic about Peter's potential.

It suddenly occurred to Dorotea to wonder if the testing routines, established by Daffyd op Owen, needed to be updated or made more sensitive. Hospitals were usually well staffed with Talents of all descriptions. Why hadn't someone spotted Peter? She really ought to discuss that notion with Rhyssa—when the mess with Barchenka was smoothed out.

"I shouldn't think there'd be much young Peter can't do if he sets his mind to it."

"Being a kinetic, you mean?"

"A rather special one, at that, since he's had to overcome severe physical limitations."

Still slightly puzzled by the fuss being made over her Peter but immensely relieved by his future prospects, Ilsa Reidinger departed.

It never occurred to Dorotea that her remarks, meant to allay a mother's natural concern, would have unexpected repercussions. Certainly she and Rhyssa were beginning to realize the boy's immense potential, but even to colleagues they had been discreet.

"It's a case of make speed slowly, Lance," Rhyssa told the Australian director, who seemed to spend more time on a spacehotel and in the Jerhattan area than arranging matters in Canberra for his leave of absence on Padrugoi. He had dropped in to see her on his way from yet another long scheming session with Dave Lehardt and Samjan.

"I've seen some fair dinkums, dealing with the Aborigines and the Maoris, Rhyssa," Lance replied in his distinctive drawl as he slouched on a chair in her tower office, "but this lad takes the peach. If he's come on this fast with only a li'l four-point-five kpm generator for him to play with, think what he could do with *real* power."

"All the more reason to make speed slowly. Control is the most vital part of his training." She projected an image of Peter, head first, zipping around Jerhattan on a whirlwind tour, with a tail of detritus, people, small vehicles, and oddments caught up in the wake of his passage.

Lance grinned, his teeth very white against his perpetual tan, his sea green eyes glittering. "Too right, mate. I get the drift. But with a Talent like his and a proper generator, we could bleeding near shift drones all the way to the nearest planet."

Think that in your most private mind, Lance, she told him sharply. *Don't let a whisper of it escape your shield.*

Lance propped his angular body upright, his expression completely serious. *I was funning!*

Rhyssa nodded slowly, and he let out a long whistle.

Yeah, but just imagine the look on Barchenka's face if we could tell her that precious Padrugoi project had just turned obsolete.

"Not quite," Rhyssa said with a vindictive grin. She had entertained a few very satisfying fantasies on that very theme herself! "A facility like Padrugoi is required for any number of valid reasons apart from a jumping-off point to the stars."

How many know *about Petey boy?*

About his potential? Main staff know he's unusual. I was too excited when I realized the possibilities inherent in his gestalt, but they only know I was excited about the boy. There are just three of us—myself, Dorotea, and Sascha—who realize that the boy might be unusual. I don't think Sascha's had the chance to appreciate the potential that Dorotea and I are

just beginning to grasp. Rick Hobson thinks the boy is inor-
dinately quick, but we had to have a kinetic in on his initial
training. Like you, Rick's got to go to Padrugoi, so we're
cramming as much technique in as possible. He and Peter mesh
well. You are my choice for his more advanced training, so
don't do anything stupid up on Padrugoi, will you?

No way! That's a mean carrot to dangle in front of me for
six long months! Lance rose. "Pure shame that Dave Lehardt's
not a real Talent. He's wizard at handling the Finn and that
slimy little Neester bloke."

Rhyssa gave a little convulsive shudder at the mere mention
of Prince Phanibal.

"You don't like him either, do you?" Lance asked.

"No!"

Lance chuckled. "Always knew you were a woman of good
sense, ducks."

R hyssa did worry about Peter—he looked so frail after so
long in a hospital bed. So did Dorotea, both keeping their
concerns from Peter, whose telepathy was steadily improving along with his kinesis. He was not limited merely to receiving or sending emotions, but was developing a true telepathy,
the ability to send and receive both abstract and lingual messages. Nor did Rhyssa or Dorotea call attention to those moments when, in sheer ebullience, Peter did not draw on the
generator in kinetic exercises.

Dorotea enjoyed cooking for his eager appetite, and once
Peter was able to perform routine tasks, she fine-tuned his kinesis with food-preparation exercises. He could pare apples and
potatoes, scrape carrots, and cut up vegetables, all kinetically.
He ate anything and everything, and his body began to fill out
with good firm flesh; Rick showed him exercises for muscle
tone, and hours spent in Dorotea's garden tanned his skin to a
healthy glow. Peter no longer looked the wasted paralytic with

atrophied muscles. Still, extreme care was needed in all his activities, since he continued to have no feeling in his extremities or lower torso and would be unaware of cutting or burning or bruising himself in some of his perambulations.

When Rick finally had to leave for his tour at Padrugoi, Peter took it hard, moping about the next day.

"Rick will be back, Peter," Rhyssa said when she joined them that evening at dinner. "He's taught you about all he knows. Now, you have to teach yourself, which'll be hard."

"Teach myself?" Peter was so shocked that his good manners briefly deserted him. His fork hovered above his plate. He and Dorotea had an agreement—he could get the food to his mouth however he chose if he was alone, but he was to observe proper etiquette with anyone else.

"Yes, teach yourself," Dorotea replied blandly.

"Rick has given you the basics," Rhyssa added with a warm smile. "Certainly you're now able to do everything for yourself and help out in the house and the garden. Now you begin the next step—testing yourself. Don't worry. Rick left a long list for you to complete by the time his tour of duty is over."

"But he didn't tell me how . . ." Peter was clearly floundering.

"You know how," Rhyssa said, acting surprised at his reaction. "All paranormal Talents come from an instinctive level. Sharpen your instinct." She smiled at him, patting his arm soothingly. "That instinct led you right to the Center, didn't it? Don't worry about the 'how'! Rely on your instinct. Use it by sending different types of inert objects to destinations farther and farther away. First to places you are familiar with. Then by memorizing tri-d visuals and maybe even using mathematical coordinates. For example, that forkful of mashed potato. Where would you like to put it?"

The fork's burden of mashed potato disappeared.

Sascha: *What is going on down there?*

Rhyssa: *Does it concern a portion of mashed potato?*

Sascha, somewhat disgusted: *It does!* He sent her an image of a white glob in the middle of his desk.

"And where did you send it, Peter?" Dorotea asked non-committally.

"Sascha's desk. But on the wood, not on anything important," Peter assured her.

"I won't require you to eat it, but do bring it back!"

The well-traveled forkful reappeared on the edge of Peter's plate.

Sascha, sarcastically: *Thank you!*

You're welcome! Peter giggled like any youngster succeeding with a practical joke.

Sascha to Rhyssa and Dorotea: *We just get Madlyn house-trained and now we have Peter! Sometimes . . . I suppose, if he's up to tricks, he's adjusting to Rick's departure.*

Peter was also up to work the next day, using the gestalt with the generator to shift various items about the Center. Dorotea started him off moving small objects from one room to another, emphasizing accuracy of placement and picking locations with which Peter was familiar. By the end of the morning he was shifting heavy bales of computer paper from storage to the Control Room, getting his placements from squares crayoned onto the floor until Budworth finally signaled that his aim was perfect.

"Weight seems to be no object," Sascha said, reviewing the achievements at lunch with Rhyssa. "How much did he have to rely on the gestalt?"

"Not much. We've got a graph on its usage," Rhyssa replied. "His need is verging on the psychological."

"Ah, but that doesn't alter the fact that he does use it," Sascha said thoughtfully. "Can and *does*. By damn, Rhyssa, he's extraordinary! Once he can really lean on generator power, there isn't anything he can't shift, is there?" His eyes were shining with excitement. "If only we could figure out just how he achieves the gestalt."

Rhyssa shook her head, with a rueful smile.

"Could Rick?" he asked.

Rhyssa sighed. "Rick did just the basic kinetic training exercises with him. He didn't have more time. Damn Barchenka. Wouldn't you just know that we'd have a promising emergent who'd benefit from training with the very kinetics that she's yanked out of our reach. Why didn't we have an earlier precog of this?"

Sascha leaned back in his chair, regarding his good friend and director with an uncharacteristically solemn expression. "Rhyssa, hon, could you follow his mind?"

She gave a short laugh. "I'm an adept at telepathy, but Peter's going where no man has gone before. Maybe another strong kinetic could follow. I'm going to dragoon Lance Baden as his advanced trainer as soon as that wretched Padrugoi is finished." She blued the mental air with assorted images of her frustration.

Sascha nodded sympathetically. "Then we'll just have to continue doing kindergarten stuff with him until Lance is free. And build him up physically. Does Don Usenik see any chance of exercise restimulating those damaged nerves? Now that—"

"Trouble!" Budworth's voice rang through the special alarm speaker in Rhyssa's office.

What kind? she asked immediately.

"Goddammit, I want to speak to Director Owen *now*!" said a voice on the room address system as Budworth patched the call through.

"You are," Rhyssa replied coolly. "Please identify yourself."

"Dammit, didn't they tell you? Bob Gaskin, Jerhattan Port Authority. You took our kinetic away from us, and now we've a container pinning three men down and no bloody way to lift it quick enough to save their lives. Right now only the safety bar on the forklift is—"

"Do you have the area on video?"

"I do—the whole yard."

"Relay it to this screen immediately," she ordered. *Dorotea, bring Peter to my office. We've got to try to help. They're patching through the image.*

Dorotea: *Dare we?*

Rhyssa: *We'll never know unless we do. Lives are at stake. He's got the potential, and he's done well enough already with bulky, heavy things.*

Dorotea: *That's halfway across the city. But . . . all right. I'll have Peter there in a dash.*

Sascha and Rhyssa kept their eyes on the screen, which was showing the container, the hoist cables at one end of it still whipping in backlash. It had come down askew across a small forklift, the sturdy frame of which was keeping it from crushing the driver and two men who had been working near him. The Talents could see the dangling arm of one man pinned at one side, the feet of a second protruding under one corner— and nothing at all of the driver.

"Why did that hoist cable part, Mr. Gaskin?" Rhyssa asked calmly. "Surely you checked all your equipment before you put it in use again." She deliberately made herself sound censorious.

The office door opened and Dorotea and Peter entered; Peter's eyes went immediately to the screen.

"If your goddamned Center hadn't pulled our kinetic," Gaskin exploded, "this wouldn't have—Holy hell! How'd you get someone here this quick?"

Rhyssa, Dorotea, and Sascha held their breath as they watched the long unwieldy mass of the container slowly rise off the crumbled forklift, revealing the driver slumped across his controls and another man sprawled flat on the ground while the third staggered to his feet, holding his injured arm. They were also aware of a humming that they could feel through the floorboards of Rhyssa's office. The hum peaked off as the container was lowered carefully to the waiting truck loadbed.

"Bravo, Peter, beautifully done! Magnificent!" Rhyssa said—and then she saw him crumpled on the floor. "Oh, Lord! Did you strain yourself, love?"

Sascha reached the boy before she did, lifting him gently and depositing him on Rhyssa's conformable chair, which instantly altered to fit the boy's limp body.

"Will the men be all right?" Peter wanted to know, his white face contorted with anguish. *They were hurting bad.*

"More to the point, young man," Sascha said, frowning, "are you all right?" *Don, get up here on the double!*

"By God, ma'am, how'd you do that?" Bob Gaskin cried. The Port Authority manager was mopping his face with shaking hands.

"You haven't been completely abandoned by Talent, Mr. Gaskin. We have a skeleton crew"—Sascha's image of Peter's frail form, bony structure emphasized, made it very hard for Rhyssa to keep her features composed—"which we can throw into gear for emergencies of this nature. Do please now overhaul your equipment. We don't have the manpower for unnecessary accidents, you know." She ignored Sascha's exaggerated grimace as she saw medics rushing to assist the injured men as a Southside heli-amb landed nearby. "Good morning, Mr. Gaskin.

"We'll check in with Southside General Hospital later, Peter," Rhyssa assured the boy.

"After Don's checked you out, young man," Dorotea added, "though your concern for the men does you credit."

I know we had to, Rhyssa, Sascha said on a tight band to Rhyssa, *but should we have?*

Rhyssa made a face. *Hobson's choice, Sascha. We maintain an official position of the skeleton crew. By the way,* don't *do that to me again real soon, huh?*

Sascha rolled his eyes, expressing remorse but no reassurance. *I'm not sure how long we'll be able to hang that lie, so would you get all uptight if I tried to follow his mind's thrust when he's lifting? I didn't realize how quickly he's emerging to full use of his Talent.*

No, after this exhibition of Peter's ability, I was about to ask you if you could spare some time to work with him. I need your insight, since you're more expert at training. If we could duplicate the gestalt, even our featherweights could move containers.

"Okay, who's done what to whom now?" Don Usenik demanded as he entered the room. He looked around, then spotted the wan Peter on Rhyssa's chair. "What have you been doing? Moving mountains?"

Which do you want first? The good news, or the bad news?" Dave Lehardt asked Rhyssa a week later.

She could tell nothing from his expression—the look of his eyes was curiously intent on her face. He might not be a Talent, but he was unusually astute at picking up minute body-language signs. She was so glad to see him that she really did not care what news he brought, but she followed his cue.

"The bad!"

"Barchenka is certain you've been holding out on her. She's heard that you have a team of kinetic Talents that are not on your official register. She's about to create a stink. And I have to tell you that I've heard some mighty peculiar rumors circulating."

Rhyssa laughed. "We're not holding out on her—Talents can't. Telempaths can always detect a lie. She has Russian telempaths on her payroll. Tell her to ask them. What's the good news?"

Dave Lehardt raised one eyebrow in a skeptical arch. "The polls are again favorable to the Talented. When businesses employing them had to cope with old-fashioned ways, Talent popularity hit a fifty-year low—worse even than after the Hawaiian volcano disaster—even though everyone was pro-

Padrugoi and everyone, meaning the Talents, was doing their share. Seems that this nonexistent team of yours has provided emergency services. Only no Talent has been observed on the scene."

"It's a remote technique that we've been developing for emergency situations," Rhyssa said, schooling her face to reveal nothing. It was not that she did not trust Dave Lehardt, but she wanted to protect Peter. "And it's the one reason we felt we could strip all our Centers of kinetics to help Padrugoi."

"A remote technique?"

"That's what I said."

"No Talent I've spoken to knows anything about it."

"I said it was remote," Rhyssa repeated, struggling to keep amusement out of her voice. "Not something we want to go public on just yet. I'm sure you can appreciate *that*!"

"So Ludmilla can't get her hands on it?"

"She's coerced almost every kinetic we have onto Padrugoi. She's got sufficient numbers and skills right now to finish her work on schedule. She shouldn't get greedier!"

"She wants to come in under schedule, and the way your Talents are working, she could."

"Is a bonus involved in early completion?" Rhyssa was annoyed. Damn the woman to a disintegrating orbit!

"Didn't you know?" Dave Lehardt seemed surprised.

"I heard a great deal about penalties and a completion bonus, but strangely enough, nothing was said, or even hinted, that *early* completion was her goal."

"I'll do what I can to squash the rumors—and, if I may be so bold, you should keep that new team out of operation if at all possible. No more cavalry charges to the rescue without warning me, huh? Please?"

That was very sound advice, which Rhyssa intended to follow. Since the emergency lift, she had been chary of using Peter's skill. It just took too much out of his not-so-sturdy body. He was strengthening himself daily—exercising was becoming almost an obsession with him. But she was still rigorously restricting the use of his Talent to life-threatening situations in the Jerhattan area, which, fortunately, were few. Meanwhile, in the ongoing training sessions, he was using fax placement photos to send items to other Centers.

"I can follow his thoughts all the way," Sascha told Rhyssa after a week of linking minds with Peter during those exercises. "I can even feel the vibrations of the generator in his cerebrum, but *how* he effects the gestalt is still beyond me. And, as nearly as I can tell, he's relying less and less on the power. At least for light stuff."

"If he keeps on this way, maybe Lance is right," Rhyssa remarked. "Plug him into a powerful enough source and he could probably obviate the need for Padrugoi."

Sascha blinked, then projected a series of images depicting Barchenka's expression, the consternation on the egg-splattered faces of the space station's major supporters, and one small boy sending out starships the way children his age launched paper planes. The last and largest image was of Sascha himself, elongated mouth wide open, chin to his chest. "Could he?"

Rhyssa laughed, rolling her eyes. "I won't say he couldn't. But you know as well as I do that all Talent has limitations. Now is not the time to put any sort of pressure on Peter. He's such a happy boy now."

"We can thank God he is!" His mental picture was of himself, patiently controlling the lovelorn Madlyn Luvaro, huge wads of cotton wool in his ears.

Rhyssa retorted with an image of stray forkfuls of potato festooning his office. "A kinetic has far more options than a telepath!"

"He's easier to keep happy than Madlyn ever was, too," Sascha said, stretching his long legs. "The odd traffic snarl or two a day, and he feels he's worth his keep. Which reminds me, I've had some pretty pointed remarks from industrial VIPs lately about this remote team of ours. My answer is that we've managed to combine the trainees with an experienced featherweight to achieve the necessary heft, but the application is limited due to the extreme youth of the participants."

Rhyssa sighed. "That old tangled-web routine, huh?"

Sascha quirked an eyebrow. "Favoring Shakespeare? Thought your family ran to Popery."

Rhyssa laughed, envisioning her illustrious grandsire, Daffyd op Owen, as she remembered him, tall, silver-haired, slender, with the face of a poet and the chin of an Italian prince. "Sometimes the Bard fits better. Which industrialists have asked?"

"Nail on the head, girl. Every one of them supplies something to Padrugoi! And, as you know, there've been delays in getting matériel up to the station, weather problems mainly, with all those freak storms messing up launch windows."

Rhyssa frowned and, in an uncharacteristic show of nervousness, flipped a stylus end over end. "Lifesaving, yes; and with the technique he's been showing over distances, I think he probably could launch a drone up to Padrugoi through any sort of weather. But there's no way Peter's going to help secure her bonus or prevent her fines."

Sascha grinned. "I won't mention the possibility of such fun and games to him, you spoilsport." He threw her an image of him hastily raising a solid barrier against the barbs emerging from her eyes. "She couldn't hire him anyway. He's only fourteen. Underage, even under existing Russian law!"

Rhyssa let out a low whistle, then grinned. "Yes, he is a minor, isn't he? And Dorotea reminded me that he's been working pretty hard with you. Tomorrow he has a day off. And I've got all these files—" She gestured resignedly at the stacks on the edge of her desk. "Testing reports to go through."

"Why don't you take a night off?" Sascha suggested, grinning drolly. "With Dave."

Rhyssa sat bolt upright, closing her mind.

"Honey, I don't have to peek," he told her.

Rhyssa groaned. "He's not a Talent."

"There's no law in the Charter that says you have to marry Talent, you know."

"But that's the way to increase . . ."

"Yeah, and where did Peter Reidinger come from? I think sometimes, my dear friend," he said, leaning over the desk toward her, "we have to look with our eyes instead of our heads. Just thought I ought to mention it. Dave's the best friend Talent's got."

"It's not up to me, Sascha," Rhyssa added, feeling uncomfortable for the first time in her old friend's presence.

"Could be. Maybe not. Lehardt's clever enough to do his own promo work." With that Sascha left her.

A s Tirla entered the Main Concourse of Linear G, she sensed an aura of excitement, telling her that something was about to happen to relieve the tedium of Linear living. As always, there were some general workers scurrying to the Plaza to see if the WorkBoard was scrolling out any jobs for able-bodieds, concerned with getting enough day work to keep out of Conscriptive Work Services. No self-respecting Linearite wanted to be sent on a hard-labor tour or, worse, spaced out to the shipyards around the Big Wheel. Few CWS ever earned a return ticket. And now even the Talents were not exempt. So most of the little knots of excited people were composed of women.

Tirla edged close enough to a group of Hispanics to pick up the drift.

"He lay hands on . . ."

"Church is always *lo mismo* . . . The singing is bad."

"My Juan now . . . when he is reminded of the purity of the Virgin, he doesn't beat me for a day or two . . ."

"The true man of God provides food for the soul . . ."

Tirla snorted to herself. Food for the soul was not high on her priorities when her belly was empty.

"I have heard," Consuela Laguna was saying earnestly, "that if he lays hands on the lame, he cures." Consuela's son was handicapped beyond remedy or repair, but she remained positive that somehow, sometime, her Manuelito would be restored to health by some new miracle treatment, and she was always asking Tirla to translate the medical bulletins for her.

So, Tirla thought, a Religious Event had been unexpectedly scheduled for Linear G. That was odd. The Public Health meeting had been only four weeks earlier. It was true that there had not been an RE in a long time, but still she was suspicious. *Two* specials within four weeks?

She moved on to the next group, all Neesters from the Levant, and they were babbling about how they could get their men to attend that night instead of adjourning to Mahmoud's squat to see his new belly dancer. Then she slipped around to an Asian gaggle who were chattering excitedly about cures and whether the RE would be bad for business. Asians provided ancient remedies for the many minor ailments that beset those in the warreny Residentials.

"He has come as promised . . ." she heard as she slid up to Mama Bobchik. The old woman's black eyes were wide; her cheeks a mottled glowing red of excitement. "You come, too, *dushka*," she said, catching Tirla's arm. "You must tell us his words, exactly. The last time I could not hear what was said, and my soul is black with sin."

"*Nakonetz,*" Tirla agreed easily. Most Religious Interpreter Groups generally said nothing, in the most ornamented phraseology. She could amuse herself by anticipating the trite phrases and flowery words. "So the Assembly extension was granted after all?" she asked, eager to maintain her reputation of knowing all that went on in the Linear.

"*Da, eto tak!*" Mama Bobchik happily reassured her. "My man was sent word to prepare late last night." Argol Bobchik was one of the Linear's sanitary engineers. "The word is that this Religious is all-seeing," Mama babbled on, "with an excellent backup group. They were well received at Linear P. Early as it is, already this morning many traders have booked space. It will be an occasion. We have not had religion here in G for some months. We are all in need of guidance. The souls of many are dark with sin and must be purged."

Tirla nodded solemnly. Mama Bobchik was certainly old enough to be facing a mystic accounting of the sins on her soul. Too bad no LEO man would be there to hear it.

But how had Tirla missed such a juicy rumor? Maybe it had been decided very late the previous night. At any rate, the presence of traders would make it easier for her to wash the tied credits for the Yassim man. She shuddered at the thought of him. She did not like to hold onto his money too long. Not that he had any reason to distrust her—she just wanted to make certain he never did. Especially if he suspected she was close to salable age. She was small and thin enough to pass for the nine years she admitted to. Someday someone would count fingers on her. From time to time she thought about what she would do then—and tried to keep enough floaters stuck inside her blouse at all times so that she could flee to another Linear if she had to. She had even managed to get her hands on a highly illegal copy of the cargo-train schedules and had found her way to the nearest access points to the subterranean concourse to eyeball escape routes.

Deftly disengaging herself from Mama Bobchik's fat fingers, she moved on to the Pakis, who were chattering about bringing in some relatives from Linear E and arguing over the advisability of such a move. Some insisted that, since the extension was legal, there would be no risk. Then Mirda Khan—a person Tirla was always careful to please—came up and quickly dismissed such stupid generosity.

"The blessings of such a Lama would be few," Mirda muttered in an intense and angry tone just audible to those around her, "for he cannot waste his holy strength on the trivial. Such as he would be gracious enough to dispense must be for us, here, in Linear G. For us," she said again, poking her thin breastbone with a broad flat thumb, "the true believers, his faithful in Linear G."

"The Very Revered Ponsit Prosit has been at Linear P," one of the other women murmured reverently. "Pandit heard of the miracles he performed."

Tirla was skeptical of miracles for, on close inspection, there were always alternate explanations for healings and savings and revelations. But they were fun to delve.

"Then we save such for ourselves!" Mirda replied fiercely, defying contradiction. Suddenly she spun around, somehow aware of being the object of scrutiny—but Tirla was quicker, moving to flatten herself against the Concourse pillar. She had heard enough anyhow and left.

So this Religious Interpreter, this RIG, had a reputation? As Tirla was quite aware, it took a real clever talker to keep from violating the variety of complex doctrines in a Linear. This Ponsit Prosit might well be worth listening to—and watching closely. In her precarious situation, Tirla was always open to pointers.

If the whole thing was legit. She mulled over the probables as she ducked into side aisles before coming out again onto the Main Concourse, far enough away from the Pakis to be screened by other groups. Then she glanced up at the nearest publi-text screen. She watched through the usual notices and announcements until it scrolled down to 2200 hours, where a legal extension for use of the Assembly was posted, with trading and drinking permitted.

The full details were being vividly proclaimed, complete with fanfares of brass instruments and snippets of the Respected Venerable Homilifier Ponsit Prosit smiling beatifically at vast audiences. A chorus was promised, and a short blast of five-part harmony and high soprano descant was presented as an enticement to attend the full show. This V R & Holy Religious Interpretation Group purportedly had only recently returned from the Eastern Cities of Faith, where Ponsit Prosit had endured "fasting meditations of great length and illumination." Linear G was fortunate in the extreme that he was able to fit that evening's assembly into his busy tour. So, he had not had a booking in a while, Tirla thought cynically. Well, Religious Interpretations were very popular in Linears, better than fights sometimes and often more showy. Tirla liked shows—and legal extensions.

There had been a Public Health roundup recently, so a second, covert one was unlikely in her experience. And while a Religious Event could be staged to mask more illicit operations than washing tieds in public, there still might not be any undercover LEOs. Crowd Controllers would be around, of course—that was standard procedure—but Tirla knew most of them despite the way they altered their appearances.

The important thing was that she had the Yassim tieds to change. She should never have agreed to do it, but Bulbar had been insistent and the "talker"—a hit man whom she would not willingly offend—had told her that she was being given the opportunity in reward for services already rendered. Having consented to a professional engagement with Mama Bobchik, who was not only another person it was unwise to offend but someone who, having presided over Tirla's birth, would always defend the girl, Tirla was committed on two counts to attend.

Prepared with several contingency plans, Tirla began her usual morning routine—bargaining for the day's meals and getting a bath and a clean issue of clothing. But as she proceeded, she was stopped by various female clients, each wanting her company during this Religious Event because the featured Lama-shaman was reputed to speak in tongues and Tirla was absolutely the only person who would faithfully tell them everything he said. There was a limit, however, to how many people Tirla could adequately represent. Surrounded by very insistent, vocal, and physically active prospective clients, none of whom she cared to antagonize, she attempted to organize them.

"Bilala, you and Pilau must come together. Anna, you team up with Marika. Zaveta, Elpidia comes as well. Chi-shu, Lao Wang with you. Cyoto, Ari-san is your partner." And so she grouped them. Ten pairs was as unmanageable as it was unavoidable. Before she got into any further difficulties, Tirla discreetly removed herself from public view. She still had to get the tied credits out of their hidey holes and secreted about her for easy access.

W e have an Incident," Sirikit said, her light, crisp voice carrying easily to Budworth, who was duty officer in the Parapsych Control Room.

"Who?" Budworth sent his gimballed chair spinning across the tiled floor to her station. Seeing him maneuver so rapidly around the Control Room made people forget that his spine had been crushed in an accident and that he had only minimal movement of his head and two fingers.

"Auer." Sirikit's surprise was reflected in her voice.

"Really!"

"And Bertha!"

"That's an unusual combination."

"Not if Ponsit Prosit the Great Flimflam is involved. I caught the p.a. for Linear G."

"It is very true she would have his guts for garters," Budworth said, grinning wryly. Bertha Zoccola was generally a relaxed and tolerant individual, but mention of that particular RIG was enough to enrage her. Budworth set himself for her fury in reporting a precog involving the man.

Whenever precognitive Talents responded to an Incident, they would flash the Center, alerting Control to receive a verbal description of what they had previewed. Budworth positioned his chair at the fingerboard next to Sirikit and scratched his chin on the rim of his head support, feeling the surge of excited anticipation that he always experienced at such moments.

"C'mon, you net-heads, report!" he exclaimed.

Sirikit glanced away from her screen to grin at him. Then a bleep sounded, startling both of them even though they were expecting an entry.

"Auer here," the emotionless voice announced, and the precog's face appeared in one of the response screens. "A real messy one. High panic, screams, mob, kids trampled, the usual thing. Why don't you grab Ponsit and space him to the shipyards? I'm tired of protecting that scuzfart."

"You saw Flimflam himself, Auer?" Sirikit asked encouragingly. At Budworth's nod, she took over the routine questions. She was one of the most deft at post-Incidental debriefing, and Auer always responded well to her. Budworth busied himself with tapping out a query for scheduled public events. More crowd control would have to be assigned to Linear G.

Auer shrugged with an indifference both observers knew was false. "He's prominent. All colored lights and glittering hands. Then running away. As usual. Never stays to calm the audiences he excites to riot pitch."

"Where?" Sirikit encouraged him.

"Your typical Residential assembly hall. Usual Ponsit backdrops. Nothing unusual . . . except—" Auer paused, frowning down at something. "Except—that's odd!"

"What's odd, Auer?"

"All over a scrawny girl?" When he looked up, his eyes were haunted.

"Yes?"

"I feel . . . and her danger is acute. It doesn't end tonight. She's Talented!" That was said in a surprised voice; then Auer passed a hand across his eyes, scrubbing downward. "It's gone now. It's gone." The screen blackened.

Another screen brightened.

"You shouldn't allow that man a *permit* at *all*!" Bertha Zoccola was bristling with indignation. "You've caught him dealing time and again! Those people don't have the credits to spend on mystical cures and miracle healings. He spouts the most appalling sort of pantheist tripe. *And* in the worst language!"

"What did you see, Bertha?" Budworth asked the plump little woman, who still cherished a worn deck of Tarot cards that her great-grandmother had once read with a high enough degree of accuracy to earn a significant credit balance.

"I keep telling you that man is nothing but trouble." Her double chin quivered, and her expression was concerned. "I don't care if the Domestic Satisfaction Index does rise after he's played a Residential. Why should we Talents protect a quacksalver, a faker, a pharisee, a hoaxer, a gyp! An arrant carnie!"

"We're not protecting him! Now, what did you see, Bertha?"

"Halfway through that—that gibberous effort of his—you never can tell *what* he's saying in that mumbo-jumble of his—there's a movement, to the left of the platform . . ." She jingled her left hand, her many wrist bracelets clacking noisily. "Or do I mean his right?" She raised the other hand, splaying fingers crammed with rings. "There's a commotion. It has to do with a large group of women." She waggled her hand again, frowning. "Then everything goes wild! A name! They're all calling a name! And I can't hear what it is! Oh, wouldn't that cause a saint to swear! The one vital detail! And I *thought* I heard it so clearly . . ." She pursed her lips in concentration and then slowly shook her head, sighing. "No, it's gone. I'm so sorry."

"Thanks, Bertha dear. You've filled in some details."

"Who else?" Bertha asked, as always.

"Auer."

"Him?" Bertha was incredulous. "Well, what'd'ya know about that? Do keep me screened, Buddy."

"You bet." Budworth was punching Sascha's office as her picture dissolved. "Sascha, we got an Incident."

"There's only one crowd controller assigned to the RIG, Budworth," Sirikit murmured to him. "Residential Linear G is listed as blue, calm."

"Well, it's about to change color unless we can neutralize. Sascha, something's going to bust wide at Ponsit's meeting at G tonight."

"Linear G?" The large blue eyes in Sascha's Slavic-cast face widened with surprise. "We'd nothing planned *there*," he murmured. "Who saw it?"

"Bertha and Auer."

"What?" Sascha raised his eyebrows. "That's a first. I'll be back to you, Buddy. I'll organize our infiltration with the Bro." *Rhyssa, we've got an incipient riot.*

That sort of thing's more your bailiwick than mine, was Rhyssa's reply. *Give my regards to Boris.*

As the contact with Sascha faded, Budworth grunted, absently scratching his jaw. He hoped there would be remote visuals set up so that he could watch what went on, and if Sascha's LEO brother, Boris, was involved, there would be. Whether his experience was vicarious or not, Budworth appreciated being involved in these unexpected spectaculars. One never knew what would happen during an Incident. He was honest enough in the back of his mind—the only safe place to think in the Center—to realize that he had not been a physically brave person even before his accident. Still and all, he found the breathless anticipation and stimulation to be very pleasant sensations for one husked by a mobility chair.

Sirikit was making rapid entries, documenting the Incident. Although the Talented had come to have immense credibility, and the meticulously kept daily files might generally be scanned only by Research, the procedures outlined by the Parapsychic Center's first administrator, Henry Darrow, were scrupulously followed. The full spectrum of Talent was far from being known and certain facets of Talent were not at all fully developed, as in the case of young Peter Reidinger's Talent for an electrical gestalt. And who knew what sort of unusual Talent might yet be discovered among emergents? Budworth sighed as he turned back to tasks which once would have seemed far from mundane.

CHAPTER 8

Tirla did not dare be late to the meeting, but she also did not want to arrive too soon and risk being hassled by even more people demanding her particular services. No matter what baksheesh was offered, she could translate for only so many at a time, especially with the other, more pressing, matter to complete. *That* had to be managed. She chose to arrive with enough time to do a quick survey and identify the best vendors, as well as any undercover LEOs or PHOs. The fortuitous scheduling of the Religious Event still bothered her.

Unless . . . It occurred to Tirla that maybe there would be some Treasury persons in the crowd, checking up on vendors, that money laundering itself was the target of this occasion. But the Ts were easy to spot. They were always so obvious about blending into the crowd.

Having arranged to meet the women at the main southeast entrance, Tirla entered the Assembly atrium from one of the side northwest gates. Someone else had already disabled the entrance eye that read IDs and counted attendance, saving her the trouble. The petty vendors had their booths up and merchandise displayed: mainly trinkets and synth clothes, goods that could be quickly shifted. But there were air-cushion carts being angled through the wider doorways, proving that some serious trading would be done. She felt somewhat easier in her mind. The big traders would not risk themselves or their merchandise at a risky-disky.

She took note of prices as she wended her way through the gathering crowd. She hoped there would be some fresh produce—well, fresh in that it had been recently nicked from the underground warehouses that supplied Jerhattan's markets. She would treat herself to a nice crisp pepper, carrot, or apple from the day's earnings, something to sink her teeth into instead of the subsistence mush or compound protein loaf. She wanted to get a stick of real chewing gum, too, to keep her mouth moist when she started translating. She spared only a glance for the activity on the platform, where hands were rushing about, draping curtains and swags and hauling lighting and sound equipment about. She was never impressed by packaging—just the quality of the contents. She found gum at Felter's stall and made him launder one of the smaller tied notes.

She was just savoring the minty flavor of her gum when she caught sight of an all too familiar profile in totally unfamiliar synth-issue clothing. Yassim was actually here? She ducked behind a large man in a stained robe that had once been the height of fashion. He was holding up both arms, wigwagging at someone on the stage. The smell of him nearly made her swallow her gum, but his outline completely obscured her.

What was Yassim doing here? Tirla wondered. Didn't he trust her? As her camouflage dropped one arm to cup his hand to his mouth to shout a direction, Tirla chanced a second look.

Yes, it was him. He was unmistakable. He had done something subtle to his face, altering its shape—probably pads in his cheeks and lower lip—but he had not, could not, alter that long thin hooked nose and the sloping forehead. He walked, as always, as if he owned the place, strutting about in a loose over-robe that had not suffered much cleaning in its long life. His headgear was also appropriately worn, torn, and stained. It was a creditable attempt to blend in, but Tirla *knew* the man was Yassim. There he was, sauntering about, inspecting trinkets, pausing to ask questions of vendors, appearing to go from one group of friends to another, friends she quickly identified as some of his multitude of ladrones, hitters, and sassins. Well and discreetly guarded though he was, why was he there?

Her odorous blocker moved and she moved with him,

keeping him as cover. When he stopped, roaring out instructions, she, too, did—and saw Yassim talking to three Neester mothers who had young children with them. Suddenly Tirla knew what he was doing there. With equal certainty, Tirla did not want to be anywhere in his vicinity while child buying was on his mind. She did, however, make a mental note of which ladrones and sassins she knew among his followers. There had to be one she could trust to give his boss the tieds she had exchanged into floaters. There was no way she could avoid that chore.

Subliminal music had started, and the lighting in the Assembly Hall began to alter subtly, heralding the beginning of the Religious Interpretation. Tirla ducked behind the nearest vendor's shillboard and slipped to the southeast entrance.

An agitated Mirda Khan seemed to have eyes in the back of her mirror-adorned headdress, for she swung around, her face as sharp as a predatory bird's, as Tirla approached. She hooked her fingers painfully into Tirla's grasp and hauled the girl to her.

"Where were you? Where were you?" Mirda shook her angrily, showering her with spittle and sour breath so that Tirla pulled back as far as she could. The other women who had commissioned her to translate the RIG's words formed a close circle around her. But since their bodies also shielded her from Yassim's notice, she did not resist.

"I was pricing the merch," she said, unrepentantly.

Bilala and Pilau were trying to edge around Mirda and pull Tirla to their segment of the circle. Mirda jammed Tirla tight against her angular body while Mama Bobchik somehow got ahold of Tirla's free arm, effectively pinning her between the two formidably large women.

"*He's* here," Tirla said to Mirda, squirming to give herself a little space. She repeated the phrase until all her customers knew.

"*He?*" Mirda stretched to peer over the heads of their little knot. She gave a snort. "Yassim'll roast in hell before I sell him another child." Her fingers tightened convulsively on Tirla's shoulder. "You stay away from him. You hear me good?"

Tirla nodded enthusiastically. If Mirda knew Yassim, was there a chance she could inveigle the woman to pass on the laundry? Not with any sure knowledge that all of it would reach him.

"He gives a good price," Elpidia whined. She had a girl child old enough to spin off. She also had a drug habit to keep, for which she exchanged the yearly fruits of her womb once they were of an age to be sold off profitably. She fretted whether or not to go back to her squat and bring down the child for him.

"I would not sell to such as him!" Mirda snapped in her own language, black eyes flashing scornfully. "Price or not. Even selling to the station is better."

"What did she say?" Elpidia demanded of Tirla.

Tirla shrugged. "I am hired to translate the speaker, not settle disputes between clients, and she is not one to annoy."

Elpidia scowled at Mirda Khan, who hauled Tirla around, nearly wrenching her left arm out of Mama Bobchik's hand.

"Come," Mirda said. Her outer robe billowing its musty folds across Tirla's face, she led the group forward, acting as a spearhead through the still thinly scattered gathering. She halted right under the stage, where no one could thrust in front of them to block their view. She was about to push Tirla forward when the girl wriggled free.

"I must be able to see him. I will stand here, where I can see, and where all of you can hear." She repeated this until it was clearly understood by all her clients.

Within the circle she felt safe from Yassim. She began to relax and even to enjoy the music despite the patchy sound of the shrill replay as it ground through a multi-ethnic repertoire. Where were the famous live backup performers? This had been publicly billed as an occasion! Tirla took note of activity on the stage, the draperies billowing suddenly here and there from movement behind them. She could just catch a glimpse of the right-hand wings and people milling about, waiting to go on. So, there was a chorus. She much preferred live singing.

Out of the corner of her eye she caught a glimpse of a big man to her right, wandering with all too apparent indifference. She sensed a penetrating assessment of her companions going on under the brim of a battered peak cap, and she leaned surreptiously into Mama Bobchik. She felt something else then, a soothing brush across her mind which caused the high, sharp chatter of the women to fall off into a less excited pitch. She was not sure what *that* was all about.

The man was not Treasury. She followed his progress, aware that he was in contact somehow with two women who gave every evidence of being oblivious to him as they chattered and laughed together, jostling through the early comers to find a good position near the stage. She peered suspiciously at the two, their faces painted with careless hands, one of them obviously pregnant, though she wore the gear of a prostitute. Their faces were unfamiliar, and Tirla was beginning to wonder if the meeting really had been staged by an authority like Treasury or PH when a third woman, well known to Tirla, greeted them effusively and stayed to gossip. Reading from their lips the commonplace remarks they exchanged soothed the girl. It was seeing Yassim here that made her so nervous. She certainly did not owe him so much that he would come after her. She was not even overdue with the laundered credits. What had happened to his stock? He was not often caught short enough to brave a public affair. She touched the little pouches of tieds in the clever vest she wore for the purpose under her issue suit and reassured herself that all were in place.

A fanfare blasted for attention, and the excited babble died down to eager anticipation. Not a bad flourish, Tirla thought, quite willing to be carried along by a good show.

Then the choir stalked out self-consciously and arranged

themselves with some poking and pulling on one side of stage center. As close as she was, Tirla could see that their costumes were neither clean nor new. Not all of them managed to find the right pitch from the final note of the recorded blurt of brass. Tirla knew the song they were singing, a really old good one, so the fact that they were singing it badly was inexcusable. She only had to translate it for Cyoto and Ari—everyone else mumbled along in their own languages.

Then the emcee came out, falsely bright, and started the pitch, waffling on about the training and merits of the Revered Venerable Ponsit Prosit. As he was merely repeating all the claptrap about mystical training in Far Asia from the public announcement, Tirla did not start to translate it until Bilala hissed at her to earn her fee.

There was another song, one which slipped from one musical ethic to another with no respect for tonality or rhythm. Perversely, the singers managed to perform the travesty competently. Tirla identified six who were spaced out on something. That they could sing at all might indeed be a minor miracle of this RIG.

There were flourishes of recorded instruments and rolls of drums, which stirred even Tirla's cynical pulses. Drums could be so exciting! A great crashing of cymbals, a painfully glaring display of assorted lights and narrow beams, an ear-blasting crescendo of bugle synths accompanied by fragrant smoke bombs, and the Revered Venerable Religious Interpreter arrived, his robes artfully gleaming.

Her clients were suitably impressed by his "magical" appearance, but Tirla had caught a glimpse of the square aperture in the floor before he shot up through the densest veil of smoke to hover on his column above the stage and the awed spectators. She preferred something more dramatic; she had seen that sort of entrance so frequently that it had lost any impact. But clearly she was a minority. Even Mirda pretended to be afraid, covering her face with a fold of her head cloth.

The Religious Interpreter went into his act immediately, face upturned so Tirla's best view was of a waggling chin and dark holes of nostrils. The light show dazzled as taped music supported his mouthings—for that was what they were, syllables meaning absolutely nothing, with random words from every language she had ever heard tossed in to confuse.

"What does he say, the holy man?" Mirda demanded.

"Tell me what he say?" Mama Bobchik pulled Tirla to her. Bilala and Pilau were equally insistent: one kicked Tirla's shin, while the other transferred a substantial amount of her weight onto Tirla's undefended toes.

"Nothing," Tirla replied, disgusted. "He says nothing!"

She was poked, pushed, and pulled.

"He's saying something." "He speaks mystically." "Tell *us* what he says." "Ah, I understand that word for myself! I will pay you nothing, bitch."

Tirla was furious at that threat. Furious at the RIG. She would translate when he said something translatable. She was pinched and tweaked and slapped. In self-defense she caught the pattern of his babble and, involuntarily mimicking his stance and delivery, rattled off the nonsensical sounds in an undertone, translating the occasional real word into as many languages as she could before picking up the gibberish again.

Then the man stopped talking and spread his arms, his beatific smile radiant in the flood of light picking him out, seemingly afloat in the air above the stage. Then Tirla realized that he was staring in her direction.

In a gesture that startled her as well as her clients, he lunged forward, eyes flashing, face contorted, his accusing finger pointing straight at her.

"Unbelievers, profaning a sacred moment with chatter. Hear, learn, obey, repent your evil uncaring ways. Be taken into the light of the world. Be admitted into the holy sepulcher. Be one with humanity and all loving, caring creatures. Be purified. Be saved! *Be!*'' His accusing hand lifted and spread open as a beam of light caught his fingers and spilled down his raised arm.

Tirla, translating as rapidly as possible in the dramatic pause, was thankful for some coherent phrases. Her clients might be listening to her, but their eyes were on him. He had the crowd's rapt attention now. Tirla was fairly sure that no one outside the circle could see her, but dared not stop talking. She kept spewing out the gibberish, worrying that such nonsense would not be worth the money promised her. They might not pay her at all. She was already regretting that she would miss the taste of the crisp green pepper she had hoped to purchase with her fee.

The Lama-shaman assumed another dramatic pose, arms out, palms upturned in entreaty.

"Bring me your sick, your weary, your wretched souls. Let me heal them. A touch will ease the tortured mind, the fevered body, the twisted limb, the blurred sight. Approach! Be not afeared. All things come to those who deserve. All creatures deserve Love. For it is Love, Love, Love that heals!''

Tirla rattled it all off easily, trying to peer through the shielding bodies to see who would be working the scam. Barney with his lizard eyelids—one blink, and his eyes were milky white blind; another, and he could "see clear once again, hallelujah!'' Maybe Mahmoud with his double joints all twisted out of shape—one touch of the Lama-shaman's healing touch and they would straighten. Or would it be Maria with her weeping sores?

The Lama-shaman threw back his head, his hands turned gold in the narrow spot-beams, glittering from some sort of paint he must have used. Her clients inhaled with awe at the sight, their faces rapt as he made mystic passes with his magical hands. Glistening strands and bits whirled from his fingertips, disappearing in brief sparks as they left the light beams. That was a new trick, Tirla thought. Not bad. Pilau tried to catch a strand, but it disintegrated, leaving no trace in her grubby fingers.

Just then another strand, stronger, shot from the stage and fell on the head of a bemused man. He was less bemused when, with another grand flourish, the Lama-shaman began to reel him in.

"You have been chosen, brother. Come to me! Embrace me!" A ramp extruded from the stage, straight toward the chosen one, who glanced about with apprehension as he was pushed onto the ramp by those behind him and propelled forward by those on either side. "Kneel, brother," the Lama-shaman intoned, and appeared to glide down the air.

Tirla could feel the faint vibration of the stage mechanism that supplied the effect, but she did not pause in her translations. It was a pretty good gimmick. She wondered where the control was. The mark appeared genuinely stunned at being chosen. He knelt obediently, a dazed expression on his face.

"Rallamadamothuriasticalligomahnozimithioapodociamoturialistashadioalisymquepodial—Omathurtodispasionatusimperadomusigena lliszweigenpolastonuchevaliskyrielisonandia. Moss pirialistusquandoruulabetodomoarigatoimustendiationallamegrachiatus . . ." the Revered Venerable intoned, holding his hand above the mark's head.

More syllables and almost-words that Tirla could not anticipate enough to mimic. She could appreciate and admire the Venerable's truly respectable breath control. Why, he sounded as if he could go on forever!

"What does he say?" Mirda pinched her sharply.

"How can I hear when you babble at me?" Tirla replied and made up suitable phrases, which she then translated. "Woops!"

Strange things were happening above the chosen one's head. How did the Lama-shaman *do* that with sleeves so tight at his wrists? Tirla wondered. Hair, face, and throat of the mark were shimmering with gold; the man's expression was first ludicrous and then ecstatic. Tirla wondered what the Venerable Prayman could be using. She was beginning to enjoy the spectacle.

The Revered slowly turned back to the audience, his face also golden-hued, the whites of his eyes visible. "The power is with me. Whom else will it touch?"

Raising his arms again and extending his hands forward, he gave the audience sufficient time to see the effect the "power" had had on the first "chosen." With a twist of his wrists, his palms turned over and strands shot out in all directions. Before Tirla could duck, one of the filaments landed on her head. Whatever it was stuck tightly in her hair despite quick efforts on her part to get rid of it. Her hands were caught by the adhesive, bound to her head now. She began to panic. There was no way she wished to be hauled up in public. Not with Yassim in the hall. Not with tieds on her, credits she had no right to possess under any circumstances.

The choir began to chant for the chosen to come forward, to receive power. The audience caught up the refrain, and Tirla could hear the ominous overtone of envy from those who felt themselves more worthy of such an honor.

"She's been chosen!" Bilala and Pilau shrieked, bursting into an ululation that shot panic through Tirla's heart as they tried to push her forward toward the ramp nearest them.

"No, she's got to stay. She's got to tell us!" Mama Bobchik and Mirda Khan were not to be cheated. They pulled Tirla back.

"Break it, Cyoto. Help me, Lao Wang. Elpidia! Zaveta!" Tirla began struggling in earnest, terror starting to chill her guts.

All the other newly chosen were making their way up to the stage. The strand tightened, pulling at her hair. She twisted. Then suddenly she was snapped free. She caught the glint of a knife blade as she fell back against the solid Mama Bobchik.

Zaveta and Mirda locked with the screaming Bilala and Pilau, who were attempting to regain control of Tirla.

As she had done before in such situations, Tirla dropped to the floor and plunged to one side, tripping someone, who fell heavily on her left foot. She ignored the stab of pain and crawled on, her breath coming in sobs. She rolled free of her encircling clients and scrambled to her feet, plowing through the chanters. Someone saw the dangling golden strand and grabbed it, nearly jerking her off her feet. To free herself she wrenched the tangled hair from her head, leaving the bit of scalp dangling in the man's hand.

"Grab her!" The chant was interrupted to set up the cry. She squeezed past several grasping hands, frantic to get to the lobby and the nearest emergency exit.

"Here, I gotcha!" She was encircled by massive forearms. She lifted her arms and slithered down; a kick was aimed at her belly, but despite being winded, she rolled, too accustomed to such dirty tactics not to have self-preserving instincts. She had a glimpse of one of Yassim's sassins, face wreathed in a witless grin of success, before she landed against the far wall, and suddenly two pairs of trousered legs shielded her.

She was helped to her feet by kind hands and made conscious of soothing thoughts of assistance, understanding, and sympathy. She recognized the aura just as her splayed fingers felt the doorframe. Managing to elude the hands, she whipped out the door and sped across the foyer, paying no heed to pleas to stop. An incredible multi-toned bellow rose behind her, an angry frustrated noise that gave impetus to her pumping legs. As she pounded down the access aisle, she heard a familiar thumping thud in the air above.

LEOs! Had they been on hand? Or had they been called? But it took time for LEO ships to assemble. She found the small square duct she needed, whipped off the cover, crawled inside, and, with some difficulty in the restricted space, snapped it back into place. She crouched in the dirt and grime, tilting her face away from the light as her lungs fought to repay her heart for the strain.

She heard people racing by, heard their exclamations as they reached the dead end, heard them turn and come back, and heard their steps continue on past her refuge. Despite the noise, Tirla fell asleep.

Rhyssa!'' The alarmed voice of the duty officer was accompanied by an impulse through her headnet that roused her instantly.

"Yes?"

"Major disaster precog," Budworth said.

Great! Rhyssa thought sleepily. Two major trouble precogs in not quite two days and not a tremble about matters which urgently concerned all Talents.

"Recorded all across Asia," Budworth went on. "Looks like Kayankira's going to get another monsoon overload. They haven't repaired the restraining dams from the last one. How're we going to cope, with all the strong kinetics on the station?"

"Is there time to bring any down?"

"That's the panic! There's time enough, but weather conditions all across the world are freaky. Even if a Padrugoi shuttle launched, the nearest clear landing site is Woomera. The kinetics have to be on site to be effective." What Budworth did not say—"if Barchenka would allow 'em to leave the station"—flashed like a neon sign in Rhyssa's mind.

"Get Sascha up for me, will you, Buddy?"

He did, Sascha assured her. *Are you considering Peter?* His mental tone mixed eagerness to try and awareness of the multiple risks involved.

I must consider Peter's unique capabilities in a situation as critical as this, she told him.

How? Without compromising Peter's security?

They both slapped up internal shields as they felt the arrival of other thoughts.

Kayankira: *Rhyssa, I've got to have all the kinetics you have left. I understand there's no chance of getting any of them down from Padrugoi?*

Rhyssa: *That's my understanding.*

Vsevolod Gebrowski: *I shall insist! I shall take this to the World Council. They have deplored the situation in India. Let them put words into action. Reducing the density of population in that area of Bangladesh also diminished the available work force, and the necessary work has not been completed on time. Now we pay for that.*

Miklos Horvath: *Not if we draft the kinetics on Padrugoi down to help. And the cleanup effort will be reduced by kinesis now!*

Rhyssa: *If we can force the weather to give us a break!*

Bessie Dundall at Canberra: *The precogs all indicate the worst flooding ever in Bangladesh. The new levees haven't been completely restored, so floodwaters will drown this year's harvest. The barriers won't work for some reason—I suspect their erection will prove that once again corruption and bribery have been widespread. We have to do something!*

Alparacin: *Rhyssa, what about that team of yours I hear about?*

Rhyssa: *They're not well-enough trained for a disaster of this magnitude, dear friend. They'd be burned out.*

Peter: *No, I wouldn't.*

Quiet! Sascha, Rhyssa, and Dorotea ordered as one.

Peter: *I was, that was just to you.*

Rhyssa held her breath. But no Talent queried the unknown voice. *Naturally Eastern will do whatever we can,* she told the others. *May we have copies of the precogs? But I assure you that highly skilled kinetics are going to have trouble coping with this sort of thing, and all I have are a handful of fourteen-year-old trainee kinetics.*

Madlyn here . . .

Sascha: *Honey, you're one voice that never has to identify. What have you heard?* He imaged to Rhyssa a vision of Madlyn Luvaro, hands to her mouth to make a megaphone, leaning out of an airlock and shouting down to a wincing Earth.

Madlyn: *Lance has been arguing with Barchenka since he got the precog. She absolutely refuses to risk a shuttle or a pilot. You gotta admit the weather's pretty freaky all over right now. I can see it clear as day: lots of turbulence, and not just over the Indian continent. Lance says there has to be one safe place on Earth they can land, and they've got to help. He's citing her for contractual violation. She says it's too danger-ous to risk so many Talents—now she's doing the matriarchal, protecting-you-against-your-own-altruism. Ha!*

And there isn't a pilot we've talked to who'll risk a drop into the soup kettle down there, she went on. *Wait! Lance says*—Madlyn's mental tone altered to a rote-recital level—*now's the time to try. He says you'll know what he means. He accepts that it could be a risk, but if ever to put it to the test, now's the time. Have you got all that?* She sounded mystified.

Sascha: *You've come through loud and clear, Madlyn, and we copy.*

Lance says that the precog indicates even more horrendous damage than the last monsoon flood caused, so Talent has got to give kinetic support. He's dragooned a pilot into coming, but the guy's scared of attempting to land anywhere. Lance has assured him that all the kinetics on board will do the land-ing okay. Is Lance gone space-crazy? All right, I'm telling them. He says he, and a contingent of the heavy-duty kinetics— enough to effect flood control—will be on the shuttle Erasmus in Hangar G at 0800. They're okay in space, but they'll need the help landing. That doesn't make sense to me, but that's what I'm supposed to tell you.

Sascha came storming into Rhyssa's room. He had pulled his pants on but was carrying his shirt in his hand. He really did have a superb body, Rhyssa thought privately. Why isn't there the necessary chemistry between us? We'd make beautiful children. He looked so magnificent angry.

"Lance is out of his wig if he thinks Peter's up to a controlled landing in Dacca weather," he announced. "Landing pallets in a warehouse is a considerably different can of worms to a shuttle full of live folk we can't afford to smear across a gale-struck concrete runway."

Rhyssa fed a direct repeat of Lance's earlier conversation on Peter's potential and a similar situation into Sascha's mind. "He was only joking at the time," she said ruefully. "Quite a legitimate extrapolation."

"We just can't risk it," Sascha said, pacing up and down the room while Rhyssa untangled herself from her pastel-covered duvet and started dressing. "As neat a solution to the lack of kinetics as it is."

Rhyssa, with ineffable sadness: *Sascha-bear, you're half-way to figuring out just how he can do it!*

They were both startled by a timorous tap on her door.

"Yes?" She and Sascha exchanged glances.

"It's Peter. Can I come in?"

Sascha threw his arms up dramatically.

"Yes, yes," Rhyssa said, shooting a comprehensive warning at Sascha.

In his distress, Peter floated rather than walked into the room.

"No one bothered to channel their thoughts," he said, both apprehensive and defensive. "I couldn't help hearing."

"No, of course you couldn't, Peter," Rhyssa said.

Is Peter there? Dorotea's anxious tone startled them.

I'm here!

Young man, if you ever leave me again in that abrupt fashion, I'll tan your bottom!

Rhyssa and Sascha had never heard that particular note in the telepath's voice before.

I was trying to explain the problem to him when he zipped out of here so fast I thought he'd actually teleported himself.

I know *the problem, Dorotea,* Peter said in a very patient tone. *To land the shuttle safely at Dacca. And, with enough power, it'd be no more difficult than that container was, or the steel I sent to San Francisco.*

"The turbulence of a monsoon is totally unpredictable," Sascha began.

Peter's expression was one of abused patience. "It'd be the same principle in spite of turbulence. And better, because the shuttle won't be powered, so that won't throw off the snatch and grab of my gestalt."

"Simple when explained in that fashion," Sascha said at his driest. Then he flung up his hands in exasperation and turned to Rhyssa.

She took a reasonable stance. "The distance, the mass involved, even the turbulence are not factors you've dealt with before. We can't, and won't, risk burning you out."

Peter grinned. "You wouldn't. Though I'd need much more than four-point-five kpm. To be safe, I'd need some real power—like the city's turbos. They might seize up—but I wouldn't."

"We don't *know* that, Peter," Rhyssa said gently, permitting him to sense her anxiety.

"But *I* know that about me," Peter said, and levitated to the bed, where he perched beside her, upright enough, but with his arms and legs draped in unnatural positions. He made adjustments when he caught Rhyssa's look. "Instinctively!"

Then she hugged him, feeling tears of pride for the shining self-confidence that had emerged in the past few weeks. She held his lax narrow body for a long moment; then, sensing his embarrassment, she ruffled his hair and released him.

"Peter," Sascha said, hunkering down by the boy, "this *is* different from the exercises we've had you do. And this gestalt ability of yours is unique! We just can't risk it."

"Dorotea said I should trust my instincts," Peter said so firmly that both Sascha and Rhyssa regarded him for a long moment. "I also read the precog report. If there aren't enough kinetics, many people will lose their lives, as well as everything they've been struggling to build over the past two years. There'll be massive ecological damage, more plague, starvation. You keep feeding me all this stuff about the responsibility we Talents have to the rest of the world, how we're supposed to reduce death and damage. If I'm willing to take a little risk, I'd be a real Talent.

"I also heard what Madlyn said to you." Peter grinned ingenuously, wincing as if avoiding a loud noise. "Mr. Baden means me, doesn't he? That it's time to really try me."

Sascha sat down on the bed on Peter's other side and looked helplessly at Rhyssa.

"As I see it," Peter went on, clearly more in charge of the situation than his adult mentors, "we Talents don't have any option. We need the ones with Mr. Baden in the *Erasmus*. Sascha, when I shifted that steel the other day, you said I had graduated into a really useful category of kinesis. With enough power in the gestalt, I *know* I can land the shuttle."

Sascha slowly shook his head. "There's another major consideration, son . . ."

"I've been studying schematics on power generation," Peter continued blithely. "Turbos in particular, as they're more reliable."

"You have?" Rhyssa was constantly being surprised by the turns of Peter's avid studying.

"Well, I thought I ought to get some sort of basic concepts from which to work . . ." He saw their expressions and gave them a little smile. "I used to watch a lot of college-level vid courses. They were a lot more interesting than most of the late-night recreational garbage. Having to think hard took my mind off myself for a while. Engineering was a good think."

Sascha and Rhyssa were reduced to nodding in belated comprehension.

"Especially," Peter added, his eyes twinkling, "as no one really seemed to *know* what to make of my gestalting. And that's the other consideration, isn't it, Sascha? Keeping gestalt kinesis under wraps?"

"He's got us there, Rhyssa," Sascha said with a chagrined expression.

"That's what you're *really* worried about, but look, if the pilot brings the shuttle down far enough, I know I can get it safely through the turbulence and land it. And even the pilot doesn't need to know it wasn't Mr. Baden and the other kinetics who steadied the shuttle." When he saw that they were seriously considering his suggestion, he added, "It isn't as if I'd be bringing the shuttle all the way down from Padrugoi by myself, you know."

"And you think the city's power system will supply the necessary gestalt for you?" Sascha asked in a wry tone.

"The East Side Jerhattan power station's turbos should be enough." Peter's eyes glowed at the prospect of all that power at his disposal.

Rhyssa and Sascha began to laugh at the sheer impudence.

"You know, I really think that'll work," Dorotea said, entering the room. She was still in her nightclothes, a fetching pale lilac that set off her lovely white hair and porcelain complexion. "Since eavesdropping is in general order today, I've been following the conversations with great interest. There won't be time to talk that idiot of a power resources commissioner into agreeing to anything of such an experimental, and highly confidential, nature. The fewer people who know what we're doing the better." Her face took on an exceedingly sly look, totally uncharacteristic. "Let's invoke a G and H!" She chortled, looking exceedingly pleased with herself. "All we have to do then is call Boris—get him to clear the power station and use his official capacity to get us in."

"Invoke a G and H?" Rhyssa stared at the elderly telepath as if she had never seen her before.

"What's a G and H?" Peter asked just as Sascha began to guffaw.

"Why didn't I think of that?" Rhyssa exclaimed in exasperation. To the mystified Peter, she explained, "That's our mayday code, for George—that's George Henner, who once owned this house—and Henry—meaning Henry Darrow, who established Talent as a verifiable paranormal skill. If a Talent invokes a G and H, he gets immediate and unquestioned cooperation from every other Talent."

Sascha rubbed his hands together. "You know, I've always wanted the excuse to invoke that mayday code." *Brother,* he called. *It's a G and H: we need escort to the East Side power station, and it's to be cleared! Shouldn't be difficult with only a minimal night crew on call.*

Boris: *A G and H? Fascinating. I'm cleaning up after a major riot and you elect this moment in time to call a George and Henry?*

Sascha: *All we need is you and a LEO heli.*

Just me? Boris responded sarcastically.

Sascha agreeably: *You to get us the cooperation we need.*

And I can expect return cooperation from you? Boris, slyly.

Sascha: *It's a George Henry mayday, Bro. You can't refuse.*

Boris: *Quid pro quo, Bro. I was about to request your presence!*

Sascha: *For a riot?*

Boris: *I could certainly use your help on this one, Bro. Some oddities have cropped up that require your particularly acute telepathic Talent.*

Sascha raised his eyebrows inquiringly at Rhyssa, who reluctantly gave an assenting nod.

"Did you follow that, Peter?" Rhyssa asked, noticing that the boy's face was still registering surprise.

"Yes," he said tentatively.

"You don't really need me, Peter," Sascha said encouragingly. "You've got Rhyssa . . ."

"And Dorotea," the lady added stoutly.

"To buffer your mind," Sascha continued. *Don, as well, I think,* he added to Rhyssa. *Why does Boris have to need me at this moment in time?*

Dorotea: *Boris always did have an awkward streak in him. Comes from being a LEO by temperament.*

Rhyssa turned briskly to Peter. "Now, you'd better get dressed. Fetch your clothes here. And what should he get for you, Dorotea? You can change in my bathroom."

"I'll get down to Budworth for the vital statistics we need," Sascha said. "The weight of the shuttle, a radar link with the shuttle, repros of Dacca—in good weather—weather reports." *If I really think about this in any detail, I'll go crackers!* he added on a very fine thread to the two women.

Rhyssa and Dorotea replied with equal fervor: *You'll have company!*

If Peter thinks he can do it, I prefer to think he can, Rhyssa added. *After all, it's the thought that counts.*

Dorotea: *That's what does the trick.*

The necessary equations, based on Peter's established use of the gestalt plus distance, weight, and optimum speed of the shuttle, atmospheric conditions, and turbulence at the landing site, were all completed by the time the LEO heli arrived to transport them.

"I thought you were having a riot of a time and we'd get a deputy," Sascha said, but he was exceedingly relieved to have his brother's support.

"I am, but I'm the best authority you have for whatever's going on." Boris smiled with white-toothed malice. "You'll want to be in on this one, Bro. We've got a lead on the kidnappings."

Sascha swore with great ingenuity.

That's as important as this, Sascha, Rhyssa conceded. *With Dorotea and Don to help me buffer him, he'll be fine.*

I wouldn't interfere with a mayday if I didn't have to, the LEO commissioner said, even as he reached down to assist Dorotea into the heli.

Sascha, the kidnappers must be stopped, Dorotea said so sternly that her tone startled all the telepaths. *There! That's settled!*

"And this is Peter Reidinger?" Boris asked, as Peter reached the steps in his treading-water gait. "Hi!"

From the stunned look on Peter's face, Rhyssa suddenly realized that no one had thought to mention to the boy that the LEO commissioner was Sascha's twin brother.

"No, you're not seeing double. I'm older by five minutes," Boris went on amiably, deftly taking Peter under the arms and hoisting him aboard. *We'll both see them safely there before I abduct you, Bro, for my less nefarious purposes. The boy's the G and H?*

Sascha waggled his finger at his brother. *Naughty, naughty!* He swung aboard and started stowing the medical equipment Don Usenik handed up, ignoring Boris's grumbling. When Don climbed in, Sascha slid the door shut, and the big heli-bus glided upward and southeast.

Boris had strapped Peter into a window seat, and utterly entranced, the boy gazed down the black canyon of the Hudson to the mass of lights that glowed from every ziggurat and ribbonway of Jerhattan.

"Rather breathtaking no matter how often you see it," Rhyssa said to Peter, who nodded without taking his eyes from the view. By the time they landed on the roof of the facility, all the Talents were subtly aware of the emptiness of the massive structure.

"Well done, Boris," Dorotea said. "This way, Peter!"

"I hope you know what you're doing," Boris remarked wryly. "My office is on the line in this!"

"Thanks, Boris," Rhyssa said. "Can you retrieve us when we shout?"

"If I can't spare Sascha, I'll send someone you can trust," the LEO commissioner said as he handed Don his monitors. Then the big heli lifted away from the helipad.

Rhyssa took one equipment case from Don as he hauled open the roof door. As soon as Peter glided inside, he began to emanate excitement, his eyes sparkling with anticipation while he maneuvered down the stairs. They entered above the huge turbines, which were humming slightly as they served the needs of the great metropolis. They turned into the control room that overlooked the turbine floor, a room lined with the equipment that registered the flow of electricity to the various substations. With an ineffable air, Peter assumed the conformable chair of the duty engineer, swinging it idly from side to side until the adults organized the monitors and started hooking him up.

Above the windows overlooking the turbines were sufficient vid screens to display what Peter needed to see. Rhyssa began entering the appropriate programs, bringing up on one screen a high-resolution fax print of the *Erasmus*; on another, a display of its specifications; then weather simulations; and finally linking the station's communications grid to the main NASA board to follow the shuttle's descent. The *Erasmus* was already in flight, having begun its descent promptly at 0800 station time, 0130 Earth time. The power-station clock read 0550 as the deep radar net began to show the shuttle's spiraling descent. The final screen pictured the Dacca airport, lashed with rain and whipped by fierce gusts of winds that shifted tree trunks, parts of cars, crates, and all sorts of debris across the concrete runway where Peter was to bring the *Erasmus* safely down.

When Don Usenik had completed his check of the equipment monitoring Peter, Rhyssa and Dorotea took seats behind them, the mind of each lightly touching the boy's. He seemed

not to notice, so intent was he on the *Erasmus*'s course. Just
as it hit the atmosphere, the generators began to whine.

Rhyssa shook her head, as unable as the others to reach
that part of Peter's mind that had linked with the enormous
power of the turbines below them. The whine built, the deci-
bels increasing to an almost unbearable pitch. Dorotea
scrunched her features up, unashamedly covering her ears with
her hands. Rhyssa was staring in disbelief at the wildly altered
readings on the control console. Don Usenik kept his eyes on
his medical monitors. Peter remained outwardly composed.
Rhyssa noticed the slightly condescending smile on his face
and just hoped he was not about to overreach himself.

Simultaneously both she and Don noticed the perspiration
on the boy's forehead, but the smile remained in place. The
generators reached a frenzied peak and maintained it. And the
touch of Peter's mind altered! It became hard as stone. Peter
had not locked mental contact out, but he had suddenly restricted the contact area, indicating intense concentration.
Rhyssa caught Dorotea's eyes, but the older woman merely
pointed to Don's patient and unalarmed watch of the monitors.
The descent of the *Erasmus* visibly steadied and slowed.

He's done it! Rhyssa, Dorotea, and Don exclaimed in muted
congratulatory tones.

Rhyssa hoped someone was recording for posterity what
was unquestionably the most dramatic moment for Talent since
a Goosegg registered Henry Darrow's delta-wave pattern during that first recorded precognitive Incident. Her mind still in
contact with that part of Peter's which was accessible to herself
and Dorotea, she watched the *Erasmus* landing, coming to a
gentle stop at the passenger terminal, seemingly untouched by
the battering wind. Peter gave a little chuckle, and suddenly
the turbulence between shuttle and terminal abated, an eerie
storm eye of absolute calm. Passengers hastily disembarked,
pausing in astonishment as they became aware of the surrounding lull. One, his face indistinct on the small screen, lifted

clasped hands above his head in a victory sign and then hurried into the dubious safety of the wind-battered terminal.

"Where should I send the shuttle, Rhyssa? Once I let go, that turbulence will just flip-flop it all over the place."

I hadn't thought that far ahead, Rhyssa admitted on the quiet to Dorotea.

"The weather charts suggest that Woomera would be the safest place, Peter, but . . ." Dorotea quickly scanned the world-wide meteorological report.

Only a slight increase in the generators indicated the effort involved as the *Erasmus* slowly turned and started back to the main runway.

"I think we'd better warn the pilot where he's going," Rhyssa said, and spoke urgently to Sirikit at the Control Center.

We've had the most unusual brownout here, Sirikit told her.

Get Main Air Control to warn the Erasmus *pilot ASAP that he's being diverted to Woomera.*

Erasmus? *Diverted?* For once the Thai woman's tranquillity slipped into astonishment. *Of course! Immediately!*

Preferably before he wets his britches, Don added as an aside, making both Rhyssa and Dorotea grin.

None of the three adults could feel any stress in the mind of the boy, who was totally wrapped in the curious process of gestalt. Physically he looked more frail than ever, and the bones of his skull seemed to expand under the thin skin of his head. They could all feel the tremendous power surging through him, but they could not deduce how he effected the control.

Slowly, against all the tenets of aerodynamics and in spite of the prevailing turbulence, the *Erasmus* sped down the runway and achieved a perfect takeoff.

"I don't believe this," Rhyssa muttered softly. "Who taught him to fly planes?"

"Every boy in this generation understands shuttle craft," Don remarked, but his expression was no less bemused than theirs. He watched as the *Erasmus* climbed slowly up into the swirling rain and clouds and out of sight. They followed it up to the supersonic level.

The generators wound down from their busy pitch.

"There!" Peter said suddenly with a note of complete satisfaction in his voice. "He's firing his engines, and he should know what to do now. I told him to land in Woomera. That was fun!" he added with less vigor. He was extremely pale and still perspiring heavily. "That was a lot of fun!" His eyes gleamed, and he grinned at Don Usenik, who shook his head with incredulity as he pointed to an almost normal pattern on the bioscan screen.

"Fun? You called that fun, Peter?" Rhyssa exclaimed almost angrily, realizing that she had been under a tremendous strain of worry even if Peter had not.

"With power like this, I could loft the shuttle much easier than the pilot could," Peter said in a voice that was suddenly hoarse with fatigue.

Dorotea, very privately to Rhyssa: *'How're you goin' keep 'em down on the farm, after they've seen Paree?'* She rolled her eyes expressively.

"Marked fatigue, low energy level, but even that's within what I'd call the normal range for a Talent," Don announced in a baffled tone. "You did great, Peter," he added proudly.

Clearing her throat, Rhyssa said wearily, "I don't think Ludmilla's going to believe that onboard Talents *also* 'ported the shuttle out again."

"Well, I couldn't leave it on the runway, Rhyssa, now could I?" Peter asked with weary irritation. "Those shuttles cost billions."

Suddenly all the telepaths were aware of other touches, vying to reach their minds.

Kayankira: *Oh, thank you, thank you. How did you manage?*

Rhyssa, Dorotea, and Don exchanged glances.

No, Rhyssa, Dorotea said on a very thin thread to the other two, *we didn't think this whole thing through very carefully.*

Rhyssa gulped and replied with an evenness in her mental tone that Dorotea applauded, *Lance is right there. It was all his idea. A real G and H. Wasn't it, Lance?*

Lance: *I'll tell her. I'd rather shout "Eureka" but accept the caveat.* He sent an image of a large crocodile, jaws wide in amazement, followed by a kangaroo bouncing from a pictorial map of Australia to the moon. *You never know till you try, do you, cobber?*

"Enough!" Dorotea said suddenly. "Let's get Peter home to bed. Don't you try to move a muscle, young man."

For one brief moment, Peter looked as if he was going to disobey. Then his expressions turned woeful. "I don't think I could right now."

"Nothing a good night's sleep and a hearty breakfast won't put right in next to no time," Dorotea said briskly, but the fierce glance she gave Rhyssa suggested that a lot more recuperation time might be required in spite of Don's optimistic interpretation of the monitors. "Now, how do we get him back to the Center? Boris and Sascha are apparently up to their eyeballs in their riot control."

The Center vehicle's coming, Sirikit said, a ripple of amusement in her voice. *Just stay put!*

Even through the heavy roof sheeting of the power station, they could hear the vibrations of the approaching heli. Then the roof door opened and a figure charged through.

"You all right down there? I was told to come pick up pieces!" Dave Lehardt cried, descending three steps at a time.

Rhyssa nearly wept with relief. What had Boris, the sly mutt, said? "Someone you could trust!"

"Hi, Peter," Dave said. "What have you all been up to that your PR man gets called out of his bed in the wee small hours of the morning?'' Then he knelt down by the boy, his expression very gentle. "You look done in. Tell me later, huh?'' With tender solicitude, he gathered up the exhausted boy and, moving with exquisite care, started up the stairs with him. Rhyssa followed, immensely grateful for his unexpected presence.

CHAPTER 9

Within minutes of the Event, an Incident Room was in place on the wide mall in front of the Assembly atrium. Crowd-control Talents and LEO specialists had quickly defused the volatile temper of the incipient mob. Although a number of attendees had managed to evade the LEO backup, the rest were being systematically ID'd.

The focus of the Incident, some twenty women of various ethnic groups, had been immediately sequestered in one of the rehearsal rooms behind the atrium and, despite their loud lamentations and protestations of innocence, were being adroitly questioned by a special Talent team.

By then Boris and Sascha had arrived in the big heli. Already the tapes from the hi-eyes, discreetly set in the high ceiling of the hall by two industrious electricians who had come with the RIG setup team, were being viewed in the Incident Room by the original precogs, Auer and Bertha Zoccola. Boris and Sascha took up observation positions. The portable's walls were packed with analyzers keyed in to the LEO mainframe. Debriefing reports by crowd-control Talents were being made at the various stations, while LEO personnel avidly read rap sheets spewed out by churning printers as the wrist-ID scans were processed. Frequently the LEO commissioner was interrupted in his viewing to initial warrants, but the main meat of the Incident eluded all. Reverend Venerable Ponsit Prosit had once again flitted off in time.

"So my precog centered on the women," Bertha was saying, studiously avoiding eye contact with Auer. The dour man was pulling at his lower lip, oblivious to her as the replay continued. "While his was for Flimflam. When are you going to bust that guy? He's obscene, a miserable maggot of a man, leeching off emotions—you know that's all he is! An emotion leech, growing fat whenever he has a mob to suck! The bigger the bunch he manipulates, the bigger his hit." She waved her arms in exaggerated circles.

"As I've explained before, Bertha, he inadvertently serves a purpose," Boris explained patiently. "He works them up, yes. He may get a vicarious pleasure holding a crowd in the palm of his hand, but his histrionics defuse a lot of pent-up garbage in a catharsis not generated by passive watching of the tri-d fare. Occasionally he runs pretty close to dogmatic insult, but usually he's innocuous and says nothing."

" 'Says nothing' is right!" Bertha muttered indignantly.

Boris went on. "He had registered sponsors for tonight, some East Indian Mystical Concept Group which is properly registered and screens as legit. We had no grounds to deny them, or him, the right of religious assembly."

"Religious assembly!" Bertha was outraged. "Religion he ain't got. And religious assemblies are supposed to be uplifting, not downtrodding. He's a rouser, a leech, a spewer of blasphemy. He's dangerous." She waggled a finger violently under Boris's nose. "There're laws against inciting to riot, and he caused one tonight."

"Unfortunately, Bertha, your precog absolves him of primary blame." Boris tried to exude pacification. Her voice was getting louder with each denunciatory remark, and she had never been noted for tact.

"Who gave him strands, Commish?" she demanded. "You can't tell me he didn't use 'em with criminal intent!"

Boris's patience snapped, and he sent a crisp summons to Sascha, who was outside helping the telepaths keep control. "On that count, we've a search-and-find warrant out for him right now."

"It was me twigged Flimflam, Bertha Zoccola," Auer said,

glaring furiously at the little woman. "He's none of your business."

Sascha arrived and deftly rendered her helpless with a heavy lean on her speech centers just long enough to escort her to a debriefing position at the opposite end of the room.

"We got another wild one manufacturing that strand stuff for Flimflam?" Auer asked Boris in a low voice.

"Could be, Auer," Boris replied unhappily. "That's the only way fringe fanatics like Ponsit Prosit could obtain strands." The tangling substance was a recent LEO invention, produced from an aberrant chemical compound to provide a fast-drying midrange restraint. Top secret, its formula and processing were of a complexity that ought not to be easily duplicatable. "There's a real smart head out there somewhere. Forensic says the stuff is pretty damned close to our formula. More toxic, which is bad, and less durable, which is fortunate. You've a good feel for technical matters, Auer. Keep your mind open for us, will you? Report even the slightest twinge. We've got to find this bozo as soon as possible. I don't care what sort of Talent emerges from Residential genes but, whatever it is, it should be registered with *us*."

"I can't imagine Flimflam having enough credit to hire that sort of smarts. Ah, and I see Yassim's got himself a new ladrone?" Auer asked cynically, pointing at the replay.

Boris regarded him with approval. "You caught that one frame of Yassim?"

Auer shook his head but pointed to the tape being played over and over on the screen. "I keep up-to-date on the LEO visitors' list. Every ladrone, hitter, and sassin known to be connected with Yassim was here tonight. He had to be, too. Didja get many?"

"A good crop but no one of particular importance," Boris said, and then grimaced. "You know those new indestructible door-eyes we've been installing? It could have been Yassim's people, or maybe the new Talent who supplied Flimflam with strands, but every one of them was disabled. Very cleverly, with a bit of wire, a hairpin, even a twisted length of foil— nothing irreparable but enough to cloud the count. We're ID'ing everyone who didn't have a chance to leave after the Incident, but we're shy counts on exactly who, and how many, came to the party."

Auer nodded again, sympathetic in his own sour way to the commissioner's frustration. "I'll keep it all in mind, Commissioner. Leave you to it."

Boris turned his attention to the head of the team questioning the focus group. *Norma, any luck?*

No, sir, they're still on the boil. We're getting anger, frustration, envy, some anxiety and worry over being detained, mainly maternal, but really, sir, we can only get the dominant emotions. They're angry at being 'done.' And not by old Ponsit Prosit Flimflam. Trouble is, none of 'em speak much Basic. Could we have a linguist down here? Someone who's got Neerest, Paki, and Asian languages? Ranjit, maybe?

I'll send him along presently. Anything else?

Yes, sir. Nine of them are involved in some kind of feud. We've had to separate them twice already to keep them from scratching each other or pulling hair. Something about being chosen and it wasn't right to intervene. Doesn't make any sense.

"Being chosen?" Boris spoke aloud as well as mentally.

Sir?

Thank you, Sergeant, you've just triggered a thought! Boris turned to the screen as yet another replay of the Incident began. He forwarded it quickly and then reduced the speed, his eyes on the screen.

You've got something? Sascha was at his shoulder.

If my theory is correct that Flimflam was fingering people for someone—Yassim probably, since his men were there in force—I want to know what the common denominator of choice was, Boris told his twin. *Most of them were males except our focus group, which were—ah, here we are!*

The two brothers watched as the reduced speed clearly showed the strand falling in the center of the focus group.

It didn't hit a woman! Unless she was a midget, Sascha said, pointing to the thin hands clawing up out of the mass. Boris tapped out an enlarge, sharpening the definition in the center of activity. *A child?*

No child in the group being held. Twenty women. I can count that many heads.

Sascha: *Are some tugging?*

Yes, and some resisting. Norma said the women are contentious. In an overlay of thought, Boris repeated Norma's exact words.

Sascha: *And feeling cheated. Look! Knife severing the strand. Now all hell breaks loose.*

"Okay, who were the nearest crowd controllers?" Boris asked.

Cass Cutler and Suzanne Nbembi were summoned, still wearing their undercover gear, although Cass had wiped off the heavy makeup and discarded the tangle of cheap jewelry. Boris spun the tape back to the relevant scene.

"Cass, Suzanne, good strong damper work today."

"It was very close, Commissioner," Cass said, rolling her eyes. "Could have been a bad one without that precog."

"Either of you two see a child with our focus group?"

"No," Cass replied quickly, and then frowned. "At least, I don't think she was with *them*. We first noticed her trying to get away from Bulbar."

"We would have intervened—no girl child should be caught by that scuz—but she freed herself," Suz added. "Knew well enough how."

"She dodged behind us for a moment, on her way to an exit. Just then the Incident erupted. Funny about that . . ." Cass faltered, frowning. "I felt *something*, Commissioner, when I touched her. A shield solid as a wall, and that's odd enough for a Linear kid. She might even have some latent Talent."

"We still haven't found the reason for the riot. Could she have something to do with it if she's a possible latent Talent?" Boris mused, tapping the monitor.

Cass gave a diffident shrug, but both she and Suz watched the replay closely. Boris speeded it up, stopping at the moment when the hands appeared, looking more balletic in slow motion than frantic as the slender fingers splayed in panic; then the sequence went on, showing fingers clutching at the strand, the flash of the knife, and the scrimmage of the women.

"Can you get the perimeter of the scene just before they started to boil?" Cass asked.

Boris tried every combination of review, but the hi-eye had been fixed on the precogged site of the Incident, and although the definition was sharp, the angle obscured what Cass wanted to see.

"Ranjit Youssef reporting as requested, sir." The young LEO officer presented himself a respectful distance from the absorbed cluster around the screen.

"And what did the search of the assigned quarters reveal, Lieutenant?" Boris asked formally.

"Commissioner, the count of illegal children under the age of ten is eight hundred and three, including five newborns. In fact, all the children apprehended are under ten."

Although the LEO commissioner was not actually surprised, the total was considerably higher than estimated. He propped himself against the desk edge and folded his hands over his chest, rubbing his jaw pensively. *Eight hundred?* he repeated.

And three, Sascha added, his mental tone equally grim.

Boris: *And all to be sacrificed to produce more underfed disposable kids to be abused one way or another. How can*

146

the traffic be stopped when people blindly follow an archaic ethnic imperative?

"Any with legal wrist IDs?" Boris asked Ranjit aloud.

"The nine-year-olds, sir, but so far no IDs match the genetic print registered for the number. There are also far fewer preteens and teens than a Residential population should generate."

"As usual. How many of the illegals under ten were found in the quarters of the focus women?"

"Thirty-two, some too young to run for it. The older ones had some warning—they always do. But a clamp is already initiated. No one without a wristband will move out of this Linear," Ranjit said, "even through disposal chutes."

"Ah, yes, disposal chutes," Boris added with a further sigh of resignation. "And, I trust, the cargo lines? Good." He tapped a sequence and the screen showed the architectural schematic of Linear G, slowly rotating to display every angle of the immense ziggurat. "Norma Banfield needs your linguistic abilities, Lieutenant. She's in the rehearsal hall to the left of the stage. She's got a mess of ethnics with little Basic, and there are two factions at least willing to pull hair."

"Pull hair?" Cass sat upright, a wisp of a memory surfacing from the recent explosion.

"Got something, Cass?" Boris asked.

"I'll work on it." She sagged into as much of a relaxed state as the activity in the room permitted. Suz began a soothing massage of her neck muscles to encourage recall.

"I'll do what I can to help Lieutenant Banfield." Ranjit saluted and left.

Cass stood. "I wanna check something in the hall, sir, unless some officious moron has sent the cleaners in already."

"Go to it." Boris gestured broadly and turned back to the schematic to try and figure out where refugees might hide in the maze of corridors, closets, and conduits. *Sascha, get your teams to start searching ducts. Scared kids can squeeze into the damnedest places. I don't want a single illegal to get caught by Yassim's slimy hooks.*

Done. Sascha's eyes blanked briefly as he gave the orders.

"I got it," Cass cried, reentering the room. She gave an eerie yodel and held the trophy up. "Her scalp, by all that's holy!"

With two fastidious fingers, Boris took the hank of hair, the dull severed strand tangled right to the bloody patch of skull skin. *Loufan! Find out all you can about the person who grew this!*

The technician hurried to the commissioner's side, received the tress without expression, and went back to his cubicle.

Commissioner, Ranjit said. After a polite pause to be sure he was not interrupting, he went on. *They're hiding something.*

Norma: *Someone. I concur. Someone important to them.*

Ranjit: *I think that's the reason for the dissension, sir.*

Norma: *I would go along with that. May I nudge them, sir?*

Boris: *By any fair means, Lieutenant.* Boris told them. He grinned to himself, knowing Ranjit's scrupulous sense of honor, and then felt the mental touch that meant Sascha had overhead the exchange.

Dealing with the unTalented took heroic efforts, Boris thought. On the other hand, did he really want everyone to have paranormal abilities? Or at least some minor paranormal quirk, so that there would be less hassle? But that gave rise to envy—envy of someone more Talented than oneself, which only increased dissension and prejudice. No, far better to have a small minority, dedicated—and disciplined—to perform functions that the mind-numb could not. And all of the peculiar and unusual quirks *registered*!

Sir? Loufan paused. *I removed the strand from the scalp, as it interfered with the reading and is certainly irrelevant. The subject is a Eurasian ethnic mix, preadolescent female. Good strong genoprint, good immune factors, healthy, unusually so.* The technician sounded surprised. Linear G subsistence fare was nutritionally adequate, of course, but if the child was illegal, as Boris suspected, how had she managed to be healthy? *And there's no match of birth ID.*

Boris: *Did you really expect to find one?*

Loufan: *Yes, sir.*

It was Boris's turn to be surprised.

Loufan: *She could have been a runaway or a kidnap.*

Boris: *Okay. File the data, Loufan, and give the hair to Bertha. Ask her—in your ineffably polite style—if this artifact sparks anything off in her mind?*

Moments later Bertha came storming back to him. "Oh, the poor thing! Hair torn right out of her scalp! Commish, who did it?"

"Possibly Bulbar. Sense anything?"

Bertha pressed the lock against her ample bosom, closed her eyes, and concentrated. "Not a thing, but it's there in my mind now." She grimaced in sudden revulsion and thrust it back to him. "Take it away!"

Sascha intercepted the lock. "Black, good length," he murmured. "Some of those women never cut their hair. Healthy, and much cleaner than you'd expect. Shouldn't be too hard to find a juvenile with a hunk torn out of her scalp."

"I'd rather you give it to Carmen," Boris told him. *Ranjit thinks quite a few of the older illegal kids eluded the search teams,* he added. *Could she be one of them? She might lead us to the rest.*

Carmen Stein laid the lock across her thighs and stroked it flat, using her long fingernails to separate the tangled hairs. For several more minutes she fingered them, softly coaxing a sense of their grower's whereabouts. Carmen always looked so placid and imperturbable when she was evoking her Talent as finder. Better than most, Sascha knew just how much activity her brain was generating at such moments. She was one of the best searchers he had ever encountered and, because her Talent was intense and exhausting, he protected her as much as he could, limiting her assignments.

"The incident occurred how long ago?" she asked without taking her eyes from the hair.

"Approximately sixty-two minutes."

"Ah, she is hiding. That accounts for the darkness. I cannot see where. There is no light. A constricted space."

"A conduit?"

"That's possible." Carmen sounded dubious. "I think she sleeps."

"That's a cool one."

"No," Carmen said, taking him literally. "Not cool. Tired." She offered him the hair.

"No, keep it, Carmen, for now. We'll need to know if she moves."

Calmly Carmen leaned forward, took a clip from the brightly enameled jar on the table, and fastened the tress, the scalp end now coated with a protective film, high on the right side of her head.

Sascha had relayed Carmen's comments to Boris.

A conduit, huh? There's so few of those in a Linear. The LEO Commissioner's mental tone was facetious. *We're flushing kids out of every available space. I hate this, Sascha, I hate it.* Sascha sent quick soothing thoughts to ease the turmoil in his brother's mind, but Boris went on. *The miracle of life should be a blessing, not a curse. How can people be so irresponsible as to produce countless unwanted children and* waste *them?*

Even illegal kids have rights, Sascha responded, gently quoting his brother his own words. *See that even the least of them get that much.*

Illegals go to the space station. Boris sounded defeated.

*They don't go as grunts. They're trained to do something
a lot more constructive than their parents ever did. Leave it,
brother.*

I scratch your back, Bro, not your nose, Boris said wryly.
*Now, I'm putting in an appearance to scare some sense out of
those flipping focus females!*

*No one better. By the way, when you have a spare mo-
ment, listen to a news update. Then you'll know why we
twisted your arm with a G and H.*

*I congratulate the triumph I sense in your mind, but I'll
have to wait on a replay of the event,* Boris said as he entered
the rehearsal hall, thinking what a scarce commodity time was
right then.

He crossed the threshold, assuming his most awe-inspiring
official manner. Tall, handsome, the strength in his powerful
frame shown off even by the bulky action uniform, he succeeded in scaring the gaggle of women silent, a silence that did
not last too long, though the renewed bursts of argumentative
crosstalk were considerably subdued.

I just got something, Commissioner, Ranjit told him. *A flash
from the woman fourth on the left, the plump young one with
the caste mark. "It's all Tirla's fault." Tirla is, I think, a fem-
inine name.*

"Translate for me, Lieutenant," Boris said, striding imperiously in front of the women, his tone haughty. "I am LEO
Commissioner Boris Roznine. Where is the girl child you had
with you this evening?"

Boris had no trouble picking up the reactions of resentment, envy, anger, dismay, and fear as he gave Ranjit time
enough to repeat his words in the various languages. The
women had had time to realize that they were in deep trouble
with Authority. Several had vivid worries about their children,
left too long alone in their squats. Others concentrated on nurs-
ing their sense of grievance. He caught occasional variations on
the phrase Ranjit had twigged, but no one else volunteered a

name. "It was all *her* fault." They contented themselves with impersonal malice.

"Let me reassure you that the children in your homes are being cared for until you can return to them," he said, smiling kindly.

As the import of his sentence was understood by each group, the wailing, breast-beating, and pulling of hair began, and more recriminations were spewed. Boris was well aware of fury, loss, resignation, and relief in one case, but he could not understand any actual linguistics used in the varied emotional reactions.

Ranjit: *This Bilala says that it is all* her *fault for resisting the Lama's choosing.* Ranjit was restraining the plump caste-marked virago from rushing at the haughty, hawk-nosed older woman on the other side of the room. *She says Mirda Khan brought all this on herself. Mirda Khan replies that—ah, the name again, Tirla—would not have been able to translate for any of them up on the stage. She had done little enough to earn baksheesh, a tip.*

Boris: *Lieutenant, ask them who is Tirla's mother.*

The question shut the women up and briefly closed down their mental perturbations. Then they all launched into personal lamentations again. The answer was also quick. None of them was Tirla's mother, and without exception, just as Boris had hoped, every one of them flashed a quick mental image of the girl in question.

Got it, Ranjit and Norma told him in unison.

As I did. With a gesture to signify that the women could be processed or released as their condition warranted, the LEO commissioner hurried back to the Incident Room.

Loufan awaited him there in front of the graphics pad, stylus ready. For this sort of transference, Boris grasped the technician's thin shoulder and concentrated on the vivid image of the Tirla child. Loufan sketched quickly, capturing in a few clever lines the intense face—remembered by most in its panic at being stranded—the wide-set, slightly tilted huge dark eyes above prominent cheekbones, the abundant waving dark hair framing it, the fine straight nose, the small cautious mouth, the long sweep of a determined jawline, the odd cleft in the chin. A charming face, if one discounted the fright, intelligent despite the fear. Tirla looked no more than eight or nine, but some wisp of thought—from the fat old woman—suggested that she was older. The woman's memory of her went back quite a few years.

"Is that her?" Loufan asked, transferring the sketch to the screen.

The LEO commissioner allowed himself a good long look, matching the image on the screen to the consensus in the minds of twenty women. "Yes, that's it. Print it, circulate it to all officers and Talents. I think we should find that child. Cass might be right about latent Talent. And if Flimflam was after her, there may be more to her than we realize. I also need to file an intelligent reason why a RIG damned near turned into a full-scale riot, and she just might provide the answer," he concluded. *Sascha, could someone be an instantaneous translator?*

Sascha considered that. *I'd say that she displayed more than a mere language facility—quite possibly Talent. Anyone who could translate ten different languages as she apparently could would be valuable to either or both of us.* He grinned at his brother. *First we'll have to find her. Then we can evaluate her abilities.*

T*irla!*
    Tirla woke suddenly, jolted out of her exhausted sleep by someone calling her name softly and appealingly. Tirla did not move, or so much as open her eyes.

Clever little trinket, isn't she? Call her again.

Won't work, Boris. She's alert now.

It had to have been part of a dream. She often dreamed

that she heard her mother calling her name. It had to be a dream, because no one could know where she was, despite LEOs searching the main conduits and sending drone units down the smaller ones. On her way home from the debacle of the meeting, she had escaped all types of earnest hunters. She had seen the numbers of children being flushed from hidey-holes.

Her hunch about the meeting had been correct. It had served as an excuse to sweep down on the pads, collect illegal children, and check all IDs. No one, absolutely no one, had ever known where she squatted. She did not even think to herself where she was. And no one was likely to discover her even in this intensive search.

Somewhat reassured, Tirla nestled back into the warmth of her sleep sack. Suddenly she heard noises nearby and froze. She heard the doors into the closed section being opened. This search was unusually thorough. Not even she had been able to get into the engineering space, and yet it was being checked.

Not even Yassim's men could find her, and they knew all the ducks and dodges that any subbie had ever figured out. She had been so lucky not to be caught by Bulbar. He was wicked dangerous. Her head still throbbed where the hair had been torn away. She had dabbed on some dis-wipe. Bulbar could have been carrying any kind of 'mune to infect her, scabby old scuz.

Her problem with Yassim remained. She had not washed the tieds. How would he expect her to when he, and every trader, had been lucky to escape the bust? Not that he took excuses. What awful luck to be singled out by the Lama-shaman! Which of the women had he really been after? And why? It made no sense to Tirla. None of them was pretty or young, or even on the lay—not with *their* husbands!

The noise of search was diminishing, and carefully Tirla reached unerringly for the water jug and food that she kept for such emergencies. Chewing the dry-eat made terrible noises in her head. She had heard about the wide-range ultrasensitive gear that was said to pick up breathing in a radius of five klicks, but there should be enough minor noises from the generators and air-conditioning units to mask her chewing, and she was terribly hungry. Finally, thirst and hunger assuaged, Tirla snuggled deeper into her sack and went to sleep again.

T ake a break, Carmen," Sascha told the finder. "She won't venture out until night. If then."

Carmen rubbed delicately at her temples and sighed. "You're right. I'll rest. She's unusual, isn't she, Sascha?"

"We believe so, even if we don't know specifically why."

Carmen regarded him with some surprise. "It's a lovely clear mind. Like a bell—when she's asleep. She's wary and cautious awake, that one. I can touch her but not read her. And with her in the darkness, I can't even help you home in on her."

"She'll come out in good time."

Carmen shot a look that suggested that Sascha Roznine might—this once—be wrong. He grinned and winked as he turned to leave her quarters.

F rankly, Sascha, we've run everything we got on the people Flimflam fingered for Yassim," Boris Roznine said, tossing a sheaf of hard copy onto the desktop, "and we can't find a common denominator. They're mostly able-bodies, doing enough work to keep away from Conscriptive Work Services, only minor misdemeanors on their sheets, none of 'em known to gamble or dip."

Sascha smiled knowingly and felt his brother poke at his mind, but he kept his shield in place. He could do that to Boris, whereas Boris could not keep him out at all. "You've had a hard thirty hours, so I'll tell you. They were all fathers."

"What?" Blood suffused Boris's face.

"Flimflam had accessed ordinary info on residents of the Linear. Mind you, it was so simple we didn't see it at first. Bertha's sensitive to females and children, Auer to the blacker side of life."

Boris scrubbed at his head. "Sometimes it is the simple things we miss. So Flimflam was fingering fathers with likely youngsters, and the girl was a bonus?"

"I guess, and we're still in the dark about her," Sascha added, aware of his brother's next query. "Carmen's latched, but the girl's cautious and hasn't moved since she went to ground."

"Scared?"

"Strangely enough, no. I'd hazard that she's had to keep a low profile before. She's a preteen and illegal."

"That will sharpen the senses."

"How're you doing with Yassim's operation?"

"We figure he picked up at least nineteen children, maybe a few more." Boris grimaced. "We collected eight hundred and three illegal kids from Linear G. If what Harv believes is possible—that every one of the related mothers has been having a kid a year—we're minus a possible forty. We located eighteen of that forty in a storage basement, but they've got the entry jammed. We're working on it." Boris shook his head. "They really will be better off in hostels."

"And in space?" Sascha asked wryly.

"Even in space they have a better chance than stalemated in a Linear."

"But they won't be able to reproduce themselves." Sascha had never approved of the law that required the sterilization of illegal offspring.

Boris raised his hands in resignation. "I don't make the laws, Sascha. I only enforce them." Then he leaned forward and tapped up a new program on his big screen. "All right.

Now, we have to find Yassim in *his* warren and save nineteen kids or more from him."

S he's moved, Sascha," Carmen said, her tone half-triumphant, half-anxious.

Sascha consulted his watch. "This time of day?"

"Linear will be crowded with those coming off work."

"Keep as close as you can to her."

"It's very difficult, Sascha. It's almost as if she isn't *seeing* the things she's looking at. I can't get a real fix, except that there are people all around her. Wait! She's stopped. No, that's no good. All I get is a mass of standard-issue clothing. She's still in a crowd."

"I'm in touch with our teams on the main levels of G. Just give us a direction, Carmen. Any direction." *Alert to our quarry!* he added in a mental call to Cass and Suz.

T irla was relieved that it had been Mirda Khan she first came across. Mirda was full of the whole affair, her black eyes snapping with indignation and a certain sly malice that she had not suffered at the hands of the Public Health—it had been a long time since her womb had borne fruit. But she had the grace to mourn her friends' losses, of both their existing children and their hope of more.

"They will see how hard it is for those of us who have no children to sell."

"Was that why Yassim was there? To buy children?"

"Why else?" Mirda lifted her shoulders in an eloquent shrug. "He would have no interest in spiritual things."

"Did he get them all?" Tirla was aghast. Yet if a big score put Yassim in a very good mood, he would be easier for her to deal with over the matter of the tieds she had been unable to wash.

"No, *they* got most of them. Yassim cannot have many, but those he got he got for nothing!" Mirda was indignant. "No price was paid to their grieving mothers and fathers. They ran into his arms to escape the LEOs. Ran! And no credits exchanged, not even a bargain made. Oh, he will not dare to enter G again." Then suddenly Mirda latched steely fingers into Tirla's shoulder. "*What* was the Lama-shaman saying? You didn't tell us. Aiiiye, and to increase insult, you did not even have the grace to accept the strand that chose you. You have earned the undying hatred of Bilala and Pilau for not accepting his choice."

Tirla wrenched herself free. "Choice? I am nothing—why would he choose me? I think he missed. Tell Bilala that I think he was aiming for her and missed. But, as for what he said, you missed nothing. That Lama-shaman spewed stupid syllables only. Not a proper word in any language. Even in his head he wasn't using real words. He didn't mean to. He is a sham man, not a shaman. It was all set up for the Public Health to raid Linear G."

"How could that be?" Mirda was startled. "No, it could not be. Not with traders there with all their goods and some of it not things the LEOs should discover on them. And certainly not when Yassim, and every ladrone, hitter, and sassin he employs, were also present. *They* would have known. Perhaps the strand was meant for Bilala, as you said. She felt that was proper for her, too, you understand, for she has been worthy. A woman who has borne a child every year for her husband. Aiyyee, and they have taken that from her now, and his pride from him. He will reproach her until the day of her death." Mirda began to beat herself across her breasts, and Tirla used the distraction to slip away.

So, Yassim had children from G and had not paid for them. And she had tieds that she could not deal for him, which she had better return. If he had enough children, then with luck he would not take her.

It was wrong of Bilala to hate her. Tirla wished that she had asked Mirda if any more of her clients did. It was essential for Tirla to stay on good terms with everyone in Linear G. She was just as illegal. Bilala or Pilau could be spiteful enough to turn her in, as a token revenge for the loss of their own children. Unless . . .

Unless Tirla could get a price for the children who had run into Yassim's clutches. She knew where he kept such merchandise. It would depend on who he had taken.

She skipped down a side aisle where, looking around to be sure she was not observed, she yanked at a conduit grille. It resisted, and she saw that the screws had been replaced. She felt inside the grille to be sure there were no wires or eyes, but this was a small opening, one only a very small or thin child could have used, and had not been staked out. She got out the vibro-blade she had earned for some long-forgotten favor and sheered off two screws. Then she climbed into the dark conduit.

Carmen was exasperated. *Just when I had a good placement—or thought I did—she's gone into the dark again. No, wait, Sascha, there's light around her now. She's in some sort of a cramped tunnel.*

Sascha: *Uses the bloody conduits like a subway. I'll have the schematic of G on my screen for the next year at this rate.*

Carmen: *Think how well you'll know the innards of a Residential by then.*

Sascha: *Thanks. Keep track of our mole.*

Carmen: *Wait a minute, Sascha, I think she's moving out of G.*

Sascha, startled: *How can she?*

Carmen: *She's in the underground. Red light. The freight subways are the only tunnels illuminated in red, aren't they?*

Sascha: *Omigod, which direction has she gone?*

Sascha, Cass here. Mirda Khan was just seen talking with our quarry. Khan insists that the girl escaped from her. I'll believe that when pigs fly.

Sascha: *What were they talking about?*

The meeting, Flimflam, Yassim. Khan has gone into panic and isn't making much sense. She's afraid—there's suddenly a real big dollop of guilt, anxiety, mainly fear. For herself and just a little for Tirla.

Sascha: *Boris! Our quarry may be venturing into one of Yassim's industrial territories. Alert your surveillance.*

At his desk in the Parapsychic Tower, Sascha Roznine experienced the sort of frustration that plagued few Talents. Hardened criminals were easier to apprehend than one preadolescent child who looked nearly half her actual age. And what on earth was the child doing in Yassim's territory? She would have done better to crawl back into her very secret hidey-hole. He was tormented with memories of the pix of vivisected child bodies.

CHAPTER 10

Barchenka was furious when informed that she would be deprived of her strongest kinetics for the week it would take to mitigate the monsoon flooding. She first cried mutiny, then grand larceny, but was brought up short by her own Station Authority, who pointed out that the Talents had a legal right to attend major disasters such as the one that undeniably existed in the Bangladesh flooding. Also, the pilot was an off-duty volunteer, and there had been no damage to the *Erasmus*, which he had returned to Padrugoi as soon as Woomera cleared him for a launch.

Massive efforts in shoring up the levees and careful manipulation of the barriers and dams prevented the Ganges from turning the lower portion of Bangladesh into a vast lagoon from Bogra to the sea. Still, whole towns had to be evacuated and necessary supplies shifted, difficult even kinetically in the appalling conditions. The force of the channeled flood did inundate Chittagong and coastal towns below it, but not as disastrously as the precog had predicted. Talent once again had reduced the impact of a major natural catastrophe.

Peter Reidinger, on the other hand, slept late into the next morning, but when Don Usenik checked him over, he seemed none the worse for his major gestalt effort. But there was no doubt that his achievement had altered him: he neither floated nor essayed to walk—he strutted, chin high, with a slightly superior smirk on his face.

"What was the saying? 'Power tends to corrupt, and absolute power corrupts absolutely'?" Sascha asked Rhyssa, peevish in his frustration over the lost girl. "He's insufferably smug this morning."

Dorotea gave a snort. "Don't overreact, Sascha! He's got a right to crow. Perfectly natural in anyone, especially a fourteen-year-old boy whose only available movement until recently was tonguing a switch or blinking his eyes at tri-d to change channels. Pretty heady stuff to save a country. I scanned him pretty deeply at brunch while he was still sleepy, and there's nothing in his mind that smacks of corruption." She grinned. "A bigger generator, more derring-do, and plenty of self-satisfaction."

"Lighten up, Sascha-bear," Rhyssa said, smiling encouragingly. "Or don't you remember some of the tricks you and Boris pulled at that age?"

"A telepath can't get into quite the same sort of trouble a kinetic can," Sascha said, grimly thinking of a girl fumbling in red-lit freightways. What was her Talent?

"Peter's got a fine sense of integrity, Sascha," Rhyssa said. "He's sensitive and sensible. We have to think *how* to bring him back to cruel reality after his minor miracle."

"A diversion usually helps," Dorotea remarked with a gleam in her eyes. "I used that ploy often with my lads." She wrinkled her nose and sighed. "All too often."

"It's going to have to be pretty good to distract him from the *Erasmus* stunt," Sascha said with uncharacteristic gloom.

Rhyssa was distracted from the conversation by the mental hail of Johnny Greene. *Rhyssa, you guys called a G and H. Did it have something to do with the spectacular landing and takeoff of the* Erasmus?

One of the phones on Rhyssa's desk rang, and being nearest, Sascha picked it up.

"Yes, Dave? No, Rhyssa's got a call on her mind. Can I help?" He listened for a moment and then replaced the handset, his face grimmer than ever.

Johnny, Rhyssa was saying, *it's very complicated.*

Sascha: *You haven't heard the half yet, dear. Dave's got*

bad news for us, too. Ludmilla's claiming that we've perjured our immortal souls and deliberately falsified our Register.

Johnny: *Vernon's had all kinds of flak from NASA, the Space Authorities, the Padrugoi Authority . . .*

Rhyssa, fiercely: *Remind Vernon what kinetics are doing on the Indian continent. Sascha, tell Dave that his public pitch is that, despite all odds, Talent has kept its covenant of disaster assistance. And I want Johnny and Dave up here as fast as they can make it. Particularly you, Greene.* To Dorotea, she said, "I think Peter's immediate illusions of grandeur are going to be heavily dampened."

Boris entered the telepathic conference. *The Power Resources commissioner is also demanding an explanation for a G and H that caused last night's brownout and wiped out all his power reserves,* he said plaintively. *The city commish wants a lot of answers. Sascha, you heard anything?*

Sascha, savagely: *No!*

Vsevolod Gebrowski, urgently: *Rhyssa, Barchenka is out to get you! And there's nothing I can do to distract her. I told her G and H. Her telempaths have explained that this is a Talent emergency code which needs no elaboration. She does not accept that.*

Rhyssa: *You tell Ludmilla from me that she's had plenty of secrets she doesn't share, like early-completion bonuses, as well as fines on delays. I don't question her; she doesn't question me.*

Vsevolod: *She does. I warn you.*

Dorotea, helpfully: *Amalda Vaden sees nothing untoward.*

Rhyssa: *Why did you bring her in on this?*

Dorotea: *I think we need all the reassurance we can get.*

Sascha: *Dave Lehardt, Gordie Havers, and two top NASA generals are on the same heli with Johnny.*

Rhyssa remembered how satisfied Peter had looked after dealing so beautifully with the *Erasmus* crisis. She groaned. "He's only fourteen."

Carmen: *Sascha, I've got a fix on her.*

Sascha was out the door in a flash. *Good luck!*

Rhyssa: *Right back at you!*

"Peter's far more mature than most fourteen-year-olds I've dealt with," Dorotea mused. "Including you," she added, favoring Rhyssa with an admonitory glance. "And he's got all the right instincts for being Talented."

Tirla did *not* like using the freight subways. The red light was off-putting. However, a cargo train servicing the automatic industrial complexes all along the riverside was the only way to get to the secreted holding place Yassim used to stash his merchandise, a train going into the J industrial. Then she would have to walk to the correct shunt. There were emergency alcoves set at intervals all along the right-hand side, so she could avoid being crushed by any passing cars. Dead unthinking things like tram trains did not frighten her. Live unthinking things like some of Yassim's sassins and hitters did.

She waited a hundred meters from the yawning red-and-black mouth of the G shunt for nearly an hour before a J train arrived. It would have to slow as it reached the junction, so it was no problem for an agile person to drop onto the first segment, catch a good hold of the flange, and settle down for the trip. Flattened on the top, she was small enough to have several centimeters' clearance from the curved ceiling of the tunnel. She reset her grip as the train picked up speed again, vibrating under her. The fetid wind, a noxious combination of overheating metal, grease, and the acrid stink of electricity, roared down across her body, and she angled her face down.

When the J train finally slowed with screeching brakes and made the left-hand turn into the cargo docks of its destination, she readied herself to jump off. She had to land clear of the coding machinery that opened and sorted out the goods to be delivered from the load. But she had done it with no problem before and did it again, dropping lightly down and running up the narrow ledge by the various chutes and moving ramps that began the unloading.

When she came to the first curve in the narrow tunnel and the last of the red light was gone, she used her handlight, glad that she had filched a fresh charge for it only the previous week. With the dim beam to light her way, she trotted along in a half crouch until the muscles in her legs and back ached. She dropped to her knees then and rested a moment before continuing on.

Motivated by her keen sense of self-preservation, Tirla had once taken the precaution of investigating his holding cell, a room hidden behind a false wall of barrels at the back of an automated factory, where the noise of the ill-tuned machinery would drown any screaming. But he did keep the children reasonably well cared for, since purchasers could view them on a closed-circuit system he provided. Disabling the archaic scanner would be no problem for Tirla, and she knew the precise location of the ventilator hatch in the room's ceiling.

The kids had been in there nearly two days. They would be rested, she knew, and possibly feeling pretty good about their new conditions, which were, after all, a considerable improvement over squats. They might not want to leave. She wished she knew whom Yassim had grabbed—then she could figure out how to stir them to leave Yassim's hospitality long enough to force him to pay their parents proper compensation.

She loosened the appropriate wires on the ancient scanner so that the static would snow the visual. Then, gaining entrance through the ventilator hatch, she dangled from the ceiling to the excited clamor of young voices.

"Hey there, cool it way down!" she ordered in Basic, repeating the message for those who might be slow to translate or need to be reassured. "Yushi, pull a mattress down so I can land soft. It's a drop."

While Yushi and his younger brother complied, she did a

quick estimate. Yassim must have been quite pleased at his catch: twenty-four prime kids to sell. The remains of a recent meal relieved her of one obstacle—the guards were not likely to check soon again—but it meant that the kids would have one less reason to *want* to leave such a cushy setup. Why, there were only two kids per bunk. They all had new gear on, and the girls were tarted up like their mothers.

"Yassim take any of you yet?" Tirla asked, imbuing her voice with trembling urgency and widening her eyes with real fear. "I got here as quick as I could!" she added, implying that maybe she had not been quick enough.

"Huh?" Yushi was good at taking orders but not at thinking.

"They took my sister!" Suddenly little Mirmalar's painted face screwed up into tears. "They took her an hour ago. And she had on the prettiest things—orange and brown with gold, and new earrings . . ."

"Oh, I'm so sorry, Mirmalar. I did everything I could to get here in time." As Tirla lavished sympathy on the weeping seven-year-old, she could see panic beginning to spread to the others. She got madder than ever at Yassim. It was one thing to take ten-year-olds, but not seven- and eight-year-old *babies*! What kind of pervs did he supply?

"Whaddya mean?" Tombi, Bilala's eldest son, asked, his manner slightly aggressive. He was nibbling at a sweetbar; judging from the smears on his face, it was one of a series.

"We gotta git out of here," Tirla said, releasing Mirmalar with a reassuring pat. "This place has a baaaad stink."

"It ain't got any at all," Tombi replied, though he turned his head immediately to the rudimentary sanitary unit in the corner.

"They take Raina already, you all are in biiiiig trouble. I'm gonna get you all out. Now. Before more bad men come. You girls know what I mean," she added, waggling a stern finger at them. Tombi and Dik snickered. "Same thing happens you guys, too, and you know you too small for that carry-on yet."

Tombi stopped nibbling the sweet and looked apprehensively at the door.

"Sure they feed you up good. Sweet stuff coming out your ass, giving you a bellyache," she said, dismissing the remains of the recent meal. "This place's good to keep you from crying much. You cry plenty soon and no one hear you ever. Stick it up you good, every which way, and that's the best of it. You know what your mothers tol' you. You know what to watch out for." She was succeeding in scaring them—the younger ones were beginning to weep. She did not want them so scared that they could not move. "Yushi, Dik, Tombi, help me move the bunks. We make a stepstair. There's room up there to stand."

"I ain't goin'," Tombi said, glaring defiance at her. He was heavier and taller than Tirla, but she kicked him so hard that he doubled up.

"You're going 'cause your mother sent me to get you," Tirla knew how scared Tombi was of Bilala. "So you're coming. Now, move! And crying won't do no good, so stop. You need your breath for climbing and walking."

Just then the enormity of moving twenty-four scared and perhaps unwilling kids sank in. Tirla allowed herself only a moment to reflect on it. She had to do it, somehow, because otherwise she would have to leave G, and she did not want to. Linear G was home. She had made herself a place there, she had a business—she was safe there. Well, safe enough, if she laid low for a while.

She chivvied and bullied all the kids up into the ventilation shaft, kicked the telltale bunk over, and replaced the grille. Someone might think that the kids were small enough to escape through it, but where would twenty-four of them *go?*

She led the way, grouping the kids so that there were bigger ones holding the hands of the smallest. She made Tombi rear guard to give him some responsibility and put Yushi in the middle. He would always follow orders.

The unloading platform with its eerie red light gave her no comfort—she knew that some of the kids would not be able to manage the acrobatics needed to get on one of the drones. They could, of course, straddle tracks all the way back to G, but it was a long, long walk, and there would be danger every time one of the speeding trains went by.

Well, maybe they could all make it back one station to I and get lost in that industrial complex. It was safer than staying in J. Or was it? Maybe she would just take the older ones, who would be in more danger? No, they were all in danger, because whoever was left could be made to tell who had rescued the others. Maybe if she put the younger ones in a safe place and went back for help . . . Mirmalar's father adored his daughters and would do anything to save the remaining one. And Yushi's father was one of the strongest men in G.

The vibrations that told her a train was on the tracks beyond the shunt alerted her. How much time did they have before they would know if its destination was J?

"Hide in the tunnels! Quickly! Stand on the ledges!" She took Mirmalar herself, for the little girl was puckering up to cry again.

"Ah, there's never anyone on goods trains," Tombi said.

"Yeah, and how d'you think Yassim's people get back and forth? Dumper cars are big enough to hold a dozen people."

That shut Tombi silent and lost him more face in the eyes of the other boys. Tirla shoved him toward a tunnel as she pulled Mirmalar after her.

The screech of distressed metal announced another goods train being shunted into J from the north. She had not counted on one arriving quite so soon. She would never get the kids

on this one even if it *was* going in the right direction for them
to get home—unless there was a dumper car.

But there was something odd here: Tirla realized with a
sinking feeling that there was no cargo waiting on the platform
to be loaded onto the arriving train. If a goods train was coming in here, what was it coming *for*? Could Yassim have someone in the main Dispatch office? Could he know that she had
emptied his cage?

There were five cars on the double-ended train. Two
looked like empty dumpers. Without waiting to question such
great good fortune, Tirla hauled Mirmalar out onto the platform.

"Quickly. It won't stop long. We must all get in."

They were, therefore, all on the platform when the train
stopped. So none of them escaped the sleep gas that suddenly
spewed out, catching them all in its mist. They fell like wilted
flowers onto the plastic-coated loading surface.

S he's some kid," Sascha said as he and Carmen carefully
placed the object of their intensive search on a blanket pad
and covered her. "Christ, but she's a bit of nothing."

Carmen smiled slowly and turned the sleeping child's head
to one side to see where the lock of hair had been wrenched
out. Her other hand reached halfway to touch it but then
stopped. "She's nothing but skin and bones, Sascha. We'll have
to improve her."

Sascha frowned a bit, looking around to see the rest of the
team attending the other children. "We may not want to, Carmen. Boris and I have a feeling about this one."

"So do I." Carmen smiled at him with her most mysterious
smile.

Boris: *Did you catch her?*

Yes, Brother dear, her and them. She'd sprung the lot of

'em. She must have known exactly where to go. Sascha spoke aloud. "I'm wondering how."

What the hell possessed her? Boris swore with frustration. He and Sascha had followed Carmen's lead, and while Tirla was haranguing the kids, a team had been cautiously organized, aware that Yassim had interests in Industrial J.

How about we find out where they were kept? Sascha asked.

What good will that do now? He's not likely to reuse a holding area that's been breached.

He might if he thought the kids had escaped on their own.

Can you manage that? Boris's tone leaped to hopefulness.

I can try.

If you could, and rigged it, we'd have one more bolthole filed on Yassim. Why *did she do it?*

"Let's wake Tirla up," Sascha said to Carmen, reaching for the oxygen. "If she can show us where, we can get some good out of this operation."

"We already have. We've found more than we hoped, haven't we?"

"Yes, and no. Bear with me, Carmen. There's a lot more than this valuable young girl at stake."

Revived, Tirla went immediately on the defensive, wary and contained, her dark eyes darting around, taking in the unconscious bodies and noticing the medic, who was daubing scrapes and bruises with nu-skin. Carmen offered a restorative drink, deliberately taking a long swallow of it before handing the cup to Tirla.

Sascha, lightly trying to get inside the girl's mind, could sense only her fierce thirst. With great restraint, she took a very small sip, rolling it around in her mouth before drinking more deeply. Her bright dark eyes challenged him. He sat down beside her in a relaxed position, hooking his hands around his knees and leaning back against the wall.

"Tirla," he began. He saw her start of surprise. "Oh, you're well known in G. And your bravery in releasing the children will be appreciated, and not just by their grieving families.''

"How could you find me here, with them?" She glanced inquiringly from him to Carmen and then saw the lock of her hair, which Carmen still wore as talisman. Involuntarily her hand started to the scabby patch on her head. Her shoulders sagged around her narrow chest, but any emotional reaction was carefully guarded in her mind. "I've heard of people like you. You found me because you had my hair."

"It's not witchcraft, Tirla," Carmen said gently. She handed the strand back to the girl. "I have a Talent which allows me to find lost people and things."

"I wasn't lost."

"No," Sascha said conversationally, with an approving grin, "but you found what was missing from Linear G."

"He hadn't paid for them."

Carmen gasped. "You mean, once he's paid for them, he can have them again?"

"Sure. The parents live on subsistence. They need the money for extras only floaters can buy."

Sascha was well aware that the girl's seeming callousness distressed Carmen, who had seen the child in a much different light. "Also puts you in well with your clients, who were rather upset with your abrupt departure from the meeting," he said amiably.

Eyes never leaving his, Tirla nodded once.

"They're all illegal, aren't they?"

Tirla's thin shoulders lifted in an indifferent shrug. "Sure, so it's no credit out of your stash what happens to them."

"Oh, no," Carmen said, pained. "They're alive. They have rights!"

Tirla gave her a quick look before resuming her scrutiny of Sascha. "Illegals don't have rights."

"Only their births are illegal, Tirla," Sascha said. "They're alive. They *have* the right to shelter, food, clothing, training,

and useful occupation. They do not have the right to reproduce themselves.'' Sascha was about to explain the legal anom-
aly in simple terms when he realized that she understood
perfectly. She was mature far in excess of her chronological
age, and well conditioned to the realities of Residential life. She
was not a romantic like Carmen. ''But they do not deserve the
occupations Yassim had in mind for them.'' Sascha caught that
instant spurt of fear, followed by the hardening of the young
eyes and the flick of hatred. ''You don't like Yassim either.''

Again one of her indifferent shrugs.

''Would you by any chance help us disable him?''

She had been wary before, but now she appeared to Sascha
to coil in on herself. ''You're not LEO. Why do you want to
queer Yassim?''

''No, I'm not LEO myself, but we have a connection. Especially against someone like Yassim.''

Tirla gave a snort. ''Someone like Yassim buys himself off
every time LEO collars him. He has powerful friends. LEO can
never make it stick.''

''You wish that LEO could?''

She hesitated briefly, then gave him a candid look. ''There
will always be men like Yassim, but I could do without *him*
very much, thank you.''

Sascha would have given a great deal then to have been
able to read her mind, to delve that reply. Tirla was far deeper
than they'd had any reason to suspect. She sat there in front
of him, cross-legged, completely composed, alert—and bargaining just as if she could get up and leave the scene at any
moment.

''I want to get rid of Yassim, too, Tirla. Will you help me?''

A glimmer of a smile touched her eyes and mouth. ''What's
in it for me?''

Carmen inhaled in surprise. Sascha sent the finder soothing
thoughts, urging her to let him handle the situation his way.
He flicked his fingers, fanning out crisp new floater notes.

"How did you manage that?" Her eyes widened in surprise and indignation.

Sascha did not often employ his kinetic ability, but this trick was always effective. "You help me now—and we must be quick about it before Yassim discovers his birds have flown—and these are yours."

She eyed the notes. Casually she scratched about her ribs. Sascha kept his grin to himself, knowing that she was checking on the tied notes hidden there. She considered his offer with all the solemnity of a computer analyst.

"There's the little matter of your legality, Tirla," he added gently.

Boris nudged him mentally. *C'mon, Brother, we don't have time for amiable lipflap.*

On the contrary, we have all the time we need, Brother. This is a strong personality and a deep one. I'm not rushing her.

Get on with it then.

Tirla gave him a wide-eyed bright smile. "I am the only child of my mother."

"But not her legally registered issue."

"How would you know?"

Sascha touched her hair. "That told us. But it is a small matter that can be quickly remedied."

She regarded him from narrowed eyes. "A small matter?" The twist of her lips was cynical. "You must be in real good with LEO." She considered, obliquely watching Carmen's expression. "And I get to keep the floaters, as well?" Her tone was ingenuous.

Sascha suppressed a grin. Legality would be the most valuable reward he could offer, and still her fingers itched to relieve him of the money. Not that he had offered a large sum, but the amount would keep her in extras for several months.

"If we get a move on—now!" he said, drawing out his acceptance.

She spat in her right palm and held it out to him. Without a second thought, he accepted the deal in archaic ritual. Her grip was unusually strong for the delicacy of her bones. Physical contact with the conscious and vibrant personality startled Sascha with an odd jolt—a sense of precognition that was gone too fast for him to pin it down.

Boris caught the edge of it. *What did she do to you, Sascha?*

I'm not sure, Brother, but this one we handle very, very carefully. I want a special ID for Tirla when we get back. Hear me?

To hear is to obey! Boris might sound facetious, but Sascha was relieved by his compliance. *Keep the bargain, but I want this wild one under control.*

The deal struck, Tirla rose with lithe grace to her feet and tilted her head back to look appraisingly up at Sascha. "So how do we disable Yassim?"

"Can you lead me to where he kept the children?" When she nodded, he went on. "We want to fix it so that he will think the children escaped by themselves."

Tirla snorted contemptuously. "I had to frighten them to make them leave at all. Such things I had to tell them. Though it was all very true."

"How would Yassim know that they were all docile? It need only look as if they had broken out. That one of the guards had been careless locking them in."

She considered that. "Yes, that could have happened. They had only just brought food." She gave him a shrewdly appraising glance. "You will have to crawl." That seemed to amuse her.

"Up this tunnel?"

She nodded, then looked over her shoulder, for the first time betraying some apprehension. "What happens to them?"

"They can sleep on until we get back," he replied. "We've got to move now."

She led him into the tunnel, and he did have to crawl, won-

174

dering how she had managed her initial trip until he saw the small circle of light that guided her steps. She had the courtesy not to go faster than he could follow, and he had time to reflect: she might not have an ounce of telempathy, or was perhaps too wary to let down the shield that had protected her so long in her young life, but there was no question that she possessed considerable Talent.

She halted at the end of the tunnel and turned to him. "You wouldn't fit down the hatch I used, but if you know how to open that inspection door, that's an easier way to get to where he held the kids."

Sascha took the scrambler from his belt and decoded the door. He opened it cautiously, aware of the hissing intake of her breath, and listened—on another level than Tirla, who was kneeling at the lower half of the opening. The level and complexity of noise in the main industrial complex was appropriate for an automated factory. He sensed nothing human, but it was Tirla who first slid through the door. He opened it enough for his larger frame and closed it carefully behind them.

Though the industrial space was lit only by occasional green lights of operational machinery, Tirla moved confidently forward. Sascha would have passed right by the false wall, but she went unerringly to the double drum and pinpointed the lock mechanism with her pencil light. She glanced questioningly at him.

"Electronic, I hope?" he murmured, and she nodded.

He scrambled the circuit, and the door swung back to reveal the deserted room, the overturned bunk bed, and the table with the empty food packages. She pulled the door shut behind them, shooting him a disapproving look for his careless entry.

"How did you get them out?" he asked.

She pointed to the darker square of the grille in the ceiling.

"Good work." He righted the bunk bed and pushed it back into its former position, managing to stick a minuscule device on the wall behind it. Then he looked about the place. It stank of many things, not all tangible. "I think you'd better master-mind this escape, Tirla. Make it look like a kid had done it."

Tirla's upper lip curled in derision. "None of them would have!"

"Point taken, but for Yassim's benefit it should *seem* so."

With her eyes half-veiled, Tirla considered the problem. Sascha waited patiently, wishing he could have been in her head, noting her thought processes.

"Okay," she said finally, leading across the room to the corner where pieces of clothing had been discarded. Deliberately she tore strips from several garments, her hands clever in finding the break in a hem or seam that would rip. "There'll be a fight . . ." She hauled mattress pads off two of the lower bunks, and the soiled blankets off the upper ones. She went back to the corner and, using a shirt, gathered up some of the containers and the remaining food before she knocked over the makeshift table. "Now, we open the door just enough to let kids out, and start leaving trails. Come out, I'll just close the door over a bit. Now, you drop stuff halfway to that wall. Then circle around. I'm going this way. I'll meet you at the maintenance door."

He did as she directed, and they met again in the chucking, clanking dark of the automated manufactory.

"Lock it?" Sascha held the door ajar.

"Yes."

"But how will Yassim know how they got out?"

"They're not there, are they? The cage door is open." Sascha saw her shrug and felt, rather than saw, her malicious smile. "Why should I make it easy for him?"

By the time they reached the loading dock, Sascha's muscles were protesting their abuse. The team had loaded the children into the cars, and the dock was full of cargo to be transshipped.

"You cut that fine, Sascha," the team leader told him.

"There'll be a goods train through here in two minutes. We're not supposed to disrupt the service."

Tirla tugged imperiously at Sascha's sleeve. "My floaters."

With one hand he passed them to her, with the other he grabbed her wrist. "No tricks now. There's more business we can do together. We'll discuss it back in G."

Sascha did not know whether it was her surprise that allowed him to capture her or if she was willingly cooperating with him. But she entered the car ahead of him as he tried to keep his grip from breaking fragile bones.

Go! he told the driver, and the starting pressure of the special train pushed him against the padded end of his car.

"Are you taking us all to G?" Her tone was casual.

"That's what you wanted, wasn't it? To get the kids back to G?"

"I kept our bargain." Her voice held an element of antagonism.

"So will I. Back at G. Then we deal again."

She was silent for a long time, thinking that over.

CHAPTER 11

Peter tried to follow the tri-d meteorologist's report on the latest freak weather conditions that seemed world-wide, Bangladesh being the worst example. It was difficult to concentrate when he felt "problem" hovering in the air. He *knew* he had done nothing wrong; in fact, he knew that he had done something most extraordinary, about which he felt very good indeed. But it was hard not to be worried. He could sense the nebulous anxiety emanating from Rhyssa, Dorotea, and Sascha. He should not have asked Dorotea about a bigger generator. The moment the words were out of his mouth, he knew it was the wrong time. But he had *proved* what he could do with enough power to increase the gestalt, and that 4.5 felt like puny kid stuff now.

Kid stuff! Peter grinned to himself and gave the 4.5 a little shove; it whined obediently. Like a dog. And who was he kidding? He was still only a fourteen-year-old boy. He had already absorbed enough Talent discipline and seen enough examples of the sort of people Talents were to realize that he had rushed the gate. One did not climb mountains when one could not walk. Rhyssa, Sascha, and Dorotea had supported him throughout the entire *Erasmus* incident, ready to help him, ready to keep him from burning himself out. And he hadn't. But had it been *because* they had been right there to protect him? Think about *that*, Petey boy, and get your swelled head back to normal. There are a lot of things you *can't* do just yet.

He poured himself another glass of orange juice and brought it to the living room as the broadcaster announced that once again supply shuttles for Padrugoi had been grounded by

weather conditions. The screen depicted the rank of four per-
pendicular space vehicles, locked into their gantries, waiting
for lift-off conditions with urgently needed matériel so that the
First World Project would be finished in time.

Talents were helping to do that, Peter thought with a little
thrill of corporate pride. He had just started wondering how
big a generator he would need to send a shuttle safely through
the foul weather when the program switched to coverage of
the flooding in Bangladesh. There were no scenes actually
showing the Talents at work; teams of doctors and rescue
workers were filmed rushing about. There was also no mention
of exactly how the *Erasmus* had landed so safely at Dacca. He
had not really expected to be mentioned publicly. But one
would think that there would have been some comment that
Talents were risking their lives in the appalling monsoon conditions. The results of their work was shown, all right enough,
but somehow that did not seem to be enough.

Rhyssa and Dorotea were always subtly mentioning how
important it was not to rub Talent into people's noses. People
resented differences. Talent had always to be discreet. The way
his mother looked at him had demonstrated *that*! Peter grimaced. His own mother was scared of him now. When he had
been totally helpless, she had been so good about coming to
see him, hugging him, kissing him, always bringing him something: a fax clip about his favorite ball team, a couple of her
special cookies, a few flowers. Now when she visited she would
not hug him; she sat bolt upright in the chair and tried not to
look at him when he wanted so much to show her what Talent
allowed him to do.

When Mum was there he redoubled his efforts to appear to
walk normally and carry things properly so it would not freak
her out. How often had she said she prayed every night to see
Petey on his feet and walking around? And she never *looked*
at him now. She never once mentioned his ball team. Not that
he would ever play sandlot baseball again . . . Then Peter

grinned, thinking what homers he could whack and how fast he could run the bases. Maybe now he could be the pitcher he had always wanted to be . . . His fastball would be *something else*! Even if he only used the 4.5!

But he had gone past that sort of *ordinary* thing, hadn't he? When one could zap shuttles about like gameboard pieces, *ordinary* accomplishments no longer satisfied.

He drank his orange juice. Not *all* ordinary things, though. Some very ordinary and extremely homely actions—like getting himself an orange juice when he felt thirsty for it—were, in a special way, far more important than what he had done with the *Erasmus*.

He sent the empty glass back to the kitchen, rinsed it out, and put it upside-down on the drainboard.

He had to keep things in perspective. It was more important to have the freedom to do little things and the *option* to do bigger ones. But, jeez, it had been a wonderful feeling to have all that power and do something no one else could have done with it—just when help was needed.

The tri-d was showing floodwater flowing obediently away from a small town and its surrounding fields. The sandbags and barriers along its torrent seemed to be containing it, but Peter could recognize the subtle signs of kinetic force. He wondered which Talent was at work. Rick Hobson? Mr. Baden? Now, if he'd had access to a generator, he would have been able to do that. He settled down to learn what he could about flood control from the program. Next time he would be ready to help. The 4.5-kpm was portable, wasn't it?

His thoughts were interrupted by Rhyssa's mental call. *Peter, would you come up to my office, please?*

Sure! He leaned briefly into the generator and sped out to Rhyssa's building and in through the front door, slowing to maneuver the staircase; he got his feet to the ground as he reached the carpeted hallway leading to Rhyssa's office. No effort!

Show-off. Rhyssa was standing by her office door, but she was smiling. "We don't have any mountains for you to move today, but there's trouble in the wind, dear boy, there's trouble in the wind."

Peter stumbled in his forward motion and corrected himself.

Trouble? Why? We didn't do anything wrong!

Her touch reassured him, as it always did. Dorotea was great: she treated him casually, as she would any of her grandchildren, and that relaxed attitude made many things easier for him. But Rhyssa was different: her mind had so much depth—not that he had disobeyed the prime rule of mental privacy, but he could not help but sense the depth and purity that was there. She was also the most beautiful woman Peter had ever seen, on or off the tri-d. And she was so *good!* Everything about her was shining and brilliant. She made him feel whole and strong.

"We did something a shade too right," Rhyssa said. "And we were not quite as discreet as we should have been."

Momentarily afraid, he reached out to see exactly what they had done wrong.

Peter!

"Sorry."

Rhyssa, more fiercely than Peter had ever heard her: *Damn that Barchenka woman!*

"Was I *supposed* to hear that?" Peter was confused.

"Yes, and double-damn Barchenka!" Rhyssa said aloud, and waved him on through to her office, closing the door behind them.

He halted, sensing the aura of crisis. Dorotea, who was rarely perturbed, was brushing imaginary threads from her slacks. Things must really be bad. He zigged sideways, aware that Rhyssa just missed bumping into him.

Dorotea: *Well done, Peter!*

"This is a strategy council, Peter," Rhyssa said, gesturing for him to sit as she resumed her chair in the tower bay window.

Peter floated over to the conformable seat, grateful for its automatically adjusted support.

"Don't ever forget just how proud we all are of you," Rhyssa said, her gesture including the entire Center. "You've added a brand new dimension to Talent." She gave him an impish smile. "And reminded this Center's manager not to get too complacent."

Without violating etiquette, Peter could hear what she was not saying aloud: Talent was very happy; the unTalented were not.

Dorotea: *The unTalented always resist a new Talent which we haven't carefully led them to expect. In this instance, you!*

Rhyssa: *We don't do something right, Peter, without doing something wrong!* Peter sensed a second qualification behind the thought and, remembering his manners, broke the contact.

Dorotea: And *we've got to figure out how to improve our testing methods!* She cleared her throat in a businesslike manner, then winked at Peter.

He thought, very privately to himself, that something bad was definitely about to happen, but he was assured of their love and approval and that was all that really mattered to him.

"If your main desire right now," Rhyssa said, smiling with that special twinkle in her eye which she saved for Peter, "is to have the biggest generator on the planet at your disposal"— Peter flushed, looking hard at his bony knees—"then the main desire of half the industries on Earth *and* in space is to have you using theirs, and theirs alone."

Space? He could get into space? He looked up in surprise, staring at her. Clearly she did not mean *his* way.

"How do they know about me?" He felt suddenly very defenseless. His father was always talking about the managers working a man to death with no consideration for him as a human being, only how productive he was, a cipher in a gigantic program.

"They don't know it's *you*," Dorotea said.

"That's the problem," Rhyssa went on.

"Why?" Peter asked, thinking of *big* generators.

"Candidly," Dorotea said, "you're fourteen, you're only just beginning to understand your Talent, and premature exposure could—"

"Burn me out," Peter finished for her, though privately he did not think he *could* burn out—if he had the right power source for anything he wanted to shift. "But I didn't burn out . . ."

"Without in the least diminishing your achievement, Peter, we were closely monitoring you the other night," Rhyssa went on. "What *they* have in mind for you is another can of worms altogether. Speaking as a Center director, I must tell you that it has never been the policy of the Centers to assign trainees even part-time work until they're at least eighteen."

"Even I," Dorotea put in, her hand gracefully sweeping her chest, "wasn't permitted to do much until I was eighteen!" She made a face. "As a child, I thought I was just playing a game, guessing which ones in the room could hear me—people who *thought* they might be Talented." She shot Peter an image of herself as a five-year-old, prettily dressed—and her early beauty was still apparent in her face and manner—walking through the Center's crowded reception area.

"But I've *proved* what I can do," Peter said. "And I was the only one who could land the *Erasmus*."

"The situation is not about right or wrong, Peter," Rhyssa said, leaning toward him, a sad expression in her eyes and face, "or even a moral obligation to reduce suffering and mitigate disaster." Then she opened her mind to him so he could directly assess the current problem.

Peter had known, of course, that the Parapsychic Centers had had to send the best kinetics to Padrugoi to help complete the station on time. He had not realized all the undercurrents beneath the carefully contrived public image of Padrugoi, much less the machinations of Ludmilla Barchenka, who had forced the capitulation of Centers, ruthlessly stripping them of kinetics in what was basically a face-saving operation. He fumed when he saw that this Barchenka woman was threatening *his* Rhyssa with all kinds of offenses when it was now patently clear to him that Barchenka was at fault. And he was part of the problem. No, at the moment, he was *all* of the problem, because Barchenka was out to add him to her force of Talent.

"And I used to think working on the station would be the most special thing you could do," he said slowly. It just was not fair!

"No, not fair, Peter," Rhyssa replied, "but Talent recognizes that completing the station is far more important than individual personal considerations. Completing it on time is obviously Ludmilla's personal goal. I can't deny her that, only her means of achieving it, since by her achievement, mankind has made another giant step to the stars. Don't be deflected too much by the skeletons in the space lockers. There's been no major forward progress in all of human history that has not been accompanied by some problems."

"Like letting people float out into space and die because rescue would put her behind schedule?" Peter was aghast.

"That's been taken care of," Dorotea reminded him.

"By Talents, and now she thinks she can conscript me?" Peter was so agitated that he floated above the chair.

Dorotea, prosaically: *You're drifting, dear.*

Peter settled down. *Well, I just won't work for a person like her. And you're not going to ask me to!*

"Indeed and we're not," Rhyssa assured him. "But first," she said with a grin, her eyes twinkling, "we have to prove to *them* that you're *you*! We've been trying very hard to keep you sheltered until you've more control . . . "

How much control do I need if I can move a shuttle about the world?

"Peter!" Despite the sharpness in her voice, Peter knew that Rhyssa was amused by his outrage, proud of his achievement, and concerned for his future all at once. He subsided. "Thank you. Now, we were warned to expect visitors of high rank and great prestige. We wanted to brief you, since you are the cat we are about to let out of the bag."

"I rather think he's the cat among the pigeons," Dorotea said with a sarcastic snort.

"Pigeons? War hawks, Dorotea," Rhyssa corrected, settling into her chair. Then they all heard the unmistakable thunking of a big helicopter landing on the X outside Henner House. "Peter, don't let the fuss get to you. There's bound to be some bruised feelings and outraged sensibilities. You just pay them no heed!"

But he could not help but heed the fine but controlled aura of apprehension. They were worried. About him! *For* him.

Ragnar's voice came through on the intercom. He was duty officer, and twenty years in the Center had made him impervious to rank and prestige. "Rhyssa, there's a bunch here to see you. Do I send 'em up?"

"Yes, I'm expecting them, Ragnar."

His "humph" came over the speaker, and Peter noticed Rhyssa's little smile. He also noticed that she was nervously running the stylus through her fingers. Dorotea sat even straighter in her chair and managed to look not only larger and more imposing but very, very queenly.

There was a polite knock on the door, and Rhyssa pressed the release button. The first man in the room was a telepath, Peter realized, and he was directing tight private warnings at Rhyssa. The second man, very tall, thin, and wise-looking, gazed directly at Peter and nodded. He *knew* who Peter was even if Peter did not know him, and he was also a telepath. He courteously identified himself to Peter as Justice Gordon Havers.

Peter knew the third man, Dave Lehardt, who immediately moved to stand by Rhyssa's desk, facing the others as they filed in. He made his partisanship very clear. He exchanged a glance with Rhyssa and gave an almost imperceptible nod of his head. She had a slight smile on her face, and Peter sensed that she was very glad to have Dave Lehardt so close by. But knowing that Dave was not a Talent, Peter was surprised by the intimate exchange. He felt a flair of jealousy.

The next six men to enter were obviously important people; four were in uniform and only one of them was Talented. That one appeared very nervous and kept looking from Rhyssa to Dorotea. The last man to enter gaped at Rhyssa in a fashion that made Peter very uneasy—his eyes and his manner made Peter wonder if he was one of those perverts his mother used to warn him about.

As Rhyssa asked them all to be seated, Peter picked up names: Vernon Altenbach, who was secretary of space; the Russian officer was General Shevchenko, Padrugoi liaison official, and even with the shield he wore, he was bristling with aggression. The telempath was Andrei Grushkov, and Peter felt sorry for him—he had to be truthful to his employer, the general, but he felt obscurely that he was betraying Talent in doing so. There were two NASA officers, a general and a colonel, and that pervert was the world-famous Josephson-junction specialist, and a Malaysian prince besides, who did such fantastic programming of air and space traffic. Peter did not like the man any better once he knew he was a genius, not when the man kept sloppily ogling Rhyssa. The man who had come in first was Colonel John Greene, and Peter watched in some awe as the most successful etop pilot of the early days of the Padrugoi Project placed a chair next to him, Peter Reidinger, and smiled quite pleasantly at him. Colonel Greene seemed to be the only one who was smiling. Even Justice Havers looked solemn.

"It would be pointless for me to deny that I am aware of the reason for your visit," Rhyssa said calmly. "Shall I call up the Eastern Center Register for you to check on our memberships?" She placed her fingers over the keyboard.

Peter regarded her with pride. She even had a little smile on her face. And that pervert kept smarming at her.

The Russian liaison general cleared his throat. "We have already seen it, Madame. But we believe that you have not honestly declared your full kinetic strength." He crooked his head to see his telempath's face.

"Andrei can certainly assure you that our declaration is honest and complete. We have nothing to hide. No Talent does."

"Andrei has also assured me, Madame Owen," the general continued ponderously, "that no kinetic anywhere could have successfully landed the *Erasmus*, not even the twenty-two on board her, or—" He paused dramatically. "—assisted its takeoff from the Dacca field in the weather conditions prevailing that day." His chest seemed to deflate slightly once he had delivered his accusation.

"It was me," Peter said. He wanted to get it all over with, and get that smarmy-faced man out of the room and away from Rhyssa. "I mean, it was I."

The stunned silence was worse than noisy disclaimers. Then Colonel Greene started to chuckle and Dave Lehardt began to laugh. He also winked approvingly at Peter. Not one of the other visitors appeared to be the least bit amused.

"And tell me just how, young man," Vernon Altenbach asked, skeptically, "you accomplished such a feat?"

Stick to the facts, man, the facts, Rhyssa said, mental laughter rippling her tone.

"Well, the *Erasmus* needed help landing at Dacca because

the kinetics *had* to be there to reduce the disaster potential. So Rhyssa called a G and H—that's a Talent mayday—and I got to use the generators at the East Side power station," Peter replied. He kept his face straight, but he was enjoying the incredulity of the non-Talented in his audience; even the Russian telempath was admiring, and Peter sat himself even straighter in the chair.

Dorotea: *Well said, Peter!*

Gordon Havers: *In times of doubt, honesty is the best policy.*

Johnny Greene: *You better believe it, because they're not!* Unobtrusively, he patted Peter's knee.

"You have, I must assume, a kinetic Talent?" Vernon continued.

"Yes, sir. I'm in training as a kinetic, but I can't do as much as I'd like because the people who should be training me are all up on the station."

Rhyssa: *Don't spread it on too thick, Peter.*

Johnny: *Nonsense. They deserve that kick in the shins.*

"How much training have you had then?" the general asked.

"Well, Rhyssa and Dorotea do the best they can, but they're telepaths . . ."

Rhyssa, dryly: *Thank you!*

Gordon: *He's sticking to the truth.*

"Initially Rick Hobson was helping me," Peter went on, "but we'd only just gotten past the necessary stuff when he got conscripted to the station."

"Talents were *not* conscripted," General Shevchenko objected forcefully. "They volunteered to assist in the completion of the first Great World Project."

Peter gave a contemptuous little snort. "If you're not given a choice, you've been conscripted."

"And you expect us to believe that a frail boy manipulated

the *Erasmus?*" Prince Phanibal Shimaz shot out of his chair and stood belligerently in front of Peter, shaking his finger at him. "I, Phanibal Shimaz, prince of Malaysia West, know that this would have been impossible from such a source! Tell us the truth, little boy!" he demanded, making the adjective pejorative.

"He *is* telling the truth," Johnny Greene said, rising to his feet to look down at the much shorter prince. Dave Lehardt and Rhyssa jumped to their feet angrily, ready to leap into the fray if need be.

"As Andrei confirms to me," General Shevchenko said in a hard voice. "You exceed your authority, Your Highness."

"And I shall prove it," Peter added, glaring back at the prince. Just because he could do games with Josephson junctions and traffic-flow patterns that no one else could do did not make him an authority on Talent. "Look!" And Peter raised his right arm, wishing he had enough small motor control to point a finger, but he had not quite mastered that yet.

Actually, it was easy enough with power diverted from the Center's equipment to raise and hold the big helicopter just outside Rhyssa's bay window so that all could see it—and see that the huge rotor blades moved idly in the breeze of its ascent.

"Do be careful with it, Peter," Johnny Greene said amiably, one of the few in the room enjoying the moment. "It's government property."

"I'm always careful, Colonel Greene," Peter replied, feeling the euphoria of potency. He was almost sorry that he could not think of an even more convincing demonstration of his kinetic Talent. Dorotea was glaring at him significantly in her enough-is-enough look. He returned the vehicle gently to the ground.

"How old are you, Peter?" Colonel Greene asked, just as if he and Peter were the only ones in the room.

"I was fourteen on the eighth of September."

"And you get about now yourself under your own power?" the colonel inquired.

Peter could see in his eyes that the man knew the true extent of his handicap.

"I was that much"—his fingers measured a two-centimeter gap—"away from paraplegia myself after Mission Number 20," Greene continued.

Peter realized that Colonel Greene was very much on their side and making it very clear to everyone else that Peter's Talent was off limits. "I've learned how to compensate just fine," he replied, and a glance at the colonel told him that that was the right answer to make. "Rick Hobson really helped me. We were just beginning to go on to tougher things when he had to go to Padrugoi."

"So you've been Rhyssa's skeleton crew? All by yourself?" Colonel Greene chuckled and looked across at the secretary of space.

"I'm not nearly as much of a skeleton as I used to be." Peter extended his arms and legs and regarded them dispassionately. "I'll get some muscle on them yet. I've got to build slowly, you see, and it takes time."

Colonel Greene rose. "I think that's the answer, gentlemen. It takes time to build muscle, any kind of muscle, and you build slowly to last longer."

"Now wait just a moment here," Prince Phanibal said, recovering from his initial surprise. "That is not the answer I came to find. You have indeed concealed from the world a kinetic Talent of demonstrated ability. He can take the place of those at Bangladesh . . ." He leaned across Rhyssa's desk, and Peter saw her flinch back from such a menacing posture.

Peter could not stand it. Kinetically he dragged Prince Phanibal backward from Rhyssa, the prince's face set in a paralyzed rictus of amazement. The door that opened to allow his exit closed firmly behind him.

"Peter!" Rhyssa could not quite disguise her relief or her consternation at his breach of courtesy.

"He's got no right to threaten you, Rhyssa! No right at all!"

Dorotea: *Bravo, Peter, though I shouldn't encourage you!*

"Now see here, young man—" Shevchenko took one step toward Peter and stopped, blinking in astonishment when some invisible force prevented him from moving farther forward.

"That's enough, Peter," Rhyssa said with appropriate severity. *That was rather clever of you, dear, even if you wouldn't realize it.* The mental image in her mind showed suppressed laughter. "The general will not intimidate you any further. General, I think Peter has inadvertently displayed another cogent reason why the Center is unwilling to utilize his unique abilities except in a crisis. At fourteen, he does not always abide by the courtesies that a more mature personality has learned."

"I demand that the boy apologize to His Highness Prince Phanibal immediately."

"You may demand all you wish, General," Rhyssa said sharply, "but I don't even know why a traffic manager, royal or not, was included in this gathering."

"Engineer Barchenka insisted on his inclusion," Vernon Altenbach remarked, attempting some diplomacy.

"I insist that he be *excluded* from any future meetings involving the Center or myself."

Peter: *He's a slimeball!*

Johnny Green and Gordon Havers, simultaneously: *Where did you stash him?*

Peter: *He's in the helicopter, and he can't seem to get the seat buckle undone.* He could not help grinning. *I won't let him.*

Johnny: *Buckle down, Winsockie, buckle down!*

Dorotea: *I didn't think anyone in your generation knew that old song.*

"Now, gentlemen, you have, I trust, seen to your own satisfaction that we have only been protecting young Peter, not deliberately denying the platform his Talent. I'm sorry that you had a long trip for nothing," Rhyssa said, coming around her desk to shake hands with Andrei Grushkov. "However, when Peter is fully trained and we have a better understanding of the parameters of his potential, we will, of course, be obliged to let prospective employers bid for his contractual services."

Vernon Altenbach eased the disgruntled Russian general out the door, the NASA colonel and the telempath assisting. But the others lingered until the first group had entered the elevator.

"Ms. Owen," the NASA general began. "Is it possible, given the boy's display of incredible ability, that he could—from time to time, that is . . . Well, we do have a serious crisis right now . . ."

"What kind?" Rhyssa asked in an unencouraging tone.

"NASA's supply schedule is at a standstill with the current worldwide weather conditions . . ."

Peter zoomed out of his chair, hovering between Rhyssa and the general. *Please consider it, Rhyssa. Working for NASA wouldn't be the same as working for Barchenka, would it? But it would be almost as good as being in space.* He exerted all his mind's pressure against hers, begging her consideration. He felt her stern resolve not to exploit him.

Johnny: *It's something to consider, Rhyssa, though we won't be pushy about it. If you say no, we'll go quietly. But it would gall me personally, and professionally, to have Barchenka saying that the Americans couldn't meet their contractual obligations.* He cocked his head at Rhyssa, grinning wryly.

Peter could feel Rhyssa beginning to relent.

Dorotea: *Consider it a training diversion, Rhyssa.*

Rhyssa: *But that's it! He's had hardly any training!*

Johnny: *Repetition hones skills, gal, and it sure reduces the glamour quotient.*

Peter did not understand that but felt Dorotea's approval

become more urgent. He sensed that at last Rhyssa was seriously considering the suggestion.

"Look," Johnny said aloud, "this is so important that Vernon would actually get himself another minder for a few weeks. I know all the technical data that Peter needs to understand if he's flinging shuttles about the stratosphere. Hell, I'd get a vicarious thrill out of it myself, getting back into space by proxy. And if Peter's working for NASA, Barchenka can't say Talent has been obstructing Padrugoi's timely completion."

"I know it appears that it's always we who compromise," Gordon Havers said, entering the discussion, "but we put a wedge in her works if suddenly we insure delivery of the matériel she needs."

"You'd have to go with Peter, Rhyssa. I'm no longer up to that sort of sustained effort," Dorotea said. "Sascha's too involved in the present crisis at Linear G to leave that. And frankly, my dear, you *are* the stronger telepath and, I think, more tuned in to Peter's mind than Sascha is. Someone has to monitor him during the gestalts. I can see you squirming to go, Peter Reidinger. Is it what you really want? Will you behave like a mature Talent?"

Peter managed to curl his fingers around Rhyssa's. "I'll behave. I'll do just as I'm told. I promise! And I'd learn a lot."

"You'd call the moves, Rhyssa," Johnny Greene said.

"I don't think we have any choice in this either," Rhyssa said, and Peter leaned against her, wishing for her not to sound so defeated. She looked down at him and cupped his head with one hand, smiling tenderly at him. "I'm not defeated, Peter dear, but I intensely dislike being left with no options."

"Think of the options that you've canceled," Johnny Greene said with a malicious note in his voice as he lifted his middle finger skyward.

"Put like that," Gordie said, grinning, "we're one up on Barchenka."

Rhyssa turned to Dave Lehardt, her expression severe. "And you keep Peter's name out of the 'casts and the fax."

"Your skeleton crew at work again?" Dave asked, pretending to ward off an attack.

" 'Dem bones, dem bones, dem dry bones, and hear the word of the Lord!' " Johnny Greene sang, doing an intricate breakdance step.

CHAPTER 12

The blond man had an air about him that fascinated Tirla. She had never had much to do with Talents, and she surreptitiously crossed her wrists. She had heard such folk discussed in the Residential often enough, in fearful, awed whispers, but she had not believed half of the powers alleged to them: finders of persons and things, seers of souls, readers of secrets, prophets of future things, and movers of mountains.

She stole a look at him where he sat with his head leaned back against the padded wall and his eyes closed; daring to observe him more closely, she noticed the quick flow of facial muscles, as if he were having an argument in his head. His jaw tightened in anger, and his lips thinned. He should have been pleased with his day's work, Tirla thought. She was startled then, when his mouth relaxed into a half smile, a clever sort of smile, and his eyebrows twitched. Had he won his internal argument? He was a strange man, she thought, even though outwardly he appeared no different from others.

He was not LEO, and yet he was, and she could not figure out where he fit in, or how he and his teams had appeared so conveniently at the J shunt—especially when she had just realized the difficulty of cajoling scared whiney brats like Tombi into riding cargo pods back to G. Without that unexpected rescue, Yassim's ladrones would surely have recaptured them, herself included. She shuddered.

So they had been rescued from Yassim. But not from Authority. She wanted no part of Authority: too many conflicting rules and regulations and silly restrictions that only begged to be ignored or evaded. The prospect of a new ID briefly dazzled her, to the point where she could feel the narrow plastic strip knocking against her wrist bone. But she did not—quite—believe that the man would be able to produce any such ID, no matter how well he seemed in with the LEOs.

No matter! She had clean floaters—more than she needed for the tieds she had been supposed to launder for Yassim—so she was well ahead in the game. The matter of the hot tieds bothered her, but she was loath to face Yassim as long as he was in the market for kids. And it was very likely that the LEOs could not collar Yassim, and that he would go into deep hiding somewhere to wait out the furor. So, morally, she could hide the tieds for a while and discreetly exchange them, especially if Yassim was out of circulation, over the next several months. This was the biggest hit she had ever made.

But still she was uneasy. She was trapped in the closed cargo pod and did not really know where they were going, though she had been keeping mental count of the rail junctions. The blond man could just as easily leave her off at the hostel with the others. Who would belie· that she had an arrangement with him? The train began to decelerate, and Tirla, with a spurt of dread anticipation, waited for the shunt connect. They were going to the G platform. She was both comforted and concerned.

"Where are we now?" she asked.

Sascha opened his eyes, and she saw that they were an unusual shade of light blue. He looked amused. "You know we're at G. So now we return the lost children to their grieving parents. That is important to you, isn't it, Tirla? That Bilala, Zaveta, Pilau, and especially Mirda Khan and Mama Bobchik know that you helped retrieve their lost ones?"

Now how could he know that? How much did he know about her? Why was he playing her along this way? He was a sharp one indeed. What sort of a scam was he running? Not all of this action had to do with that perv Yassim.

She refused to be drawn by what could just be a shrewd

guess on his part. LEOs were not above putting surveillance on Meetings, even a silly RIG with that Lama-shaman. Perhaps there had been eyes on her clients, although why such a gaggle of silly women would be the object of LEO interest she did not know—unless it had to do with selling kids. But none of them had been there to deal kids—most of theirs were too young yet. They had all been looking for "messages" and "salvations." Yet Sascha had identified her clients, and he had even known that Mirda Khan and Mama Bobchik were especially important.

"It just pays to be a good neighbor," she answered diffidently.

"Oh, you have definitely been a good neighbor today, Tirla. And a very good citizen!" He laughed softly, throwing his head back and showing large white even teeth. It would be a very nice laugh, Tirla thought, if it had not worried her that he was laughing at all. Perversely she liked him, for his strong grip and his droll words, but she did not trust him any further than she could have thrown Bulbar.

She gave him a quick stare for calling her "citizen." Citizens lived across the river in the beautiful hives, luxury cones, platforms, and complexes, not in Linears.

"Trust me, Tirla?" His eyes were not laughing, nor was his mouth, and his voice was gentle and entreating.

"I have no reason to."

"If I give you one?"

She snorted scornfully. Just then the train braked to an easy stop, and the lids of the pods opened to reveal a group of adults, waiting to lift out the unconscious children. A slim woman in a LEO uniform standing at the edge of the platform spotted Sascha and thrust a narrow plastic case at him.

"Here's a reason, Tirla." Sascha showed her the ID bracelet in the case. He took advantage of her surprise to clasp it around her wrist.

She stared at it, holding her arms away from her, trying to

absorb the significance of having a legal identity and then the slowly dawning knowledge that the bracelet was not banded in the usual Residential colors. Green banding meant that one could travel between Linears, but what did the gold and black stripes mean?

"You are now legal, Tirla."

Just then the four freight elevators reached the cargo level. A mass of women flowed out onto the platform, raising loud lamentations when they saw limp bodies on medipads. Sascha drew Tirla to one side as Public Health personnel circulated, establishing the parentage of those Tirla had rescued.

"What happens to them?" Tirla asked. This was not what she had had in mind when she set out on her mad venture. Parents would not be pleased that their children were in the hands of Authority. Nor would they profit as she had intended. She had an ID bracelet and more credit than she had ever possessed in her life—but what good would it do her if the tenuous position she had carved for herself, her clients, her means of supporting herself, were gone? Suddenly her future seemed as bleak as that of the children she had saved from Yassim.

A tall, slender, very handsome young man in a LEO uniform planted himself squarely in front of the Sascha person and saluted. "What do you wish me to tell the women, sir?" he asked.

"That Tirla here," Sascha said, moving her to stand in front of him, his hands lightly—and, she felt, kindly—on her shoulders, "found where Yassim had hidden their children. She was leading them back home, to their mothers and fathers, when we, also searching, came upon them."

In a voice that penetrated the tumult of wailing women, the young man rattled off the announcement in the required languages—a task that made Tirla restless under Sascha's hands. As each of the linguistic groups understood, they fell to whispering among themselves. When the translator had finished, Mirda Khan and Mama Bobchik waded forward, their expressions grim. Under Sascha's hands, Tirla's narrow shoulders tensed, and surreptitiously she shielded her brand-new ID bracelet by moving her arm slightly behind her.

"And the children?" Mirda Khan demanded in Basic, jutting her chin out. She stared pointedly at Tirla.

"The records have been checked," Sascha said, his voice diplomatically apologetic. "Their births were illegal."

When Mirda Khan frowned, Sascha signaled for Ranjit to translate. The wave of hysterical weeping was punctuated as mothers of now officially illegal children threw themselves across the unconscious bodies, obviously determined to resist attempts to remove them. Sascha ordered the crowd-control partners to neutralize the incipient hysterics. He dampened his own reception, but he could not remain immune to the intense emotional agitation that battered his senses. He was perplexed. These same women would have sold their sons and daughters in a few years.

Boris, he said, *it's going to be a lot easier to buy these women off with something.*

How about the truth? Isn't a hostel a better fate than the future Yassim planned for them?

I would think so, Sascha replied, *but I do not think they'll see it in the same light. I'll tap our slush fund if you won't ante up.* Anything, Sascha thought, to shut up the spine-crawling ululations. He was not used to having to deal on this level.

Getting soft, Brother?

You're not here and listening. And there's Tirla to think of.

You're taking charge of her, aren't you? Boris asked.

I'd rather she wasn't jeopardized. Her Talent could be very useful in multilanguage groups.

The noise was fearful, the aura exceedingly unpleasant for any Talents with the least modicum of empathy. Tears were streaming down Carmen's face.

"How much, Tirla?" Sascha asked.

Startled, she twisted in his hands to see his expression.

"How much will stop their tears and relieve their loss?" he went on.

"You'd pay?"

He saw the leap of astonishment in her velvety brown eyes before a canny veil settled over her expression. *Brother, this one's going to deal for the hairs on our chests.*

"For the youngest, you don't have to give much." She named a figure. "Add ten percent for each year they have, and that should be enough."

"I'd say five percent for each year."

"Seven!" she retorted. "The bigger they are the more it takes to fill their bellies."

He spit in his hand and held it out. She closed the deal and then stepped four paces nearer to Mirda Khan.

Ranjit, monitor this for me! Sascha ordered.

She's speaking Arabic, Ranjit said. *She's saying that she has been arguing hard for the grieving mothers ever since they were caught in the tunnel. Only because she has spoken out so forcefully has a way been made to ease the sorrow of the mothers. Illegal children have rights, the big man says, and she believes him. They will be much safer than with Yassim, for which every mother should be thankful, knowing perfectly well the fate which awaited the children, despite the grief it causes. For how else can people survive on mere subsistence alone? A price has been agreed, as they must have seen, and she has acted in good faith. Sascha,* Ranjit added as Tirla turned to face another section of the women, *this child is amazing. She's speaking Urdu now as glibly as she did Arabic. Oho!*

There was a commotion, and a plump little woman, her face contorted with conflicting emotions until her beady eyes were hidden in the folds of her cheeks, pushed through. Sascha recognized her from her caste mark and the vindictiveness of her roiling thoughts. She would have leaped upon Tirla if Mirda Khan and Mama Bobchik had not intervened. Sascha sprang forward to protect Tirla, berating himself for not anticipating an attack.

"Unwanted bitch," the woman shrieked in Basic. "Illegal, you! The bint is illegal! She is illegal!" She struggled against the restraining hands. "Take her. You take her if you take my Tombi. You take her!"

"Of course I am illegal, wasted barren woman whose husband will beat her morning, noon, and evening for refusing a fair price that will feed him for many days to come on lamb and papadums." Tirla leaned with fervor into the task of returning verbal abuse. She had, Sascha noted, managed to run her bracelet up under her sleeve, out of sight.

Sascha restrained Tirla by her shoulders. "She is illegal, woman. She comes with us. Tell them, Ranjit!" When the message had been translated, he added, "The deal she spoke of will be good for only three more minutes." He looked pointedly at his digital watch. "Then there is no more to talk about. Let each mother who accepts the offer stand by her child."

Then, to shut up the renewal of Bilala's caterwauling, Sascha shot a strong silencing command compulsion on the hysterical woman. She fell back in the arms of the women who held her, her mouth working soundlessly. An awed hush fell over the platform.

The business was quickly concluded then, and Tirla watched solemnly as crisp floaters changed hands. She had never seen so much money in circulation at one time and in front of everyone. It was better so. No one could claim afterward that one had received more than another. Some of the women lingered, displaying real distress as their children were loaded back into the front four cars. Sascha propelled Tirla towards the last car, which the search group was boarding.

Tirla held up her braceleted arm. "You keep the bargain in fact but not in spirit?" she demanded as the drone cover slid shut. She tugged at the coveted wristband.

"The bargain is kept in fact and in spirit, Tirla, but you can't go back to G, not with Bilala your enemy."

"Huh! That one!" Tirla snorted derisively. "She wouldn't find me if I didn't want her to. I'm not afraid of that stupid woman."

"Frankly, I would be, were I you," Sascha said. "She'll certainly make sure Yassim knows what part you had in clearing out his hide."

That caused her to reflect, although Sascha still could not nudge his way past her shields.

"Then what was the point of making it seem as if they'd escaped?" she demanded with some exasperation.

"That seemed a sensible safeguard at the time. Up until you'd wanted to be such a good neighbor. C'mon . . ." Sascha held out his hand. "I think I can find you a safe squat for a few days with a friend of mine." *Dorotea?* he called. *Can you spare a moment for this waif?*

Tirla looked at his hand as if it were covered in acid. "At the hostel? With *them*?"

"You're legal, remember?" he reassured her with a little smile. "Technically, you're free to move anywhere you want to now. You've got a wad of floaters, but—" He raised his hand in a cautionary gesture. "—you know as well as I do that an unattached kid in a Linear right now is in jeopardy. Yassim has got to find replacements, and Mirda Khan and Mama Bobchik wouldn't be there to defend you."

"Defend me?" Tirla was both indignant and astonished.

"Oh, they did, in their own ways. And if a ladrone didn't snap you up, the Public Health would, as you're underage and should be in school." *Wow!* he exclaimed to Dorotea as he sensed Tirla's sudden reaction. *That opened up an excited crack.*

Dorotea: *Keep working it then!*

"Frankly, I would be wary, were I you," Sascha said.

Tirla fingered her precious ID. "School? I could access Teacher?"

"You've the right to all the education you can stuff into your head—that is, once you overcome the little problem of being an unattached minor. C'mon, get into the pod. It's ready to go, and I want you out of this hostile environment."

Tirla cast a look over her shoulder at the knot of women around Bilala and said "Stupid cunt" under her breath, but she did not resist Sascha's guiding hand.

"Once you've caught up with the grade level, you could even go to a regular school."

"Me? In a school?" Tirla was skeptical as well as contemptuous.

"I suspect you've got a lot more talent than you realize, Tirla."

Dorotea, acidly: *You were never one to understate a cause.*

Tirla hunkered down beside him, balancing her torso between spread knees, hands dangling limply between her legs, her butt against the padded end of the cargo pod. She cocked her head up at him, hauling the strands of dark hair off her face, her dark eyes sparkling with, it seemed to Sascha, a private amusement that, for all his telepathic skill, he could not penetrate.

"Talent?" she repeated.

"Yes," he said. "Talent." He settled down beside her just as the train began to ease forward.

"I'm nothing like *you*," Tirla said warily, swaying a little.

"No, you're not. I cannot talk to everyone in their own language as glibly as you do."

Tirla thought for a moment and then shrugged. "That's not hard to do."

"Not for you. Ranjit, who's quite a linguist, was making heavy weather of the translations just now."

Tirla shrugged again, dismissively.

"In a few years, you could earn a big wage just translating." He could feel her attention. "Enough to live at the top of any Linear and never have to worry about the Yassims of this world."

"Working for LEO?" She was plainly unwilling.

"For someone with your gift of languages, there are far better opportunities than LEO. You do need some schooling."

"I got schooling." Her tone was both rebellious and indignant. At Sascha's prompting, she added, "I used my brother's ID—as long as I had it. I got schooling."

Dorotea, would you check that out? The brother's name and ID are on the Incident report.

I caught a glimpse again, Sascha, Dorotea said. *I'm going to need personal contact with her to get past that shield. I gather you plan to bring her to my place and I'm to play sweet frail harmless grandmama? Boy, this has been a day! In for a penny, in for a pound. Did you get any of the high-level interview?*

Caught most of it! Sascha sent an image of him cheering like a mad soccer supporter.

When all the excitement dies down, Sascha, we are going through the testing procedures with the proverbial fine-tooth comb.

Just then Sascha felt the jar as the four forward cars were detached to go on to the western hostel that would accommodate the illegal children. He caught the look of apprehension on Tirla's face and her quick glance at him.

I'll take her to my spare room if you'd rather, he told Dorotea.

Nonsense. I may hate typecasting but I'm far more suitable. Though you're doing rather well, Dorotea allowed somewhat grudgingly.

Sascha smiled and resettled himself. "It'll be smoother from now on," he said to Tirla. "We're being shunted to the commuter track."

"Where are you taking me?"

"To my grandmother."

I'm not sure I care to be related to a glib philanderer like you, Sascha Roznine. No morals.

"If she'll have you for a few days until I can find the right Residential school for you," he amended. "That would solve the problem of nosy Public Health officials and keep you out of Yassim's notice." The mention of school briefly opened her shield and he saw a fearful startlement—a hunger and a withdrawal—before it lowered. He went on casually. "But, as I said, you've a legal ID, floaters enough for months, and you can suit yourself."

Their car had been shunted several times, and the progress became smoother and faster. Tirla noticed it, and she also noticed how the other people in the car were relaxing, smiling and chatting comfortably with one another.

Residential school, my ass! Boris's disgusted tone echoed in Sascha's mind. *I can just see Fairmont or Holyoke taking in that subbie.*

Tolerance, Bro, tolerance. She's clean and healthy, and that tight mind might conceal a genius.

Boris: *For scams!*

Dorotea, steel in her tone: *You just let us handle one of our own.*

Since when am I disowned? Boris asked.

Dorotea: *When you're wearing nothing but your LEO hat!*

Sascha had a mental image of his brother withdrawing quietly, offending hat in hand. No one took on Dorotea in a crusading mood. He glanced down at Tirla, who was deep in thought, staring down at the floor, though her body appeared relaxed. When the cargo-pod door opened as they reached the vehicle park in the quiet grounds of the Eastern Center for

Parapsychics, she reacted with amazement and disbelief. As the other members of Sascha's team piled out, laughing and chatting over the successful assignment, Tirla just stood, her large eyes wide and white as she stared around her. Sascha did not hurry her. The old Henner estate, with its big old beeches, maples, and oaks, the wide lawns and the attractive two-story residential units, was unusual enough in modern Jerhattan and had to be a revelation to a Linear resident. Tirla looked appalled.

"My grandmother lives over there," Sascha said, pointing to the dwelling that had once been the gardener's lodge. "There she is, weeding the border." *You are the most complete ham, Dorotea. Weeding?*

True enough, but I wasn't going to swathe myself in black subsistence and bedeck myself with bracelets and nose rings to make her feel at ease. And the border does need weeding.

What about your arthritis?

I always suffer for my art, m'dear. I've recruited Peter, too. He needs to climb down from rarefied atmospheres, and something homely will help. Also, he may be older than she is, but he looks young. He's to appear with eats. Refreshments are always a good way to start off a conversation, particularly for someone with a Near East background. "Why, Sascha, what a pleasant surprise!" Dorotea hoisted herself to her feet and held out her arms to him. *Kiss me, you lout. Even grandmothers need a ration of passion now and again!*

"Grandmother, this is Tirla . . . Tunnelle."

Inventive boy! Dorotea commented.

"She needs a place to stay for a few days. Would it be too much of an imposition?"

Dorotea extracted herself from Sascha's enthusiastic embrace and extended a mud-daubed hand to Tirla. Since Dorotea had been accepted and acceptable from the moment of her birth, she had about her an aura that made rejection from anyone impossible; Tirla delayed only a moment before grasping the extended hand. *She's got bones like a bird's, Sascha. How could she possibly do all she's just done?*

"Tirla, this is Dorotea Horvath." *There's nothing frail about Tirla's mind, Dorotea.*

"Actually, I was just about to quit and have something to eat and drink. The sun's warm today. Peter, is the juice ready?" she called, and gestured for her guests to precede her into the little house.

Sascha was glad that he had thought of Dorotea, instead of taking Tirla to the far more daunting manor house and its formality. Judging by the girl's stunned expression, even this homey room was far outside her experience.

"I expect you'll want to wash up, and I need to," Dorotea said gently, touching Tirla's arm and pointing to the little hall. "Lavatory's second door on the left, dear, plenty of towels. Peter," she said as she made for the small kitchen, "we have two more guests."

Peter: *What's she like?*

Sascha: *Scared.*

Peter, wryly: *Know the feeling!*

Dorotea: *Tight shield.*

Peter, earnestly: *I'll be careful.*

Dorotea: *And don't show off. You'll terrify her.*

Peter: *I did all the showing off I'm going to do this morning.*

An apprehensive Tirla reentered the room, surreptitiously trailing fingers along wooden surfaces and across the sofa backs. Sascha noticed that she had washed hands, arms, neck, face, and that portion of her chest that was visible above the round neck of her rather worn clothing. She had brushed her long hair neatly back over her shoulders. Sascha thought of the cheerless functionality of subsistence living quarters and gave Tirla another full mark for nonchalance.

"Here we are," Dorotea said, arriving with a large tray laden with all sorts of fingerfoods: savories, small open-faced sandwiches, wedges of fruit, and strips of fresh vegetables. "Peter, don't drop the glasses!" Fortunately, Tirla's back was to the boy who, with both hands on the huge pitcher of orange juice, was allowing four large tumblers to float along beside him.

"Hold it while I pour," Peter said, handing Tirla a glass, a diversion that kept her from noticing the other glasses sliding to positions on the low table near Dorotea and Sascha.

Dorotea: *Peter!*

Peter: *She didn't see it.*

When all had been served with juice, Peter bounced into the chair beside Tirla and took a long drink of the juice, wiping his mouth and exclaiming with satisfaction at the taste.

"Don't inhale the juice, Peter," Dorotea said as she offered Tirla the tray of snacks. *An uncommon fondness for green pepper,* she noted when she saw Tirla's eyes brighten at the sight of the slices. Closely watching Dorotea, the girl had closed her fingers about three, then increased her haul to six when there was no reaction. "The cheese puffs are hot and fresh," Dorotea said, pushing them toward Tirla. "You'd better get them now before Sascha or Peter hog them all."

Tirla let the pepper strips fall into her lap and obediently took a cheese puff.

I couldn't make myself some coffee, could I, Doro? Sascha asked plaintively.

Drink! Anything. She won't until we all do. "Peter, this is just what I needed. I must have dehydrated in the sun. Sascha, there're asparagus in the breadrolls. I know you like them! And Peter, you are not to eat all the chicken sandwiches. He would, you know," Dorotea rattled on, nibbling at a cheese puff which she then put to one side to take a bite of a pâtéd cracker. *Well, we've all sampled everything to prove there's no poison or drugs. Ah, good! Oh, my word! She's starved!*

Tirla had started to drink and eat with quick sharp bites and snatched swallows, as if she was torn between eating and drinking and afraid that the food would suddenly disappear. All three telepaths were aware of a sudden lightening of her carefully guarded thoughts as she made inroads on the snacks. The pastry melted in her mouth, releasing tastes that satisfied unknown cravings with textures that titillated her tongue, from the reassuring crisp watery tang of the green peppers to the bite of sharp cheese and savory meat fillings.

Food would be a trigger, Dorotea went on wryly, *when you consider she's probably been hungry all her life.* She took a long drink of the orange juice. "I hope you've more in the kitchen, Peter, because it tastes marvelous. But then, fresh-squeezed orange juice always does, don't you think so, Tirla?"

Sascha! Boris's tone was authoritative. *Your waif's in good hands. Someone just snatched one of the Jerhattan schoolkids we stranded three weeks ago.*

"Well," Sascha said, rising and dusting crumbs off his fingers. "I'll leave you to it, Tirla. You're safe enough here for a few days, and Peter can show you how to log on to Teacher. Right?"

As he strode across the lawn to the main house, Dorotea told him, *She paused in her eating when you left, but I fear the snack tray and the orange juice pitcher are of far greater moment than you, honey.*

Sascha was not certain, in his private mind, if he liked taking second place to a batch of canapés, even with a preadolescent.

CHAPTER 13

"Y ou been here long?" Tirla asked Peter the next morning as they ate breakfast in the pleasant and, to Tirla, amazing kitchen room. Dorotea was preparing eggs—fresh eggs—in a pan at the stove, using, of all things, a naked flame. Tirla did not wish to distract her from the dangerous procedure, so she spoke in a low voice.

"Hmm," Peter said amiably, taking neat spoonfuls of the ripe melon. "Ever since I got out of the hospital."

Tirla watched to see how he dealt with the food—she would have sliced it thin and eaten down to the rind. "Why were you in the hospital?" she asked. Hospitals were fearsome places to Tirla, who had always made a practice of avoiding medics, as well as quacks. She also had a wary distrust of sick people, never having been ill or injured herself.

Peter gave a diffident shrug of one shoulder. "A wall collapsed all over me."

"You must have been hurt bad." In Tirla's experience people did not survive walls coming down on them.

"Couldn't walk for months. Couldn't even feed myself." His eyes took on an unfocused cast.

"And they let you live?" Tirla was stunned at such good fortune.

Peter regarded her with some surprise. "Of course, though for a while there, I really didn't want to live."

Tirla absorbed that remarkable statement as she bent to the task of eating melon. It was really good—not gone off like most of those she scrounged. She flicked careful glances at Dorotea to make sure the fire was under control. Why didn't the woman

use the hotter she had right there in the wall? One of the first
things one learned in the Linears was not to mess with naked
flames. Fire was a sure way to bring down the wrath of the
LEOs.

"Why did you?" Tirla asked, realizing that Peter was waiting for her to comment. "Live, I mean."

"Rhyssa taught me how to move again."

"You do move sort of oddly," she said, having noticed the
peculiar gliding motion he used. He did not, in fact, seem to
take real steps, though his legs moved.

Peter snickered, his mouth full of melon. He swallowed
and grinned broadly. "That's because I'm not really walking. I
impel myself kinetically." His eyes glinted with mischief at her
mystification. "I make my body move. It can't."

Tirla stopped eating, staring at him until she recalled that
even in Linears a lengthy stare was impolite. "Your body
doesn't move? But you're eating. You're using your arm and
your hand—just like me." She held her own hand up.

"I'm pretty good at it, aren't I?" Peter was delighted with
his effect on Tirla. "I've done some other stuff, too, moving—"
He broke off, with a slightly rueful grin. "I hear you're pretty
good at your Talent, too. That was larky—getting the kids away
from the pervert."

Tirla slowly shook her head, dismissing her achievement.
"Nothing like what you do. I don't have much Talent at all."

Peter snorted with good-natured contempt. "That's what
you think. It's not what Rhyssa said. I'm good at what I do.
But you're very very good at what *you* do. Don't knock it."

Slightly embarrassed by the sincerity of Peter's tone, Tirla
changed the subject, eager to pump him on puzzling topics.
"You said Rhyssa helped you? Is she the dark-haired one who
was here last night after Sascha left?"

Peter nodded his head. "She's the director here."

"Not Sascha?"

Peter shook his head, grinning. "Sascha's the deputy chief.

He takes over when Rhyssa's involved with someone. Like me! I'm her special project—'' He broke off, blinking his eyes rapidly, and flashed a quick, almost apologetic glance at Dorotea before he grinned. "Rhyssa has lots of special duties, being the director. I'm not the only one.''

Tirla noticed that his cheeks flamed briefly. What could embarrass a boy like Peter? Then Dorotea was passing plates with freshly cooked eggs and bacon and urging Tirla to sample the hot toast. Tirla ate until she was stuffed. She thanked Dorotea profusely for the effort of handcooking.

"I enjoy it,'' Dorotea replied, smiling gently. "Especially for appreciative appetites. Peter, why don't you take Tirla to the study and log her in? You've got to go through some assessments first, honey, but once your standard's been decided, you'll be expected to be present for all the classes you're assigned.''

Tirla nodded briefly, far more interested in the way Peter got down from his chair—indeed he did glide as he conducted her to the study, and the curious fluidity of his movements fascinated her.

"And you aren't really walking?'' she asked.

"Nope, it's all kinetic. My spinal cord got severed when the wall fell on me. Medical science can't splice that—yet—but kinetic science gives me movement. Better'n being stuck in a support chair,'' he assured her blithely. "Here's your terminal, and here're your earplugs. I've got to do my hours with Teacher, too. Can't slip out of that with kinesis!'' He made a face as she slid into the chair he indicated. When she had slipped the plugs into her ears, he typed a sequence with an odd finger movement, and suddenly the blank screen cleared.

"Tirla Tunnelle, may I, as your personal Teacher, welcome you to this Educational Program.'' The screen showed the School Room and a pleasant-faced woman seated at the desk. Tirla knew that the Teacher was a construct, devised to reproduce the old teacher-pupil confrontation, but she had always liked the look of Teacher; someone a person could trust, who would not laugh at questions or honest mistakes, who was there to help one learn. "Sascha Roznine told us that you have had some credits under the name of Kail, Linear G resident, Flat 8732a. Today, if you will bear with me, Tirla, we will just see how much of those early lessons you remember. Now, shall we begin? If you need to be refreshed about the function keys, please type H for help. Or, if you're ready to begin, strike RE-TURN, and we'll begin the assessment."

With conflicting emotions—awe at realizing a long-held dream and fear that the miracle might be withdrawn for some capricious reason—Tirla touched RETURN.

I think," Dorotea began, drumming her fingers rapidly on the kitchen table, "Tirla is going into an education-overkill phase. She won't leave the terminal, though Peter has been as slyly devious as you, Sascha, in getting her outside. I also think she finds the grounds daunting instead of pleasant. She sticks to the paths and won't use the playground facilities. But all this study and no play is not an improvement."

Don Usenik, who had joined the informal meeting as medical advisor, shook his head, mildly amused by Dorotea's fervor. "According to the medical reports, she's in excellent shape. Amazingly so when you consider the conditions under which she's lived."

"Well, I think it's wrong for a child her age to try and absorb two years' education in four days," Dorotea maintained.

"Any improvement in receptivity?" Rhyssa asked.

"What does Peter say?" Dorotea countered with some heat.

Rhyssa laughed. "Peter thinks she could if she would. When she's involved in her studying, he can hear an ongoing mental commentary. She has amazing retentive powers, visual as well as auditory. She's answered him telepathically once or twice when she didn't realize it."

"We have got to make her aware of her potential," Sascha said, frustrated.

Rhyssa leaned across the table. "It will take time, Sascha. There's no need to force scope to her Talent."

"Boris would like a hundred more like her," Sascha said, frowning.

"But I thought you and Boris had found the Jerhattan child," Rhyssa said, having followed his thought. She did not like what she read: that Boris wanted Tirla to work undercover with Cass.

"Oh, we found and rescued her all right enough," Sascha replied with no sense of achievement, "and two others, but there were no leads whatever of any use. Only a minor ladrone who reports by phone—another of those conveniently illegal connects. So a dead end. The girls could tell us nothing; they had been gassed, blindfolded, stuck in some sort of smooth plastic cocoon. Their trauma went pretty deep."

"The psychological scarring of their incarceration is going to be difficult to neutralize," Don remarked, frowning. "A new wrinkle in rendering the abducted docile—tactile disorientation. Villainous trick." He shook his head. "You and Peter are off today, aren't you? So that leaves Dorotea and me to come up with some brilliant ideas on sharpening up the Tests, huh?"

"And me," Sascha said, coming out of his gloom. "I am after all, director of training for this Center. The trouble with a unique like Tirla is that she doesn't realize she's got Talent in the first place. And in the second, how can you test children that aren't supposed to exist?"

"What training have you planned for Tirla then?" Rhyssa said.

Sascha shrugged. "Training? She's a natural at what she

does—getting into the communication center of anyone's brain and adapting to whatever language they're using." He spread his hands wide. "How can we improve on that? And she can't explain any more than Peter can explain how he does what he does."

"I'd do it myself, but I hate crowds and I can't walk far," Dorotea said suddenly, "but Sascha, why don't you start by hauling her away from Teacher for an afternoon? Those issue shoes are useless, and while she might feel happy in subsistence issue, I would like to see her dressed in something nicer. Several something nicers."

"Me?" Sascha glanced first at Dorotea and then at Rhyssa and pretended not to see Don's amused expression.

"You!" Dorotea pointed a stern finger at him. "She trusts you."

"But I've never bought clothes for a kid."

"No need to panic," Dorotea replied unfeelingly. "I'm sure Tirla knows what she'd be comfortable wearing, and that's all you need to go by. She's still a trifle young to want to bedeck herself alluringly."

Wanna bet? Rhyssa said in a tight aside to Dorotea, who gave her an unfathomable glance without betraying a mental explanation.

"Take her to one of the good malls. Let her see how the other half lives—the one she's inhabiting now," Dorotea went on. "And then treat her to something tooth-rottening and utterly satiating. Spoil her a bit. Show her there's more to life on this level than a square box and a wrist ID."

"She might know of other kids with unusual aptitudes," Rhyssa added. "She doesn't miss much."

"That's for sure," Sascha replied heartily. "Your heli just landed, Rhyssa. I'll just see you all off."

"Peter!" Rhyssa called. "Dave and Johnny are on their way. Are you all packed?"

Dorotea snorted. "He's been ready since before you thought of the—" She paused and grinned wickedly. "—distraction."

"I'm coming," Peter called. He glided to Tirla's room. "I'll see you," he told her. "Keep clocking in the study time."

She hit the HOLD and regarded him in surprise. "You going somewhere?"

Peter grinned mischievously. "Rhyssa's got a job for me." He winked.

"Job? For you?"

"Sure. I'm very useful, I'll have you know."

Tirla gave him a long disbelieving look. "Doing what?"

"More of what I'm good at."

Tirla gave him a look of profound disbelief. "What could you be good at?"

Peter made a clicking sound in his mouth, since he could not snap his fingers. "I just wish I could tell you, Tirla. But it's a professional secret."

"So don't tell me. I got better things to do than guess secrets!" Tirla turned back to the monitor.

"But I'll be gone weeks."

Tirla wriggled her fingers at him over her shoulder. "Have a good time," she said, keeping her eyes on the screen. The Teacher on hold had her mouth open and hand half-raised as she was making a particular point in the lesson. Tirla tried to resume her studying, but the truth of the matter, though she could not let on to Peter, was that she would miss him. Weeks?

He was the first boy she had ever met who had some sense. She knew he was supposed to be a very clever kinetic—he had talked to her about thought transfer and telepathy, which made her a bit nervous—but he had also been good about helping her with some of the harder problems Teacher set her. At least Sascha would be around. She would not like Sascha to be gone for weeks.

She was surprised to have her lesson interrupted a second time—and by Sascha.

"Tirla! Have you stirred out of this room today?"

"No," she said, tapping out the answer to the problem on the screen.

"Tirla! Turn that damned thing off! We've got something better to do with the afternoon."

She rolled over on her side to look up at him. "What?"

"Buy you some new shoes and clothes."

Tirla looked down at the toes that were visible through the latest cracks in her footwear. "I did try to find the issue slot, but Dorotea doesn't have one."

Sascha hunkered down and firmly punched the Off switch.

"Hey!" Tirla regarded him with astonishment that quickly turned to antagonism. She reached for the switch, and he caught her hand.

"You can pick up where you left off when we get back. On your feet!" Sascha gave her hand a warning pull. "We don't have issue slots at the Center. Generally we get ordinary stuff from the Remote Mall, but as I haven't a notion of your shoe size or what colors you like, I think this once, we'll go in the flesh. When we're done, we're going to have a treat."

That got Tirla's interest. She bounced to her feet, her black eyes sparkling. "What kind of treat?"

"That'll be entirely up to you, my dear," he said, leading the way to the transport lot. "In our malls there's a lot to choose from," he added in a provocative tone.

Whatever misgivings Sascha might have entertained about shopping for a child were swiftly compounded. First Tirla had to recover from her initial shock at the size of the mall that Sascha had chosen. Then she led him a dance through every department of the twelve-story complex, eyes and head constantly on the move as she did an initial reconnaissance.

Back on the first floor, she mused at length over the various items that had caught her attention the first time and then began a second tar. On the fourth level, fortunately the one dealing with shoes and apparel for young people, the sole of one shoe disintegrated—"From the heat of the speed at which she was traveling," Sascha told Dorotea later.

When an officious floor walker moved in on Tirla with the obvious intent of removing the waif from the elegant premises, Sascha intercepted him.

"I wouldn't," Sascha said in a low voice, pushing out his sleeve so the special design of his wrist ID was visible. "I'm escorting her. Is she acceptable as a patron now?"

"Yes, sir, I'm sorry, sir, but you must admit . . ."

"That's why we're shopping."

The man walked quickly out of Sascha's vicinity with several anxious backward glances.

"You weren't going to hex him, were you, Sascha?" an amused voice beside him asked.

He turned to see Cass Cutler grinning up at him. "If I could, I'd put a hurry one on Tirla," he said. "We went through all twelve levels of this place like a dose of salts, and now she's settling down for a second tour."

Cass laughed at his discomfort. "And they sent you out on your own with your protégée?" She laughed again. "That's unkind."

"It's supposed to be mutually instructive."

Tirla reappeared and latched onto Sascha's hand, regarding Cass very narrowly from her suddenly inscrutable eyes.

"I remember you," Cass said. "You ricocheted off me and my partner at Linear G. And you messed up Flimflam's scam to a fare-thee-well. My congratulations!"

"You're one of him," Tirla accused, jerking her head toward Sascha.

Cass laughed again, a throaty, genuine laugh. Sascha could feel Tirla's fingers relaxing. "Not quite, chip. We're on the same side, but right now I'm assigned to LEO, crowd control."

Tirla looked about her, slightly contemptuous. "Not much of a crowd here today."

"I'm not on duty today," Cass replied, grinning down at Tirla. "I see you're on a day off, too. What've you found that appeals to you?"

Will you help me, Cass? Please say yes! Sascha pleaded. *I've a hideous presentiment that that child intends to case the entire mall again before she'll even try something on.*

"If you don't mind me saying it, Tirla, you'll be able to walk further with a decent pair of shoes on your feet. There're some good bargains to be had right now. What strikes your fancy?"

With a sense of reprieve, Sascha followed Cass and Tirla to the shoe department. An hour later, after two harried human clerks had replaced the mechanical fitter, Tirla's small, narrow, and very dainty feet ended up in soft purple leather boots, in the only pair that would fit her feet.

Totally unsuitable for a child, of course, Cass said, *but they do fit.*

And she adores them! Sascha saw how Tirla's face glowed as she strutted from mirror to mirror, regarding her feet.

"Mr. Roznine," the head clerk said wearily as the docket spun out of the teller machine, "your young companion has a most delicate and unusual foot to fit. May I recommend this concern? They do very fine custom work."

Sascha read the man easily and caught the unspoken message: "So we won't have to go through this again." But he was just as grateful to take the card, which could be inserted in Dorotea's mall machine for home shopping.

He blessed Cass with every new purchase, for the woman actually seemed to enjoy the looking, the trying, and the endless discussions of fit, style, and color.

"The concept of having unlimited funds to spend is foreign to the child, Sascha," Cass said at one point, "but you must admit that she knows what suits her."

Tirla was modeling a one-piece outfit as different from subsistence issue as diamonds from rhinestones. The main color was a soft blue with purple accents in seamstitching, pocket trim, and fasteners. Once Tirla found that outfit to her taste and Sascha's—it was always Sascha to whom she turned for approval—it took the combined efforts of both Sascha and Cass to get her to buy additional clothing.

"Why do I need more? I've boots, and this material's hard wearing. It'll do for weeks. Even if I had to catch freights again," Tirla added, peering mischievously up at Sascha.

He had to chuckle at her impudence. "It's a fetching outfit, Tirla, there's no question of it. But even Teacher will get tired of seeing you in it."

Tirla gave him a long hard look. "Teacher doesn't *see* me."

"No, but Dorotea and I do, so do Sirikit, Budworth, Don, and Peter, and Rhyssa. You never see *them* wearing the same clothes two days in a row."

"Oh, they have lots of clothes. Dorotea has closets full." Tirla did not sound envious—if anything her tone was slightly censorious, as if she felt it was improper for people to have so many things to wear.

"A few changes are in order," Cass said. "I've got quite a few myself," she added encouragingly while Tirla merely stared back, her hands plunged into the deep pockets and her shoulders hunched under the smooth fabric.

"This isn't coming out of your floaters, Tirla," Sascha began, suddenly realizing what might be causing her hesitation. "Dorotea and Rhyssa want you to be suitably dressed now that you're a Talent. You're not a subbie anymore, you know." He pointed to her wrist ID.

"Oh." There was look of surprised wonderment on the girl's face as she regarded her bracelet with dawning comprehension. "Is that why those salespersons were so nice to me?"

"Quite likely," Cass said in a dry tone of voice. "Everyone in malls like these recognizes the distinctive pattern."

Tirla twirled hers on her fragile wrist. "They do?" She settled the band outside the cuff of her new clothes. "How much
can I buy with just this?"

Sascha disguised a choke of dismay with a cough just as
Cass caught him in the ribs with her elbow.

"Let's find out, shall we, chip?" Cass asked cheerfully and
held out her hand.

Tirla took it readily enough, but her other hand immediately sought Sascha's, and then she was dragging them after her
toward a rack of brilliantly colored trousers.

She was not as profligate as Sascha feared, but she ended
up with "something different to wear every day of the week."
Then Sascha made good his promise of a treat, inviting Cass to
join them in the Old-Fashioned Parlor of Gastronomical Confections and Irresistible Desserts.

Tirla managed to get through three immense, rich concoctions that Sascha privately thought revolting.

Cass: *Let her enjoy, Sascha. Ice cream is something she's
only heard about.*

Sascha: *What if she comes home sick? Dorotea will skin me
alive.*

Cass: *This child has an iron constitution if she's survived
subbie slop until now. And look at how much pleasure she's
having.*

Sascha, groaning: *I'll be sick!*

It was then that Tirla realized there were other girls and
boys enjoying the parlor. Her spoon on automatic, she took
full note of the other youngsters.

*That blonde ought never to wear bright colors. She'd look
better in pastel shades. Boy, what's he wearing such tight pants
for? He'll squeeze 'em dry. Now that red outfit might look
good on me. Maybe I can get something like that next time
Sascha wants to spend money.*

Sascha glanced surreptitiously at Cass, who rolled her
eyes.

Sascha: *Stream of consciousness and loud and clear. Does she realize she's broadcasting?*

Cass, busily spooning up the last of her treat: *Highly unlikely. That child's had to be on the* qui vive *all her life. Frankly, Sascha, I take it as a high compliment that she's relaxed enough in our presence to do some unguarded thinking.*

Sascha: *Good point.*

As nonchalantly as he could, Sascha observed Tirla, listening to her pithy and acute remarks about physical appearances, style, clothing, manners, and a range of other subjects that flowed across her alert and fascinating mind.

Then Cass, with apparent reluctance, rose and said that she had to get back to the Center, as she had an evening assignment. Tirla even looked disappointed that their threesome had to break up.

"Look, chip, anytime you want to have a gawk round some of the other malls—" Cass started.

"There are *other* ones?" Tirla exclaimed, shooting an accusing glare at Sascha.

"Thousands," Cass told her with an unrepentant grin. "But you can't really do more than one at a time, or it all gets jumbled up in your head as to what you saw where and which price. Believe me, I know!"

Tirla saw the merit of that and, tucking her hand in Sascha's, was content to return to their transport and the Center.

By the time they reached Dorotea's, their purchases had arrived by express package tube and were piled neatly about the room.

"What a charming combination!" Dorotea exclaimed on seeing Tirla's clothes. *Did you buy the mall out, Sascha?*

Give her a little while and she probably will. Cass made the mistake of informing her there are a thousand more just like Grafton's, and we may never be able to pay her bills.

Dorotea laughed. "I'll expect a fashion show after supper, Tirla."

"Show? Why? I can put on something new every day this week. That'll show you," Tirla replied. "What's for supper? It smells good!"

"After all you just finished eating?" Sascha demanded.

"That was the treat. Don't I get supper after a treat?"

"Of course you do," Dorotea assured her, glaring at Sascha.

If you'd seen the three huge, gooey, sickeningly sweet things she consumed only a half hour ago, you might not be so quick to stuff her with supper, Sascha cautioned.

"Wash your hands, Tirla, and I'll serve immediately. Are you staying, Sascha?"

"No, thanks," he said, managing to sound polite. *Peter was right about her being telepathic. But she doesn't know she is.*

Hmmm. You see, you did learn something from her today. What did she learn from you?

How to spend money, Sascha replied sourly, and left.

I f the official spectators at the launch even noticed the youngster seated to one side in the upper control room, they would have supposed him to be a child on a special tour, his youth according him a treat. The men certainly noticed the woman who sat beside him, for she had an arresting beauty and an unusual silver streak in her dark hair. However, her attention never strayed from the boy. Equally involved in him was the tall dark-haired man in fatigues with a colonel's eagle on one collar tab. So few spared the trio more than a passing glance. The real action was taking place out by the massive towering gantry, where gale-force winds whipped the steam from the shuttle's rocket end. All recent launches had been pretty tricky, the bad weather causing havoc with all air transport but none more so than the critical first minutes of a shuttle launch.

The countdown echoed through the shielded room—at the count of eight, the spectators were jockeying for position for an unimpeded view through the treated slit windows, eager for ignition and takeoff. Fingers were surreptitiously crossed, for this was the thirteenth successive shuttle flight.

"We have ignition!" As often as that phrase was uttered, it was always said with a ring of quiet triumph.

As the shuttle engines began their full-throated roar, none of the spectators would be able to hear another noise, that of power generators pulsing at ever-increasing speed: a subtle whine that built and then leveled off just as the shuttle, one of the majestic new Rigel class, began its first imperceptible upward thrust. The final link to the launch tower fell away. Everyone held his or her breath. Then, despite the howling wind and the lashing rain, the shuttle crept upward from the reinforced concrete without deviating a centimeter from the optimum takeoff trajectory. Lift became obvious with increasing acceleration, and suddenly the bird was up and running, disappearing, except for the radiance of its rockets, into the lowering ceiling of dark gray swirling clouds.

Immediately all eyes turned to the newly installed infrared monitors that continued to track the shuttle on its unswerving path through the atmosphere and safely above the turbulence, well on its way to Padrugoi Station, where its payload was urgently needed.

"The pilot has the conn," Peter Reidinger said, opening his eyes. He glanced first at Rhyssa and she nodded, smiling reassurance as she removed her hand from his. He liked her to be touching him in these moments, even if he could not feel it.

"You have the conn, Crosbie," the controller said, letting out a small sight of relief. "Good thrust, Pete. You're working like a charm. Got the whole thing down to a science."

"It is," Johnny Greene reminded him, grinning.

"You know what I mean, Colonel," the controller said, flapping his hand.

"He's teasing you," Peter said, turning his attention to the monitor. He did not really need it—he could follow the ascent of the shuttle like a pulse in his vein, a tingle of power running up and down his bones. He could *feel* that.

"Very economical thrust, Peter," Johnny said, perusing the printout on the generator control panel. "That's the third one in a row at that level gestalt. I think we can now establish certain parameters to power usage in bad-weather launches— even if I still can't tell *how* you do it." He made a disgruntled noise in his throat. The ex-etop pilot had been hoping that he could learn Peter's gestalt link by following his mind during a launch. He and Rhyssa had decided that the fact that he had only latent kinetic Talent might be all to the good—for a pure kinetic might be unable to adapt to Peter's ways. But he had had no more luck than Sascha at discerning the boy's method.

"Maybe you're trying too hard, JG," Peter suggested. "I keep as open as I can . . ."

"I know you do, lad. Wide open. I'm just too clumsy to get through the door. I think it's going to *have* to be a trained kinetic."

"Second-stage ignition," the controller said, alerted by his board. "On its way! You do good work, Pete. Good work."

"C'mon, time for your swimming lesson, Pete," Johnny said. "Gotta keep you fit enough to launch these birds."

"Can't I stay? To be sure it docks okay?" Peter would not admit, even deep in his skull where Rhyssa might see, that he did not have enough energy left immediately after a launch to move from the couch. He grasped at any excuse to gain the few necessary moments to reenergize himself.

"The bird's okay," the controller assured him.

"Look all you want," Johnny said, reseating himself. If he had guessed Peter's secret, he never let on.

The spectators below were beginning to file out of the gallery, hunching into wet-weather gear, bracing themselves for the stiff winds. With a wink, the controller turned on the intercom.

"I tell you, Senator, it is a measure of the state of the art in space technology that we're now able to launch *despite* the weather."

"If I had a nickel for every hold I've had to wait through, m'boy, I'd be able to buy drinks for the entire base. Just how much did you say this new technology cost us?"

The figure mentioned by the congressman was three times as much as Peter's contract had actually cost. And nearly one hundred percent more than the generator.

Peter grinned broadly, thoroughly enjoying the eavesdropping. He had been appalled at how much a big generator cost—though Colonel Greene assured him that it was a pittance when compared to other items purchased for Canaveral—and he could not believe the contract figure for his short-term services. Not to mention the bonuses for every successful launch. He had been even more delighted when Rhyssa suggested that the Center increase the pension that was being sent to his parents.

Talents were generally not contracted until they were at least eighteen years old, but the circumstances and his unusual ability had been construed as sufficient to make an exception— a brief exception.

Vernon's advice to the Center had been that if the technology *cost*, it was bound to be considered more efficient than something in the medium range. The difference between fact and fiction went into the Center's research fund.

At that, it had taken some finagling on Altenbach's part to get the Canaveral staff to consider the "new technology," even with the enthusiastic assistance of General Halloway and Colonel Straub. Peter had not been mentioned; the generators had, plus some very odd "instrumentation." Peter, in fact, had been hidden behind a screen with Rhyssa when the "new technology" had had its first test. He had kinetically flown a drone from Canaveral to Eglin Field despite gale-force winds and a ceiling of 100 meters. He had landed it right on the target painted on the runway—to show the precision of the "new technology." He was then allowed to launch a loaded drone into orbit, where it could be retrieved by a Padrugoi-based craft. His precision again was the deciding factor: so many drones had wandered off course that the drone program had been drastically curtailed.

Two days later a proper shuttle launch was grudgingly permitted. There was no foreseeable change in the terrible weather patterns, and shipments had fallen weeks behind delivery. That first morning, Peter had been a trifle anxious, and the shuttle had ascended at such an astonishing rate that the controllers had thought that a misfire had occurred, and they had been about to abort the mission. Peter, with Johnny telepathically assisting him, had reduced the thrust and the mission had continued. The pilot later was heard to mention that his instrumentation had registered a g-force of 11 for the first few moments—he had been scared shitless thinking he would not even be able to activate the escape-pod control on his armrest.

The "new technology" improved in finesse over the ensuing launches, and NASA breathed a corporate sigh of relief that it could complete all the programmed supply runs to Padrugoi.

Rhyssa and Johnny watched the expression on the boy's rapt face as he followed the current shuttle's progress. The controller handed them coffee as they waited through Peter's absorption.

"Okay," the boy said finally, as the screen showed the shuttle nearing its docking rendezvous and he had recovered sufficiently. "The new technology is ready for its swim." Though still a bit weak, he managed a proper descent from his chair, raising his right hand in a creditable wave to the controller as he maneuvered the steps to the ground exit of the room.

It had taken four launches before the mission launch controller was comfortable with "new technology" and Peter's peculiar part in its schematics, but he had come to like the youngster and had given up trying to figure out how he did what he did—whatever it was.

"Get your slicker on, Pete," Johnny said.

Peter had discovered that he could kinetically keep rain from soaking him, but he tried to resist the temptation to show off unnecessarily. Dutifully he flipped the slicker over him. Exiting the concrete bunker, they all made a dash for their waiting aircar.

Two weeks after Rhyssa and Peter went to Florida, Boris made one of his rare visits to the Center to apprise Sascha of the fact that undercover agents believed more children had been sold. The agents had noticed a lot of floaters being spent in Linears A, B, and C. So Cass and Suz were sent on assignment to Linear E. As the two women frequented all the Jersey Linears, they were known to the inhabitants. Cass's pregnancy made her even less suspicious, and she pretended ill health to account for Suz's company. So far they had nothing to report, not even a ripple of expectation. Whenever contact permitted, they stuck a locating strand in the hair of each child they encountered.

Similar teams were stranding Linear children throughout the Jerhattan area. Scan teams worked around the clock, waiting for a strand to show up in an unlikely area.

Boris made one of his rare visits to the Center. "You know, Bro," he said, "we've got nothing but stopgap techniques. Planting a telempath won't stop kids being abducted." Sascha was in Rhyssa's office, attending to routine administration de-

tails as he took a break from formulating new testing procedures. Boris was standing at the window, looking out on the
peaceful scene below.

"No, no, no, and no, Bro," Sascha said without looking up
from the monitor. He made a rapid motion across the keyboard, then swiveled about to give his brother a hard stare.
"There is no way in which I'll permit Tirla to be used as bait!"

"But she's a natural," Boris said. "She knows how to decipher Linear rumors the way no other operative available to
us can."

"You think I,"—Sascha jabbed his chest with his fingers—
"would risk her?"

"Candidly, I don't think Tirla would be at risk," Boris went
on, beginning to pace. "We could put her in with Cass and
Suz, set her up with every telltale known to technology. She
knows Linears, she can speak any lingo, she's clever as can
stare, and—"

"She's twelve years old and you're not using her as bait,"
Sascha roared, not bothering to dampen his outrage and fury.

Boris regarded him with surprise. "That kid was never
twelve! And what's the matter with using the one advantage
we've found in dealing with Linear abductions? She's got a
unique Talent, a natural camouflage, and an ability for this sort
of thing. Look how she managed in Linear G."

"Linear G was a once-off. I'm not putting her at risk like
that again."

"She was never at risk. Except maybe from you!" Boris
glared right back at his brother. "And this was Cass's idea. I
think it has potential. One thing sure, Bro—unless we can get
at the mastermind behind this despicable traffic, we're going
to be losing kids. Kids who might well be Talented, too."

"You step up your search-and-seizes, Boris. Leave Tirla out
of your calculations. There are other ways, ethical and tech-
nological ways, to solve LEO problems."

"Sascha, if I had the personnel to do it the hard way, I would," Boris replied, his face reddening in an effort to keep his temper in the face of his twin's intransigence.

"Use some of the Linear G kids as bait then. They'd love a chance to get out of the hostel!"

Boris gave his brother one long look. "You know, that's not a bad idea. I'll check 'em out." With that he strode out of the room.

CHAPTER 14

espite the work, those last three weeks in Florida had been almost vacation time for Rhyssa, John Greene, and Peter. Launching thirteen of the eighteen supply shuttles occupied two or three hours of a day at the most for Peter.

When Johnny Greene started to explain the mechanics of lift, trajectory, orbiting, and other such matters pertaining to the job at hand, he and Rhyssa discovered that there were woeful gaps in Peter's education. He had not even had bedside schooling during his months in the hospital. So a telempathic tutor was immediately hired.

Alan Eton quickly discovered that Peter had the usual boyish disregard for grammar, spelling, and syntax, though his vocabulary skills were, in technical areas, beyond his age group. His mathematics were well into first-year university, and his understanding of certain aspects of physics was curiously advanced. With the colonel as his role model, Peter was eager to progress in those sciences. Taking advantage of the boy's admiration, John Greene suggested that he had better improve his computer and English skills, as well, even if he was kinetically superior. While Peter understood some chemical and biological concepts—particularly those that had a bearing on his accident—he had, naturally, had no laboratory experience. A course of study was initiated and regular school hours kept, with Alan guiding Peter deftly into independent study of whatever the boy wanted to learn while filling in the more obvious lacks. A university degree, bachelor or advanced, was not at issue for Peter Reidinger: his career was well underway, but if he was to develop to his full potential, it was essential for him to have an overall understanding of many disciplines. Occasionally, as he struggled through his lessons, he wondered how Tirla was doing and what sort of training Sascha was giving her.

Physiotherapy was still a necessity, and without the inhibiting body brace Peter had no trouble exercising his limbs, which he did religiously, hoping to acquire some muscle.

"There have been instances," the physiotherapist had told Rhyssa and Johnny, "where even badly damaged neural tissue has been stimulated. That's what we can wish for Peter. To feel and to move normally."

"What's the probability?" Rhyssa asked.

The physiotherapist had shrugged ruefully. "Who knows? It certainly does no harm for him to exercise kinetically. Improves muscle tone and fluidity of movement. I'll be honest, I wouldn't have guessed he was walking kinetically when he entered the gym the first time."

Swimming was Peter's favorite sport. Water supported his body, and with minimal effort he could give the illusion of swimming. He could even do incredible dives off the board, hovering in the air as he made his body twist and then entering the water cleanly. There had not been enough sun in those weeks to produce a tan, but surrogate facilities had given him an excellent color. Rhyssa had benefited, as well.

"You needed this rest," Johnny told her as they lounged on the sunbeds while keeping an eye on Peter, who was splashing happily about in the pool, pretending he was a dolphin.

"You know," she said with a deep sigh, "I think I did. It's been pretty hectic the last few months." She sighed again. "But that's the rigors of being Center director—and I wouldn't be anything else in *spite* of the negatives."

"You ever going to marry, or have kids?" Johnny asked at his most casual.

"Johnny Greene, what are you leading up to?" She cocked an eyebrow, which warned him that, if he was not straight with her, she would probably winkle the information out of his mind.

Johnny gave her a rakish grin. "Nothing—except that Dave Lehardt just arrived." His grin broadened as he saw her reaction. "Ah! So! You're not entirely immune to his charm, after all."

Rhyssa managed a laugh, though she could not hide the sudden flush of pleasure at the news. "How do you know? You can't 'hear' him if I can't."

"I saw him get out of the car. He's coming around through the house." The gleam in Johnny's eyes was intolerable to her.

"We're just working friends," she said, and heard a mental ha-ha from Johnny as Dave Lehardt strode into the pool room. Johnny chuckled again as Dave's glance rested on her just that moment longer before he greeted the others.

"Hi there, Skeleteam," Dave called to Peter, who had an arm looped around the pool stair rail. "Need a hand out?"

"I think you'd better, Pete," Rhyssa said. "Your lips are blue, and your skin's wrinkled. Hi, Dave."

Johnny, on a tight band: *You'd make a good team, you know. His beauty and your intelligence!*

Rhyssa projected an image of herself chasing Johnny with an outsized hunk of wood with the words "blunt instrument" carved on it.

Johnny: *Dorotea thinks so, too.*

Rhyssa: *You guys let me do my own thinking.*

Johnny: *Dave will, because he can't hear you. And that's about the only drawback. He lusts after you, you know.*

"Really impressive launch today, Pete," Dave went on,

hauling the boy out of the pool by one arm and deftly covering him with a huge towel.

"He gets better every time," Johnny said, latching onto a spare lounger with his artificial foot and hauling it closer to where he and Rhyssa were sitting.

Rhyssa: *You watch yourself, John Greene. I've my own minder,* she recalled with amusement Peter's handy treatment of the annoying Prince Phanibal, *and I'll tell him to dunk you if you misbehave.*

Johnny sent her an image of wide-eyed innocence. *Me? Step out of line—especially if you threaten to short-circuit my cybernetic limbs in a lousy pool? D'you know what salt water does to my spare parts?* He imaged a violent shudder that sent bits and pieces spinning off his artificial arm and leg.

"Actually, the last three shoots have been within a jog of the same power settings," Rhyssa said to the new arrival.

Dave Lehardt periscoped his lean length to seat himself on a lounger and grinned at Rhyssa. Was she imagining that his eyes were warmer when he looked at her? Damn him for not having a Talent! Damn him for having such a naturally dense mental shield! She had no real clue—except in blue eyes she wanted to drown in—to go on. No wonder the unTalented regularly bungled relationships. And yet . . .

"NASA is delighted with the effectiveness of its new guidance-and-tracking system," Dave was saying, looking well pleased, "and they're quite happy to leave it in the 'need to know' category. More queries from Padrugoi, requesting details of this top-secret G and T as a possible adjunct to their systems."

"And?" Johnny queried, flipping over on the sunbed, eyes narrowed to slits and his body relaxing in the warmth.

"General Halloway hems and haws with the best of them about a trial model, with a formidable test schedule ahead of it, by no means a totally proven system . . ."

"I am too a proven system," Peter said, looking disgruntled

as he floated over, an eerie-looking maneuver since his feet
were invisible under the swathing of towel that he was trying
to keep out of the puddles around the pool. His teeth chattered.

"Oh here," Rhyssa said, making room for him on the
sunbed. She would have fallen off if Dave had not quickly prevented it with hands and knees. She felt warm where he
touched her, a warmth that was nothing generated by a sunbed.
Then she settled Peter beside her, adjusting his limbs. "You're
up to fifteen minutes' sunning today, aren't you?"

"Tell you one thing," Dave went on, still supporting Rhyssa's body. "I'm going to have to change the nickname Skeleteam. You don't look so much like one anymore."

"All this good wholesome Florida sunshine," Peter said,
grinning at Dave. He had finally gotten over his jealousy of the
PR man: it was difficult to be jealous of a guy he liked so much,
who could think up neat treats and found the best places to
eat. Johnny often argued to Rhyssa—when Dave was not
around—that the man had to have Talent but that it simply
wasn't measurable. Then he discussed things like traumatic
breakthroughs and psychological reluctances, and Rhyssa replied that sometimes it was nice to know someone who could
always surprise you.

"If you see any of that wholesome sunshine, let me know,
huh?" Dave remarked, referring to the fact that the rain had
lifted only briefly in the past three weeks. "When are you guys
going to develop a reliable Weather Talent?"

"Look, we just got one minor miracle up and running,"
Rhyssa replied. "Give us at least three days!"

"God only rested one day," Dave said, deepening his voice
to a bass register and looking pious.

"Three weeks, three months, three years, three decades,"
Johnny replied in a sepulchral tone. "Can't even figure ol'
Petey boy out, and I've been busting my buns for weeks
now." ·

"Pete," Dave began, "how do you see what you do? Might as well ask the source right out straight," he added in a broad aside to Rhyssa.

Peter laughed and pretended to consider the question, knotting his brows and rubbing his chin the way Johnny sometimes did. "It's like I think that's what I want to do—move the shuttle up—and I sort of lean into the generators, revving them up, and then I sort of"—he shrugged his thin shoulders—"let go."

"Like a stone from a slingshot?" Dave asked.

"Yeah, sort of like that."

"You don't sound sure."

"I'm not. It needs doing. I do it."

Rhyssa, sensing Peter's distress about being unable to explain adequately, put a warning hand on Dave's knee. His hand immediately covered hers, keeping her arm in a slightly awkward position. Over Peter's prone body, Johnny grinned at her.

"There are many operations," Rhyssa went on quickly, "that one accomplishes strictly on an involuntary basis. Like breathing. You don't consciously go through the steps of drawing breath in and exhaling it—it's an involuntary procedure. Or take reaching for a glass. You don't consciously tell your hand to extend the required distance, tell your fingers to encircle it and your arm to lift the light weight. The task is accomplished without much conscious effort. Peter is working on such a deeply involuntary basis that he cannot—yet—analyze the requisite steps. Once Lance Baden is released from durance vile on the station, I think we'll see progress in understanding what Skeleteam does as easily as he breathes."

"It's not quite that easy," Peter said.

"Don't hurt Skeleteam's feelings," Johnny said in mock affront. "He'll strike!"

"Not with his contract, he won't," Rhyssa said feelingly.

"You know, Pete," Johnny began in a thoughtful tone,

"what you said about something needing to be done and doing it. You really *don't* stop to think how? You just do it?"

"As you yourself, if I may remind you, landed a badly damaged shuttle on your twenty-first mission," Dave put in. "Experts still haven't figured out how you did that!"

John Greene grinned at him. "Neither have I. Sorry, Pete."

"You were using kinesis?" Peter asked.

"Nothing else would have gotten us down that day with one wing crumpled and the tail assembly blown off. Technically I had what they call a traumatic explosion of Talent necessitated by an intense urge to survive."

"What hit you?" Peter asked then. He had always wanted to ask, but it had never been quite the right moment and he was not sure if the colonel liked to reminded of how he had lost an arm and a leg.

"Some damned-fool half-trained clowns, doing aerobatics through the flight path," Johnny told him, cursing fluently and inventively on both audible and telepathic levels. Peter's eyes rounded with awe at the flavorful language. "Fortunately they didn't survive to answer to me, or the law, for their antics."

"Oh!" was Peter's reaction to John's uncharacteristic bitterness.

"You're not going to waste the pool, are you, Dave?" Rhyssa asked, to change the subject, and in the hope of regaining control of her hand before her arm fell asleep.

"You're stuck with me for a few days at any rate," Dave replied. "Without benefit of the Skeleteam, the airport's socked in solid." He rose and, whistling a jaunty tune, began to pick his way through the puddles in the direction of the changing room.

Johnny heaved a sigh and resettled himself on the sunbed, hands cushioning his head. The nu-skin sheathing his artificial arm looked real enough except, Rhyssa noticed, that it did not take a tan. Peter, however, was becoming a rich brown that made him appear like any other healthy, if scrawny, boy his age. He was also falling asleep, considerably more tired by the morning's activities than he would ever admit. Smiling tenderly down at the boy, Rhyssa eased herself off the sunbed and onto the lounger that Dave had just vacated. She checked the timer: Peter had ten minutes to go. She relaxed on the soft mattress.

"*Je*-sus *Christ!*"

Dave's sudden expletive roused her, and she watched helplessly as, in midair, he flailed with arms and legs from a slip in a puddle, his long body poised to come down right across the corner of the tiled pool in what would be a serious fall. The sunbed lights went off, and the next instant his abrupt descent was halted and he came to rest gently on the poolside, unharmed, unbruised, but considerably shaken.

"How the hell . . ."

"My God!" Johnny Greene exclaimed. "Did you do that, Pete?" he asked. The very slightest of snores answered him. "My *God*! I did it! I did it! *I did it!*" His voice rose in a crescendo as he stared at Rhyssa in a state of shocked delight and surprise.

Rhyssa began to shake her head, grinning so hard at the breakthrough that she thought her face would split.

"That was all you," she assured him. "Once again Johnny on the spot!"

The moment Dave Lehardt entered the kitchen that evening as Rhyssa was clearing up the debris of their celebratory meal, she knew "a moment" had come. Over the last few months of their close association, she had learned to pick up the subtle hints of his body language and her own responses to him. She felt her heartbeat begin to speed up, and she tried not to crash dishes about or drop things. Worse, she could extract no helpful clues from this man's mind. Perhaps that was

why Dave appeared to be so much more romantic than any of
her Talented associations.

He came right up to her so that she had to look about, to
acknowledge his proximity.

"The hardest thing in dealing with you Talents is to catch
you when no one else is listening," he began. His blue eyes
held a very intense look. He took the saucepan away from her
and returned it to the soapy water, then put both hands on her
arms and turned her slightly but decisively toward him. "Pete
and Johnny are so involved in a rehash of my pratfall, they
couldn't be paying attention to anything else." With a little
pressure of his hands, he pulled her against him.

Johnny: *Don't you dare be coy!*

Rhyssa: *Get out of my head, Johnny Greene.*

Peter: *Ah, just when it's getting interesting. How'll I ever
learn how it's done!*

Rhyssa: *Break off! Both of you! If I feel so much as a ten-
dril of thought . . .*

Johnny: *I think she means it!*

Peter: *I* know *she does!*

Her mind was filled with a deafening silence.

"They're not," Rhyssa assured him.

"I've been told and warned, obliquely and right to my face,
that I've no right to ask a woman of your obvious Talent, and
talents, to marry a man without an ounce of the right stuff in
him."

Rhyssa felt a surge of anger flare deep inside. She wondered who had been inhibiting this wonderful, caring man—
especially considering all he had done to aid Talents. Then she
willed him not to stop talking such marvelously romantic stuff
and tilted her head up encouragingly. She shivered with anticipation.

"But I think such a decision is up to you and me," he went
on. "And I'm so totally besotted with you that I can't think
straight when you're in the same room with me, and I don't

think of much else but you when we're apart. Rhyssa Owen, would you even consider marrying me?"

"What took you so many eons to ask?" she replied, folding her arms about his neck and grinning up at him.

With a gladness that seemed to emanate from every pore of him, he clasped her firmly in his arms and kissed her with a great deal of entirely satisfactory expertise, just as if he had read her mind.

CHAPTER 15

Sascha!
He could not ignore Dorotea's call, but it was coming at an awkward moment. He lifted his hand to signal to Budworth and Sirikit for a slight break in their discussion.

Dorotea's mental tone was colored by vexation. *As you showed her how to use her wristband to purchase damned near anything anywhere, you may now teach her thrift and budgeting. And some sense of order in her own room! There's not an inch of space that isn't stacked ceiling-high with "bargains."*

Sascha: *Where is she?*

Dorotea, at the end of her patience: *Trying on clothes while viewing today's lessons!*

"Look, Bud, run those ethnic groupings again," Sascha ordered. "We've at least got a statistical forecast of how many psionic Talents each generation has produced since Darrow and op Owen's time. Now let's break it down into individual Talent manifestations: precogs, finders, affinities, kinetics, telepaths, telempaths."

Budworth shrugged equably and began to formulate the program.

"I still don't know *how*," Sirikit said in her soft, lilting tones, "that's going to help us discover Talent in the Linears."

"Where there's smoke, there's gotta be a fire or two," Sascha commented cryptically as he exited. But his mind was already on one particular Talent who had come so far from her early years in the Linears.

Since that fateful shopping trip three weeks before, Tirla

had discovered a new pastime that almost rivaled her hunger for learning. At first, Dorotea had been amused. "It's hunger of another sort: acquisition. It'll pass."

Cass had accompanied her on two more expeditions, showing her how to use the subway transport, and thought it was fun to watch Tirla slip into the most exclusive shops and boutiques. Then she had started shopping on her own, and scoffed when Dorotea worried that child-stealers would snatch her.

"Snatch me? Not likely," Tirla replied scathingly. "I can smell their sort coming on the streets. I'm safe in the malls."

But the malls were not free from all peril, for she was detained twice by overzealous officials and, to her credit, had waited patiently until someone—usually Sascha—arrived from the Center to verify her right to wear the ID bracelet and make charges against the Center's account.

She was more amused by the detentions than alarmed, and determined to enjoy her new pastime. Certainly she was not deterred from her expeditions, and since Sascha backed Cass's opinion that Tirla was capable of handling herself, Dorotea's apprehension waned. Invariably, Tirla ended her afternoons at the Old-Fashioned Parlor. When Tirla announced that she was going to work her way right through the five pages of confectionery selections, Dorotea had laughed.

"It might put a little weight on those bird bones of hers, and she always eats her dinner," she said. "I wish she would put on weight. What must those shop attendants think when that child looks half-starved all the time?"

Dorotea was standing in the living room when Sascha arrived in answer to her summons, and she pointed sternly toward Tirla's room. Sascha tapped on the door, and Tirla's cheerful hum broke off.

"Who is it?" There was always that note of apprehension when the girl was caught unawares. Once she could break into the telepathic mode that Sascha was certain she possessed, she would rarely be caught off-guard again.

"Sascha!"

"Just a minute."

For just a moment, Sascha thought he caught a stray coy thought, and then the door opened, in stages, because Tirla had to rearrange things to get it wide enough for him to enter. Sascha looked in and groaned.

"Tirla, what happened to the kid who had to be coaxed into buying more than one outfit?" It was the first thing that came into his head, and it was probably not at all the way to handle the situation.

Dorotea, in disgust: *Ham-handed twit!*

Tirla blinked at Sascha. "But you told me I could shop whenever I wanted to. Just look what I found today!" And she held up a pair of stiletto-heeled sandals with jeweled straps. "And they fit. They didn't cost much, because the shopkeeper had had them around for decades and practically gave them to me. Aren't they lovely? D'you want to see them on? They make me much taller."

"I'm sure they do, Tirla, but to be candid, they're not the sort of thing a girl your age should wear."

"They fit!" she repeated as if that were the most important aspect.

"Tirla! Is there no place I can sit down in here? And that's what has Dorotea so upset. You know how neat she keeps everything in the house."

Dorotea: *That's right. Blame me.*

"While Talents may have what they need, and also what they want, *within reason*," he went on, "that's the operative phrase. This—" He gestured broadly, hooking a hanger and its layers of clothing off the door. The pile tumbled to enlarge a mass of colorful blouses lying beside the door. "This is no longer reasonable!"

Tirla merely looked up at him, her face expressionless, but

he sensed so deep a hurt and disappointment that he relented instantly. "I don't think I can send it all back," she said. "I've tried everything on."

"Look, chip," he said, using Cass's affectionate nickname for her, "sending it all back is not the answer."

It's a start! Dorotea put in.

"Learning to buy wisely is. Some of this stuff—" Sascha pointed to items of intimate apparel in lace and gauze that were far too sophisticated for even a twenty-year-old. "—can be packed up and stored . . ."

Dorotea, acidly: *Where?*

"In the vaults." He began picking up other inappropriate garments. "And we'll get the clutter down to manageable proportions." In doing so he exposed a small hill of shoes, of all colors and in a variety of styles that astonished him—and all of them small enough to fit Tirla's dainty feet.

Dorotea: *Cinderella complex?*

Sascha: *Pairs, every single one of them,* he said wryly.

Dorotea: *Then how can they be pairs?*

"Five pairs of shoes, no more, Tirla." He saw her sulky expression. "Five pairs at one time. And ten different outfits in the closet. None of this . . ." He held up an emerald green ball gown with exquisitely detailed beadwork in silver and leaf green. It was exceedingly stylish, and the color was perfect for Tirla—but not until she reached twenty. Eighteen, at least. "I'll have some trunks sent over so you can put everything away. Then we're going to sit down and work out a budget."

"Budget? Like they do for cities and projects?" Surprised, Tirla came out of her sulk.

"Yes. The Center has a budget, I have a budget, Peter has a budget . . ."

Dorotea: *All God's chillun got budgets!*

"Then I won't be able to go shopping again?"

Sascha was not impervious to her broken voice and her sad

expression. "Shop all you want. Look in every damned mall on Manhattan, Long Island, and the Jersey Shore. Just don't buy anything. Window shop to your heart's content."

"Never buy anything again?"

La da da, da da da dah! Dorotea sang, mimicking a nostalgic violin air.

All right, Sascha retorted. *And how would you curb a kid who's never had much in her life and suddenly can have anything she wants?*

More or less as you're doing, Dorotea admitted. *Just don't waver at the sight of tears in her big black eyes!*

Sascha caught an undertone in Dorotea's voice that puzzled him. But he ignored it and returned his full attention to Tirla. "No, chip, not never. Just not so much so constantly, things you don't really need right now, because you've got enough— of practically everything, as far as I can see."

She sank to the edge of her barely visible bed. "But it's not fun to window shop unless you've got someone with you. Where's Cass? She loves to shop."

"Cass is out on assignment."

Tirla cocked her head up at him, no longer a disappointed and confused twelve-year-old. "More kids missing?"

"Not yet," he said mendaciously. "We want to keep it that way."

"Is she in a Linear?" Excitement brightened her expression. Sascha nodded.

Dorotea: *For the love of little apples, don't tell her where, or she'll track Cass down.*

"Why don't you let me work undercover with her? I could be her kid and—"

"No!"

Tirla rocked back on the bed at the vehemence of his response. She looked hurt and confused again and even younger than her chronological age.

"Sorry, chip." Sascha ruffled her sleek and shining hair in an effort to compensate for his tactlessness. "Give yourself a little break. We didn't catch Yassim, and if he spots you, he'd have you wasted so fast, none of us could help you."

Tirla noticeably paled.

Dorotea: *Well, she's still afraid of Yassim!*

Tirla seemed so afraid that Sascha gathered her up in his arms and rocked her. "Yassim can't get you here in the Center, Tirla. You're safe here. I want to keep you safe so you can grow up and use that rare Talent you have . . . to earn enough money to pay for all you've been buying." He tried to make a joke of it. He felt her stiffen in his arms. "No, not your float-ers!" And he had to laugh. The little witch. Her hoard was precious to her, never to be broached. "Just think how little you'd have left if you *had* spent your stash. Think of that the next time you want to buy something. Pretend you're spending *your* money."

"I *wouldn't* spend *my* money," she mumbled against his chest.

With the slender little body curled trustfully in his lap, Sascha permitted himself just a few moments to caress her hair and savor the feel of her in his arms. Why Tirla? Of all the women in the world, how could this little waif, streetwise and precocious, have become so entangled in his emotions and heart? She could not possibly understand how much she meant to him. She was far too young for that aspect of maturing to have touched her. And yet . . . she responded to him as she did to no one else. With a final little hug, he put her from him as gently as he could. One day, eight or nine years in the future . . .

Dorotea had no comment to make. To his surprise, Tirla obediently began to fold up her possessions, neatly and care-fully. Sascha watched for a few more moments and then went to arrange for trunks.

P eter and Rhyssa returned in quiet triumph the day that Cass
Cutler reported to Boris that three Neesters and two Hispanics in Linear E were suspiciously more affluent than they
had any right to be. Boris decided that he would not darken
the happy return with such news and did not even inform Sascha of the event.

Dorotea and Tirla both exclaimed over how well Peter
looked, tanned and healthy and moving with more confidence,
while Rhyssa listened, an oddly soft smile on her face. Dave
Lehardt had remained behind in Florida to finalize his PR campaign, setting the stage for Colonel Johnny Greene to assume
the role of Skeleteam.

In his turn, Peter took full notice of Tirla's new elegance
and was amazed that she had shopped the malls herself.

"Well, Sascha took me the first time," she admitted.

Dorotea, privately to Rhyssa: *And said "Open Sesame,"*
and in a week Tirla's room was as full as a bazaar.

Sascha: *I heard that. Knock it off!*

Rhyssa: *Did she pick that outfit herself?*

Dorotea: *She picked out everything herself and a lot of*
things a twelve-year-old girl has no need of—yet.

Rhyssa: *She's got good taste—in what she's wearing now.*

Dorotea: *Good taste all round. Just a trifle sophisticated.*

Aware that Sascha was seething, Dorotea changed the subject.

Peter and Tirla slipped out of the room.

"How come you're allowed to go to the mall all the time?"
Peter asked Tirla, envious of her freedom. *He* was never allowed to go anywhere on his own.

Tirla shrugged. "Oh, they tried to tell me how dangerous
it was." She giggled. "As if I didn't know how to take care of
myself in any old Linear. Particularly one as straight as the ones
here in Jerhattan."

"And you go whenever you want?"

"Nearly every day." She cocked her head at him. "You

ever been to the Old-Fashioned Parlor of Gastronomical Delights?''

"Me?" Peter thumped his hand against his chest, then grimaced. He still didn't have the small-muscle control needed to use just a thumb or a finger. He was feeling aggrieved on several counts. "Oh, I heard about the Parlor." He pretended indifference, but then his pose faltered. "Is it really that good?"

"Good?" Tirla's enthusiasm bubbled out of her. "It's spectacular. You wouldn't believe the concoctions they serve. 'The most,' " she quoted from the menu, " 'scrumptious, delectable monstrosities of confections you'll ever experience.' " Sensing Peter's longing, Tirla deliberately encouraged it. "Any kind of flavor of ice cream, all homemade, every topping known to man . . ."

"And you just go?"

"Sure. Why not? It's only four stops away on the subway." She jerked her thumb at the murmur of adult voices coming from the living room. "Who'd miss us for half an hour, anyway?" When she saw the hesitation on his face, she added almost challengingly, "They're busy. We'd be back before they'd know we'd gone!"

That decided Peter, though he knew perfectly well that his physical circumstances were far different from Tirla's. Nevertheless, she was younger than he was, and if she was allowed, he was, too.

They left the house by the side door, Tirla skipping beside Peter in delight at his company. It was going to be such fun showing him just how well she knew her way around.

Peter could sense how pleased Tirla was to be able to take him someplace familiar to her but new to him. So he just smiled as they took their seats on the subway from the Center platform. Other Talents on the same car grinned at the two, sending telepathic greetings and congratulations to Peter, who had learned to assume a modest demeanor in public, even among other Talents.

Tirla was describing in great detail her favorite gastronomical delight—the one with four kinds of ice cream, four kinds of toppings, four kinds of nuts, and cherries, coconut, and multicolored sprinkles.

"My mother took me to a place like that," Peter said, "oh, a long time ago now. For my tenth birthday. My sister goes a lot; Mother says that's why she has spots so often."

"Spots?"

"Pimples. Zits. Facial eruptions."

"Oh," Tirla replied in a tone that expressed unenlightenment. Peter imaged a pimpled face at her. "Oh! That sort." Surreptitiously she ran her hand over her face.

Peter laughed. "You may never get spots, Tirla," Peter said encouragingly. "They keep us on a healthy diet anyhow. Not subbie food."

"What was Florida like?" Tirla asked.

Peter had learned a lot from watching Dave Lehardt answer difficult questions tactfully. So he told her about the flat land and the palm trees, the sand, the good food, the pool, and the sunbeds, and she seemed quite content at his implication that he and Rhyssa had been taking a holiday.

She assumed leadership as soon as they reached the right station and eagerly started running up the steps ahead of him before she remembered his disability. When she stopped, he was right beside her.

"Your vacation did you a lot of good, didn't it?" she said, and plowed on upward. "See—there's the Parlor, just inside the mall entrance," she added, pointing.

Neither youngster noticed that their progress was being closely observed by two men, just descending from an elegant private hopper parked on the mall's helipad. The shorter man took a small black instrument from his pocket and pointed it at them.

"How exceedingly careless. Neither of them has been stranded! I want them taken! Especially that odious little boy! I want no slipup, no excuses. You won't have too much trouble with the boy, but his companion mustn't be allowed to spread an alarm. Do it as fast as you can assemble a crew. Have I made myself plain?"

"Yes, sir."

P eter was able to shout just once, his cry more indignant than alarmed. Then an ominous silence descended despite Rhyssa's attempts to reestablish communications. She wasted no more time on the silence but broadcast on the widest band possible.

ALERT, ALL TALENTS, ALL LEO PERSONNEL! Peter Reidinger may have been abducted. Presumably in vicinity of Old-Fashioned Parlor. Tirla was with him.

TIRLA! Sascha's blast was nearly as loud as hers.

Complying! came Boris's calming bass tone. *All units in the area are to commence search procedures. Fax photos of the children are being dispatched to all vehicles. I'm proceeding immediately to question any possible witnesses. This is a Top Priority.*

This is a G and H Priority! Sascha added with bitter vehemence. *Sirikit, what does Budworth have on the strand scanner?* There was a long and stunned pause. *Oh, my God. I never stranded Tirla. Rhyssa?*

Peter neither, was Rhyssa's horrified reply. *How could we have been so* stupid?

You weren't, Dorotea said in a bracing tone. *Their ID bracelets can be traced far more accurately than a stranded kid.*

The exchanges had taken bare seconds while Rhyssa, Sascha, and Dorotea sped toward the Control Room, where the monitoring equipment would, they hoped, be able to give them some indication of where the children were.

Budworth was in front of the appropriate screen, his face twisted by anger and distress. "Bracelets were cut off. Scanner has 'em in a sewer drain in the mall heli-lot."

"Oh, my God!" Sascha's exclamation came out in a sob, then he shook himself. *Carmen, get in here. Bertha, Auer, you come, too. Dorotea, any chance that you can reach Tirla?*

If you can't, I'm not likely to. There was a quality of ineffable sorrow in her response. *She's keyed to you like no one else.*

"There's nothing, nothing there at all," Rhyssa murmured, her voice breaking. "I've always been able to hear Peter's mind."

"Not if he's been anesthetized, my dear," Dorotea said. "That's the only time he couldn't hear or answer." Then she spoke to Sirikit on a very tight band. *Phone Dave Lehardt and tell him to get here as fast as he can.*

Sirikit, her own eyes bleak, discreetly complied.

"C'mon, Bro, c'mon! How long does it take your squads to get moving!" Sascha demanded, pacing anxiously.

The Talents had to wait another five agonizing minutes before Boris contacted them.

The kids sat by themselves. Tirla's well known here, and she introduced her friend, Peter, to her usual waitress. She saw them leave the place. She caught a glimpse of them entering a small hopper with the Talent Center emblem. There were four men, but she didn't see their faces. She didn't see anything odd, except that the boy walked funny and then seemed to be assisted by one of the men. And no, she didn't notice the registration. I've an APB on small hoppers with Talent emblems in Jerhattan, but it'd be helpful if your scanners have picked up their bracelets.

Sascha: *The IDs were cut off. Left in the sewer outside the mall.*

Boris: *That would be the first thing. So, can you pick some-thing up yet on the strand scanners?*

Rhyssa, heavily: *Neither Peter nor Tirla was stranded.*

Boris, exploding: *In the name of all that's holy, why not? The two most important young Talents? You have everyone running about like lunatics, stranding dumb subbie kids and pampered hive children, and you don't strand Peter and Tirla?* The silence following his outburst was more eloquent than anything he could have added.

Rhyssa began to weep, and Dorotea tried to comfort her, tactilely and telepathically.

All right, then, Boris went on in a calmer tone. *We have to assume the abductors are following their latest procedures. That's the only thing that would account for total telepathic silence. The kids were gassed. They're going to be stashed someplace and in those neat little cocoons. Sorry, Rhyssa, but I'm too angry to be diplomatic. Sascha, have you called Car-men in? My finders are all on the case. Somehow, we'll find 'em. Those kids are smart. Once they wake up, they'll be able to help us find them.*

Suz and Cass further dampened the spirits of the Talents by reporting that in excess of thirty children in each Residential had been sold, or just taken. Ranjit, working covertly in Residential W, also confirmed evidence of more activity in the mall markets than could be discreetly ignored. Such scope and audacity was more than LEO or the Center had anticipated. All had happened so smoothly and simultaneously that both the Center and LEO had been caught unawares.

"My sympathies go out to Rhyssa and the other Talents. It's incredible that two valuable young people like that could also be vulnerable to this despicable group," the city manager told Boris, who passed her message on to Sascha and Rhyssa. "This has top priority, and all the resources of the city are at your disposal. No effort will be spared. Is there anything I, personally, can do? Offer a reward? Trade immunity for information?"

"Get your department heads thinking," Boris told City Commissioner Teresa Aiello, "where such a significant number of children could be detained. I've got every available person on transport surveillance. They can't have been moved out of the Jerhattan area, not in a group or singly. I put a hold on all rail freight and every container is being examined. Any cargo of a suspicious size is being opened. They've got to be somewhere nearby—for a while."

"Everyone on this staff will start examining possibilities— unused warehouses, old buildings, underground stores," Teresa assured Boris grimly.

Boris Roznine did not have quite all his people on transport duty—he had a good third picking up as many ladrones and sassins as his teams found in mall or factory areas. LEO might just luck out and dislodge a clue from an apprehensive subbie.

"Peter is alive, isn't he?" Budworth asked, too concerned to be tactful.

"He's alive. It's not a dead silence," Rhyssa said, wincing at her choice of adjective, her voice low with tension. "But he's not conscious."

"Nothing yet, Carmen?" Sascha asked the finder, whose hands were stroking the lock of Tirla's hair. She could not meet his eyes as she shook her head slowly.

"Christ on a crutch! How could we be so arrogant as to believe we could protect them with an ID bracelet!" Sascha demanded explosively, stalking around what free floor space there was. "*Why* on *Earth* didn't we think to strand them?" He pounded one fist into the other hand. "We've wall-to-wall Talents," he said, gesturing almost scornfully at the various teams clustered about monitors or swiftly feeding programs into the mainframe. "Where could they have got to? That many bodies are too hard to hide. The kids have to be fed. They can't have been whisked off to their—" Sascha could not find the appropriate noun and grimaced. "Wherever. Boris initiated transport surveillance within minutes. Dammit, the subways and cargo routes have been wired since the incident in G.''

Sascha, ease up, Dorotea told him, her warning a very narrow quiet thought. *Rhyssa's feeling guilty enough as it is . . .*

Sascha: *And you think I feel none for not stranding Tirla, for encouraging her to go to the bloody mall? To that unmentionable bloody confectionery parlor?* Sascha's response was loaded with derision. *She'd've been bloody safer if I* had *let Boris use her for bait!*

Dorotea: *Stop castigating yourself, Sascha. Tirla's been safely in and out of the mall and the parlor for weeks now.*

Rhyssa, brokenly: *Peter's worked so hard . . . What could have possessed him to take such a risk?*

Dorotea: *He is just a boy, for all his power. Don't worry, we'll hear. The least whisper, and we'll hear them.* Dorotea's mind cast restlessly for a trace of Tirla's. After nearly five weeks of proximity with the girl, she should be able to spot her consciousness.

MAY ALL YOUR ORIFICES BE CLOGGED WITH CAMEL DUNG, YOUR BELLY ETERNALLY FULL OF VOMIT! MAY YOUR TONGUE ROT AND YOUR TEETH FALL OUT AND YOUR GUMS SWELL WITH BOILS! MAY YOUR LIVER ROT AND YOUR BLADDER DRY UP AND YOUR GLANDS SHRIVEL AND PUTREFY!

"Good God!" Dorotea was jolted to her feet. "Did you all hear that? It was loud enough!"

"Peter doesn't know that kind of language!" Rhyssa said, with a slight grin.

"Tirla would," Sascha replied, beaming from ear to ear. "Pungent, isn't she? Damn, where's she got to? I can't hear her anymore."

"Well, I can, and she's still in fine form," Dorotea said. "Neither of you hear her now? She can certainly broadcast when she's of a mind to." She held up her hand, listening, every muscle taut. *Dorotea here, Tirla. Can you hear me?* Dorotea's mental tone was tranquil and reassuring.

Tirla: *Dorotea? Where are* you?

Dorotea: *More to the point, where are you?* "Can you hear her now, Sascha, Rhyssa?" she asked. Two brief head-shakes confirmed Dorotea as the primary contact. She felt the light, firm mental touches of Rhyssa and Sascha, listening in.

Tirla, savagely: *You tell me. I can't see a thing. I can't feel a thing. I can smell, and the stench is worse than the bottom level of a factory bilge. Couldn't you guys track me?*

No, we couldn't, Tirla. Your bracelets were discarded right at the mall when you and Peter were taken. Is Peter nearby? Sascha had motioned Carmen over, but Carmen kept shaking her head at her continued inability to find Tirla. *Can you remember what happened?* Dorotea went on.

Tirla's disgust was obvious. *I can't remember anything. Peter and I finished the new spectacular they just added to the menu. He paid for it himself. Said it was his treat this time 'cause he'd just had a vacation. We left the Parlor and were walking toward the subway when something covered my face, and I don't remember a thing more. Awful stuff. Sweet icky smell. How come I can talk to you all of a sudden?*

Sometimes it's a case of need-to, Tirla, Dorotea said, putting a smile of approval into her mental tone.

You needed me to? Tirla asked. *Or I needed you to hear me? Peter? Peter, answer me!* Dorotea caught the conflicting emotions in Tirla's question, but such competitiveness was not a bad sign.

You and Peter were not the only two taken today. Cass and Suz reported that a number must have been taken from E, as well. A very well-organized affair. That's why anything you can tell us will help, Tirla. Anything, no matter how trivial.

Peter's not answering me in here. Maybe he's just not awake yet. My stomach's sour. I shouldn't've had that spectacular. Peter? Peeeeter!

Dorotea spoke gently. *Don't panic, Tirla. Peter will wake up soon enough if he was gassed the same time as you were. We're very relieved to hear from you, believe me.*

Tirla, mildly surprised: *I do believe you. You can't lie in your mind, can you?*

Not to me, you can't, Dorotea replied, gesturing imperiously for Rhyssa and Sascha to stop trying to insinuate questions into her head. Tirla's voice was clear but, after the first burst of psychic outrage, neither as strong nor as loud. She could not risk losing the link. *Now, tell me what you can about your surroundings.*

They stink!

We've already established that. What of? Besides, I assume, the unpleasant bodily discharges of frightened children. What can you hear?

Tirla, disgusted: *A lot of crying.*

Even that tells me something, Tirla. Can you isolate the individual crying enough to estimate how many children are around you?

Dorotea could sense Tirla's concentration and did not interrupt.

Tirla: *I think there's a lot of kids. There's sure a lot of crying and moaning, and someone's hiccuping. All around me, all sides, above, but none below. Why'd they blindfold us and tie us down like this? Most of these kids wouldn't even try to escape.*

Dorotea: *Yassim lost all the G children, didn't he? I think that, unfortunately, that caused him to change his tactics. He's now employing a disorientation technique, sensory deprivation, to reduce the children to compliance when they are released. You're not afraid, are you?*

Tirla, candidly: *I don't like it, but I'm not scared. I'm mad.* Her tone strengthened. *I missed my math class.*

Dorotea broke into relieved laughter. An angry Tirla would

be far more useful than a frightened one. Sascha managed a relieved chuckle, and the tension in Rhyssa's stance eased.

Dorotea: *Stay mad, Tirla. Anger can be a valuable asset. Now what I want you to do is try and calm the children. Get them to tell you their names and, if possible, where they came from. E and R were not the only Linears hit. We estimate that upward of a hundred children were taken.*

Including Peter and me?

A hundred and two. Look, Tirla, we're going to have to rely heavily on you to help us find you, Peter, and the others. Dorotea gave Rhyssa a raised eyebrow at her smothered protest. "Candidly, that child is lot better able to take care of herself."

Rely on me? How? I'm blind and strapped in like cargo! Hey, you lot! Shut up! Quit your grizzling, stupid Neesters. Tirla then dropped into languages that Dorotea could not understand. *They prefer crying for their mommies! Mommies who sold 'em!* Tirla said, suddenly dropping into Basic again. *Some half dozen are from E, seven are from W, and two from C. How they bleat! None of 'em's Peter.*

Dorotea: *Ask them their names.*

Tirla could give ten names of the estimated fifteen children in with her. These were instantly forwarded to Boris.

"Where can Peter be?" Rhyssa murmured softly. At some point while she had been concentrating on Dorotea's conversations, Dave Lehardt had joined the anxious group in the Control Room. He linked his fingers in hers, and the physical contact was almost more reassuring than the aura of encouragement that emanated from all the telepaths about her.

"Ask her again about the various smells," Sascha prompted Dorotea. "There may be *something* that'll give us a clue to where."

Well, there's a sort of metal stink, Tirla replied when Dorotea relayed the question. *And there's a moldy mildewing rot-*

ten stink that's stronger. There's another smell I can't identify. Oily. I'm stuffed into something—feels like plastic foam. Even my fingers are separated into slots. I'm bound at the wrists, ankles, waist, and across my chest. If I was shorter, I'd be choking. Oh, cut the caterwauling! No one's hurting you! She roared out repetitions in other dialects, continuing to broadcast mentally as she shouted at the other children.

"Her predicament is beginning to get to her," Dorotea said grimly. *Tirla, I'm with you. Even if you can't hear them, Rhyssa, Sascha, Boris, Sirikit, Budworth, Dave—we're all here. We'll get you out of there, I promise.*

Tirla: *Soon, please. If I have to listen to all this crying and moaning much longer, I'll space out. What about that woman who wore my hair? Why don't you ask her where I am?*

Carmen is right here and reminds you that she needs light to find you! Remember? That's why she couldn't locate you in the Linear—you were in the dark.

Tirla, wryly: *I'm a lot more in the dark now than I was then. What if they don't turn any lights on?* For the first time, her voice was tinged more with fear than with outrage.

Dorotea: *It may be no consolation to you right now, Tirla, but they'll want you to be in good condition. They'll also have to feed you and keep you clean.*

Tirla: *Yeah? When? Next week sometime?*

You were taken at approximately three. It's ten-thirty now. You can't be left without food and water much longer.

Tirla: *You're right. That's not much consolation. Dorotea, don't stop talking to me, will you? I don't care what you say. Just don't stop talking.*

I'm totally at your command, Tirla. Dorotea projected an image of a flourish and a curtsy. She was rewarded by a little chuckle. *Shall we start with the math lesson you missed?*

Tirla, surprised: *In my head?*

Dorotea: *Write it on the board in my mind. I'll remember for you.*

"And also increase her telepathic facility," Rhyssa said with a genuine smile. "You are incorrigible, Dorotea."

"Also very good at what I do," the old woman replied smugly.

Rhyssa? Rhyssa?

Rhyssa gasped with incredulity, stricken by the faintness of Peter's call. Dave wrapped an arm about her shoulders, supporting her as she held up her hand to stop all noise in the room as the weak voice reached her mind. *Yes, Peter. I've been listening for you.*

Peter: *I can't see anything. They gassed me. I'm going to be sick.*

Rhyssa kept her mental tone calm and firm as she clung to Dave's hands. *Easy, Peter. Remember our drills. Reduce the nausea.*

It's never been this hard before, Rhyssa. There was an edge of despair in his voice. Rhyssa knew so well how he hated anesthetics. He had reactions to most of the common ones. It was going to take time—which she did not think they had—for him to shake off the residual disorientation and nausea in order to bring his kinesis into use.

Rhyssa: *Focus your mind, Peter, just as you used to do in the hospital. Focus your thoughts; ignore the extraneous.*

Peter: *There're other kids in here with me. Some of 'em are pretty scared.*

Rhyssa: *Call out for Tirla. She's somewhere—maybe very nearby.*

Dorotea, urgently: *Tirla, Peter's awake. Call his name.*

Neither heard the other.

"Christ! Fine team of Talents we are when our kids are vulnerable!" Sascha remarked caustically.

Tirla, echoing Sascha's frustration: *Why doesn't Peter just glide out of this contraption, Dorotea?* Tirla asked, unconsciously echoing Sascha's frustration. *He's the kinetic!* When Dorotea explained Peter's problem with the anesthesia, Tirla gave a bark of laughter. *So it's up to me again, I guess. Don't forget the answers to my equations, will you, Dorotea?*

Dorotea: *Tirla, what are you planning to do?*

Tirla: *Get out of this coffin.*

Dorotea: *How?*

Tirla: *They made one mistake when they strapped me in here. They strapped my fingers down, not up where I couldn't reach anything. I should be able to dig out enough plastic to free my hands.*

Dorotea felt the effort in Tirla's mind, effort and fringes of pain. "Could she do that?" she asked Sascha.

"According to the Bro, the kids retrieved in Manhattan had been wrapped in foamed plastic cocoons. She might be able to scratch at it with her fingers."

You have made contact with Tirla and Peter? Boris's voice was excited.

Contact, Bro, but not release. Both kids are cocooned. And Peter's having a bad reaction to whatever gas they used. Sascha made another face, mimicking the aggravation his brother was mentally expressing. *He'll need a little time before he recovers completely.*

Boris: *Is there time? I've got the city manager,* and *all her deputies on my back for action. Some of the other kids were legal, too.*

Rhyssa was concentrating on strengthening her link with Peter, helping him to dissipate the residue of the anesthetic. Her face mirrored his desperation and sense of failure, and she leaned heavily against Dave.

There! The triumph in Tirla's voice was evident to Dorotea, and she held up her hand, repeating the girl's words for the others. *Camel-gutted tripe! Miserable dung-eaters! Descendants of snake offal. Scuzfarts! Maggots!*

Good heavens! How pungent. Tirla, how have you hurt yourself? Dorotea demanded, sensing pain.

Tirla: *Never you mind. I'm out of this cocoon. There are*

nineteen other kids stuck in 'em here, some of 'em still knocked out. Peter's not one of 'em. Tell Carmen not to fracture her skull finding me. This place is black as the bottom of an elevator pit. Ugh. I slipped in junk. Ugh! I've reached one wall. Faugh. It's slimy and gritty. Too smooth and cold for metal. Ah, an opening. A window. Plastic-coated. I can't even scratch a sliver off. Look, I'm going to try something, Tirla went on. *They always forget about ceilings. There's air coming in here from someplace.* She was silent for a long while, though Dorotea was aware of strenuous physical activity. *I am not hurting you. Just using you as a stepladder. And I won't let you go, crybaby. You're no use to me. Quit your grizzling.* Another period of silence followed, and Dorotea reported more physical effort, punctuated by inadvertent grunts of pain.

Tirla: *Well, I was right. There is a ceiling hatch. And I can see, a little. Well, whaddya know? I'm in a shunting yard. There are rows and rows of train cars, old ones. Can't have been moved in years. And someplace down to my right there's light. Sort of around an edge, like of a window or a door. Any idea where I could be?*

From the moment Tirla mentioned a shunting yard, the description was forwarded to everyone concerned.

Tirla: *I'm going along the tops of cars toward the light,* the girl reported. *I can't hear anyone, and no one would be stupid enough to walk around this place without a light.*

Tell us how many cars have children, Tirla, Dorotea urged.

Tirla: *Peter! Peter! Answer me! Peter! It's Tirla! Answer me! Wow! I nearly fell off the edge of the car. Slippery surface, moist. Whole place is damp!*

"Try for yards by the river, by the sea. Along the Sound," Sascha said, prowling up and down the bank of monitors, checking patterns.

Tirla! Peter cried exultantly. His voice echoed from Tirla's mind to Dorotea and lifted the anxieties of every Talent in the room. Rhyssa sank into a chair that Dave pulled over for her.

Then he handed her a stimulant drink, gesturing her to toss it down quickly.

Tirla: *So here's where they stashed you, huh? Now, I'll just drop in beside you. There! The tape'll sting coming off—oh, I forgot. Sorry.*

Peter: *I won't feel it anyway—do your worst. Just don't take all the skin off my wrists! Isn't there any light in this place?*

Tirla: *I guess not. There—you're free. Only the tan came off. Here! Don't go faint. Lie back. Stay easy. Get your breath. Now look, you'd better rest some more.* Dorotea could hear the nervous concern in Tirla's voice, a matter she did not impart to Rhyssa. *I'm going to look around this place, Peter,* Tirla went on. *You get your kinetics working again, 'cause there's no way I can haul you up by myself.*

Peter: *I'll be okay, Tirla. I'll be okay. Just—just come back.*

Tirla: *Oho! Aircar! Big bugger. Expensive! No lights!* There was a long moment of silence. *That was too close.*

"Ask her if she saw a number, a description, anything!" Sascha prompted Dorotea.

Tirla: *I'd say that it's a metallic blue jetter, twelve-seater, no lights. But I got a glimpse—a three, a dash, and R-I-G—I think. Could have been a B, but the I and the G were clear enough.*

When Dorotea repeated what Tirla had said, Sascha exploded to his feet. "R-I-G! We couldn't be so lucky!" He slapped his right palm against his forehead. "Budworth, get through to Auer and Bertha and see if they have any tickles about Filmflam."

"Flimflam?" Rhyssa and Dorotea said together, both reaching into Sascha's mind for confirmation, but he was involved in a tight conversation with Boris and would not let them in.

"Boris is doing a search on the registration," Sascha said aloud, holding up one hand, his expression intent and eager. "Dorotea, tell Tirla she's a star!"

Tirla, surprised: *Was that enough for you? Oops. There's another one coming in, from another direction. Also running dark. I'll see if I can get a better reading.*

Tirla, Dorotea replied hastily, *don't risk discovery. And Rhyssa says she'd rather have you stay with Peter.*

Tirla, blithely: *Peter's okay. Working on it. I'm going to find out who the other dark-flier is!*

Tirla! Dorotea was momentarily stunned by the independence. *Tirla!* She turned to Rhyssa, hands outstretched in appeal. "The little witch has cut me off! Oh, just wait till I get my hands on that child! The impudence of her."

Rhyssa was also irritated. *Peter, stop her!*

Peter on his dignity: *I don't need a minder, Rhyssa. I really don't. Just enough time to catch my breath. 'Sides, no one could stop Tirla.*

"Rather admirable of the child, I think," Sascha replied. For a palpable moment he and Rhyssa locked wills. Then he continued in a gentler tone. "I do realize, Rhyssa, that Peter's inhibited by the gassing he took. If Tirla can manage an ID on the second car, too, we'll maybe catch more than just the well-deserving Revered Ponsit Prosit."

"Has Boris confirmed the owner of that jetcar?" Rhyssa asked, only marginally appeased.

"Registered to Ponsit Prosit, a.k.a. Flimflam," Sascha said with a grin. "Complete with vanity plate—VRPP/2403/RIG—at a Riverside address that is more palatial than reverential. Boris is sending out surveillance and standby teams. I'd like the Center to muster Talent as of right now!" Sascha waited long enough for Rhyssa's assent and then pointed a finger at Budworth to punch the Alert button. "We can move once we've got a definite fix."

"Neither Auer or Bertha have anything for us," Sirikit told them.

"That's odd," Rhyssa said with a frown. "There should be something!"

"I find a precog silence reassuring," Sascha remarked, buckling on his utility belt and checking his trank gun. "Flim-flam is at least not going to trigger panic in the immediate future, so we have a very good chance of catching him *in flagrante delicto*. Dorotea, is Tirla available again?"

Dorotea shook her head, her lips pursed in an aggrieved moue. "Wretched little snip of a thing!" she said with a certain amount of reluctant admiration in her tone.

"Got it!" Carmen cried suddenly, jumping out of her chair, rushing to the map terminal, and punching coordinates that brought up the South Shore area. "Tirla's come through again. There simply can't be two such similar situations. She's heading toward an old railway switchhouse. I can just make it out. There's a crack of light coming through a window that opens onto a platform. There seem to be hundreds of cars of old rolling stock rusting there. Here we are!" She pointed to the marked area on the map. "Here're tracks. Acres of them. And obsolete railcars waiting to be recycled."

The others all converged to look at the area magnified on the screen.

"It couldn't be better, could it," Dorotea said slowly, "as a place to hide terrified kids!" *Tirla! Answer me! We know where you are now.*

When Tirla did not reply, Sascha gave Rhyssa a long look and then, Dave Lehardt at their heels, the telepaths left the Control Room, jogging to the stairs that would take them to the aircars and teams waiting on the landing roof.

CHAPTER 16

Tirla's night vision had adjusted to the gloom—part mist and part lightlessness despite the angry red-orange glow of Jerhattan that lit the rim of the horizon on all sides. The upper levels of distant Linears, majestic in the night, punctuated the halo of the city with their long silhouettes. From top stories, with aerials and stacks, aircraft-warning signals blinked their light patterns. She moved forward carefully along the curved tops of the railcars. If she slipped, there would be nothing for her to catch on to. The surface was gritty with dirt and slippery in the moist air. She headed toward that thin band of light and the dark bulk of the building that framed it.

She had safely traversed five cars, two more with children moaning and weeping inside them, when she felt a pressure in her mind that she recognized as Dorotea trying to contact her.

Go 'way. I've got to concentrate.

She cursed softly as she slithered for a panicky moment between cars, then waited until her heart had stopped thudding, and she was fairly sure that her scrambling had not been heard. Her sharp ears had caught the sound of muted voices from the building. The line of cars continued past a long platform, and she debated slipping down and getting close enough to the building to overhear the conversations.

But conversations were useless tender; the registration number of an aircar was undeniable proof. She crawled forward on her belly, conscious of every noise she made, the dryness of her mouth, and the increasingly painful stiffness of her fingers.

There was a sudden break in the murk and there, parked

beside the less distinct blue jetter, was an expensive sports jet-car, its hull a crisp white, its tail ID equally visible. The two cars were balanced on the one junction of rail that was free of rolling stock.

Tirla: *Peter, I got the second one. The number is CD-08-MAL, clear as day. And the other car is right beyond it. Peter?*

Peter: *I heard you, Tirla. I told them. You come back here. They're mad at you for closing Dorotea out. You're going to have to apologize to her.* Peter sounded fierce.

Apologize? Why? Tirla was so surprised that she slipped, banging down on the railcar. *Now you've done it!* She flattened herself on the far side of the car as light flooded out of the building, illuminating the platform and the slightly bulging side of the car on which she lay.

"I tell you I heard something!" said the man silhouetted in the doorway. He peered around the doorframe, and Tirla had a good view of the scene behind him: two men, one of whom idly swung a short stick, clipping it against his boot with an air of indolent diffidence.

"Shut the door, you cretin!" The door abruptly closed and then opened in a much thinner crack. ". . . a good look around. Up, over, under, in. Mess up once more, maggot—you can be eagle-spread, too."

The door closed a second time, but not before Tirla recognized the angry voice. Her guts froze. She heard the ladrone moving, his shoes crunching the grit on the platform. She heard him haul back one of the warped carriage doors, the plastic creaking as he looked in the carriage. He moved on down the platform, cursing softly under his breath as he dropped down to flash his light beneath the car. Tirla could take no chances. Quickly she moved at a crouch and jumped to the next car. She was just in time—the red pinpoint of a filtered handlight shone briefly where she had just been. She held her breath, hoping against hope that the searcher would not notice her outline on the dusty top.

As he cautiously opened the door of the building, she watched. The stick swinger was nearest the door—she got another good look at his haughty face, with its beaked nose and thin-plucked brows. And she saw a table piled with credits which two other men were counting—floaters, by the size of them. One of the counters looked vaguely familiar, but her attention was caught by the face of the other man as he turned his head; he had a cruel face, and a hungry one. He was idly tapping his black boot with the stick; she caught the gleam of gold around the handle. Only then did the significance of the pile of floaters dawn on her.

Tirla: *Dorotea! The payoff's being made! Floaters. More than I've ever seen in my life!*

Dorotea, her voice hard-edged: *Tirla, don't you ever dare cut me out again.* Tirla was momentarily dismayed. Wasn't she doing what they needed done? How could such a sweet old lady come on so tough and hard?

Tirla: *Well, if you crazy Talents don't move your asses, you're going to mess everything up and I'll have nothing more to do with you.*

Peter! Help Peter now! Dorotea did not sound apologetic, but she did sound anxious.

Tirla knew very well that Peter—not to mention all the other kids—needed help. As quickly as she could, she moved back along the line of cars. If the payoff had been made, some of the kids might be shifted soon. She had to get Peter out and free as many of the others as she could. If they all scattered and hid, it would take all night to recapture them—if she could stop them from crying long enough to help themselves.

Tirla slipped and this time could not recover her balance, sliding down the dirt-encrusted side of the car and landing painfully on stones and cinders that bruised and cut her feet. Cursing her clumsiness and hoping that she had gotten far enough away so that the noise of her fall had not been heard, she made her way along the ground, cursing the bastards who had removed the beautiful purple boots that she had bought on her first trip to the mall.

Crying had been reduced to whimpering in the first two cars. Tirla winced. How much time did she have to get Peter out if the payoff had been made? Could he make use of that special Talent of his now?

Yes, I can, Peter said, appearing out of the darkness between two cars. He touched her hand. *And I know exactly how. C'mon.* He led her along the track until she nearly stumbled over a big handle attached to one side of the track. *We're going to do a switcheroo.* He laughed softly out loud. *Much faster than letting all those kids loose. There's a hundred of them.*

They heard a muffled thrumming and saw the whiteness of the aircar lifting slowly from behind the building.

C'mon, Peter urged. *I've got to get to that transformer box or my idea won't work! I need the gestalt for this. You know how to uncouple cars?* Suddenly the process was driven into Tirla's mind and she staggered a bit, stunned by the vivid intrusion. *Then go back and uncouple the last car with kids in it. Stay there and warn me if anyone's coming.*

"You mean like, upstairs?" Tirla asked in a hoarse whisper, pointing to the sky.

No, them! Peter pointed at the building.

"When are we getting some help?" Tirla demanded in an acid-whisper, refusing to talk in her mind when she was nose-to-nose with Peter. "My feet hurt!"

"Soon," Peter hissed and then gave her a shove to help her on her way. "Try walking my way!"

She couldn't but wished she could. Her feet hurt and her hands ached. She did not quite understand how he could possibly do what she thought he was going to do. Railcars that had not moved in years were going to make the most awful racket. Peter was stupid! She hurried, hoping that the sound of the aircar might cover some of the noise the railcars were sure to make.

She identified the last car from the moaning inside it and struggled with couplings encrusted with caked oil and dirt. *Peter, it's—* Suddenly the stiff coupling released itself and she was knocked off balance, staggering back into the end of the car. *Well, thanks!* A wail arose from within. *Shut your faces, you stupid gits,* she ordered, forgetting that the other children could not hear her. *I'm doing my best to save your innards and your virtue.* She banged her fist once against the side of the car and felt the pain worth it when the warning achieved an instant drop in the mewling. That did much to soothe her aggravations.

Nervously she glanced up to see the aircar's slow upward progress. Running dark like that, the pilot had to be careful not to get tangled in the wires that festooned the area around the building. If Peter could just get moving . . . He was! She heard the squeal, rattle, and clanking as wheels long locked on rails reluctantly began to turn. She swung up to sit on the tongue of the coupling, watching the building for any sign that someone within had heard the metallic protest. But the building was two hundred meters or so away, and the aircar was whooshing and thrumming.

She peered at the skyline, yearning to see some subtle movement that hinted of the approach of help. Those Talents were so slow. How soon was "soon"? Her car moved all too jerkily with rattlings and clankings, but it was making progress along the track. The dark building with the telltale band of light was slowly receding. She felt the car clack across the junction, veering right, and experienced partial relief. If that ladrone looked outside and saw half the train missing . . .

She saw the white blur of Peter's face as the car inched past the transformer box; there was no disguise in the dark night for the audible hum emanating from it. What was Peter doing?

She jumped down from the coupling, wincing as her cut feet hit the stony, cindery ground. The cars continued to move obliquely away from danger, down an empty track.

"You can't leave just empty track. They'll know . . ." Tirla put an urgent hand on his arm and then could not release it. She could feel him shaking from the effort he had already made, shaking and more—and she was affected by his shaking and whatever else it was that raced through him.

"I'm trying," he said tensely. "A gestalt's hard with all that anesthesia still slowing me down. Help me!"

"Gestalt?" Tirla stuttered over the unfamiliar word, and then Peter put the explanation in her mind. Before she could ask how she could possibly help with that, she was. Her body seemed alive with the current racing through her, like the time she had caught a jolt from an exposed wire. Only this was not as painful as that shock had been. But it was . . . what was it?

The metallic protest was startlingly loud on the still air. The white jet had moved beyond visibility into the swirling mist. Tirla felt both stronger and weaker, clutching at Peter with both hands, wanting to help him make the gestalt and needing his support. Suddenly she was aware of movement behind her as car after car began to slide past them onto the track—*clickety click, clickety click*—far too loudly. Suddenly, with a resounding clank, the new cars bounced against those near the platform, and Tirla's heart clenched when she heard the shouts of alarm as men piled out to investigate.

Tell me! Did you let all those other kids loose?" Flimflam asked, his nose inches from Tirla's face. She wished he would bend just a little closer so she could bite him. But he would probably poison her, the greasy, coarse, evil scuz.

Unfortunately, before Tirla could help Peter to hide, two of the faster ladrones had caught them. They had been roughly hauled back to the building and into the presence of a seething

Flimflam, so enraged that flecks of foam had gathered at the corners of his mouth. Screaming with exasperation, Tirla had been shoved in front of the raging man as Peter collapsed on the floor, groaning.

"We didn't see no others," one of the ladrones said anxiously. "There wasn't a sign of them, nor those cocoons in the cars neither."

"Tell me where the children are!" Flimflam repeated in one of the more common Neester dialects, squeezing hard on her swollen fingers. "Did you let them loose?"

Despite herself, Tirla let out a howl of pain, trying to pull her hand out of his grasp. It hurt so much that she could not even think of a suitable malediction to fling at him. He let her go but scooped a stick off the table and began to slash it across her back.

"Hey, boss, the merch! Don't mark the merch!"

"Tell me where the children went!" he demanded in the most common Asian language.

Tirla let tears run down her cheeks as she glanced quickly around the room, as if seeking help. Then in one of the most obscure languages she knew, she answered him in a piteously appealing tone. "Don't beat me. I don't understand you! Don't beat me again!"

"Of all the—" Flimflam roared, swiveling about to the ladrones and hitters in the room. "What did she say? One of you must understand her! Just what I need. A dumb kid! Well?"

There were murmurs and shrugs as no one admitted to understanding.

Dorotea, reassuringly: *We're nearly there, Tirla. We have the yard on the nightscope.*

"Where—" Flimflam was making ludicrously broad, pantomine gestures, so unlike his polished performance as a RIG that Tirla nearly laughed even though he kept poking her painfully with his stick to emphasize his words. "Where—are—the others? Can no one talk to her? Rouse the other one. We can't waste time. That bloody His Highness will be sending the transports. We must have the merchandise ready. Months of planning, everything goes without a hitch, we've got the money—*where are the others?*"

A ladrone poured water over Peter, who did not even moan. Tirla watched him anxiously. He looked terribly pale, crumpled up like that. He had been fine until they had been recaptured. Perhaps the effort of moving those heavy railcars . . . She gasped as the whip sliced her again right over the previous welt. Tirla tried to back away but hands clamped on her shoulders, holding her fast. She kicked backward with her heels, jarring feet already sore, but her captor had heavy boots on and she only achieved more bruises.

"Let's really put some fear into her," Flimflam said, gesturing, and she was flung facedown to the hard surface of the table where she had recently seen piles of floaters. Cruel hard hands grasped her by wrists and ankles. Suddenly pain exploded across her already lacerated feet. She screamed and screamed again at the second horrific stab of pain, then fainted for the first time in her life.

So she missed seeing Flimflam violently propelled backward to crash against the wall. She missed the explosive entrance of Sascha, Rhyssa, Dave Lehardt, and the Talent teams. And she missed the other excitements that would have given her immense satisfaction.

CHAPTER 17

"ommissioner," Ranjit said, "that's a diplomatic registration."

"I wouldn't care if it was God himself, Lieutenant," the LEO commissioner answered. "Law Enforcement and Order means just that from bottom to top, and right on down the line again. Or it's privilege, not law enforcement and order!" He measured the distance on the huge display map, from the South Shore train yard to the Riverside address. "Assign the best driver we've got to shadow that CD. And I want that beehive—not just the penthouse lift or the domestic floors but that entire complex—secured. Whoever is in that car could go to ground anywhere. Pack all entries with sensitives. Tell them to home in on any strong emotion—we may get a lot of wash on this. You know how hivers hate to have their privacy broached." He turned to another aide. "Barry, get me the city manager and tell her this is a sensitive affair. I want her forewarned so she can back us with the Corps. Feed the situation through Judicial and get me four—no, make it five—John Does and a search warrant. And let's hope that Sascha's efficient."

He shrugged on his tunic top, resplendent with the "bravery bars" and braid, then strapped on sidearms and gestured for Ranjit and his other aides to follow him to the rooftop garage. Jet- and aircars were spinning off along usual routes, having been instructed to move circumspectly.

Sascha? Boris linked with his brother as his aircar took off.

Nearly there, Bro. It still takes time to drive a car from there to here. The other bird has not flown—holy hell, what's happening? Back to you later.

273

Boris felt the abruptness of the mental break and cursed under his breath as his aircar plowed on to his destination. The pause lengthened, causing him some anxiety. Surely Sascha was competent enough . . . Should he have sent men with the Center teams? If the child-dealers at the railyard should get a warning through to his own quarry, the whole operation might be jeopardized.

My God, Boris—Sascha's voice burst in on him like a bellow—*if you let that Shimaz slime ooze out of this, Highness, Prince, manager, or whatever, I promise you that the Talents will handle him* ex officio!

The LEO commissioner had never before heard such vindictiveness in his brother's voice.

Boris: *What happened?*

Sascha: *The Venerable Revered Ponsit Prosit used a bastinado on Tirla's feet. And Peter's collapsed!*

Boris: *Flimflam didn't get a message off, did he?* If the man had, they might lose the most important criminal.

Sascha, livid with rage: *No, not when he had a little girl to interrogate! Make it stick on that other bastard, will you? Or, by all that's holy, I will. Myself with no help from any other agency, dear LEO Bro.*

Boris: *LEO is on the move, Sascha. You hang onto your temper. Have you got the other children? Have we any proof of complicity?*

Sascha, sarcastically: *I don't suppose Tirla's bloody feet count for more than assault and GBH. But we also took possession of a case full of many too many floaters, ready for a night deposit, complete with an account number I'll bet can be traced to the Venerable Revered.*

Boris: *That should be enough to convict Flimflam. But is there enough to catch this—what did you call him?*

Sascha: *Shimaz, Prince Phanibal Shimaz, who seems to be a whiz at more than Josephson junctions. Flimflam's spilling his guts: His Highness has rather an extensive operation—child labor in his rice paddies and mines, child prostitution, and a child farm where the healthiest are kept that way until someone can pay for the organ they need.*

Boris, growling: *Get me something to link him to that yard. Something that will stick!*

They were well on the way when the comlink heralded a connection from Commissioner Aiello. She appeared on the cabin screen dressed in formal attire. Hovering beside her was her protocol officer, Jak, who, for all his empathy, could at times be quite tiresome about details.

"Do you have incontrovertible proof, Roznine?" she asked.

"We have proof of a connection which is incompatible with any diplomatic occupation," Boris replied, setting his jaw.

"Who? Surely not the ambassador!" At that moment, Teresa Aiello was depressed with pessimism.

"We are not after his Excellency, so Jak can relax. Members of his Corps, certainly, and an embassy vehicle has been identified and traced from the abduction site. There's no problem of proving involvement. Is the DA there, too? Well, give the old dog a comforting word in his shell-like ear. The Talents have cracked this abduction ring." The last he admitted ruefully, for despite protests to the contrary, he and his brother were in constant competition.

The massive beehive was aptly nicknamed. Its bottom levels along the block-square bulk, where other buildings obscured views, housed maintenance, storage, and worker accommodations. Where the hive rose above its neighbors, there were great curved plasglas panels that were part solar-heating, part prestigious display of wealth. Each pie-shaped apartment boasted luxuriant gardens and views from the outer wall, and where the hive had an atrium core, rare plants and trees festooned the inner walls. Naturally the top apartments were the most exclusive and expensive, with one whole floor given over to private garden and garage facilities, swimming pools, game courts, and whatever other amenities the residents expected, to secure the ultimate of comfort.

Is the surround complete yet, Ranjit? Boris asked on his helmet com unit.

Just now—completely ringed, sir. No one can get in or out without being observed.

"Commissioner," Boris's pilot said, "here comes the suspect vehicle now."

The sleek white jetcar swooped to settle and deposit its passengers on the roof of the hive.

"Three men!"

"I can see that myself," Boris said. "Secure that jetter the moment it's garaged. See what you can get the pilot to say. Grab the log, and any garage records. And now—" He could not keep the satisfaction out of his voice. "Let's get the bastards."

The LEO pilot put them down on the hive roof, and Boris Roznine and his squad made for the ramp down to the entrance level of the penthouse. Seeing the formal and formidable attire of the LEO commissioner and his aide, the door attendant hurried to open it. His bow was respectful and nervous.

"What are you doing, you naga? I'm not expecting guests!" exclaimed the man at the other end of the magnificent white marbled reception hall. A servant was just assisting the removal of his elegant blue suede long coat while a second man was also shrugging, unassisted, out of his own outerwear. "Exclude them immediately."

"I think not, Prince Phanibal," Boris said, stepping forward while sending Ranjit a quick thought about reinforcements.

The prince's companion moved with astonishing speed out the nearest of the many doors leading from the entry hall while the paralyzed doorman gaped.

"Is His Excellency at home?" Boris asked, some glimmer

of Jak's protocol lessons seeping through his anger. The door-man fearfully nodded before the prince ordered him not to respond.

"How dare you—whoever you are—enter a diplomatic res-idence without invitation?" Prince Phanibal demanded, his ex-pression haughty and totally confident. His gaze ignored the lieutenant by Boris's side and the detachment standing just out-side the door.

"Boris Roznine, commissioner for Law Enforcement and Order in Jerhattan!" Boris turned to the awed and shaking doorman. "Please beg His Excellency's indulgence and request an immediate interview on a matter of grave urgency."

The attendant, ignoring the prince's countermands and threats, opened a hidden door and disappeared. He had no sooner gone than all the other doors of the entrance hall swung open and a number of large men filed in with military preci-sion. Three, black-robed and turbaned, with silver-mounted belts and daggers which were exactly the legal length permitted display guards, immediately flanked the prince.

Boris did not need to look over his shoulder to know that the LEO officers just outside the doorway, carrying the weap-onry legal for them, outnumbered the embassy guards and were quite ready to force an entry. He waited a moment for the prince to absorb that fact.

"I believe that we now await His Excellency's appearance," he said with a grim and ungenial smile and, in studied insult to a royal person, seated himself on the nearest decorative bench.

"Do you not understand the repercussions this unwar-ranted intrusion—" Prince Phanibal began imperiously. "I am not only a royal prince of my house but a manager of the Pad-rugoi. I am due back on the platform on the next shuttle."

"That is why I, as LEO commissioner, am here to explain personally to the ambassador," Boris replied. *Is this the guy who's been giving Rhyssa so much grief? Perhaps if we both try, we can probe his mind,* he sent to Sascha. *It's not admissible evidence in court since it's under duress, but it'll give us some clues.*

There was a brief pause as the brothers tried to breach the prince's mind. Then Boris pulled back. *He's got a dense mind shield. He's had careful conditioning, and I'd love to know where. No, we can't break it, not without breaking the law.*

The slightest of smiles tugged at the corner of the prince's mouth and his eyes narrowed, hiding smug pleasure at deflecting the mental intrusion. He raised his left hand briefly, his fingers closing as if on some accustomed possession. Then he threw his fingers open in vexation and raised the arm indolently across his chest, the smile broadening.

"Perhaps you have mislaid your little stick," Boris heard himself saying. Sascha was there! *Saving time and effort, brother?* Boris asked.

The little stick which made raw meat of Tirla's feet, Sascha said savagely.

Prince Phanibal stiffened in surprise. "I—what?"

"The little switch that you are fond of carrying as an affectation, for you don't own any—animals—I believe," the Boris/Sascha link continued. "The one with the ivory handle and the rather unusual filigree design."

"I do not have to account for my possessions to such as you," Prince Phanibal replied as he angled himself obliquely from Boris, tilting his chin arrogantly to display what many probably considered a handsome profile.

At that point the ambassador, clad in a deep purple velvet robe with exquisite gold designs, entered from the central door. He cast one startled look at the prince and his pose, another at the group by the door, then signaled for the guards to withdraw. Boris Roznine rose and walked forward to meet the Malaysian.

"Due to the gravity of this situation, Your Excellency," he said, speaking on his own although he knew that Sascha was listening avidly, "you will permit me to dispense with formalities. This man"—he gestured to the aloof prince—"and another have been involved in activities incompatible with any function in your embassy. I must ask you to instruct His Highness and his companion to accompany me to the LEO headquarters."

"With what could the Prince Phanibal be charged?" the ambassador asked with great dignity.

"The charge is indeed grave, Your Excellency, for there has been traffic in abducting minors and subjecting them to illicit bondage for the purpose of slave labor, unlawful intercourse, and organ removal."

"You have proof of such a heinous crime?" The ambassador drew himself more erect, but he did not appear to be all that surprised.

"Yes, Your Excellency." Boris inclined his head with a nod of regret. The ambassador was too fine an old man to be saddled with such a scandal. "There are witnesses!" the Boris/Sascha link continued, supporting Boris's reply. "Talented witnesses."

The prince snorted his disbelief, his poise undisturbed. "Such a claim tries all patience. You will dismiss these deceivers, Uncle."

Sascha: *This bugger's clever.*

Boris: *He hasn't turned a hair or admitted a thing.*

Sascha: *Does he think all Talents are adults?*

Boris: *Tirla is on the official Register, is she not?*

Sascha: *Didn't you read the ID bracelet you got her six weeks ago? And there are four of the ladrones, spilling their guts to avoid being spaced, confirming what we've got out of Flimflam for turning State's evidence—his mind took very little pressure when he regained consciousness. That was some scam they had going. Furthermore, it was the dear prince who infiltrated LEO programs and filched the strand formula. He had all the special clearance passwords because he was work-*

ing on Padrugoi and doing all that fine work with the Joseph-
son junctions. He browsed and took what he needed. Got his
island laboratory to perfect a variation for Flimflam to use
as a special effect in those REs he put on. We have all the
details needed to implicate the prince and that secretary of
his. Returned from the religious institutions and a period of
meditation in the Far East? He was planning the whole thing
with Prince Phanibal's backing. Sascha's snort of contempt
was so strong that Boris grunted.

The ambassador turned his head slightly over one shoulder
in Prince Phanibal's direction. "I will not dismiss them,
Nephew. Talent cannot be forsworn." Then he regarded Boris
steadily for a moment and beckoned for the prince to step
forward. "You will go with them."

"But I cannot be arrested like a common criminal!"

"Oh, indeed, Nephew, you are an uncommon criminal, for
diplomatic immunity does not shield pederasts," the old man
said in a voice that was leached of all emotion.

"You cannot permit such insult to our name," the prince
said, slapping his fists to his legs in his barely contained frustration and anger. "My father will hear of this. You will hear
of this. You will be disgraced! You will never return to your
home. Your children and your children's children are dog
meat . . ."

Ignoring him, the Malaysian ambassador strode to the nearest door and closed it firmly behind him. The guards moved
to cover each of the doorways, subtly removing official protection from the prince.

Commissioner? Ranjit said politely. *The pilot has been ar-*
rested, and we have the jetter's logs and the garage log. Also,
Prince Shimaz's companion was apprehended, attempting to
escape.

"If you will come with us . . ." Boris began formally, gesturing toward the roof landing steps.

The prince suddenly erupted into action, his face contorted

in rage, flinging himself toward the opening Boris had made. Ranjit, with great presence of mind, neatly tripped the man as he passed.

At that, it took three officers to subdue the raving man.

"**S**o, despite appeals from his grieving father, and protests from Ludmilla Barchenka that His Highness Manager Phanibal Shimaz *must* be released until the station is completed," Sascha told Tirla, sitting on the edge of her bed in Dorotea's house, "that scuzball will spend the rest of his life at hard labor on the moon."

"And Flimflam?" Tirla's eyes flashed with an anger and hatred that startled Sascha, even though he understood it.

"Oh, turning State's evidence gave him a choice of occupations," he said with a grin. "He elected to take a job as a sanitation engineer on the Big Station. Not exactly spaced out, but near enough."

"How many of the kids *were* illegals?" she asked after relishing Flimflam's future for a long and satisfactory moment. She and Peter had both been in court to give their evidence but had not heard the sentencing. She still was not comfortable walking very far on her tender feet, and despite Peter's patient instruction in kinetics, she had been unable to levitate as he did. Peter was baffled, sure that she had some latent kinetic ability; he maintained that he had been unconscious when Flimflam had been thrown kinetically across the room just as the rescuers arrived.

"Eighty-seven children," Sascha replied brusquely.

"In the hostels, huh?" Tirla gave a long sigh.

"Just think what you and Peter saved them from, Tirla. You had a taste of it."

"And there haven't been any more deals or abductions?"
Sascha shook his head.

The apathy that had settled over Tirla after the trial worried everyone in the Center. Obediently she had worked with the physiotherapist to regain movement in her damaged feet—she had been more severely injured than had first been apparent. She had dutifully tried to improve her telepathic range, but Dorotea and Peter were the only ones she could hear at any distance; even Sascha she could hear only if he was within a hundred meters. She did test to an astounding degree of empathy, the source of her unusual linguistic feats.

She was assiduous in following her education program, opting for a very wide variety of courses, some of which Dorotea was certain she could not yet comprehend. Her reports proved that she was more precocious than anticipated. She took no joy in the freedom of the Center's grounds and played with no other children despite their repeated attempts to interest her. She had even refused to go on shopping trips with either Sascha or Cass. She tended to become more animated in Peter's company, but she saw him only rarely, as he and Rhyssa were deeply involved in his highly specialized training. She was virtually recovered from the abduction, but her morale was extremely low, so Dorotea had insisted that Sascha come for a visit.

"What does it take to strand a kid?" Tirla asked him.

"Look, chip," he said, laying a gentle hand on her knee and noting that she felt no less fragile to him, though she had put on weight since she had first come to the Center. "You can't save all the illegals. And for the moment the danger is over."

"But not the appetites," Tirla said, brooding. "Like that scuzzy prince." In the privacy of her room, her face took on a malicious expression. "*Is* it difficult to strand a kid? Cass and Suz said they were stranding kids in Linear E. Have they improved the strand for a long-term use?"

"I know you're biologically twelve years old, Tirla, but you sound fifty." Sascha was exasperated.

She tilted her head up at him, regarding him through slightly

narrowed eyes, a little smile playing at her lips. "In the
Linears I am. You surely don't want another scam like that RIG,
do you? And like you said, even illegal kids have rights! I know
Cass has had her baby and wouldn't want to go undercover so
soon. But I'd bet my last credit—"

"All of them are the Center's now, remember?" Sascha
teased, and caught a sly gleam in her eyes. So Dorotea was
right about her squirreling some floaters away. Old habits died
hard.

"And the Center also has to give me anything I want—"

"Within reason."

"Well, I'll be reasonable. I'm good at languages—anyone's—
but I can't keep sharp if I'm here," she said, gesturing out the
window at the lawn. "And Teacher says I don't know all the
languages of the world—yet. I'll do you a deal, Sascha Roznine." She cocked her head at him in what he had come to call
her "haggling manner." "I'll strand illegals in every Jerhattan
Linear. I'll strand 'em, but I won't report 'em." She gave a
mirthless grin. "If there're sweeps, and I was blamed for 'em,
I'd lose my—what do you call it—credibility? I got ethics, too,
you know. But I'd know when trouble was brewing, and that
I would report. That'd help, wouldn't it? I'd be a better trouble-
spotter than any of those LEO plants of your brother's!" The
notion seemed to amuse her, and certainly she had become
more animated. "I always knew who was LEO—even who was
Talent."

While there was no question of her affection for Sascha,
she was never easy in Boris's presence, though he had tried to
be ingratiating. An ingrained distrust of all LEOs was Sascha's
diagnosis, not wishing Tirla to be at odds with his twin.

"You really wouldn't consider staying here with Dorotea
and extending your Talents?"

Tirla wagged her head, grimacing. "It's not that I don't like
Dorotea. She's the best ever. It's just—I don't feel comfortable
in all of this." Her glance swept around the well-appointed

room. "I'm a Linear brat. My Talent, as you call it," she said, wrinkling her nose in self-deprecation, "works best in a Linear environment." Her eyes twinkled.

"You can't live all your life in a Linear," Dorotea said, entering the room, her expression worried. She radiated affection, reassurance, and support.

"Why not?" Tirla demanded, lifting her hands in a quick gesture of exasperation.

"Indeed, why not?" Sascha echoed.

"Cass and Suz live on the high side of Linears when they're undercover. I'd really like my own squat on, say, Level 19, so I'd have a view and not so much smog." Her grin was sheer impudence. "In case he hasn't been listening in, ask your brother if I wouldn't be more use to him living in a Linear."

Sascha laughed. *Bro? Did you hear that?*

Little bint! You'll never know where you are with that one, will you? It's demonstrable that she's superb as a pulse-keeper. There are far more squabbles and arguments in Linear G than while she was there. I could use a Tirla in all the big Linears. If Rhyssa doesn't mind . . .

Dorotea: *I mind!*

Boris: *Sorry, Dorotea, but Tirla's a Registered Talent and too damned vital to lay about until she's of age. But there's nothing that says she has to live at the Center while she's waiting for her eighteenth birthday to come around. If she'd be much happier in a Linear, she could live in one. With Lessud and his family in Island K? Go to school properly and still keep her ears and eyes open for the general well-being of the community. With the scam dried up in Jerhattan, Long Island is the next logical pool to fish in for illegal kids. We could use a reliable pulse-keeper like Tirla.*

"Did you get any of that, Tirla?" Sascha asked her, grinning. Sitting beside her, he could feel her concentrating on "listening," but her mind echoed nothing but the desire to hear.

She shook her head and gave a sad little sigh, with a look of apology to Dorotea, who had been trying so hard to train her.

"The Bro wants to know if you'd prefer to live in a Long Island Residential while you're waiting to grow up," Sascha explained.

"A Residential in Long Island?" Tirla became animated at once, sitting up in her bed, her big dark eyes glittering, a delicate tinge of color suffusing her cheeks, and a hopeful smile on her lips. "That'd be living in high style!"

EPILOGUE

Three months later.

Rhyssa?

The tone, apologetic but firm, roused Rhyssa from one of those intense sleeps where it is difficult to move the body even when the brain has become alert. She lay heavy in the bed and managed to open one eye to see the clock; then she heard the familiar sound of Dave singing softly to himself in the bathroom. Once again she had overslept. She really did not know what was the matter with her these past few weeks—she simply could not seem to get enough sleep.

Rhyssa! The tone was more urgent, and then recognition came.

Yes, Madlyn? What's the matter?

I didn't wake you, did I? I thought I had Earth times down pat.

I overslept. What's the matter?

It's her! Disgust, frustration, anger, and exasperation packed into that one pronoun forewarned Rhyssa. *She's at it again. Saying we Talents are not doing our job! We have only pulled her out of her midden and yet she has the gall to blame us for anything that goes wrong up here.*

What is it this time? Rhyssa hauled herself up against her pillows and reached for the coffee thermos—another elegant notion of Mr. Lehardt's, and so civilized. She started to pour herself a cup and then stopped. The smell of it turned her stomach.

There's one last very critical shipment due to come up,

Madlyn went on, *only it hasn't because Johnny says he won't ship it yet.*

Won't *ship it?* That blew the last of sleep-fog from Rhyssa's mind. What was Colonel Greene up to now? *And naturally it's essential for her to complete the installation?*

Vital! It's got the last of the internal mechanisms and remotes. Very delicate stuff, I know, and not something you want bounced about. And there's only a week more before the completion date. Then we can all come down to earth! There was heartfelt relief in Madlyn's tone. *So we want to know why it's being held up. Because we are, too, you know.*

I know. I'll sort it out, Madlyn. Indeed, I will.

Dave was whistling louder now that he knew she was awake. He might not have been telepathic, but he displayed a keen sensitivity where she was concerned that more than made up for it in ways she could never have anticipated. She grinned to herself and then recalled the task at hand. Eight-thirty was not too early to rouse Colonel John Greene out of his Floridian sack.

Johnny boy, phone me! He was too far away to link telepathically with her, but her call would reach him easily enough. She looked at the phone, counting down. It rang in exactly ten seconds.

"You wished parlance with me, Madame Lehardt?"

"I do indeed, Colonel Greene. What hanky-panky are you pulling on poor dear Ludmilla?"

Johnny's chuckle was drenched in malice. "Only what she deserves, petal. She conscripted us Talents to be sure she finished on time, and finished on time she will be. Not one moment earlier, not one moment later. Why?"

"Oh, I see." Rhyssa chuckled. "And you have it timed to the final hour?"

"Lance and I worked out the time it would take to install those controls, and we've scheduled the kinetics needed. We know exactly how long it will take. Lance must have forgotten to clue Madlyn. I'm sorry she's getting hassled, but she's well able for it. Soothe her down, will you, Rhys? We're doing it our way!"

"Oh, I quite agree. Not an hour early and not an hour late."

As she hung up, Dave came in the room, a towel draped about his lean hips. "I did try to wake you, Rhys," he said with a rueful expression. "You just don't want to get up in the morning."

"I'm wanton enough to admit that I love being in bed with you, Dave, but preferably awake, not sleeping like the dead." She lifted her arms and began to stretch, then stopped. "And what's wrong with the coffee? The smell makes me nauseous."

Dave grinned as he sat down on the edge of the bed, looking at her. His blue eyes crinkled. "Figured it out yet?" he asked, glancing down at her abdomen.

"I thought—I mean, I haven't been ill," Rhyssa said, with dawning awareness, "just sleepy! Oh, Dave, could I really be pregnant?"

"Think about it a moment, O wise woman!" He got up, shedding his towel as he began to dress. She loved looking at him, no matter what he was doing, and the intimacy of this daily act was something special for her. "After all, I've been doing my best for several months now!"

Awed by the possibility, Rhyssa did start thinking about her body, placing her hands gently on her belly, intuiting the biofeedback.

"Oh, Dave, I am pregnant. I am!"

"I think you're the last one to have copped on, then," he replied, grinning broadly. "Dorotea knows."

"And she said nothing?" Rhyssa sat bolt upright again, startled and somewhat miffed that she had been left in the dark—and by Dorotea!

"Well, there's some things it's more fun to find out by yourself," he said, grinning as he stooped down to kiss her lovingly. "There's a sort of glow about you, too. Everyone's noticed. They've been politely waiting for an official announcement." He stroked her tangled hair, running fingers down her silver streak.

She sighed, then blurted out, "Does Sascha know?"

Dave stopped in the act of pulling on his tunic and ducked his head out of the folds to regard her with some alarm. "Sascha? I know you're close but—"

"Well . . ." Rhyssa paused. There was one of the few drawbacks to Dave's lack of Talent. Sometimes she had to explain with far more detail than a Talent would require. "Well, Sascha's got to wait, that's all, and he doesn't take waiting kindly."

"Wait?" Dave pulled the tunic down. "Wait for what?"

"For Tirla to grow up, of course," she said, gathering herself to rise from the bed. She felt oddly protective of the new life inside her, which was silly, since it was obviously well settled in.

"Tirla?" Dave's eyes nearly popped in astonishment. "He's gone on her? Dirty old man!"

"Not so old and certainly not dirty where Tirla is concerned. Bolt out of the blue on him, all right enough. He's never felt that way about any other female." Rhyssa permitted herself a little knowing smile. "But she's the one for him, and he knows it. He just has to wait a few years."

"That wight's not even—"

"Tirla is twelve now, going on two hundred," Rhyssa replied with some asperity. Tirla was a very interesting personality, and she and Sascha would deal very well together. It was incredible, really, to have found two such diverse Talents during her directorship: one macro who would shift worlds and one whose skill was a micro-Talent, eroding language barriers. "Neesters ripen a lot faster than we Northern and Occidental types. She'll be more than ready in four years to marry Sascha."

"And that's decided?" Dave was skeptical.

Rhyssa smiled. "Sascha precogged it—to his intense astonishment. Next time you see them together, notice how she looks at him. Quite proprietary that young lady is where Sascha is concerned. And she's better for him than Madlyn would ever be."

"And they'll have Talented kids?"

"That's a very high probability." Rhyssa smiled smugly.

Dave paused. In her presence he always allowed his emotions to show. He cleared his throat and asked briskly, "What about us? When will we know?"

To reassure the man she loved, Rhyssa smiled as she nodded. "No problem there."

"You sound so sure."

She put her arms around his neck, letting her gravid belly rest against him as she pulled his head down to kiss him. "I am. He just told me so."

ABOUT THE AUTHOR

Between her frequent appearances in the
United States and England as a lecturer and
guest-of-honor at science-fiction conventions, Anne McCaffrey lives at Dragonhold, in
the hills of County Wicklow, Ireland, with assorted horses, cats, and a dog. Of herself, Ms.
McCaffrey says: "I have green eyes, silver
hair, and freckles—the rest changes without
notice."